Pleasure Island

Pleasure Island

Lorie O'Clare

APHRODISIA

KENSINGTON BOOKS

http://www.kensingtonbooks.com

APHRODISIA BOOKS are published by

Kensington Publishing Corp.
119 West 40th Street
New York, NY 10018

All Kensington Titles, Imprints, and Distributed Lines are available at special quantity discounts for bulk purchases for sales promotions, premiums, fund-raising, and educational or institutional use.

Special book excerpts or customized printings can also be created to fit specific needs. For details, write or phone the office of the Kensington special sales manager: Kensington Publishing Corp., 119 West 40th Street, New York, NY 10018, attn: Special Sales Department, Phone: 1-800-221-2647.

Aphrodisia and the A logo Reg. U.S. Pat & TM Off.

ISBN-13: 978-0-7582-3447-6
ISBN-10: 0-7582-3447-3

First Kensington Trade Paperback Printing: June 2009

10 9 8 7 6 5 4 3 2 1

Printed in the United States of America

Pleasure Island

1

Natalie

"I didn't realize I'd get to choose from so many men!" This was unbelievable.

I couldn't remember the last time the sun warmed my skin without making me sweat. Not too hot, and absolutely no chill in the air. And there were no bugs. None. The smell of the salt water mixed with aromas from nearby flowers and created a tangy scent in the air that was unforgettable. But staring at the view in front of me, I could appreciate that the perfect weather and lack of bugs had nothing to do with why they called this paradise.

And, oh, my God, was this paradise!

"You can choose several." Rose Bontiki, the owner of Paradise Island and referred to as "Guardian" in the handbook, grinned at my astonished expression. "Not many of our guests manage to get through more than two though."

I could see why. "When do I have to give you my decision?"

"I need to know now." Rose gestured to the row of men, standing shoulder to shoulder, and wearing nothing more than tiny skin-colored loincloths.

"So I have to tell you right now how many men I want as my companions during my entire stay here?" I remembered the manual was clear on this, but now that I stood here, I didn't know how I would be able to decide right away.

"Yes. Then, whichever one you choose will escort you to your room. Of course if you wish to have more than one they will both escort you. I should warn you though, your choice is final."

"Final."

"Yes." Rose's pale pink skirt blew around her slender calves as a warm breeze picked up from the ocean. "Once you take your choice or choices to your room, you will enter their names on your contract."

"Oh, yeah. I read that in the handbook." The handbook, more like a thick encyclopedia, explained all the rules for the island. Everything in it was broken down like an owner's manual. I patted the top of it, which stuck out of my over-sized purse. "I think I've got all of it memorized," I added, grinning and feeling like the student craving the teacher's attention.

"Good girl." Rose nodded her approval. She then gestured to the line of men standing at attention in front of us. "So which one do you want?"

I tapped my lip with my index finger, taking my time looking at the long line of men who stood so solemnly in front of us. This was a very important decision, and one I wished I didn't have to make in a matter of minutes. The man I chose now would be my best friend, fuck me, and do anything I wanted for the next two weeks while I was on the island. There was something odd about leasing a lover, although admittedly, a flare of excitement surged through me as well.

I glanced from one guy to the next, counting them first. Twenty-three guys all gave me impassive stares. Of course, they couldn't look anxious for me to pick them. Instead they simply stared straight ahead, almost as if none of them noticed me and Rose standing there staring at them. A memory of the guards at Buckingham Palace popped into my head. Choosing one who looked interested wouldn't work. Story of my life.

I looked at each one of them again, this time comparing height, and mentally determining how many of them were taller than me. Call me silly, but I like a guy who is taller than I am, although maybe it didn't matter how tall they were if we were lying down.

Hell, it mattered to me.

Ten of them appeared quite a bit taller then my five-foot-six inches.

I was narrowing it down—on a roll now.

Out of the ten finalists, I tried to determine eye color, but I stood too far away.

"Can I get closer to them?" I asked, glancing at Rose.

It amazed me such a young looking woman owned this small island and ran this resort. She hardly met the image I had created in my mind of the shrewd business person reputed as a self-made millionaire and owner of this reclusive island. When we spoke before on the phone she sounded much older.

Rose answered the toll-free number on the pamphlet I found in the backseat of a taxi I'd taken to see a show about a month ago. She explained that Paradise Island was anything but a joke. I made my reservations and gave her my credit card number on the spot.

And I'm not a spontaneous type of gal. I honestly couldn't believe I was doing this. But maybe a soul can take boredom for only so long.

"Not too close. I prefer minimal contact before the contracts are signed. It's on page twenty-three of your handbook."

The handbook was heavy inside my purse. On the small chartered plane that brought me here to Paradise Island, I'd read every word on every page. It was the lawyer in me—automatically checking for loopholes and legalities. I was amazed at the simplicity in the wording, and how exciting it made Paradise Island sound. One thing was quite clear by the time I'd read the handbook from beginning to end, Paradise Island wasn't about finding love. It was about escaping, fulfilling fantasies with no complications. Of course now that I was here, with the sunshine warm on my bare shoulders, and breathtaking views in every direction, Perfect Island would be an even more appropriate name.

Interesting that according to the logistics carefully laid out in the handbook—paradise didn't equate love. I wasn't sure that I agreed. But, I didn't have a problem agreeing with the fact that I wasn't here to fall in love. That isn't something you can pay for—no matter how much money you have.

I remembered something and did pull the handbook out, adjusting my purse strap over my shoulder as I lifted the thick paperback book.

"Just a minute, I know it's right here somewhere." Flipping the pages with my thumb, I refused to glance at Rose and see any strain in her pretty young face. The rather large amount I charged to reserve my room here on the island had already cleared my bank. If I needed a minute, I would take it. "Okay, here it is." I glanced at the chart that explained how much everything cost. "There is an extra charge for more than one."

I ran my fingernail under the line in the handbook where it stated, $10,000 per week included a private room and bath and three meals a day in the dining room. Meals could be served in the room with advance notice. As well, the first escort was included in the package deal, but there was a $2,500 per day charge applied to the credit card on file for each additional escort.

"Of course." Rose smiled easily, and not one wrinkle appeared on her face. Standing next to her for too long would make a girl feel more than inadequate. Anytime I grinned, crow's feet appeared on either side of my eyes. I hated it.

At the rates she charged her guests Rose could afford to stay young and gorgeous for the rest of her life. I wasn't in paradise to get a complex about my looks though.

I returned my attention to the ten men I'd singled out so far. For two weeks—a package deal for twenty grand—the man I chose would be my companion, at my beck and call, to do anything I asked. Anything. No one would rush me with this decision.

Rose glanced at her watch after another minute passed although she didn't say anything. I narrowed it down to five, eliminating the men with facial hair, and with no hair on their chests. Again, my personal preferences. I wanted perfection to join me in paradise, and at this price, I would settle for nothing less.

But that still left five to choose from. Damn. No wonder Rose was a self-made millionaire. Who could choose from the selection of men who stood before me, all of them made of stuff a lady would fantasize about?

Of course it would be nice if I could see them without the loincloths. You know, get the chance to look under the hood before I bought the car—or lease it as the case may be. But that was on page one and page twelve. The men always remained dressed in public. Rose had her reputation to consider.

Finally, after another few minutes, I narrowed it down to two. It was the best I could do. One white man, well more like brown with the perfect tan he had. And the other a dark black man. Both all muscle and drop-dead gorgeous.

"I'll take those two." I pointed to my choices.

Rose smiled. Her tone was gentle and soothing, like she never cared how long it took for me to make my selections. "Perfect choices. Tomas and Nicolas are two of my favorites."

Did Rose get to enjoy all of these men? Like I would ask her that.

"Tomas?" Rose held her hand out and Tomas, the white guy,

stepped forward. "And Nicolas," she said, beckoning to the black guy.

They approached her quietly, both barefoot and walking with controlled steady paces that made them look more like predators than studs just pulled off an auction block.

Both stopped when they stood on either side of her. Rose smiled at them and then looked at me like I was her best friend. "This is Natalie Green. She just arrived here on the island and is my special guest for the next two weeks. Please escort her to room three. I'll stop by shortly to make sure your accommodations are to your liking."

And so that I could sign the contract. The handbook made it very clear. All business matters were tended to promptly as soon as the guest arrived. Then for the rest of my time here, I wouldn't be bothered with anything pertaining to money. Made sense. They would run my credit card for the additional sum of $35,000 within minutes of my settling in. I had no doubts.

One thing about being alone in life, I didn't have to explain my actions, especially when they turned insane. But I had the money. It would serve me nicely in my old age, or give me the memories and adventure of a lifetime, which would also serve me nicely in old age.

Either way, I'd cashed in a few bonds, transferred money, and used my debit card. The transaction was complete before I even touched foot on this tropical island. Of course now, with my additional man, they would charge it again. No regrets. No looking back. My life wasn't exactly anything close to exciting. In fact, there were days when I wondered if I quit existing how long it would take before anyone noticed.

Don't get me wrong. I'm not suicidal. Not even close. Working in my father's law firm for the past ten years, when all my father and grandfather wanted was for me to marry into an acceptable family, didn't exactly fulfill me. They never let me work on any of the good cases, but instead insisted that I present myself at all the charitable functions that they claimed were on behalf of the law firm. Which meant, until I became someone else's trophy to place on the mantle, my father and grandfather didn't have a problem making me their trophy to display. Being placed on display with nothing else to do is boring as hell.

Spending this kind of money to escape my life, to exist as someone else for just a couple weeks, without anyone back home knowing what I was doing, sounded better than perfect to me.

And I hadn't been the only person on the plane. There were other people on this planet just like me, willing to pay a small fortune to indulge in a life that they could never have any other way. Not that I said a word to any of them. No one spoke at all on that plane. One couple and two men walked past me when they boarded the charter plane. But it was obvious on their faces—that dismal, over-worked, humdrum expression slowly faded the closer we got to the island. By the time we landed, I was so enthralled by the captivating surroundings and the young man who escorted me to Rose to choose my companion, that I didn't pay any attention to where the other guests went.

Although I didn't see anyone else from the plane as my two men walked silently alongside me up the wide marble steps toward the huge mansion on top of the hill, I knew there were other guests around somewhere. I didn't mind the privacy. I couldn't help mentally calculating how much money this island might bring in monthly. I also pondered what laws the island would fall under, since it wasn't part of the United States, and appeared to be privately owned.

God. I closed my eyes briefly and gave myself a mental shake. Here I was in paradise, walking with my two men, who were damned near naked, to my private room to enjoy any pleasure I could imagine, and maybe even a few I couldn't. It was just like me to get lost mulling over the legalities of something. No wonder I was stuck on permanently boring and humdrum.

"Are we allowed to talk to each other?" I looked at Tomas, the white guy.

"Sure." He smiled warmly at me.

Nicolas chuckled on the other side of me and I gave him my attention. "We can talk, or do anything else you'd like to do," he said in a deep baritone.

I could listen to Nicolas talk all day. He had that deep sultry black man's voice that would curl any woman's toes as she melted like warm butter at his feet.

"I guess talking will work until we get to our room," I decided.

"What would you like to talk about?" Nicolas asked.

"Well." I thought for a minute, or tried to make it look like I was thinking. My mind was suddenly blanker than the pale blue cloudless sky above us. "Do you two like working here?"

"We don't work." Tomas gently wrapped his fingers around my arm, just above my elbow.

"Good answer," I conceded. If he acknowledged any of this as work, it would fall under the line of prostitution. The handbook must have been looked over by a fleet of lawyers before being published. Nothing in it could be construed as illegal. "I guess I should ask if you like it here."

"Trust me, this is paradise. Your room is this way."

The stairs ended and the men led me along a path surrounded by beautiful gardens on either side.

"You're right about that." I breathed in the thick perfume coming from the variety of flowers. Maybe touching on a lighter subject would force the men to sway from their scripted answers. "I'm not an expert, but aren't those orchids?"

"Among other things, the island is known for its gardens." Nicolas's hand was so warm when he pressed it between my shoulder blades. "Those are oncidium orchids," he informed me, pointing at bright yellow flowers that grew in a thick patch to our left. "And the lavender ones over here are dendrobium orchids."

"You know a lot more about flowers than I do," I offered, laughing easily at my ignorance.

The men chuckled but they weren't laughing at me. Years of analyzing people taught me when someone was relaxed or not. And Tomas and Nicholas were perfectly at ease as they escorted me along the wide sidewalk with the vibrant flowers and ivy bordering either side.

"Feel free to ask anything," Tomas said. "I know more about some things than others."

It was on the tip of my tongue to ask what he knew more about. Gorgeous was putting it mildly with him. His dark sandy blond hair waved naturally around his face and curled at his neck. There was a roguish look about him. The way he held himself, walked with such confidence wearing next to nothing, was enough to know that very little would embarrass him. I'd always wished that I could move through life with such self-assurance that every emotion I had wasn't obvious on my face.

"What do you know most about?" I had to ask.

Tomas grinned and my heart kicked in to overdrive.

"Sex, my dear," he said without hesitating.

2

Natalie

It was a damned good thing that Nicolas stepped in front of me at that moment. If he hadn't, I probably would have walked into the glass doors. Nicolas pulled open the door and held it for me while Tomas kept his hand on my arm and escorted me through a huge foyer.

"I guess that makes sense," I said quietly, my mouth suddenly dryer than sandpaper.

"We also know how to make you very comfortable," Tomas offered. "In no time, you'll be convinced you've lived here forever. We're going to show you pleasures that will make you forget you ever had another life before arriving here."

His tone was dark, and rushed over my skin, giving me goose bumps and making my nipples hard and aching for attention. At this rate, I'd be an over-sensitive, sex starved babbling idiot before we got to my room. Which, when I thought about it, might be Rose's plan of attack. Get the clients so worked up that any sex would be good sex by the time they got it. Although a quick look at my two escorts and I knew beyond any doubt that sex with them would be extraordinary.

My sandals slapped against my feet and echoed throughout the large room. I glanced up and saw a balcony that disappeared into several hallways. The foyer was two-stories tall. The walls were all glass, which showed off the incredible gardens outside. The place was stunning, captivating, and absolutely breathtaking. Walking between these two gods, wearing my shorts and tank top, I felt anything but pretty. They, on the other hand, were the perfect addition to this incredible mansion.

"The architecture is as amazing as the gardens," I murmured, looking up at a smoothly carved archway as we walked under it.

"Is that your area of expertise?" Nicolas asked.

I didn't mean to laugh. "Hardly. I'm a lawyer."

Nicolas's expression didn't change, which probably meant he'd never had to experience getting a lawyer. I was going to be with these two men every minute for the next two weeks, and although I'd planned on living out a fantasy and not dwelling on the real world, they were both making it easy to talk. And like I had anyone to talk about other than myself.

"You two already have me pulled out of my world enough that I didn't give my standard answer." For some reason, I wanted to impress them. Neither man batted an eye at my profession, and although I didn't do a damned thing all day, the office I worked in was known nationwide.

"Good," Tomas said quickly. "No standard answers required."

"I'm a junior partner with the office of Green, Green and Albert."

"Junior partner?" Tomas sounded confused and intrigued.

"Green and Green? Isn't your last name Green?" Nicolas rubbed his thumb over my bare arm and smiled down at me.

Apparently neither one of them had heard of Green, Green and Albert.

"Yes, it is. But I'm not either one of those Greens. My grandfather and father are partners with my uncle in the practice. And I don't feel I do much to earn my paycheck. I know it sounds terribly childish of me to complain, and I'm sure many would kill for my position, but I'd love a bit of the action. Unfortunately, my father and uncle take all the good cases, and I get to sit pretty in an even prettier office. My father feels he's done his duty in providing for me by employing me, although I know he wishes I would marry someone with a background that he approves of and throw lavish parties like my mother does." I realized I'd been rambling and quit talking, sucking in a breath and wondering if I'd just bored both of them to death.

"There's nothing wrong with wanting to pull your own weight." Nicolas nodded like he understood.

"Elevator or stairs?" Tomas asked when we reached a huge living room.

There were couches and overstuffed chairs everywhere, but there wasn't anyone else around. It seemed such a huge place to be so empty.

"Elevator," I decided, more than willing to change the subject. After all, this was my vacation. And if I was going to spend it with these two men, I didn't want them thinking of me as some boring stuffed shirt. That's what everyone else in my world was, not me.

"Good choice," Nicolas whispered from just behind me.

I couldn't help wonder why he liked my decision. Both men were in incredible shape. Maybe they saw that I was a bit on the pudgy side, and agreed with my mental decision that it would take every bit of stamina I possessed to take on two men. Or maybe he simply didn't want to climb the stairs. Shit. Maybe I needed to relax and quit trying to second-guess everything they said.

God. What had I been thinking? How long had it been since I'd had sex with one man? And I'd never had sex with two guys at once. Hell I'd never even dared imagine such a thing. Well . . . maybe I had imagined it once or twice. Acknowledging my own daydreams brought heat to my cheeks and I looked down at my polished nails and endured the silence as the two men stood on either side of me.

If my daydreams of kinky sex made me blush, how would I handle fucking two men in real life?

Like a bumbling fool, I told myself bitterly.

Tomas pushed the button for the elevator and the doors slid open immediately. He gestured for me to enter, and I led the way into the small space that smelled like the gardens outside. Nicolas pushed a button and the doors closed silently behind them as they continued facing me, instead of turning to stare at the closed doors like elevator etiquette required.

Suddenly I was alone, confined in a very small space with two of the most gorgeous men I'd ever laid eyes on. They would be my lovers. By the time I left this island I would know every inch of their muscle-packed bodies by heart.

Heat attacked my cheeks at the thought of it. What if I couldn't go through with it? How would I start things? I'd never been any good at flirting with men. Probably why I never dated, or got asked out on dates. Men were strange creatures, ones that I barely understood, even in the romance novels that I devoured daily while sitting behind my desk with no work to do. And now, two of them stood inches away from me, practically naked, shy of a very small piece of material that barely covered each of their cocks.

My cheeks had to be three shades of red from embarrassment and humiliation that burned my flesh with no mercy. And I was a blotcher. Anytime I got embarrassed, patches of red would cover my cheeks and neck. I bet at that moment I probably looked like I'd just contracted some rare island disease. One that left hideous red circles all over a person's face and neck.

I looked down in a feeble attempt to hide my sudden condition and got an eyeful of their loincloths. They'd either stuffed whatever was underneath those cloths with a lot of socks, or both of them were already semihard.

Oh, Lord.

"Would it be okay if I kissed you?" Nicolas's deep voice was hypnotic.

I must have looked like a deer caught in headlights. Just great. Now not only was I blotchy, I was suddenly rendered mute while goose bumps chased each other over my flesh. They would be calling a paramedic by the time we reached my room.

"Uh-huh." I couldn't believe I agreed. My answer just slipped out of my mouth.

"Good. I wasn't sure I could wait until we got to the room." Nicolas moved into my space.

I backed up until the cool hardness of the smooth wall pressed against my bare shoulders and the back of my legs. His hands touched my cheeks, and he lifted my face to his. He had the most beautiful milk chocolate-colored eyes. And his lips. They were full, soft, and looked like they would be very, very good at kissing.

Nicolas's face blurred when he brought his lips to mine. Then I realized, like a complete klutz, that I stared at him wide-eyed as he closed in for that first kiss. I must've appeared like some adolescent, who didn't know the first thing about how to even return something as simple as a kiss.

"Oh," I murmured when he pressed his mouth over mine.

I mentally kicked myself. I wasn't some girl, ignorant of how to please a man. Maybe I didn't get out every night, and unfortunately I didn't have tons of conquests under my belt. But I knew how to be romantic. And I damn sure knew how to please a man and make him enjoy himself.

Opening my mouth, I tilted my head and closed my eyes. I was going to enjoy every damned minute of this. And oh, boy, was I off to a good start. The moment my body relaxed, Nicolas growled quietly, the sound reverberating straight to the core of my body. Every inch of me tingled as his tongue moved cautiously into my mouth and his lips sealed against mine.

And then the elevator did a very neat trick. It seemed to turn sideways when he deepened the kiss, or at least I would swear that it felt like it did. He brushed his fingers over my chin and then down my neck, barely touching me, yet igniting tiny fireworks that exploded inside me and created a burning passion that instantly throbbed furiously between my legs.

Nicolas brushed his tongue over my teeth and then, tilting his head and opening his mouth a bit further until I almost collapsed into his hard packed body, he devoured me like he'd kissed me a million times. His arm wrapped around me, holding me firmly against him. I don't think I'd ever been turned on so much by just a kiss.

When he released my mouth, I was sure I would never breathe the same way again. I simply stared up at him, my jaw hanging open, and then ran my tongue over my lips and tasted him there still.

"You do that very well." And I wanted more immediately.

"My turn." Tomas took my hand and pulled me to him, then wrapped his arms around me and bent me over until I thought I'd fall on my back. Except his muscular arms kept me pinned against his virile body.

I groaned and didn't even try to hold myself up. His arms were like steel. And he used his teeth. Just a bit. But when he nibbled on my lower lip something inside me exploded, like a dam that held all of my apprehension and nervousness broke and every bit of fear and uncertainty that I had about this place flowed out of me. I was suddenly as light as the air, floating and drowning at the same time. My nipples were so hard they ached. And my breasts swelled, suddenly aching painfully while being crushed against his rock-hard body.

"Holy shit," I cried out when he straightened my body and let go of my mouth at the same time. "Who taught you to do that?"

"I'll take that as a compliment." Tomas grinned, looking very pleased with himself.

"I'm sure in for a hell of a ride." There I went babbling again, obviously no longer in control of anything that came out of my mouth with these two studs turning me into a pile of mush.

"Yes, you are," Tomas promised, his grin wicked.

My heart beat so hard I could barely breathe as I stared at my two men. Both of them looked like they couldn't wait to devour me.

"Just wait until we get to your room," Nicolas promised.

3

Natalie

The doors opened behind my two men and they reached for me, each of them taking my hand as the three of us left the elevator. Nicolas and Tomas continued holding my hands, like we were three lifelong best friends and guided me down a wide hallway with doors that were so spread out we'd passed two of them before I noticed the numbers on them.

"Here is your room." Nicolas reached for the long gold handle and turned it down. The door opened, apparently unlocked. "Let's make sure everything is to your liking. Rose will be here shortly and will make any adjustments that you wish. Once she leaves, it's just the three of us for the rest of your time here. So now is the time to speak up if you aren't pleased with something."

I remembered the handbook saying that I had a certain amount of time to request a change if my escort wasn't to my liking, or in my case now, my escorts.

"I don't see anything I don't like." I stared at their firm asses as they walked in ahead of me.

It was my first chance to take in their backsides. The loincloths didn't cover their bottoms and I got an eyeful of black and white buns of steel. Who the hell cared what the room looked like?

Rose swept into the room a few minutes later, placing my contract on the table by the balcony and bringing my brain back to matters of business. I sat at the table and didn't pay a lot of attention to the three of them as they chatted easily about the weather and how wonderful a certain type of flower looked now that it was in full bloom. It was like the three of them truly lived a life without care, or had any problems like the rest of the world had.

They left me alone while I read every word of the contract. It was verbatim to the one that was offered as an example in the handbook. The only difference was that Rose changed the wording from singular to plural when referring to my escorts. Satisfied that everything was in order, I signed at the end of the contract, and dated it.

"Here is my personal cell phone number." Rose handed me a pretty card, decorated with flowers and with her name and number etched in fancy calligraphy on it. "Paradise Island doesn't have an operator. I'll personally answer unless I'm with another client, in which case just leave a voice mail and I'll call you back immediately. Of course room service will provide your meals here if you don't wish to go to the dining hall. I'm sure you'll find everything to be perfect. But if you need anything, just call me, or Nicolas or Tomas can get you whatever you want as well."

"So far I'm very pleased," I told her and was proud of myself for not blushing.

Rose looked like I just paid her the highest of compliments, her creamy cheeks glowing a pale pink as she smiled sincerely. "Very good. Enjoy your stay here." Either she was a very skilled actress, or Rose sincerely loved her job and receiving compliments was something she took to heart. Maybe the skeptic in me leaned toward the former.

Tomas followed her to the door and closed it behind her then turned and grinned at me. "What do you want to do first?" he asked.

"Do you mind if we take these off?" Nicolas reached for his loincloth. "They really aren't as comfortable as they look."

"That's fine." Like I would tell him no. "And we can do whatever you two want to do."

"Good." Tomas slid his loincloth down his legs.

Apparently they fit like thongs, with thin elastic bands holding the small piece of material in place over their cocks.

Tomas straightened and I stared at the most perfectly shaped cock I'd ever seen in my life. "I would love to fuck you," he told me.

"Or would you like to fuck me first?" Nicolas asked, shoving his loincloth down his thick thighs and then stepping out of it. "Although if you're up to it, we could both fuck you at the same time."

I gawked at one cock, and then the other. Here came the red blotches again. And I had to be imagining this. There weren't even romance scenes in the books I loved reading that embarrassed me like this did. Worse yet, or maybe it wasn't that bad I had to admit to myself, I loved it. My heart raced and my body was tormented with need that I knew would be more than satisfied. Both of them had raging hard-ons.

I snapped my mouth shut, suddenly aware that my jaw was almost hanging to the floor, and almost bit my tongue. Two of the best looking men in the world were asking me which of them I wanted to fuck first. Or gee, would I prefer to have them both fuck me at the same time? What the hell did I say to that?

"Sure." Like that answered their question. This wasn't how I acted in my fantasies, but no matter how much I lectured myself to be the perfect seductress, I was truly out of my league.

I silently thanked both of them for pretending not to notice that once again they'd rendered me speechless.

"Maybe I could help you out of your clothes?" Tomas didn't act like my one word answer confused him in the least.

These two were definitely paid well. They had to be. Otherwise they probably both would be rolling on the floor laughing their asses off right about now.

"And how does some wine sound?" Nicolas walked over to the small refrigerator and bent over to open it.

My mouth went dry watching long corded muscles strain in his legs and ass. Every inch of him was such a perfect shade of dark brown. His ass was firm, solid, and hard packed just like the rest of him.

"Wine is good." Anything liquid would do right now. My mouth was drier than sandpaper.

"Would you look at how lucky we are?" Tomas lifted my tank top and then stared at my small breasts as if he'd just discovered gold.

I looked down at myself, confused. "What?" I asked, then glanced around me to see what he was talking about.

"I've never seen such beautiful nipples. Do you know how much I love large nipples?"

"I've got more nipples then breasts." I looked down at my 34Bs, breasts that had been the same size since the eighth grade.

"Damn." Nicolas popped the cork and simply held the bottle, gazing at me like I was some kind of goddess. "She's fucking perfect."

"I'll say." Tomas pulled my tank top over my head and then reached for my shorts. "Let's see all of you, please?"

"By all means."

"I bet she's soaked." Nicolas watched but also managed to pour wine into three glasses.

He brought mine to me and I was surprised that the glass was chilled.

He gave Tomas a glass and then lifted his to his lips, his attention riveted to me as Tomas slid my shorts down my legs.

"I love a shaved pussy," Tomas exclaimed, taking a quick drink of his wine and then putting the glass on the table next to me. He was on his knees in front of me and used both hands to pull my shorts to the floor. "I have to taste you," he said, then pressed his mouth to my clit before I could answer.

Which was a damned good thing. I couldn't have formed a single word if I had to at that moment. I did manage to grin though. How many women sipped at wine while a gorgeous hunk knelt before them and licked and stroked their pussy with a tongue skilled enough to push them toward the edge faster than they wanted to go.

I stepped out of my shorts and spread my legs, offering him room to explore with his mouth as he pressed his tongue over my clit and then put his hands on my ass to hold me in place while tasting me.

Nicolas moved next to me, still holding his wine. "The only thing better than fine wine is tasting it on a beautiful woman. May I?"

I wasn't sure what he asked to do but nodded my consent and took another quick sip of the wine, which tasted like a damned good year.

Tomas's mouth was performing some awesome tricks on my pussy. Already my legs were wobbly and I grabbed his shoulder with my free hand, stabilizing myself so that I wouldn't fall over on him.

Nicolas dipped his finger into his wine and then touched my nipple. He rubbed the cool wine over my puckered flesh and then dipped his finger into his glass again. He appeared to take the task of meticulously painting my nipple and breast with the alcohol very seriously. Then putting down the glass, he placed his hand on the middle of my back and lowered his mouth to my breast.

"Oh, my God." I would have dropped my wine right on Tomas's head if one of them, and hell if I knew which one, hadn't taken my wineglass from me.

I had two mouths on me. One sucked my breast while the other feasted on my pussy. Wave after wave of greedy desire mixed with intense satisfaction warred with each other as they rushed over my body. I was flooded with lust, not wanting either one of them to stop.

Nicolas and Tomas paid very close attention to detail. My pussy tingled and was soaked and throbbing when Tomas moved his mouth away and began planting moist kisses on my inner thighs. Nicolas moved from one breast to the other. They took their time, loving me with their mouths, until I turned into one open and very raw nerve ending. I shivered, although I was anything but cold. And as they kissed and licked, feasting on me like two starving men, the pressure built inside me until I couldn't take it any longer.

My legs gave out and I crumbled over Tomas. "Oh, my God!" I cried out, no longer caring that I had no social graces when it came to group sex. Embarrassment was the last thing I felt. "I just came!"

"I know you did." Nicolas sounded very satisfied.

"And you're going to come again, very soon." Tomas grabbed me, breaking my fall, and lifted me into his arms.

I felt the hard throb of his dick poking my ass as he carried me to the very large bed in the middle of the room. "What are you going to do to me now?" I asked.

"Absolutely everything," Tomas promised.

Nicolas was right behind me, chuckling.

Every inch of my body tingled, and my pussy started swelling all over again, anxious to learn what absolutely everything might be. I was ready to come again. And I couldn't wait to find out what they would do next.

4

Malachi

"No one ever chooses these models," Rose announced, walking in to the large warehouse with Charles, Phillip, Adrian, and Maggie. It was amazing how such an incredibly beautiful woman could bitch so much yet not develop those nag lines that so many women like her got. "Malachi, what are you going to do about this?"

I didn't see any reason to glance away from the monitor screens on the wall. "Do about what, Rose?"

"Do about what, Rose," she mimicked, then walked up and slapped my shoulder. "What are you going to do about these models that no one ever wants? They're a waste of flesh."

I did finally look past her at Charles, Phillip, Adrian, and Maggie. "How are you guys doing today?" I could kick Rose's ass for calling them wastes of flesh in front of their faces. She didn't get it. I wanted to say they were human, too. And damn it, part of me really believed they were. I was human, and I made them.

"Doing good, boss." Adrian was the most laid back of the

group. His crooked grin was a classic bonus that Rose wouldn't ever appreciate. "That is, for a waste of flesh."

When Rose gasped, Adrian winked at me, and I couldn't help laughing. "None of you are a waste of flesh, no matter what Queen Grouch says."

"Malachi!" Rose looked horrified. "Don't speak about me like that in front of them. They must always respect me completely."

"Then maybe you shouldn't insult them to their faces," I said coldly. "Why don't you all go help supervise the Adams?"

"I'm sorry we let you down," Maggie whispered when she walked by.

I wanted to kick Rose's ass more than usual. I kept my cool for the companions' sake, and didn't let any of them see how pissed Rose made me as the four of them headed over to the other end of the warehouse.

"I swear to God they've got more of a heart than you do," I hissed, glaring at her.

Rose brushed her nicely painted fingernails over her thick black hair. "Don't be silly, Malachi." She finally gathered enough intelligence in that pompous brain of hers to lower her voice to a conspiratorial whisper. "They're machines, sweetheart. Sometimes I swear that you forget that."

"They're also the reason your income is over six figures annually," I threw out at her. I shouldn't have been surprised to see no level of compassion register in her face.

Instead, she smiled softly. "Malachi, dear, don't get jealous of them."

"What?" I would never be able to follow Rose's line of thinking.

Her thin, delicate looking fingers were as cold as the rest of her when she gripped my shoulder and squeezed. "Give yourself credit. I give myself credit. In spite of how successful the companions are, I know that if I hadn't had the ingenuity to discover your talents and offer you a job, and if you hadn't been willing to make your home here and continue with your work, we wouldn't be as filthy rich as we are now."

She leaned over to kiss my cheek and if she noticed me stiffen, she ignored it. Rose didn't care about me. Her actions were simply to appease. If anything rang true and consistent about my business partner, it was that she was a cold, heartless bitch, concerned only with the almighty dollar and how many of them she could rub together.

It became clear a long time ago that telling her I didn't care about the money only made her angry. "Was there something else you needed?" I returned my attention once again to the monitors, which allowed me to watch all of the companions, and make sure nothing ever went wrong.

"There's always something I want," she purred, and then scratched my shoulders with her fingernails.

When Rose offered herself to me, she wanted something badly. After ten years on this island, she still hadn't figured out that there weren't any sparks between us. I didn't have a problem admitting that Rose Bontiki was an incredibly gorgeous woman, and on more than one occasion, guests arriving on the island requested her for their companion over one of my creations. Fortunately for our guests, Rose refused to be a companion.

"What would that be?" I asked, and adjusted one of the monitors so that I could see one of the guests in her room.

"Is this how you get your rocks off?" she hissed. "Watching our guests get laid in their rooms? You know if anyone ever caught you doing that . . ."

"Which they won't because guests aren't allowed in this part of the island." I glanced down at the printout of the guests who'd just arrived this morning. This guest was Natalie Green, from Chicago, a lawyer from one of the larger firms in the Midwest. "And no, this isn't how I get my rocks off. This is how I make sure that my companions perform properly." I looked away from the pretty lawyer before her actions did start to affect me. "What do you want, Rose?"

She immediately looked offended. Not that her pouting expression fazed me a bit. I glanced over my shoulder at her but then focused on the rest of the printouts. Then, adjusting the monitors, I focused on each companion who was matched up with our new guests. Occasionally a companion wasn't compatible with a guest, and I liked finding that out before the companion sensed trouble.

Rose grabbed my shoulder, pinching her long fingernails into my bare flesh while flashing me one of her famous, empty smiles. "I want companions that guests will fight over," she said coolly.

"Then maybe you should leave me alone so that I can work." If any guest knew that two people who hated each other's guts ran paradise, they'd laugh us right out of the Pacific. "Thanks for bringing the gang back to me," I added, putting a cheerful edge in my voice intentionally, just to get under her skin.

"You better work on your gang," she said under her breath, and gave me one of her million-dollar smiles—literally, since I knew first hand. I gave it to her with her last plastic surgery procedure. Rose turned, tossed her thick black hair over her shoulder and sashayed her way out of the warehouse.

She glanced over her shoulder when the sun hit her hair and showed off the faint red highlights. Her smile became sincere when she caught me watching her. Let her think what she wanted, it made it easier to work with her. Raising a limp hand in a gesture of good-bye, I returned my attention to the monitors.

Five guests arrived this morning. Four other guests were already here and would be for another few days. I switched channels from the hot lawyer before I forgot why I was sitting here, and found Mr. Hardister, who for some reason had turned in his last two female companions and was now working on his third. The island had a policy that guaranteed customer satisfaction, but Hardister was taking advantage of the policy. I had no doubts. Especially as he sat watching the morning news, remote in hand, with Maria on her knees in front of him giving him a blow job.

I almost pitied Maria. She was one of our more popular companions. I'd done a damned good job mixing her personality chips when I'd created her. Always a smile on her face, and up for just about anything, Maria charmed anyone she spent time with. If Hardister complained about her, I would have to talk to Rose. It would mean that Hardister was abusing policy and simply wanting to switch out companions every couple of days while he was here on the island—and complaining they didn't satisfy him got him out of paying for extra companions.

"Malachi?" Maggie brushed her fingers over my bare shoulder.

"What, sweetheart?" I asked, turning my attention from my work and adjusting the stool so I faced her.

"The Adams are acting up again." She made a quirky expression and smiled.

Maggie was best described as a living, breathing Barbie doll, complete with her tanned skin and straight, waist-length blonde hair. And she was beautiful beyond fault, although maybe I was biased.

"Those damned Adams," I said playfully, and stood, tickling her and laughing when she did.

My companions might be created to offer sexual pleasure, but to me, they were my children. I couldn't think of them any other way. Putting my arm around Maggie, I hurried over to where two of the Adams were repeatedly walking into each other.

Of all my creations, the Adams probably shouldn't hold such a special place with me. I knew no one understood why I didn't scrap them. Hell, sometimes when they created more work than they accomplished, I didn't understand why I kept them activated. But then there were times like now.

"Hold on to that Adam," I instructed Maggie, pointing to the manlike android, whose face wasn't even partially developed. "I'll grab this one. On my word, face him toward the door."

"Roger that," Maggie said, laughing as she jumped around the two Adams. "Why do they do this?" she asked, her tone proof she was curious and not condemning.

Thank God they acted up after Rose left. "Circuit malfunction," I huffed out, wrapping my arms around the waist of one of them, which wasn't an easy trick since he kept stepping forward and backward. "Okay, Maggie, now!"

I turned my Adam and Maggie turned hers. I grunted and huffed loudly. Lifting a grown man was no easy task. Maggie lifted hers, the amused grin on her face never fading. She reminded me again why I didn't regret making my later models stronger than the average human. The two androids, dressed in loincloths like the other companions on the island, walked out of the warehouse like nothing happened.

"Can you fix them?" she asked.

I started after them, deciding it would be best to see what shorted out now before they damaged anything or themselves. "They won't ever be like you or the other companions. But I'm going to do a diagnostic on both of them now, I think."

Maggie didn't say anything. And although I knew she wasn't programmed to judge, I gave personal thanks anyway that she didn't. There were times when I thought I understood parents of physically deformed children. They loved their kids just like a parent of a normal looking child would. And that's how the Adams were to me.

An hour later, after Charles and Phillip helped me carry the Adams to my laboratory, I sent the companions away, and stood in between the tables where the two Adams lay motionless. It didn't seem so long ago when I first created life, and now here my first attempt at it looked lifeless on the tables.

"Don't go getting all emotional, old man," I told myself, and walked over to the computer where I kept my logs on each model.

The Adams were my first attempt, and didn't have human faces or the ability to speak. I admitted, as I stared down at one of them and brushed my knuckles over his skinlike cheek, I'd come a long way in mastering a human nose. Nonetheless, when these Adams were "brought to life" they were a mile marker in robotics.

I remember that day like it was yesterday, and my excitement when they sat up on a table so similar to this one and walked over to the counter and poured a glass of water and brought it to me. Without the aid of a remote. My staff at the time applauded my efforts, and the next day I was on the front pages of all the national newspapers in France.

"The beginning of the end," I grumbled bitterly, returning my attention to my computer.

The last thing I expected to be doing for the next decade was mastering my creations and creating companions to offer sexual pleasure.

I typed in quick notes on their latest malfunction, hopping up several times to confirm which wires cross circuited, and then kicked back in front of the computer.

There were several blogs I kept an eye on, mainly my competitors and what they were up to these days. Sometimes spending so many years on this island made it easy to forget the rest of the world was out there. I'm not vain, not at all, but I don't want to hear that someone is getting the better of me and coming out with something that I haven't thought of yet.

A box popped up in front of the Web site I was looking at and I groaned.

"I don't like her," the instant-message box read, and the statement was followed by a link. Rose wouldn't leave me alone even when she was on the other side of the island.

I clicked on the link without responding and watched as it quickly opened in front of me. The link was to an article about a law firm in Chicago that had successfully won a lawsuit for a medical supply company that we used. I leaned forward, resting my chin on my hands and read about Green, Green and Albert, Attorneys at Law. It didn't surprise me that Rose wouldn't like our new guest, without even bothering to get to know her. Rose didn't like anyone who she viewed as competition, and any pretty lady arriving on the island, Rose viewed as a threat.

"It doesn't even mention her name," I said out loud and brought the blog I'd been scanning back up in front of the chat box. Devlin Products was still boasting their latest personality chip. I clicked a few more links, searching where I could to learn how far they'd come with it. "Not even close, my friends," I said, admitting relief and satisfaction when I leaned back in my chair, clasping my hands behind my head and grinning at the screen. "My Adams are still better than anything you've got."

Rose's chat box started flashing. I wouldn't have acknowledged it but the word "robot" was visible from behind the blog.

"Check this out. Another of our new arrivals, James Martin, did a paper for this scientific journal on robots. I did a search on his name and it came up."

Rose loved investigating all of her guests, probably as soon as their money cleared the bank.

Ignoring Rose when she sent another message, I focused on finishing my log entry on the Adams. Then standing and stretching, I headed over to the window that looked out over the courtyard between the few buildings that were my world: the warehouse to my left and the dorms where the companions stayed to the right.

I watched two of my companions walk from the dormitory

to the warehouse, more than likely headed over to finish the work that the Adams weren't able to finish.

I hated the thought of shutting down my Adams. They weren't perfect, but it wasn't their fault. Watching Adrian and Phillip disappear into the warehouse, I didn't need to see more to know they'd have the task the Adams were doing done in minutes. Unloading the boxes of supplies that arrived in the cargo area of the plane that brought our guests to the island kept the Adams busy. It was grunt work. But work they could do.

Staring past my buildings to the mountain that blocked my view of Rose's mansion, I considered going back to the warehouse and dealing with the Adams later. "Probably wouldn't be a bad idea," I mumbled to myself, glancing at the clock and noting that it would be lunchtime soon. If Maggie was anything, she was a damned good cook, and word had it she was making enchiladas for lunch. I'd check in on Adrian and Phillip in the warehouse, go over the inventory list to make sure everything I'd ordered showed up, and double-check to make sure all the companions up at the mansion were behaving themselves with our guests.

I certainly wasn't going back to the warehouse and the monitoring screens to check out our new guest, Miss Green, the lawyer. I wasn't a voyeur, and I didn't care how she looked while fucking Tomas and Nicolas at the same time.

5

Natalie

Tomas stretched out next to me. Nicolas was on the other side of me. I looked down and saw their legs brush against each other. Their arms almost touched as they reached for me. But neither of them seemed to notice that they were so close to each other. All of their attention was on me.

God. I would pay willingly for this much attention from two gorgeous men every day—if I had that kind of money.

Which I didn't.

"I'm going to remember every minute of these two weeks," I murmured, letting my head fall back on thick long pillows.

"That's the idea." Nicolas brushed his fingers over my belly and looked up at me with very dark brown eyes.

My tummy fluttered, even though his touch was casual. I couldn't believe how swollen and wet my pussy felt. It throbbed harder than the rest of me, making me feel like part of me had taken on a life of its own.

"I have a confession." My two studs for hire might as well know the truth about me now. "I've never been with two men before."

"How flattering." Tomas's sandy blond hair parted at an angle over his head. A wavy strand fell over his broad forehead, making him look rather roguish. "You seem very relaxed with us. We must be doing something right."

I made a rather humiliating snorting sound, a forced laugh that I never gave much thought to when I was at work. But right now, it seemed so unladylike and unattractive. It amazed me that neither man's expression changed. They adored me, and stared at me like I truly was a sex goddess. It was like they were the ones paying for time with me, and wanted to enjoy every minute of my perfection.

Except I was far from perfect.

"You two are doing everything right. I'm the one who's the dunce."

"Then you're the sexiest dunce I've ever seen," Nicolas muttered, his deep baritone scraping over my already raw and sensitive flesh.

"Now I know you're paid to say that."

"Nope." Nicolas looked so serious I almost believed him.

"Okay. You're right." I thought I understood his point. "This is a fantasy, a living fantasy. I should quit thinking about money, or how I really look, or any of my imperfections."

"Money doesn't matter. And as for your imperfections, if that is what you're focusing on right now, you must be getting really bored." Tomas leaned into me, nipping at my lip. "Sweetheart, I don't see any imperfections."

"You're right. I'm perfect," I whispered, smiling as I relaxed against the bed. Who wouldn't feel perfect with all this attention?

I closed my eyes, feeling every inch of me tingle and let him kiss me. When Nicolas found my breast and began suckling me, I jumped. But Tomas gripped my shoulder, pressing me farther into the large stuffed pillow behind my head, and deepened the kiss.

Their hands were everywhere, caressing and stroking me until a fire that started between my legs burned out of control throughout my entire body.

"This feels so good." I felt I had to praise them somehow, let both men know how wonderful it was to have all of their attention.

Growing up under the close scrutiny of my father, the only men who dared to get close to me were ones who saw dollar signs. They were boring, self-focused, and seemed more interested in impressing my father than me. But these two knew nothing about me. I know they blessed me with so much attention because they were paid to do just that, but I was going to enjoy my fantasy. If I was cursed to be rich for the rest of my life, the least I could do was splurge and enjoy this erotic fantasy.

I opened my eyes just in time to see Nicolas's very white teeth clasping my nipple and stretching it as he held on.

"Oh, Lord!" One of my hands was underneath Tomas's body so I only had one hand free, which instantly went to Nicolas's head.

It dawned on me this was the first time I'd touched either one of them intimately. And his black, shiny bald head was smoother than I imagined it would be. It didn't feel like he shaved his head. It was so smooth I'd swear that no hair grew there at all. He didn't let go, but looked up at me with an intensely penetrating stare that just about made me come.

"Her nipples sure crave the attention." Tomas flicked the other one with his finger just hard enough to make me jump.

"Apparently so." I hadn't noticed this about me before. "Shit."

Tomas shifted his body, touching my side everywhere as he slid down me and started feasting on my other breast.

"Watch us," he instructed, his mouth full of nipple.

I lifted my head and did as I was told. Tomas, with his blond hair, and Nicolas, with his bald black head, had their faces right next to each other. But it was like neither knew the other was there. It was the most erotic sight I'd ever seen in my life. Both of them feasting on my breasts, taking their task very seriously with their eyes closed and humming with very deep baritones as if I fed them a meal they'd been craving all their lives.

And my God! What they did for me! Sparks and tingles danced inside me, leaving my breasts and racing to my pussy. They built a pressure inside me that made me even wetter. My thighs were damp and the cream covering my shaved skin turned me on as much as what they were doing to me did.

I touched both of them. Spreading my fingers over their shoulder blades and back, it was kind of fun exploring their bodies. A bit of confidence built inside me. They seemed so pleased with me it helped me want to please them. Suddenly I wanted to know what it would look like to see them groaning with pleasure, to watch while they came.

I really wished I had more experience in this area. I guess I was paying a hell of a fee to gain that experience. And so typical— when I want something, I take it to the extreme so that I walk away fully educated in every detail. Talk about sex-ed extravaganza! I would learn all there was to know all at once.

And damn! If these two weren't eager to share with me every bit of skill that they possessed. It was impossible to say which one I enjoyed more. If I closed my eyes, and I did even though they wanted me watching, and stroked their bodies, I couldn't tell them apart. Not until I reached their faces and felt that wonderful wavy hair and smooth bald head. Of course, I knew which one was on which side of me, but still, it was an interesting discovery while brushing my fingertips back down their shoulders and to their arms. Their muscles bulged the same, rippled and stretched under smooth skin the same. My compliments to their trainer for buffing them up so perfectly.

Nicolas and Tomas continued devouring my breasts until every inch of me pulsed with need. I wanted their mouths elsewhere. More than anything, I ached to feel them inside me. If I could remember how to speak, I'd let them know that. But not only was I not sure my mouth would work at the moment, my brain didn't seem interested in forming words for me to say.

So I did the next best thing. I dragged my nails down their backs, scraping their skin with my fingernails. Both men groaned and arched their backs slightly—just enough to show me I gave them pleasure.

A sensation hit me harder than all the lust consuming my body. I could control both of these men. Not with my words. Not with manipulative behavior—but with touch. With my body.

I almost laughed out loud. My body, with my 34Bs and soft tummy that wasn't firm and trim like so many of the ladies in my world, had both of these men harder than steel. My fingernails, professionally done at my local salon before I left town, had them purring like cats.

Very dangerous and virile cats.

I raked their backs harder with my fingernails.

"Damn, baby." Nicolas bit my nipple hard enough that a shock wave rattled my entire body.

I dug into his flesh and he gripped my arm, raising his face to mine.

"A small amount of pain intensifies the pleasure, don't you think?"

I opened my mouth, but then got lost in his sultry gaze.

Tomas grunted, as if seconding the statement, and then pressed his hand over my abdomen, stretching his fingers while whipping my tender nipple with his tongue.

"Not too much," Nicolas added. "But just enough to stimulate the body, allow it to feel and experience every bit of pleasure possible."

"That makes sense." My lips were dry and I ran my tongue over them but it didn't help. I swallowed.

Nicolas smiled. "There are parts of the body," he squeezed the nipple he'd just sucked, "that will offer stimulation to other parts of the body if they are tormented just enough. Some might call it torture, without the pain."

"It's certainly stimulating me." Simply staring into his beautiful face, so dark with eyes that looked like they knew my mind better than I did, was a form of torture in itself. I ached to know more about him, learn why he was here, and how he learned so much about sexual pleasure.

As gorgeous as he was, it wasn't hard to figure out the latter.

"I can only imagine what else you might know," I prodded.

"Today you'll do more than imagine." Nicolas spoke with calm confidence. His baritone was equivalent to that of a deadly purr.

"Oh really? I can imagine a lot." I didn't blush this time. And I was damned proud of my increase in confidence.

Not that I ever thought I wasn't good. I know I am. And intelligent, and all that other stuff. But I'm no runway model, which were the kind of women I would imagine on the arms of men like Tomas and Nicolas. My father told me so many times that I was blessed with the kind of looks a man would marry and not want an affair with. As much as I know his words were meant to be kind, I understood what he truly said. The drop-dead gorgeous ladies would get all of the attention, and I would get the boring, yet secure life.

The only problem is that I didn't want boring and secure. I wanted wild, untamed, and challenging.

Tomas's hand pressed lower until he cupped my smooth pussy. It had been a last-minute decision, shaving everything off down there. But I figured what the hell! If I were going to have mind-blowing sex for two weeks, then I might as well go all the way and prepare my body for the adventure.

He spread my flesh wide open with his fingers, exposing my

clitoris to the open air. My legs stiffened, as did the rest of me, as if my body would do anything to protect that small, but incredibly sensitive part of me.

"Relax, Natalie," Tomas encouraged. "Let us show you what you've only imagined."

"And maybe a few things you've never imagined," Nicolas added.

For a second, I thought I saw a wicked glow in his eyes. It faded quickly but it was enough to make my heart race way too quickly. And I held my breath, which didn't do much in helping me relax.

Tomas pressed one finger against my clit, holding it there. My hips leapt off the bed and both men chuckled. But they weren't laughing at me. I knew that as I sailed over the edge, closing my eyes as the dam of pressure they'd created inside me while sucking my nipples exploded and a rush of moisture soaked my pussy.

"Good girl," I heard Tomas say.

My gaze blurred as I stared at the white sparkly ceiling. "I've got quite an imagination," I managed to utter in between pants.

"You aren't imagining this." Nicolas leaned into me, lifting my head and offering my wine to me. "Drink," he instructed.

The wine moistened my mouth and lips and created a soothing sensation as it washed down my esophagus. "Thank you," I whispered, taking the glass from him and taking another sip while relaxing my head against all the roped muscle in his arm.

He watched me, as if mesmerized by how I sipped wine, and didn't say a word until I swallowed my third sip and offered the glass to him. Then his small smile raised my blood pressure quickly. Although I've always been fairly good at holding my alcohol, the vapors from good wine quickly floated to my head.

Nicolas placed the glass on the table by the bed and then turned his attention to me. Without hesitating, he pressed his lips over mine.

I opened willingly for him, and felt Tomas grip my legs and spread them. I focused on not fighting him, on relaxing and allowing him to do what he wished. Damn that took some effort.

If Nicolas noticed I wasn't putting all of my attention into kissing him, it might be why he impaled me with his tongue. My mouth was so wide open that my lips stretched. Tomas lapped at my pussy with his tongue, drinking my juices while Nicolas devoured my mouth.

It was too much to concentrate on. Nicolas smiled against my mouth when I finally relaxed. "You're amazing. Do you know that?"

I was getting accustomed to their flattery. "This is amazing."

"We're just getting started."

"I don't think I have to tell you I'm enjoying every minute of this."

Nicolas chuckled. "I'm enjoying myself, too."

I believed him. Just because I didn't have sex every day didn't mean I didn't know what was involved. We were definitely just getting started. And as hard as his cock was, pressing against my leg, I believed he was having a good time with this.

And who wouldn't?

I loved the feeling of two men touching me everywhere, of our legs intertwined, their mouths adoring me while their hands caressed my flesh. Every inch of me was oversensitive. Nicolas's lips were full and soft, different than a white man's. I never kissed a black man before and although I didn't experience the taboo excitement that some might think I would, there was still something different about him. My father might have his faults, but he didn't raise me to be a racist. People were judged by the qualities inside them, and not by the color of their skin. And believe me, Nicolas possessed some qualities that were outstanding.

I ran my hand down his shoulder. His skin was so soft, just like Tomas's, like they soaked in baby oil just before coming to me. And it was smooth. But underneath that perfect flesh, hard muscles twitched and flexed when I ran my fingers over them. I pressed my palm over the bulge of his bicep. His skin was warm, perfect, and his body was hard and so well defined. Tiny black curls around his nipples and between his pectorals were coarse and contrasted the perfect smoothness of his skin.

I felt a hard thumping heartbeat but then realized it was mine. Grazing his flesh with my fingers, I searched for Nicolas's heartbeat, wanting to feel it pulse with the strength and energy I felt from the rest of his body.

Nicolas quit kissing me and moved his head back just far enough so that I could focus on his face, causing my hand to slide down his chest before finding the source of his power. I knew nothing about this man yet there was something, a bond between strangers possibly, that made me feel very comfortable and relaxed while watching him.

I grew more sated just watching him. Tomas lay at the end of the bed, with half of his body off of it. He placed gentle kisses on my inner thighs and looked up at me when I raised my head to focus on him.

"You've got an absolutely perfect pussy." He purred like a deadly cat and then ran one finger down the length of my soaked entrance.

My head fell back on the pillows. "I designed it that way just for you," I told him, groaning.

"That would make you just like us," Nicolas said, and both men chuckled.

"Would you like to put a condom on me?" Tomas asked.

Instantly my head cleared, losing all previous comments with the sobering thought of protection. "Oh. Well I've never . . ."

"Let me show you. It really can be quite sexually arousing. Some feel it breaks the mood, but if done right, it can be just as erotic as any other sexual foreplay." While Tomas explained this to me he straightened, walking around the bed naked with his hard cock protruding in front of him and leading the way.

"I'd like to learn that." I was enthralled. And at the last minute remembered that I'd requested protection be used with my companion when I filled out the questionnaire that I'd sent in with my initial payment. No way would I have sex with anyone who did this sort of thing for a living without making them wrap that baby up.

These two men weren't cheap though. They didn't act like whores. Not that I had any firsthand knowledge of how a whore might act. Giving it some thought now, I imagined they would behave just like these men were now, classy and professional, and taking in stride the very serious matter of protection while making it as erotic of an adventure as everything else we'd done so far.

Just watching Tomas move, his large muscular body like a well-oiled machine, captivated me. He picked up a small box on the side table next to the bed and opened it. Then pulling out a strip of gold-wrapped condoms, he let them fall apart from each other. For some reason, they reminded me of individually wrapped chocolates, each one promising a fulfilling treat and mouth-watering experience.

Tomas easily tore one of the foil packages free, and held it in one hand while extending his other hand to me. I placed my hand in his, feeling his strength when he easily pulled me to a sitting position.

Nicolas was right behind me, his hands never leaving me as he gently rubbed my back. But my attention was on Tomas. His large cock was in front of my face as he stood at the edge of the bed in front of me. My already soaked pussy swelled with anticipation and I glanced from his perfectly shaped dick to the square gold package in his hand.

He handed the wrapped condom to me. "Tear the foil gently

so that you don't damage the condom. Then pull it out of the package."

I did as he said. The condom had a lubricant on it, and the moistness stuck to my fingers. I was embarrassed to say that I had very little experience with this kind of sexual protection.

"Many women are on birth control, and forget about the many other reasons for using condoms." Tomas seemed to read my mind. "Condoms aren't foolproof, but they are a safety precaution and, like I mentioned, if added to the sexual play properly, can stimulate our fun even more so."

"I've been on the pill since I was eighteen." I don't know why I told him that, but it was the truth. The few sexual experiences I had were with men I had dated for a while. It was embarrassing to admit that I'd never discussed sexual diseases with any of them, or even given it much thought.

One of the prerequisites for coming to Paradise Island was proof of a full physical, which of course made sense, and I would have questioned the scruples of the place if they hadn't requested proof that I was healthy, and not harboring any sexually transmitted diseases. According to my doctor, I was clean and free of any and all nasty bugs.

"There you go," Tomas said, nodding his approval and then wrapping his fingers around his hard cock. "Hold the condom in your hand and then place it on the edge of my cock."

I held on to the round edge of the latex and then pressed it to the tip of his cock. Tomas sucked in a breath through his teeth, making a soft hissing sound. I looked up at him, seeing the amount of focus and concentration he implemented as he watched me touch him. Again it seemed his eyes glowed. I stared into them, searching for something that would show me that I affected him as much as he did me.

He opened his mouth, prepared to walk me through the rest of this new adventure, but I was kind of getting into touching him like this. Dropping my gaze to his perfectly shaped cock, I unrolled the condom and watched as it stretched thinly over his hard, smooth, thick shaft. I sheathed him with the lubricated latex, letting my fingers smooth it over him. Once it was in place, it made his dick glow, look even smoother. And an odd scent reached my nose.

"Is it flavored?"

"All of them are. The package says what each one is." Tomas spoke through his teeth.

My administration affected him, and I loved the sensation of control. Both men quit moving, quit speaking, and allowed me this moment to explore and get to know Tomas's cock. I ran my fingers over the smooth, thin covering, and then touched my index finger to my tongue.

"Oh, my God, its strawberry. How cool!" I blushed over my schoolgirl tone of voice, but then laughed at myself and touched him again. "This is going to be fun."

"That's the whole point."

Of course it was. And that cock that almost danced in front of my face was dying to show me how much fun this would be. I was definitely just as eager. Hell, eager didn't begin to describe how I felt. Dying to experience the ride I was about to embark on was more like it.

I remembered at that moment something that the handbook said. If a woman hadn't had sex in a while, and wanted to enjoy the sexual experience with her partner for as long as possible, several positions were suggested. And switching positions often was also indicated as a way to keep the pleasure going for as long as possible.

"Would you sit in that chair?" I asked Tomas, nodding to the table and chairs in front of the large window. Full, dark purple drapes offered an almost perfect backdrop of mystery and seduction.

"Wherever you like." Tomas turned his back to me, taking his sheathed dick with him.

I had a wonderful view of his tight firm ass and my mouth watered. I'd never viewed the male anatomy as something that was breathtakingly beautiful before. But watching corded muscles flex in his legs while his firm ass made my fingers itch to touch him, gave me new appreciation of his gender. Sitting on the bed gave me the perfect angle to see his balls shift as he moved. They were tight looking, full, and I imagined what it would be like to cup them in my hands.

When Tomas sat in the chair, Nicolas pressed against my back gently, encouraging me off the bed. I slid to the edge of the king-size bed and stood, my legs suddenly wobbly. Maybe riding him wasn't the best way to start this. My legs might give out before I could come. Hell, they might give out before I made it to the chair where Tomas waited.

But Nicolas stood next to me, and guided me as if he sensed that although willing, my nerves were kicking in big time. As I reached him, my tummy did serious flip-flops. His rock-hard dick looked even larger with the shiny condom stretched over it.

"Come here." Tomas reached for me.

Nicolas let go. I straddled Tomas and his hands firmly held my waist as he adjusted my pussy directly over his cock. Resting my hands on his shoulders, I slowly lowered myself until I felt his cock press against my entrance.

"That's it, baby. Take your time. Fill yourself with my dick as quickly, or as slowly, as you like."

I held on to him and closed my eyes. Bright lights popped and flashed behind my eyelids and my thighs quivered as I slowly lowered myself onto him. His cock slid inside my soaked and incredibly ready pussy. He stretched and filled me, twitching slightly the more I lowered myself. As he traveled farther inside, my muscles contracted, easing his path, encouraging him deeper into my heat.

Fireworks exploded in my mind. They turned warm, reds and auburns, flashes of orange and soft pinks. My world transformed as my pussy took in all that he could offer. And just when I knew he was all the way in me, his mouth clamped down on my nipple and his hand moved quickly to my back, holding me tightly to him and then biting me with a quick nip.

"Oh, Lord!" I sunk lower, not even thinking when my legs gave out, and felt him create a sudden pressure that quickly spread over every inch of my womb. It was more than I could take, yet I wanted every bit of it.

"Shit!" I screamed.

Tomas chuckled, the depths of his baritone sending shivers over my flesh. He quickly scraped my nipple with his teeth, torturing further the sensitive puckered flesh that he just nibbled. Then he relaxed his tongue and lapped at my nipple, pushing it up and down with his smooth even strokes. It was just enough distraction to prevent me from stopping him when he thrust his hips upward, and filled me the rest of the way.

The pressure already created stretched and traveled even further. My immediate reaction was to straighten my legs, keep him from hitting that spot that would make me explode.

"Uh-uh," he told me, chuckling and holding me tightly enough that I couldn't move.

No matter that I was on top, supposedly controlling this moment—at least according to the handbook—Tomas held me easily enough with his hands on my waist that I wasn't able to rise and escape his massive cock. He thrust again. And at the same moment, again nipped at my nipple.

"You beast!" But I laughed, and even arched into him, giving him even freer reign to enjoy my breasts.

Arching my back also allowed him to glide deeper inside me, this time stroking my inner pussy muscles from a different angle. The intensity of it all was more incredible than the handbook suggested. I squatted over him, feeling the stretch of my inner thighs. His cock stretched me open, impaling and caressing as he slid deep inside me.

I clutched his shoulders, enjoying the warmth of his body, and the hardness of it as well. Not only could I experience this about him with his cock in my pussy, but also with my hands caressing his smooth flesh. And as I stretched my legs in an effort to stand and force his cock to almost glide out of me, muscles in my legs and abdomen pulled and quivered.

This was an all-over body experience. I experienced so much from many different angles and due to so many stimuli. It really took more effort than I would have guessed to simply open my eyes, look down at his sandy hair, and see his mouth torture and tease one breast and then move to the other.

"Ride him faster. Take him harder." It was Nicolas behind me, his hand suddenly stroking my hair, as he instructed me on how to fuck Tomas.

I reached for Nicolas and pressed my hand over his hard abdomen while taking Tomas deep inside me. Nicolas guided my hand until my fingers wrapped around his cock.

Damn, it was thick. Very thick. And long. I stroked the length of it, surprised when it lengthened and got even harder. It took some effort to open my eyes, as if riding Tomas and stroking Nicolas were all the multitasking I could manage at the moment. But I did, and turned to stare at the beautiful cock in my hand.

He was so dark, and my hand so white. The contrast turned me on.

"Can you take me in your mouth, baby?" Nicolas's voice was rough.

Again that sensation of power, of knowing my actions, my body, what I was doing to these two men, got them off as much as it did me, fed my ego and confidence.

"Thought you'd never ask," I said between gasps and leaned

slightly, while Tomas kept me balanced over him, I ran my tongue over the swollen tip of Nicolas's cock.

My lips stretched and tingled when I sucked part of him into my mouth. It took a minute of feeling awkward before I created a rhythm, riding one dick while sucking the other in my mouth. And then it hit me. Two cocks were in me at the same time. A fantasy of mine. I admit it. Taking two men at once. Giving them pleasure and knowing I had what it took to get both of them off, filled me with excitement and a rush of adrenaline.

"God, she's incredible."

"This is fucking amazing."

I wasn't sure which one of them said what. And honestly, I didn't care. I sucked and fucked, loving the hell out of it. Even when my leg muscles cramped and I knew I wouldn't be able to keep the rhythm going much longer, I didn't care. That's what other positions were for.

"Let's take her to the bed."

Tomas lifted me, standing and allowing his dick to slip out of me as he carried me to the bed. I was like a cat in heat, rubbing against him and grinning when he placed me gently on the bed on top of him. I spread my legs, accepting that my muscles would scream at me for days once our lovemaking was over. Once again I sunk down on his hard and ready cock.

"Can you take both of us?" Nicolas asked from behind me.

Something brushed over my asshole and I jumped, opening my eyes wide and staring down at Tomas's focused expression. He watched me intently, his lips pressed together and his blond hair curling over his forehead. I was damp with sweat and he was still soft and smooth, and not sweaty. Which was probably a good thing. I was doing most of the work anyway, and didn't think I would like a man sweating like a pig underneath me.

"How?" I asked, even when he stroked my ass again.

"Relax and keep fucking Tomas," Nicolas instructed, without answering my question.

But then something wet, almost tingly, was rubbed over my tight asshole. I'd never given thought to having anal sex while on the island. But then every time I imagined how my sexual adventures would play out here, I got so distracted from my work, I'd forced myself not to think about it, telling myself I would just have fun and create memories for a lifetime once I got here.

"Relax and let me lubricate you," Nicolas said, his smooth deep voice stroking my senses while his finger continued stroking my ass.

He pressed against my ass just as Tomas filled me completely. Wave after wave of desire erupted inside me and both men groaned. I cried out, arching my back and squeezing my eyes closed as I turned my face to the ceiling. Whatever Nicolas was doing back there, I liked it. And God help me, I never thought I'd enjoy being fucked in the ass.

Nicolas pressed again, and whatever he rubbed on me tingled against my skin while a pressure built inside me that was from more than Tomas's cock.

"I think she's ready," Nicolas said.

"We're ready when you are," Tomas answered.

I blinked, realizing Tomas was still deep inside me, but no longer moving. There must have been a question on my face when I looked down at him.

"Just relax. Keep your legs spread like they are now and come here. I want to kiss you." Tomas didn't blink as he spoke and I noticed brown flecks in his green eyes. They were such a pretty color.

I came up with the strangest things to dwell on sometimes. Like the color of a man's eyes while his dick was buried inside me and another man was preparing to mount me from behind.

I lowered my face to Tomas's and his hands gripped my shoulders. As I brushed my lips over his, enjoying how soft and full they were, he wrapped his arms around my neck and opened for me. Our tongues danced while his cock jerked inside me. At the same time Nicolas pressed his hand against my belly while his other gripped my hip.

A sharp pain hit and I cried out, stiffening and bucking. But I couldn't form words. Nicolas must have lubricated my ass very well. He slid into my ass, stretching muscles that had never been stretched like this, pushing into my virgin asshole, and creating a pressure that built so fast I couldn't catch my breath.

Both men growled and suddenly Tomas moved inside me again. He started fucking me but Nicolas was fucking me too. Their growls and heavy pants, as they both took me and sandwiched me between corded, rock-hard muscles was hotter than I ever imagined it would be. I'd always thought of anal sex as raunchy, hot in romance novels and fantasies but not something for real life.

Nicolas and Tomas quickly changed my mind on that subject. They created a rhythm together and built pressure that overtook the pain that I experienced when Nicolas first entered me. It grew inside me to the point where I wasn't sure I could take it any longer.

"God. Please." I wasn't even sure what I was begging for. But I managed to raise my head, which caused me to arch into their thrusts. They both hit spots inside me at the same time that broke a dam holding my orgasm back. It ripped through me brutally, exploding and rushing inside me with an intensity that took me over the edge faster than I'd ever gone before.

"Damn it! Shit," I cried out, howling as they impaled me again and again.

"My turn," Nicolas growled, gripping my hips with his long, strong fingers.

"I'm right there with you," Tomas groaned, moving his hands to my breasts while staring up at me with glazed eyes.

I stared down at him, noticing how muscles tightened in his jaw when he grit his teeth and continued watching me. I wasn't moving, but then again there wasn't a lot I could do sandwiched between my two men. It's the one downfall of condoms, I'm sure, but I didn't feel either of them come. Not that I needed to, their growls and their bodies tightening around me was so damned hot, it was almost the best part of the experience. Another wave of desire rushed over me, giving me chills and making me feel way too hot at the same time.

My arms gave out, and I collapsed on Tomas's chest, my heart pounding a mile a minute when I couldn't catch my breath. I'd just fucked two men at once and lived through the experience to talk about it.

Nicolas slid out of me, and I suddenly felt light as a feather. My ass burned and throbbed, but for some reason, although I could acknowledge a biting pain for a moment, it wasn't something that bothered me. Instead, I tingled and pulsed, feeling stretched and hot—and very, very satisfied.

Tomas's arms wrapped around me, holding me while I remained collapsed against his virile body. He stayed lodged deep inside me, still hard, hot, and pulsing, while he crushed me against him and nestled his head between my shoulder and neck. It was strange. I was sure I wasn't thinking clearly, and it would make perfect sense if I wasn't, but as I relaxed against Tomas, my heart pounding wildly, the oddest thought came to me. I didn't notice his heart beating along with mine.

6

Malachi

"Malachi, what are you doing here in the gardens? Everything okay?" Jonah looked up from his gardening with his watery gray eyes.

The old servant had a shade of eyes that I had tried matching more than once and simply couldn't. I'd determined a long time ago that what I wasn't able to duplicate was the look of wisdom and serenity that gave depth to his shade of gray.

"Just thought I'd get some fresh air," I lied, visions of Natalie Green fucking Tomas and Nicolas still too damned fresh in my head. "Looks like it might rain."

"It's that time of year." Jonah straightened slowly, glancing up at the sky while pulling a handkerchief from his back pocket and rubbing sweat from his forehead. "That's why everything is in such full bloom. The gardens are beautiful right now, at their glory."

"That they are, old man," I agreed, and walked around the area he'd been grooming. I collapsed on a stone bench nearby and stretched out, breathing in the salt air and gazing out toward the ocean. "I forgot how incredible the view is up here."

"Beautiful and dangerous." Jonah turned to look toward the cliff that was nearby. Neither of us could see it from where we were, but the drop to the ocean was indeed a deadly one and we both knew it was there.

From my vantage point though, the vast ocean and the many different shades of blues stretched on forever. The illusions of paradise. Sometimes I forgot that was where I was. Maybe I needed more moments like this, to stop, breathe in the atmosphere, and actually enjoy it. The physical beauty of the island was beyond captivating. It was the humans on the island that destroyed paradise. And besides the guests, there were only three of us.

Natalie was human. I squeezed my eyes closed and pinched the bridge of my nose, but that didn't cause the picture in my mind of her hot fucking body trapped between two men while her cries of pleasure filled my brain. Goddamn. I needed to dwell on how perfectly those two companions pleased her and not how fucking sexy she looked enjoying both of them.

"How are things back at the ranch?" I asked, doing my best to shove images of her out of my head and shifting so I could watch the older man continue with his gardening. God only knew why Jonah focused on this small patch of earth so far from the mansion. More than likely so he could get away from the Queen Bitch and all of the guests for a few.

Jonah stabbed the earth with his small shovel and overturned the dark soil. "It would be smart for you to go to the mansion more often."

"Why is that?"

"Seems a man should look out for what is his," he said.

I watched his gnarled hands pull weeds from around one of the flowers. His leathery skin was filled with deep wrinkles and his white hair raised off his shoulders when a breeze whipped in from the ocean. If it weren't for Jonah, I probably would have gone insane on this island knowing Rose was the only other human here. I wondered sometimes if he didn't go nuts from loneliness. Granted, he wasn't probably too often alone, and overseeing the companions who worked in the mansion probably kept him busy, but a man does well with a partner in life. More than once he'd declined my offer to create a woman just for him. Although every time I offered, I was sincere, I somehow respected him more for saying no. Companions weren't the same as knowing the touch of a real woman. And a man needed that.

Like I was one to talk.

"I might head up that way." Maybe I'd run into Natalie. Although she'd be with Nicolas and Tomas, and probably head over heels infatuated with both of them by now. They were both modeled after me.

I blew out a breath and raked my fingers through my hair, realizing that I hadn't brushed it yet today. I didn't make a habit out of talking to the guests. Rose hated it when I did, and sometimes a man needed to pick and choose his battles. Staying out of her realm of the island made it easier to argue that she should stay out of mine.

Jonah looked up at me quickly and held my gaze for a long moment. I felt like I couldn't look away until he did. Maybe he was dubbed the servant and me the master but there was something about Jonah, something that held my respect and, yes, even envy.

"Do that," he said slowly, and then returned to his garden.

I was about to ask him what he meant. Jonah never came out and explained himself. You had to ask the right questions, and then still interpret the answers. There were days when I just wanted to shake him until he shared what he knew without making me pry it out of him. I actually gave it some thought when my cell phone rang.

"Malachi, it's Darcy," Rose said quickly, sounding winded. "She's damaged. One of the guests got too rough with her."

"Goddamn it!" I jumped to my feet.

Jonah stood faster than I'd seen him move in a while. "What's wrong?" he demanded.

"Darcy," I explained, and apparently, unlike me, my simple answers made perfect sense to him.

"My cart is over here," he instructed, gesturing for me to follow as he hurried down the path. He whistled once and Pluto, his golden retriever, a gift I'd given him one Christmas after he'd refused a companion, leapt up from the stretch of sun he'd been basking in and hurried after Jonah.

He slipped behind the driver's wheel of the golf cart, our chosen means of transportation on the island, and Pluto leapt on the narrow backseat/cargo area. The golf carts were aesthetically pleasing to the guests. Cars stole from the captive aura the island offered. And golf carts were easier to have flown out here than cars were.

I climbed in on the passenger side, encouraging him to go faster as we hurried to the mansion. Jonah pulled around back and we both ignored happy guests who laughed and carried on in the gardens surrounding the place.

Rose was already at the back door. Unfortunately, this wasn't the first time this had happened, although lately my companions didn't just break down. If something went wrong it was due to abuse by a guest.

"Thank God we aren't compromised," Rose said, offering me a relieved smile as she gestured for Sharay, her personal companion, who easily lifted the long box and carried it toward the trailer we used to hitch to the golf carts and haul supplies when necessary. "Of course, if you'd been at your station where you belong instead of God knows where, Sharay and I wouldn't have had to resort to plan B."

"Which is why plan B exists," I growled, wanting to smack her for her indifference to shutting down Darcy. Sharay slid the box, which was shaped a bit too much like a coffin for my tastes, onto the trailer. I snapped it open and stared down at Darcy's blank expression. She appeared to be sleeping, which for all arguments' sake, she might as well be.

Every companion had a shut down switch that could be activated by a remote to make them go into sleep mode. Wherever they were, whatever they were doing, if the switch was triggered, manually or by the remote, they would slump over, appearing to the unknowing guest that they'd passed out or fallen asleep.

"It's okay, sweetheart," I whispered to Darcy, reaching into the box and stroking her cheek. "We'll have you back to new in no time."

"I guess I'll send Maggie over to Mr. Holloway," Rose said, sighing. "He and his wife just want a plaything anyway."

I looked over at her, ready to pounce. In fact, it took so much control not to attack that for a moment I couldn't say a word. She had the nerve to straighten and look at me defiantly. Jonah shifted, burying his fists deep into his pants pockets while scowling at the ground. Jonah understood that my companions weren't created to be abused, but Rose didn't. Rose thought the world was at her disposal, existing solely for her to prance through and do as she pleased.

"You talk to the Holloways, or I will," I snapped. "The companions aren't going to be abused, or your guests can just go home."

"I'm not going to discuss this with you. You obviously have no business sense and you never have. Please Mr. Holloway and he'll either come back or tell his friends to visit us, or both," she said, turning toward the door and gesturing for Sharay to follow her. "I expect Maggie to be here within the hour."

She headed inside and closed the service door with a bang.

"Want help taking Darcy home?" Jonah looked up at me with those watery gray eyes.

"That's okay, old man." I looked down at Darcy and then

gently closed the lid on the box. "Help me attach the trailer to the cart and I'll drive her home. I'll head up that way now."

"What about Maggie?" Jonah needed to know and I understood. As soon as I left, Rose would be questioning him.

"I'll see if she's available." It wasn't a good answer and I knew it. But damn it, my companions weren't for people to abuse.

Jonah didn't say anything but moved to the other side of the trailer and the two of us rolled it over to the golf cart. Jonah connected it to the hitch. One of the few things Rose and I agreed on, the golf carts were better for the large paths we'd had built on the island shortly after I moved here. They didn't tear up the cobblestone paths. There really wasn't anywhere for guests to go that they couldn't walk, and having gasoline delivered to the island was getting damned expensive.

"Pluto," Jonah said, and the dog wagged his tail as he ran to the old man. "I guess you'll have to postpone that visit," he said, reminding me I'd planned on scoping out the mansion for a bit, and possibly seeing Miss Green in person, even if I hadn't decided on whether I'd say anything to her, or not. "Our new arrivals will be here for a couple of weeks. You'll have time," he added, turning before I could ask him why he would say what he just did.

Climbing behind the wheel of the cart, I watched as Jonah headed for his cabin, which was a cozy looking small home and his private sanctuary behind the mansion. I assured myself that I misunderstood Jonah's meaning as I accelerated and turned the cart toward my home. I'd done nothing, and said nothing, that would have implied I had any interest in meeting, or even seeing, any of our new arrivals.

The companions acted pretty much as I expected. They were upset. I paid close attention to their reactions when situations were critical. It offered an incredible opportunity to note what stimuli they could handle and what needed work.

Charles, Phillip, and Adrian were quiet and quick to jump in and help lift Darcy out of the box and carry her into the laboratory.

"What happened?" Adrian asked, while the other two stood silently, watching.

"Apparently there was an accident." I glanced up when Maggie appeared in the doorway. If I told them the truth, I'd be sending a crying companion up to the mansion. My stomach tightened with anger at the thought of making Maggie replace Darcy. "She'll be fine."

No one said anything, but they didn't leave me alone either. Curiosity was one of the easiest programs to master. And I didn't mind the company. They all jumped in eagerly when I asked for a certain tool, or for extra light.

When I took her shirt off and rolled her to her stomach, Maggie hurried over and pulled a hospital gown out of the closet then walked over to the table. "She'll die if you turn her on and she's half naked in front of all of us," she informed me quietly.

I accepted the gown and covered her torn flesh with it. Anger ripped through me at the welts on her body. No woman, machine or human, should be abused like this. It pissed me off even further thinking about sending Maggie to the brutal assholes who'd done this to Darcy.

For the life of me I didn't understand why anyone would turn down Maggie. I'd designed her after a girl I'd had a serious crush on in college, the first woman who dumped me. Now there was a line of women that was endless. But not something I planned on dwelling on at the moment.

"You're a sweetheart, Maggie," I told her, smiling.

She immediately grinned back at me. "I just know I'd die if I woke up with a bunch of guys staring down at me naked."

"Really?" I asked, half teasing, and waited for her response. I needed to take the back panel off of Darcy, but that wasn't something I would do in front of the other companions. No one liked watching one of their own kind being opened up and repaired.

"Well," she said slowly, matching my teasing expression, "maybe it would depend on the circumstances."

"Kind of what I thought," I grumbled, but then grinned at her. "Okay, all of you, Darcy and I need some privacy," I announced and then watched as they slowly left my laboratory. "Oh, Maggie."

"Yes?" She turned around, her pretty blue eyes so bright.

I hated telling her this but kept my emotions intact. My companions didn't always read emotions accurately, but they mimicked them beautifully. I didn't want her learning resentment.

"Head over to the mansion and take Darcy's place for now, please," I said calmly.

My insides twisted further when her face lit up. "Really? Did Rose ask for me?"

What I wouldn't do to strangle the life out of Rose. "Yes, dear. Actually she did." I couldn't look away from Maggie's delighted expression. "And Maggie?"

"Yes."

"If Mr. Holloway tries to hurt you, kick his ass."

"Really?"

"Really."

Maggie nearly skipped out of the room, calling after the other companions to announce her exciting news as the laboratory door closed behind her. I closed my eyes, vowing silently to turn Rose off if Maggie came back to me in the same condition that Darcy was in right now.

Although, there was only one way to turn Rose off. I wasn't a murderer, but imagining it sometimes sure seemed easier to do the longer I worked with her.

I placed my hand on the middle of Darcy's slender back, focusing on how warm her skin still was, and the smoothness of it. My companions were perfect, better than human in almost every way. I stroked her blonde hair, and a rush of pride filled me. It also hit me how long it had been since I'd been with a woman. The five-finger lover sure as hell wasn't what it was cracked up to be, especially when too much time had passed since the real thing. There wasn't anything morally or ethically wrong with fucking one of my companions. But anytime I tried letting my mind drift there, something stopped me.

"She's your creation, part of you," I explained to myself, knowing that was the reason why I couldn't have sex with Darcy, or Maggie, or any of my females. They were my children.

Clearing my throat, I walked away from Darcy and over to my computer on the other side of the room. "A few notes," I began, pushing the record button that automatically started typing everything I said. "Note that when Maggie experienced embarrassment over being teased about waking up with several men staring down at her, she managed the appropriate expression, but that was it. Memo to self to work on brain receivers acknowledging embarrassing moments and creating color alterations under the flesh so that companions will blush."

There was something sultry about a woman blushing. I should experiment with that some, possibly find one of the guests and toy with them a bit. Once again, the young lawyer from Chicago, Natalie Green, popped into my head. I turned back to Darcy and stroked her blonde hair away from her face, but saw Miss Green with her brown hair that she'd pulled back in a hair tie at her nape while fucking Nicolas and Tomas. I wondered what it would look like down.

My cell phone rang and I reached for it, more than willing to send it to voice mail if it were Rose. "Smart bitch," I muttered, recognizing Jonah's number. Rose knew I wouldn't refuse Jonah's calls. "What can I do for you, old man?"

"Are you through with Darcy yet?" Jonah asked, his scratchy voice one I'd love to be able to copy someday. "Lord is stuttering. I'd say it's rather entertaining, but Rose disagrees."

"He's stuttering?" I didn't know a dog could stutter.

"Don't know how else to explain it. It's like he's barking with the hiccups."

I shook my head, and turned to Darcy. "I'll be right up, old man." Hanging up, I caressed Darcy's bare shoulder. She'd been abused pretty badly and I wouldn't rush to fix her. "Enjoy a nice nap, my dear. I'll be back and get you up and running in no time."

The ocean brought in a moist breeze that almost had my hair damp as I rounded the side of the mansion in the golf cart and parked alongside Jonah's cabin. Bright yellow hibiscus almost blinded me with the sun shining on them as I parked and climbed out.

Our guilty culprit came leaping toward me with a tongue and tooth greeting. "How you doing, Lord?" I asked, squatting down and allowing the dog to greet me with a tongue bath.

Lord, who was something close to a collie-spaniel mix I'd made for Jonah when he decided Pluto needed a companion, barked eagerly, and showed me what it sounds like when a dog stutters. I laughed out loud, the malfunctioning voice box so entertaining it was tempting to leave him like this. Pluto bounded out of the cabin, running around me and Lord with his tongue hanging out of the side of his mouth.

"You like how he sounds too, don't you, Pluto?" I asked, reaching to scratch behind Pluto's ear.

"I got a chuckle out of it, too," Jonah said from behind me. "Needless to say, you and I are the only ones who find Lord's unique condition entertaining."

"Come here, boy." I patted the golf cart seat and Lord eagerly jumped into the cart, his thick long tail wagging a mile a minute.

Lord looked from me to Jonah, as if to make sure we both knew that he was ready for the ride, and excited to embark on any adventure. Lord and Pluto were one of my prize pieces of work. In fact, if I were still active in the robotics community, what I wouldn't do to show them off. I'd be shocked if I didn't win recognition for one of the groundbreakers on android science. Both dogs' coats felt just like real dogs. They were guaranteed to be nonallergenic though, and I'd proven the fact quickly since I was one of those unfortunate souls who grew up deathly allergic and deprived of enjoying man's best friend for most of my life. Even without my human companions, these better-than-perfect dogs would be a gold mine on the market. But part of moving here and working here was agreeing to keep all of my work a secret. Paradise Island wouldn't be the same if the guests knew they were having sex with machines.

My smile faded when Jonah scowled. "How long are you taking him for?" he asked.

I glanced at Lord who sat in the passenger seat, panting and looking like he was grinning from ear to ear.

"Oh." I should have guessed Jonah wouldn't go for parting with his roommate. Ever since I gave Lord and Pluto to Jonah, the three of them were nearly inseparable, even when Rose insisted Jonah not take his dogs with him when he worked in the gardens. Pluto was better at lying still and unnoticed, but Lord tended to be a bit friendlier when he saw a new face to greet. "Well." I scratched my head and realized my hair was still a mess of tangles. "Let me see if there is a supply kit inside. Maybe I can get him fixed up right here."

Jonah let out a low sharp whistle and Lord bounded out of the golf cart and to his master's side. The old man patted his head and grinned at me as his phone rang. "Check the lockers in the supply closet," he told me and pulled his phone from his belt.

Leaving the three of them, I headed into the mansion from

the back service entrance. A handful of cooks worked in the kitchen, and the sweet and sour smells of a tangy sauce filled the air and my stomach grumbled eagerly. Maybe before I left I could raid the kitchen even though Maggie might take offense if I declined her food after snacking here at the mansion. However, it would be good to know that the companions I created, and then drilled in special classes to fine-tune their culinary skills, were doing their job right.

I paused when I entered the grand foyer behind the wide, winding staircase. I was always taken aback when I entered this lavish mansion. Rose spared no expense in having the place built. Although I knew half of everything on the island belonged to me, I still felt I was intruding in someone else's home when I stepped foot inside this place. I was out of my element and didn't want to change to make this my element. The place reeked of wealth and pretentious behavior. Granted, it was a place for fantasies, but not my kind of fantasies.

For some reason, I stopped and backed up against the wall when three people walked down the stairs. It was Natalie and she had Tomas and Nicolas with her. Her hair was down, and damp, and the sundress she wore clung to her voluptous figure. She wasn't smiling, but not scowling either. Instead, she appeared lost in thought as she focused on the steps in front of her. Tomas and Nicolas talked quietly to each other. Damn. She was sexy as fucking hell; much prettier in person than on a monitor screen. Her hair curled at the end and parted over her practically bare shoulders. She wasn't tan, but not pale as a ghost either. Nor was she one of those starved, toothpick looking kind of women. Although far from fat, her slender figure appeared to be perfect. Shapely hips and small, perky breasts helped create curves that her dress hugged, creating an enticing picture. I continued gawking when she reached the bottom of the stairs, which would be damned hard to explain if she caught me doing it. And I had plenty of work to do. I didn't have time to stand in the shadows and hope to watch how her ass swayed in that dress when she walked away from me.

She wasn't runway-model material but I never did like women who were nothing more than skin and bone. I'd designed some of my companions like that, intentionally making them almost gaunt since some men liked that. Skinny with big boobs—like any woman came that way without surgery. That didn't describe the woman I watched across the hallway. She had curves, and damn nice ones at that. And her breasts weren't so large that they'd sag by the time she was forty. She was perfect, my definition of exactly how a lady should be.

Miss Green and my guys reached the bottom of the stairs and turned to enter the dining room. I blew out a breath of exasperation and stalked toward the lockers. It probably wouldn't do me any harm to find a real woman sometime in the near future. Maybe take a day and fly over to Hawaii. I needed to get laid.

7

Natalie

The vast variety of food, arranged buffet style, was over-whelming. A sweet-smelling breeze lifted my still-damp hair from my shoulders, and the loose fitting sundress made me feel like I wasn't wearing anything at all.

"You haven't tried shrimp until you've had some of this." Nicolas reached around me, taking my porcelain plate from my hands. "This is on a sugarcane stick. You dip it in the pineapple-mango jam." He pointed to a bowl next to the shrimp. "There is mahimahi, which is very sweet and mild, if you haven't tried it. Also the swordfish. And of course, the finest sashimi ahi tuna that money can buy."

"It all looks so good." And I was sure every bit of it was very fresh, and very pricey. No expense was spared anywhere on the island. Truly a paradise, albeit a very expensive paradise.

I had attended numerous political fund-raisers where delicacies from around the world were served. But growing up in Chicago, I didn't have a lot of exposure to seafood like this. The aromas that drifted to my nose made me anxious to try every-thing. I was starving but didn't have a clue where to begin.

"You aren't putting a thing on your plate." Nicolas's bare chest brushed against my backside, sending tingles down my spine, a silent reminder of how wonderful he'd made me feel earlier.

I looked up into his chocolate-colored eyes, but couldn't help letting my gaze wander over the rest of his perfectly sculpted body. All of us showered after having sex, but apparently I was the only one expected to dress for dinner. Both of my men donned their loincloths and moved around me with ease, as if they were very accustomed to wearing them. Granted if I had a body as perfect as either one of them, maybe I would be willing to saunter around publicly with next to nothing on as well.

In spite of the wonderful time I had earlier, taking in Nicolas's dark face, broad shoulders, and his incredibly muscular chest and arms, created a yearning inside me so powerful I completely forgot what I was about to say.

"We'll choose the best foods for you," Tomas suggested as he stood on the other side of me. He pointed to the sashimi ahi tuna. "Put some of that on her plate."

"And the swordfish." Nicolas picked up a bamboo stick with glazed meat speared on it. "Don't forget the shrimp. And have you ever had seaweed salad? Chef makes it taste sinfully good."

"Not too much." I couldn't help laughing as my two men eagerly dished enough food on to my plate for the three of us.

"You've got to eat, my dear." Nicolas's gaze bore through me, seeming to find the source of the heat that simmered deep inside my womb. "We won't have it said we didn't take proper care of you."

"I doubt anyone has ever accused you of mistreating them." My cheeks warmed and he gave me a knowing smile before returning to the task of filling my plate.

"There isn't anyone else but you," Nicolas said quietly, although he didn't look at me but instead focused on the entrees enticingly arranged on the table before us.

I almost commented that he probably said that to every guest he spent time with. But this was my fantasy, right? And paradise wasn't paradise if it got clogged up with too much reality. I let the comment slide and moved in between the two of them as we worked our way down the buffet line.

Muscular bodies flexed and stretched as both men reached around me, teasing and torturing me whenever our bodies touched. Nicolas and Tomas got into creating a feast for me, and themselves, from the endless variety of foods laid out before us.

A lot of work went into displaying each food item. Several long tables were covered with colorful tablecloths. I never knew there were so many varieties of seafood. I discovered I loved octopus salad—Tako Poki. There were also many different kinds of vegetables and fruits, professionally displayed in ornate serving dishes. Every bit of it looked so good.

The island was the epitome of perfection. Tomas and Nicolas with their loincloths, which amazingly managed to cover their large cocks, and at the same time revealed buns of steel, put perfection over the top. Or at least my idea of it. When either of them leaned over the buffet table, muscles stretched, I got an incredible view of their backsides. Not an ounce of fat anywhere, and rear ends that were packed with as much steel as the rest of them. My two guys were lethal weapons, mouth watering eye candy, the best of the best.

"Where would you like to sit?" Tomas held my plate and his.

"It doesn't matter to me. You know the place better than me. Lead the way." I smiled when Nicolas offered his arm to escort me.

"Anywhere is fine with me," he said, keeping his voice low. "I'm starving."

"Me, too." I grinned easily and felt like I was hanging out with my best friends when he smiled back at me.

I glanced around at the many tables and then past them at the screen walls that I could see through to the view of the yard. Meticulously landscaped gardens, with bright green grass, incredibly bright flowers in every color imaginable, and an endless deep blue sky offered a panoramic view that was picturesque. It looked like some clever photographer touched up the colors to make the scene surreal. I swore the shades of everything around me, from the grass to the gray sidewalks, were more vivid than they should be.

Unless kick-ass sex did that to a soul. Maybe my retinas were damaged from too much sex and from here out I would be forced to stare at the world with too much color washing over everything. It wasn't such a bad side effect.

"Maybe we should sit inside. Soon we'll rub lotions into your skin and prepare you for our sun. If we lounge outside too long before doing that, you might get burned." Tomas winked at me and held our plates like they were sacred and started across the room.

One of the women who'd flown on the small chartered plane with me to Paradise Island walked hand in hand with a tall slender man. They strolled lazily, like comfortable lovers, across the middle of the yard toward a group of palm trees. Her laughter drifted across the yard, and I looked away, not wanting her to notice me. Although why should I be embarrassed of the others seeing that I'd chosen two men, instead of one?

Like I would see any of these people ever again once I returned home.

"You've got a point. I should get outside more." I glanced down at my rather white arm, but then looked at the couple walking outside. She did look a lot more pale than he did. "She was on the plane with me," I mused out loud, and then wondered why I did.

Tomas wrapped his arms around me in a hug that was friendly, like one would give another when they'd been best friends forever. "We definitely got lucky then," he said, speaking in a low tone that almost made it sound like he growled.

An older, dark-skinned gentleman stood on the other side of Tomas. I must have been lost in thought and too busy adoring the surroundings to notice him join us. But he stood silently, holding a large silver tray with our three plates on it.

"Why did you get lucky?" I returned my attention to Tomas.

"Because you are a hell of a lot prettier than she is."

"I'm the one who got lucky. There's no way she could be getting more attention than I am." I couldn't help grinning at the older guy, who winked at me, giving away that in spite of his stiffly starched white uniform, he was as relaxed and comfortable as my two escorts were. "Obviously her escort isn't taking into consideration that she might suffer a sunburn."

"Then may I suggest the dining room?" The servant spoke with a breathtaking accent. "It's very comfortable and I'll never be too far if you wish for something more."

"Sounds great," I told him.

"And I certainly hope that you'll wish for something more," Nicolas whispered into my ear.

He traced a line down my spine with his fingers as I walked by his side. Even though both of them fucked me better than I'd ever known sex to be my entire life, Nicolas's touch created shivers of desire that rushed over my flesh.

"I do. I mean, I will," I stammered.

His fingers brushed over my tailbone, such a small movement, yet enough to stir rushes of need that swelled between my legs. I got so flustered I worried I wouldn't be able to follow the servant with our food without crashing into him—or a wall.

"Where do you want it?" Nicolas asked, continuing to speak in a low, hushed tone.

Every inch of me tingled with a charged energy. I looked up at him, certain I would start floating if my legs gave out underneath me. My brain seemed to be creeping back into that won-

derful world of lustful fog. Maybe that was why I didn't understand his question.

"Where?" I asked, whispering since there were others around
us. "What do you mean?"

"I mean here?" His fingers stimulated every nerve ending in
my back when he moved them lazily to the base of my neck.
"You might be surprised at the pleasures you could enjoy while
eating your food."

"The dining room? Is that allowed?"

If Tomas or the servant overheard our conversation, they
didn't give any indication.

"Anything is allowed, as long as you wish it." Nicolas's attention remained fixed on me. "I would love to show you how
enjoyable eating can be. Unless you prefer to only have sex in a
bedroom."

"Oh, my." I was starving but his suggestions made my tummy
twist with nervous excitement. "Sex doesn't have to happen in
the bedroom only."

"Good girl." Nicolas's deep baritone chuckle pushed that
swelling inside me dangerously near the edge. "Then allow me
to seat you. I want this to be a meal you won't soon forget."

Our servant made a show of placing our plates around our
table. He left briefly, long enough for Nicolas to pull my chair
out for me. For an upright chair, it was amazingly comfortable.
The cushion I sat on was thick, and covered with smooth cool
velvet. And the back of the chair was also padded, soft yet firm
and so easy to relax in. The table setting also surpassed anything I'd ever seen at the country club my family had belonged
to all of my life. I never quite understood the importance of
polishing silver when you planned on dunking it into food. But
I could easily have used my knife as a mirror if I were inclined
to check my makeup.

"What would you like to drink, miss?" the servant asked and
stood solemnly next to me, his hands clasped behind his back.

"We have any kind of iced tea you can imagine, fruit juices, iced water or coffee, or if you prefer, whatever alcoholic beverage appeals to you."

"Ice water with lemon sounds very good." My mouth went dry while my brain struggled to imagine what forms of debauchery Nicolas might have in mind during our meal.

"If I may." Nicolas took the chair next to me and placed his hand over mine, squeezing gently. "I think a chardonnay will accompany the meal perfectly. When we have our dessert, I think you will love the Spanish coffee. "

"That does sound good." I wasn't much of a drinker, and almost said as much. Getting a buzz on with these two studs around me could get me in trouble. I almost laughed. I'd already fucked both of them, planned on fucking them again—possibly sooner than I originally thought. What trouble could I get into? "The chardonnay sounds perfect. Although Baileys and coffee will do for dessert."

"Excellent choice," the servant told me and smiled.

I glanced at Tomas and Nicolas, ready to give them a knowing smile. They glanced at each other, their expressions serious, and for a moment my stomach tightened while my mind suddenly spiraled with thoughts of some serious scenario they might be plotting.

"Enjoy your meal. I'll check on you in a bit to make sure everything is to your liking." The servant gave me his complete attention while he spoke with his incredibly romantic accent. "If there is anything else you need I'll be sure and get it for you."

"Thank you." That's when I noticed no one else dined in the large dining area. It was probably for the best with my brain working around possibilities that Nicolas might suggest.

His brown eyes glowed, offering answers to more than the one question that I asked. "Are you ready?" His baritone was like a rush of warm wind over my cool flesh.

I glanced at Tomas, who focused on his food. "What for?"

I wanted to ask why we were the only ones in the dining room but Nicolas's smile gave me goose bumps.

"For a meal that you'll never forget."

"Bring it on, sweetheart," I said, trying to sound confident while my stomach suddenly filled with butterflies. How was I supposed to enjoy the food?

His chuckle sent shivers down my spine. I couldn't look away from his smile. White teeth glowed against his shiny black skin. And his bald head gave him an authoritative look, not to mention made him sexy as hell.

"Allow me to feed you." He moved his chair closer to mine, and then took his time unwrapping silver from a thick cloth napkin. He ran his finger down the length of the fork, stroking its handle as he looked at it almost adoringly. For such a muscular man, it was odd how the sophisticated action fit him like he did it every day. "There's something incredibly erotic about watching a lady take food from a man's hand, or in this case from his fork."

I couldn't answer. And I no longer cared why we were alone in the large dining room. More than likely, it was a damned good idea there weren't other people sitting close enough to see what we were doing—or about to do. I had no idea what to say. All I could do was watch as he pushed the fork into a strawberry. Pale red juice trickled over the prongs as he lifted the fruit. He dipped it into a rich, thick cream, twisting it slowly until the fruit was well covered with smooth white decadence and then lifted.

"Open your mouth," he whispered.

I'd already parted my lips, and opened for him anxiously. I couldn't wait to taste the rich treat he offered. He slid the cream-covered fruit past my lips and an array of flavor exploded on my tongue. I hummed my approval, which made him growl with satisfaction.

"Good girl," he purred, his gaze hooded with long, thick black lashes as he focused on my mouth. "The Romanof sauce is cream, brandy, vanilla, and sugar. Always a delight with straw-berries. I knew you'd love it."

Sweet juices mixed with the rich cream and practically slid down my throat. He pulled the fork out of my mouth, looking incredibly pleased as he once again poked a piece of fruit, this time melon, and again dipped it in the succulent cream sauce. I was going to be toasted before sunset. Not that I thought I'd be paying much attention to the sun.

"I don't even want to know how many calories are in each bite," I said, licking my lips and preparing for my next bite.

"Don't worry about calories." He offered the cream-covered fruit and I bit down eagerly. "You'll work them off before they can do damage. I promise."

The melon almost got stuck in my throat as I took in his meaning. Desperately trying not to ruin the moment by cough-ing and gagging on the fruit, I looked down, lowering my face so that I could chew and keep juices from dribbling down my chin.

"I think you're ready for something a bit more substantial now." Nicolas held the fork in front of me with a thin slice of tuna twisted around the prongs.

Tomas ate silently, watching me intently when I glanced his way. The way he looked at me, sated and content, a man who knew with satisfaction what I had to offer in bed, sent a warm sensation rushing through me. Like being submerged into a perfectly hot bath.

"Eat your meat," Tomas instructed, reaching for a damp strand of hair and brushing it behind my shoulder. "Protein is an im-portant part of your diet."

I stared at Tomas's perfectly chiseled features. He looked so serious although there was no missing the double meaning in his words.

"Take the tuna," Nicolas instructed.

I opened my mouth, shifting my attention to him, and allowed Nicolas to feed me the slice of fish. The unique flavoring brought out the best in the meat.

"Oh, my God, that's wonderful."

"The lady likes." Nicolas grinned, plucking up another slice and flipping it over the fork before offering it to me.

"I like it very much."

"Now you should have something to wash it down with." Nicolas lifted my glass and handed it to me.

The wineglass was covered with condensation, which instantly made my fingertips wet. I sipped at it, amazed at how perfectly chilled it was and how its smooth texture complemented the fish more than I would have imagined. My mother would kill to know the names of these chefs when planning her parties. I, on the other hand—I simply was thrilled to be able to enjoy the perfect dishes in front of me.

Both men took a healthy drink with me. Nicolas's glass was just a bit over half full when he put it down. I only managed a few sips before the alcohol floated around in my brain. "This is a bit too good," I mused, knowing it would go straight to my head within minutes if I didn't sip slowly. As many parties that I'd been to throughout my life, I'd never indulged much in alcohol. Although mix it with something sweet, and I wanted to devour it like chocolate.

"It's supposed to be." Nicolas's smile was almost wicked.

He picked up the fork and surveyed my plate before scooping up octopus salad and holding the bite to my lips. No one had ever fed me before and honestly, if asked, I would decline on the offer. It just sounds so embarrassing. But the way Nicolas lifted each bite to my mouth, and then slid the fork over my lips, made the process very erotic.

He then lifted a roasted shrimp by the tail, using his fingers this time. Holding it to my mouth, he kept his fingers against my lips while I pulled the meat free from the tail and enjoyed the perfectly seasoned seafood. Other wonderfully spiced foods passed my lips. Just a small portion of each, a teasing and torture session for my palette. And with each morsel of food, he watched, devouring me as my mouth closed over the fork and then when I licked my lips afterward.

"Enough," I finally said, holding my hand up when he put the fork to the plate. "If I eat any more the only thing I'll want for dessert is a nap."

"Naptime will come, my dear. And when it does, you'll sleep like a baby, I promise." Nicolas put the fork down and lifted my wineglass, offering it to me.

"I have no doubts." I sipped too eagerly, forgetting for just a moment how quickly wine could go to my head. The alcohol drifted into my brain. It tasted so good that after a couple sips and pausing, I brought it to my lips again.

"You enjoyed your lunch?"

"Yes. But you haven't eaten."

"I will." He pulled his plate closer to him.

Tomas nearly had his plate cleared and leaned back, lifting his glass to his lips and watching me with those bedroom eyes. Something told me he already knew the agenda for the afternoon and simply made himself comfortable, although even relaxed he reminded me of a predator waiting for his moment to pounce.

I took another sip, not having a clue what to expect. My mind didn't seem able to work its way around any possible fantasies that might be carried out in our present setting. As the alcohol worked its way through my system, I didn't care as much what might happen. Just knowing that something would happen made the moment perfect. I put my glass down, then licked my lips that seemed a bit numb, and stared into Nicolas's eyes.

"Do you want me to feed you?" I teased, feeling relaxed and buzzed enough to be a little daring.

"If you want to, you can. I did have something else in mind though."

"What?" I couldn't wait to hear.

"Give me your hand."

I didn't hesitate. I should have, although I'm not sure why. Maybe because decent young ladies were supposed to at least make a show of hesitating before entering a sexual situation. I'm not sure if it was the alcohol, or simply because I'd already enjoyed wonderful sex this afternoon and felt a bit more comfortable with these two men, but giving thought to his request didn't even enter my mind. Not to mention, I told myself to bat away the moment of hesitation that crept into my brain, social sexual expectations didn't apply here on Paradise Island. I was in a different world, one where men comfortably lounged in loincloths, and all looked like Greek gods, and I was free to do, and behave, how I pleased, publicly or privately.

That was easy enough to tell my brain, but just try and live outside the circle we're all raised in. It's not as easy. But I sure was willing to give it heck!

He gripped my hand, wrapping his strong fingers around mine. My fingers looked so frail and white in his. Nicolas massaged the top of my hand with his fingertips until I met his gaze. It was then that he moved our linked hands toward him.

"Touch me," he whispered. "Feel me grow while you watch me. I want you to know beyond any doubt exactly what you are in for."

"What do you mean?" His words swam around in my brain, sounding like mumble jumble.

His meaning became clear when he pressed my hand over his cock. Beneath the loincloth, a rod of steel grew under my touch, thick and round and very, very long. When he let go of my hand, I ran my fingers over the bulge that definitely grew the more I stroked.

I gulped.

Nicolas lifted his fork.

I didn't move my hand, or pull my gaze from his, as he ate his food and I caressed his cock. A cock getting larger and harder than I'd ever seen it before. And soon it would be inside me.

It was a damned good thing he fed me before asking me to touch him. I wouldn't have been able to enjoy all the wonderful food before us while stroking Nicolas's cock. And the way it grew, getting harder, thicker, longer, from my touch made my mouth water. Maybe I should start worrying that something on this island put my sex drive in turbo mode. There wasn't any reason that I should feel so damned horny after just having such incredible sex.

I sighed and glanced around the quiet dining room.

"Is something wrong?" Nicolas sounded concerned.

I stared into his smoldering dark eyes. His skin glowed a beautiful caramel shade, and his bald head gave him such a superior look. God! He was absolutely, perfectly gorgeous.

"I was just thinking that I've turned into a demented sex fiend." Honesty came so easily on this island.

Tomas chuckled and the side of Nicolas's mouth curved up slightly.

"Maybe it's the company," Nicolas suggested.

"I'm sure that it is." Both of them were so wonderful. I couldn't have selected better escorts.

The dining room doors opened and a couple entered, hand in hand, following the same servant who'd seated us. They selected a table along the wall, far away enough that we couldn't be heard. Nonetheless, we no longer had our own private dining room.

"What kind of sex do you view as demented?" As he asked, Nicolas's cock jumped under the loincloth.

"Oh." Good thing I wasn't trying to eat anything. If I were, it would have choked against the lump that was suddenly in my throat. "Having sex in a dining room with other people eating here would be demented."

"Sounds kinky to me." He grinned and his white teeth flashed beautifully against his dark skin.

"And scary." I looked around the room and my hand slid down the length of Nicolas's steel shaft.

The dining room doors opened again and another couple entered. This time a different servant carried their plates and sat them on the opposite side of Nicolas, Tomas, and me. I started pulling my hand away from Nicolas's crotch but he clasped his hand on top of mine.

"There's nothing to be scared of," he whispered, leaning closer to me while pressing both of our hands over his dick.

"People will see us," I told him.

"They might enjoy the show." His eyes glowed like black onyx. But it was the honesty in his expression that made him appear so sincere.

"A show?" My lips were suddenly so dry I knew they would crack if I moved my mouth to say more. Not that I could think of a damned thing to say.

"A show that you control. You call the shots, and do whatever you want to do." He lifted my drink to my lips so that I smelled the enticing wine before accepting, and sipping. He grinned, satisfied. "Drink and enjoy yourself."

He handed me the glass and I took a large unladylike gulp. Then followed it up with a few more smaller sips. The alcohol drifted upward to my brain, instead of down to my stomach where it belonged. When I set my glass down, it was almost empty. And I felt comfortably numb.

Which made it easier to smile. "Now, how am I supposed to decide what I want to do?"

"Find out for yourself." He continued pressing our hands against his thick cock. "Raise your dress and see how wet you are. If you're soaked, you should do something about it."

"That logic is tempting to follow." I giggled and lifted my dress, pulling it up my thighs with my free hand which was also damp from holding my glass.

When I spread my legs, turning toward him slightly so that his legs ended up between mine, I knew I was wet before I even touched myself. As my fingers moved over my smooth pussy, I moved my other hand down the length of his cock. I picked up a rhythm without even thinking about it. And better yet, doing this while watching him, and not quite sure if anyone in the room watched us or not, created a pressure inside me that threatened to explode any moment.

"Let's adjust this." Nicolas's fingertips were cool and smooth when he touched my thighs and pushed the fabric of my dress up around my hips, exposing me thoroughly.

Tomas's hands snaked around my waist, helping to adjust my dress and then rubbing his hands over my thighs. "Relax, enjoy yourself," he whispered, his breath torturing the side of my neck.

Nicolas straightened and squeezed my hand that was wrapped around his cock. For all the intimacy we shared, I stared into a stranger's face. It was an odd sensation and one I wouldn't dwell on right now. If I wanted compassion, intimacy, I would have to open my heart to a man. Paying someone eliminated that complication. I shoved the twang of regret that I wasn't doing this with a lover out of my mind.

"That's it, sweetheart. Makes for a much better show." He smiled with his lips closed, his eyes turning bright as he met mine. "Would it be easier for you to stroke me if I took off my loincloth?"

"It might be more comfortable for you." I was stuck on what I'd seen in his face. I wasn't some love-starved woman. Life was good. And fulfilling. I wasn't thrilled that there wasn't a man in my life, or that I never got the cases that mattered, but overall, I would be a spoiled child to complain. There wasn't any reason for me to want to see something more than mild friendship occur between me and Nicolas and Tomas. We were from different worlds, and always would be.

God, now I sounded like my father. Heaven help me.

"You're right at that. I would definitely be more comfortable without restrictions." He leaned back slightly, and worked his fingers without looking down until his cock sprang free. With the small amount of clothing he wore, it didn't take much.

"Oh, my." I couldn't help but think his comment matched my thoughts and meant more than simply moving his loincloth out of the way.

Tomas reached around me further, helping spread my pussy open and moving his fingers with mine. I could look down at what our hands were doing, or focus on Nicolas and those dreamy, dark brown eyes that added to his intense expression. So many sensations ripped through me our surroundings seemed to fade and there was only Nicolas and Tomas. I actually considered fucking both of them again today.

But where? When? I glanced around the dining room, pulling it back into my world, looking at the couple on one side of us and then those on the other side. All parties were engrossed in conversation, holding hands and flirting and smiling. They weren't looking our way.

"What are you thinking?" he asked.

"How are we going to do this?"

"Do what?"

I met his gaze. Heat washed over my face. The ugly red blotches were back. I made a face but his expression remained serious. He probably was so affected by my stroking his cock in public that soothing my embarrassment was too much to ask.

"Do anything," I whispered. "I mean anything more than this."

"What do you want to do?"

I shot a sideways glance at Tomas. He watched me intently and tilted his head slightly, and his smooth cheek brushed against mine while his fingers rubbed moisture around my already sensitive pussy. I turned my attention back to Nicolas.

"I doubt we could do anything here." I cleared my voice.

"Are you content with this?" His gaze dropped to my fingers. "You're so beautiful when you stroke yourself like that. But is that all you want? All that matters is that you're satisfied."

8

Natalie

"I'm satisfied from eating," I said honestly. I knew my answer was a cop-out, but honestly, I didn't know what else to say.

Hell yes, I was satisfied from the awesome sex I had with Tomas and Nicolas. The food was awesome. Sex again with both of them sounded wonderful. But here, with so many people so close, I wasn't sure I could do it.

Nicolas nodded once. "We can leave then," he said, grabbing his cloth napkin and wiping his face.

"Wait. You aren't done eating." I grabbed his hand when he would have stood. "Don't tell me that's all you want to eat."

These men had sex with so many different women. Surely I couldn't mean that much to them that they would give up eating. My mind warred with itself while I stared into his beautiful chocolate-colored eyes. Eyes that I wouldn't forget any time soon.

"This is about you, my dear."

I stared at him, deciding I loved the dark shade of his skin, and the way his full lips pressed into a determined line when he was serious about something. And he was right. I paid a hell of a lot of money for him; for both of them. But I didn't want to look at it that way. That would ruin my fantasy if Nicolas and Tomas just became purchased dick.

"This is about us," I reiterated. "All three of us. If one of us isn't happy, then all three of us will know and feel it. So eat until you are full," I ordered. His expression remained solemn, but his cock danced with excitement. Maybe being ordered around got him off. Nicolas didn't strike me as the kind of man who would enjoy submitting to anyone though. "Please," I added.

His brooding expression didn't fade when he gave me a small smile. "You're the boss," he whispered, and turned his attention to his food.

I worried I'd offended him and pondered over his comment when we walked outside after eating. Somehow, I doubted I would get a straight answer if I asked. And even that created a bit of guilt inside me. I professed to all three of us needing to be happy, and wanted a bond of sorts to form between us, yet at the same time, was convinced they put on a show for me.

Okay, I knew they did. So what did it matter what they really thought of me? Because I was curious, that's why. Probably why I became a lawyer, and why I craved cases where I could explore and investigate. Privately, I committed myself to learning more about my scrumptious men.

"I don't know that I feel like going back to the room yet," I told them, walking in between them slowly as we meandered along a cobblestone path through the gardens. "The handbook said the island is one hundred acres of paradise. Is all of it open to clients?"

"Most of it, yes. What would you like to do?" Nicolas asked.

I glanced up to see him watching me carefully, as if he could guess my desires before I spoke them.

"There is a wonderful swimming area. Maybe we could try that," Tomas suggested.

"I love to swim. But not right after all that food and wine."
The dessert coffee, perfectly laced with Baileys, made me feel
lighter than the warm air surrounding me.

"Let's explore the gardens. I would kill to have such beauty
at my home." The air wasn't just warm, it was spiked with
beautiful fragrances. This truly was paradise.

"I know just the place." Nicolas suddenly sounded excited
when he grabbed my hand and wandered off of the cobblestone
path.

I found myself laughing when he came to a hill and the three
of us ran down it. My hair would be a mess, and I was sure I
would be sweaty and disheveled, and you know what? I didn't
care. I ran so fast I would have fallen on my face for sure if Nicolas hadn't swooped me into his arms at the bottom of the hill.

He spun me around and I knew I probably wouldn't have
laughed so hard if it weren't for the alcohol. Tomas and Nicolas
must have had incredibly high tolerances. They both drank at least
as much as I did, but neither of them were breaking a sweat,
and they both seemed focused on only giving me pleasure,
nothing else.

Nicolas found my mouth, and at that moment, I was certain
all one hundred acres tilted to the side. The ocean would flow
over the land and take us all away with it. His mouth was that
good as he branded me with his soft lips. Heat swarmed throughout my body, and I wrapped my arms and legs around him, letting my laughter fade into a sigh, as I opened up to him.

His touch was commanding, dominating yet gentle. Never
in my life did I ever think a man could kiss me so thoroughly
that when he let me up for air, I was as satisfied as if he'd just
fucked me for hours.

"Natalie, I can't wait any longer to be inside you again," he
whispered into my mouth, his chocolate eyes almost black with
desire. "I want to feel your soaked pussy wrapped around my
cock."

I could hardly breathe. I tried answering by kissing him again. My body slid down his and when I made an effort to get my legs to hold me, he again moved me as if I were lighter than the sweet air around us and held me until I lay on the ground.

You would guess that on a tropical island, the insects would be thrilled to find a sweaty body lying on the ground—food for the taking. Somehow Paradise Island managed to be insect free though. The soft moss underneath me didn't even itch when he raised my dress and then positioned me so that my legs wrapped around his firm waist.

"What about condoms?" I asked, suddenly warring with the thought of allowing him to fuck me without them. Which was proof I was drugged by paradise. I couldn't allow this man who had sex with so many people fuck me without protection. "We really should . . ."

Tomas knelt next to me while Nicolas remained positioned between my legs. "We're always prepared, my dear," he said, producing several wrapped packages in his hand.

I blinked. All these men wore were loincloths. They didn't have pockets or anywhere on their body to stash so much as a form of ID, let alone condoms.

He smiled at my confused expression. "I grabbed some from the counter on the way out of the dining hall. At Paradise Island, we're always prepared."

I swear to God I didn't remember him grabbing anything on our way out. Obvious proof that I was more than a little distracted by my two men. Tomas lowered his mouth to mine, kissing me. He placed the wrapped condoms on my belly and I felt Nicolas scoop one of them off of me while Tomas impaled my mouth.

"I want you now," Nicolas said while Tomas continued kissing me.

I groaned and apparently that was all the answer Nicolas needed.

That massive beast glided so deep inside me I was positive I wouldn't walk again. I cried out, reaching up with my arms, and probably raked Tomas's shoulders with my nails. He growled into my mouth while Nicolas started fucking me.

Tomas bit my lower lip and then ended the kiss. My vision was so blurred his blond hair seemed to glow with the sun behind him. He moved then and I shifted my attention to Nicolas. Tomas created a pillow for me with his thigh and then moved his hands over my breasts, caressing while Nicolas eased in deeper.

Nicolas closed his eyes, his expression so serious that gazing up at him robbed me of my ability to form a single thought. The sun made his skin glow and he tilted his head slightly, making the view I had before me one that surpassed perfection. So much muscle, every inch of him trim and solid. From his perfectly shaped neck, to his broad shoulders, and then that chest of his—holy shit!

All I could do was stare, and probably drool, not that I would have noticed if I did. That incredibly large cock of his did things to my insides that I never dreamed possible. He filled me, moving steadily in and out, while more muscles than I knew I possessed twitched and stretched, creating room for all of that hard, solid cock of his.

I turned my head and felt roped muscle flex next to my cheek. The coarse hairs on Tomas's leg tickled my flesh, adding to the pleasure offered by my heightened senses. Lord, if I could truly put into words how both of these men made me feel. Well, it's enough to say that I can't do it. Hell, I couldn't utter a word, let alone remember how to spell, the pleasure taking over every inch of my body was too much.

And the pressure building inside robbed me of any coherent functions at all. I could feel Nicolas moving, was more than aware of every inch of his cock, the way it bulged along his shaft, and how the tip of it seemed incredibly swollen. Although part of me wanted to pull him out of me, take him in my hands and learn more about his cock, there was no way I would pass up on how incredible he made me feel.

"I love how you glow when you're getting it good," Tomas murmured, brushing hair out of my face and then running his fingertips down to my shoulders.

"Getting it good," I began, taking heavy breaths in between each word. "That's an understatement."

Both men chuckled and I fought to focus on their beautiful, sexy faces staring down at me.

"I'll take that as a compliment," Nicolas said, not sounding a bit winded. "I can't help but wonder how much you can take."

He didn't offer any more explanation. But then he didn't have to. Suddenly he thrust harder, showing me that up until that moment, he'd been holding back considerably.

"Holy crap!" I screamed, and dug my fingernails into Tomas's arms. White light flashed before my eyes while Nicolas's cock actually grew harder, more defined, as he impaled me again and again.

I could actually feel the veins that wrapped around his massive shaft as he buried himself deep inside my womb. Roped muscle twitched under my hands as Tomas's fingers pushed the straps of my dress off my shoulders and then exposed my breasts.

"There's a view to die for," Tomas hissed and then barely touched my breasts.

I arched into him, wanting him to say more, give me more, but scared I wouldn't be able to handle what their definition of more might be.

Nicolas held on to my legs firmly and rode me hard and fast. I couldn't slide away from him with Tomas holding me on his lap.

"Look at how her breasts jiggle," Nicolas said, still not sounding out of breath and his deep baritone smoother and richer than warm syrup.

"I know, they're absolutely perfect."

I wanted to laugh, to tell both of them they were full of it, and that they had to have seen better than what I had to offer. But they made me feel so beautiful, so desirable. And I loved feeling that way. I didn't want to crush the moment by throwing in some reality.

Maybe I was perfect to them. Maybe all they'd had while working on this island were a bunch of old hags. That worked for me. I was the best either of these gorgeous men ever had. It wasn't my fault they worked here and couldn't go choose ladies who were suitable for men that were beyond ideal stud material.

I was glad to make their day and give them a shot of perfection like they were giving me. Yea, right!

Regardless, at the moment I wasn't going to argue with them. Just then, Nicolas raised my legs slightly, and his thick cock sunk deep into my soaked pussy. I glanced down, got an eyeful of his massive, sheathed cock sinking farther and farther, disappearing as I watched, and filling me, creating sensations I'd never known before.

I could feel him pressing deeper, the heat from him building, and at the same time Tomas brushing his fingertips over the swell of my breasts. It was all too much, too many of my senses heightened. There was no controlling it.

I came in waves and waves, crying out loud enough that my throat burned. And I didn't care. It didn't bother me if everyone on the damned island were watching. These two men were so damned good that all that mattered was riding out the relief that came with my orgasm finally releasing.

"That's it, baby," Nicolas encouraged. Again his soft deep voice stroked over me just as Tomas's fingers did. "Come as hard as you can. All those tiny little muscles of yours are stroking my cock so perfectly. There isn't a better feeling in the entire world."

Maybe that was it. Maybe these two were nymphomaniacs and so any woman they were with was perfect if they could fuck. And maybe I needed to quit trying to analyze all of this and just enjoy it.

Although damn, I was already doing that. In fact, I'm pretty sure I left enjoyment back at the dining room and quickly moved into loving the hell out of it.

"You feel so good, too." Talking was harder to do than I realized.

And it wasn't fair that Nicolas did all the work, yet spoke with a calm, cool ease. Although his smooth deep voice sure did add to his sex appeal.

"Oh, sweetheart, I'm feeling very good," he practically purred.

I focused on his face, smiling the best I could while he plummeted again, deeper this time, and created sparks before my eyes.

"Oh, God," I cried. "Too much. It's too much."

His chuckle created goose bumps that raced over my flesh.

"There's no such thing, sweetheart," he said, but then his expression hardened, his jawbone seeming suddenly more pronounced and his full lips pressing into a firm, strong line, while thick black lashes fluttered over his chocolate eyes. "But damn, baby. You feel too damned good. I'm going to come."

His large cock twitched inside me, and his pace slowed considerably while muscles protruded in his chest. The fine outline of every inch of him, covered with his smooth, dark flesh, was so beautiful I almost cried. But the way he made me feel when he slowed, suddenly taking deliberate effort to move in and out of me with such cautious precision, pushed me to the edge.

I couldn't take it. Couldn't handle it another second. I let go of Tomas and scraped my nails over Nicolas's chest, feeling his coarse curly hair torture the ends of my fingers.

"Now, Nicolas. Damn it, now!" I'd never been so demanding, so brazen, in all of my life.

When he pierced me with his gaze, bore through me with

those dark eyes of his, I couldn't tell whether he liked my orders or not. But then a rumble started inside him, deep enough that I could feel it vibrating as it grew. It spread through him, up into his throat, and down into his cock.

He shook inside me, and I watched while the rest of him started to quake as well. Then the rumble turned to a roar as his eyes widened and he started to come.

Once again I regretted that we had to use condoms because I couldn't feel him come, just his cock throbbing. I was sure I would have been able to feel his warmth fill me without them, but I wasn't complaining. My pussy tightened, and I reached for him, wanting him closer, as he made me come with him again.

"My turn," Tomas said, sounding so excited all I could do was allow him to lift me, balance me while I settled on all fours.

I didn't know a man could sheathe himself so quickly. Tomas unwrapped a condom and slid it on his rock-hard cock and then pressed into my soaked, burning hot pussy. When he entered me I howled, convinced I'd have a sore throat before the day was over.

Tomas fucked me hard, not waiting to build up the momentum. "She's burning me alive, man," he grunted, gripping my hips and impaling me while I stared at the ground between my hands and enjoyed once again how damned good it felt.

It amazed the hell out of me that I was still horny. But as he fucked me, rode me like a warrior who would never tire, the pressure inside me built once again. Had I ever come more than once while making love to any man? And now, here I was, coming how many times today?

"Lord, it's so fucking good," I mumbled while panting, my hair flying around my face.

He rode me hard, holding on so I couldn't move. Nicolas's strong hand rubbed my back, as if soothing me while I took all Tomas had to offer. And damn, he had a hell of a lot to give. I didn't care that I was on my hands and knees outside. It didn't bother me that my dress was now twisted around my waist. And I no longer worried that anyone could walk over the hill and see me taking one man, and then the other. All that mattered was that Tomas was getting damn close to hitting that spot. And I needed it hit bad.

"She's going to come for me," Tomas announced, sounding triumphant.

I was surprised he knew before I did. But analyzing either of them was too damned hard to do. I let the dam break inside me, not even trying to control my needs when they peaked, and then exploded with enough intensity that my arms gave out. I pressed my cheek against the ground, taking him even deeper as I arched my back and let him fill me.

Life was good. So fucking good. And I knew now why they called this paradise.

I didn't mean to fall asleep when we returned to the room. But after another quick shower, and then donning the comfortable bathrobe that was provided with the room, my men surprised me with snacks from the dining room. I munched a little, but when I woke up, with them lying on either side of me, the large tray covered with a variety of healthy snacks and "to-die-for" sinfully scrumptious chocolate desserts was over half eaten.

I was tempted by a couple of the remaining pieces of fudge, the all-American standard recipe made with milk chocolate and no nuts, just the way I loved it. And in fact, I stood at the end of the bed, staring at the small squares, before forcing myself to take one step, and then another, away from the snack tray.

Included in the extensive questionnaire I was required to fill out were questions about my favorite desserts. I shouldn't have been surprised that when the tray appeared, it was loaded with everything I put down, plus a few surprises.

What I did find interesting was how Nicolas and Tomas were as excited about the treats as I was, commenting on how they loved the items selected. Either Rose had all of her men memorize every guest's questionnaire so they would be well rehearsed no matter who selected them, or it was a mighty uncanny coincidence that we all loved the same foods.

I glanced back at the room, which was heavy with shadows and lit only from the light coming out of the bathroom. Tomas and Nicolas were both turned, facing the edge of their sides of the bed, and appeared to be sleeping soundly. Neither of them snored, but their slow heavy breathing and relaxed bodies were proof enough that they possibly exerted themselves more today than they'd led me to believe by always appearing so calm and ready for more.

It was hard to pull my gaze away from them. The blankets were pulled down some from my sneaking out from in between them, and muscles rippled and bulged even as they slept. Damn if I could tell which was the better looking man. Nicolas with his bald head and perfect smooth, chocolate skin was packed with steel muscles that would make any woman weak in the knees. And Tomas, with his wavy blond hair that was just long enough to give him that roguish, irresistible look, was the kind of man who I would be scared to take home to meet Mother. Either she would chase him off or try stealing him behind my back. And Father, well all he cared about was a guy's family tree. I didn't have a clue if either of these men even had family, let alone a single branch to a tree. Nor did I care. They were perfect, and for two weeks, they were mine.

I snuck out of the room, not with any direction in mind, but needing to stretch my legs and clear my head a bit after my first day of mind-boggling sex. It wasn't until I reached the large rooms downstairs, with their glass walls that I realized how dark it was outside. The thought occurred to me that I might run into other guests who might be having sex in various parts of the island. That thought scared and excited me at the same time. Not that I ever thought of myself as a Peeping Tom or a voyeur, but this was Paradise Island. And as Nicolas pointed out earlier, sometimes it was erotic to be watched, or to watch. Either way, I wasn't sure what I would do if I came across anyone doing the hot and heavy.

Probably turn tail and run.

In Chicago, one didn't take walks alone at night. Not even in the neighborhoods I grew up in. Although I reassured myself that this wasn't a town, and that every single person here was either an employee of the island, or a guest, my stomach tightened nervously when I stepped outside into the warm night air.

I'm not sure how long I walked, I quickly got lost in the beauty of the gardens. There was something so tranquil, so appealing about them. On either side of me, arrangements of the most beautiful plants and shrubbery, with small statues and fountains arranged around them, made me ache to take up the hobby and create such beauty in my own yard. I wished for an escort who could identify the plants. Most had their flowers closed, but some, even at night, showed off their gorgeous flowers. I stepped off the path more than once to breathe in their perfumed fragrance.

Like I said, I don't know how far I walked because I lost track of time. I pulled my cell phone from my waist and pushed a button on it so it would glow. At least it was good for something since I didn't have a signal. Unfortunately, I didn't look at the time when I left, but it was just after midnight, and turning around, I no longer saw the mansion. At least I knew all I had to do was follow the cobblestone path back. But nicely organized gardens no longer surrounded me. Instead, large trees with even larger leaves created a canopy over the path, which I noticed was no longer cobblestone, but simply cement.

A weird sense of excitement filled me, tightening my tummy and making my palms sweat, but it was like an adventure. One where I was sure I wouldn't get hurt—which was the best kind of adventure to have. I was in a part of the island where the guests probably didn't go. It crossed my mind to turn around and go back, but it wasn't like there were DO NOT ENTER signs. The sidewalk continued on in the darkness ahead of me.

Yes, it was dark. Very dark. The tree branches and leaves overhead blocked out the moonlight. And I didn't realize until this moment that the gardens were lit, obviously set up for moonlight strolls. This part of the island didn't have lights to guide my way. I couldn't see ten feet in front of me. An eerie sense of being wrapped up in a blanket, or walking blindfolded, filled me with trepidation. I don't know why I kept going. It's not like I'm some super sleuth by nature.

My father would not give me any of the tough cases that required the least bit of research. All I ever got were easy, fluffy, you-could-do-them-in-your-sleep-type cases. Paperwork and more paperwork. No exploration. No investigation. Nothing but filling out forms and filing them with the right department. The least I could do tonight was prove to myself that I was strong enough, tough enough, to handle walking into the unknown.

One foot in front of the other, my flats tapping on the smooth pavement beneath my feet. I kept going.

I'd hardly noticed the vibration against my shoes when a light shone behind me. I jumped off the sidewalk, instantly feeling itchy from dew-covered leaves that slapped my arms, as if to say, this is our terrain, get back on the sidewalk!

But they hid me from the golf cart that drove along the sidewalk and passed by without noticing me. A man I didn't know drove it, his expression blank as he kept on going.

Once I managed to swallow my heart, I stepped back on the sidewalk, this time looking behind me, as well as in front of me, before I picked up my pace and followed the cart. Walking quickly when it's pitch-black isn't easy. Your senses become incredibly acute. I swear I could hear dew landing on the large leaves above and around me. But when my cell phone rang . . .

"Shit," I hissed, grabbing it and then struggling to free it from my waist. Odd, now I had a signal.

For some reason, its quiet buzz violated the night silence, and it was imperative that I make it stop as quickly as possible.

"Hello," I said, sounding incredibly out of breath.

"Natalie, where are you?" The deep baritone on the other end of the line sounded not only worried and anxious, but sent creepy crawlies rushing over my flesh.

I suddenly felt like I'd been busted doing something that I shouldn't be doing. But I wasn't I told myself firmly.

"Who is this?" I asked, although I was pretty sure I knew.

"Nicolas. We woke up and couldn't find you." The worried edge in his tone was gone. Now he simply sounded hurt. Like living without me, even for a minute, was more than he could handle.

"I'm fine," I told him, picking up a motherly tone that I didn't know I possessed.

"Where are you?"

I laughed but then grew silent when I stepped off the pavement accidentally. It was all I could do not to cry out and alarm him when my ankle twisted on the edge of the pavement. Flinging my arms out, and managing not to send my phone flying, I regained my balance before I could fall on my face. So my night vision sucks—especially when the stars are the only source of light.

"To be honest with you, I'm not quite sure," I said, then realizing I was whispering, I cleared my voice. But now I was barely moving, gingerly putting one foot in front of the other since obviously I couldn't tell when the sidewalk curved. "I started walking, and I just kept going. It was so beautiful outside. But now its pitch-black and I might as well be blind."

There was silence on the other end of the line, but only for a moment. "You need to turn around and come back. Return to the mansion immediately." Nicolas used a tone that I hadn't heard out of him before. He sounded stern, almost angry.

I knew he was simply concerned though. "I'll be back soon. Enjoy the snacks and relax. Watch TV. I'm out exploring." I laughed again, intentionally this time, to show him I wasn't worried.

"You aren't supposed to be walking outside by yourself. It's in the handbook. Natalie, turn around and come back now." He sounded so stern that I stopped.

Silly me for turning around to take in my surroundings. I couldn't see a damned thing. "I don't remember that being in the handbook." I read every word of that book, and I was pretty good at holding things to memory.

"Turn around and start walking back. We're coming to get you. There is nothing at the end of the sidewalk anyway. It simply ends at a cliff. It's not safe." Again his commanding tone was so different than the playboy persona he'd held on to since I met him.

Which I told myself was just earlier today, or maybe yesterday by now. It shouldn't surprise me that there were a lot of sides to my men that I didn't know. And in truth, they were only my men for two weeks. No matter the amount of money I paid to be here, after that time, they would belong to someone else. That much, I knew, was in the contract—well, in so many words.

I believe it said, during the duration of your stay on Paradise Island, your companion, or companions as my case may be, would be at my beck and call to serve me in whatever manner pleased me.

Okay, so reciting the handbook to myself in the dark wasn't getting me anywhere. And damn it, I didn't want to turn back. I couldn't say if it was because my curiosity was piqued, or because I didn't like being told what to do. I did know in my heart that it was a bit of both. If I didn't mind being ordered about, I would be content with my life back in Chicago, and I wasn't.

"Natalie, are you there?" Nicolas asked.

"I'm here. I'll turn around and meet you two in a bit. You're sweethearts to come out and join me. The night is beautiful."

"I can't wait to see you." Once again, the deep masculine purr returned to his tone.

"See you soon," I said cheerfully, and ended the call.

Then I started walking as quickly as I could in the same direction I'd been going. Nicolas and Tomas didn't know how far I'd been walking. And suddenly I really wanted to know what was at the end of this sidewalk.

Nicolas told me there wasn't anything there. But if that were the case, why would someone be driving this direction in a golf cart?

There was light up ahead. I swore there was. Squinting, I'd slowed my pace before I realized it and then came to a complete stop when the trees ended. For some reason, in spite of it being a bit creepy, the darkness was now my protector. And the sight in front of me wasn't what I expected.

Not only were the trees gone, but all of the fancy foliage and beautiful plants. If I didn't know better, I would think I wasn't on the island anymore, but in some city somewhere. The grass was cut short, and although the sidewalk continued, it didn't look as clean. And ahead of me there were buildings. Nothing fancy. Almost like a factory, or something out of an industrial part of a town.

"I'm not supposed to be here." I wondered if Nicolas knew this was out here, and that was why he sounded so stern. It wasn't like I would sabotage anything. "Why can't I be here?"

Hell, I paid an incredible amount of money to come to this island. And no matter what Nicolas insisted, it didn't say anywhere in the handbook that a guest couldn't wander around alone. That simply confirmed my first statement. They didn't want me to see this place, whatever it was.

I ordered my legs to quit shaking as I walked away from the

trees. At least I could see now. The sky was clear. Stars shone so brightly that in spite of the almost-full moon that shed a fair amount of light on the darkness, I would believe that the stars could offer enough light on their own.

Now that I made my decision to continue exploring, I moved faster, breathing in the wonderfully salty aroma from the ocean. The sidewalk was wider now, and darker. I guessed those golf carts might use this as a road, and that explained the different shade.

The first building that I passed looked like nothing more than a small booth, although there wasn't anyone inside. I did notice a small camera hung at the corner pointing toward the sidewalk in front of me. Pausing, I cringed. Maybe I really wasn't supposed to be here. But what could be so secretive? In all honesty, I couldn't imagine the place being anything more than maintenance buildings for the island. But what would they be maintaining? The island could have its own power plant. That would make sense. And I'm no expert or anything, but none of the buildings in front of me looked like power plants.

Just to see if I could get away with it, I walked around the back side of the small booth, and then remained on the grass long enough until I thought I was out of range of the camera. By the time I hopped back onto the pavement, my flats were soaked from the dew and squished when I walked. I hate having wet feet in shoes.

There were streetlights now, and enough of them that I couldn't avoid their glow. I froze when I saw someone in a golf cart. He drove, looking directly ahead, along another sidewalk that went from one tall square building to another. He stopped outside the building, got out of his cart, and then pushed several buttons on a pad next to a garage door. Instantly, the garage door lifted and two other men stepped outside and began unloading boxes that were stacked on the back of the cart.

I wasn't sure what struck me as more odd, the fact that all

men wore loincloths, and nothing more, or that I stood in the open, with nothing to shield me, and none of them noticed me. That or they weren't bothered by my presence.

Something inside encouraged me to run—run like hell. The cowardly part of me consumed a majority of my thoughts. I admit it. I may dream about being Olivia Benson from *Law and Order: SVU,* but some fantasies, even on Paradise Island, aren't going to come true. The only reason I didn't turn around and scoot my ass out of there was plain and simple. I couldn't move. Fear and anxiety attacked my central nervous system and had me shaking like a leaf and nearly hyperventilating, while I waited to be discovered.

Another part of me surfaced, the part that had the nerve to come here in the first place, to have sex with two strange men at the same time and enjoy the hell out of it. That took courage in itself, damn it.

I wasn't doing anything wrong. I hadn't crossed any DO NOT ENTER signs. And no matter what Nicolas said, there wasn't anything in that handbook that said I couldn't wander the grounds by myself. So, the only way not to get busted with your hand in the cookie jar was to announce your hand was there, and ask if anyone else wanted anything while you were helping yourself.

I managed to suck in a deep breath, and walked toward the men and the golf cart.

9

Natalie

"Hi there." My voice cracked slightly, but I sounded cheerful.

Then my gaze landed on the sides of one of the boxes. There wasn't anything unusual about the boxes themselves. It was the manufacturer's name, Pewitt Blanch, printed on the side of the box that grabbed my attention.

The only reason I recognized it was because I'd done some work for them in the past. Nothing too serious. Just drawn up some amendments to their existing contracts. They were a company that supplied materials to hospitals, anything from forceps to baby incubators, to orthopedic implants.

Not exactly the kind of items that one would expect to be shipped to Paradise Island.

"I was just out taking a walk," I explained, gesturing at the sidewalk behind me. "I didn't mean to interrupt."

And apparently, I wasn't. Because none of the three men acknowledged me at all. In fact, they continued unloading the boxes, walking into the garage and setting them down, and returning for more. Not once did any of them look my way. It was hard to suck in a breath. This was totally creeping me out.

I dared to move closer to the golf cart. The driver leaned against the steering wheel. The two men picked up the last of the rather large boxes, each of them carrying two, which almost covered their faces as they walked into the garage. I leapt out of the way to avoid being trampled. It was damned unnerving suddenly feeling invisible. In spite of the warm saltwater-scented air, chills rushed down my spine. Crossing my arms over my chest, I tilted my head and squinted to better see into the warehouse.

This time the men didn't come back out. The door slid down and the man in the cart pushed it into reverse and backed away from the building, the monotonous repetitive beeping sound the cart made the only noise around me. Not once did he look at me, or act like he even knew I was there.

"Have a good evening," I yelled out, louder than necessary, and waved as I walked toward him. I stopped dumbfounded, when he turned the cart around and drove away without acknowledging me. "Now that's odd," I began, but then frowned when the streetlight caught his face. There was something wrong.

I gawked, swearing his face wasn't shaped right. When I blinked, knowing it was rude to stare, he drove the cart between the two buildings across the large courtyard and disappeared. Something was seriously not right here and damned if I knew what it was. The chills that rushed down my spine a moment ago now raced over my body with a vengeance.

This was more than creeping me out. I realized at that moment that I'd never really known fear in my life. But right then, I couldn't move, could hardly think, and simply stared while trying to decide if I should run like hell. Panic caused a nasty bile to rush to my throat as my heart started pounding so hard I could barely breathe.

I snapped my head to the right when someone else walked out of the building alongside me, and I didn't give much further thought to being ignored by the three men I just saw. This man strolled out of the building, closed his cell phone, and attached it to his hip as he headed in my direction. He looked normal. His actions were normal. Maybe being alone in the dark was making my imagination run rampant.

"Excuse me," I said, which immediately grabbed his attention. In fact, he stopped dead in his tracks and then simply stared at me as if I had two noses or something. Nervously, I pressed my palms against my robe and rubbed them against the smooth material. But I was no longer cold. In fact, suddenly it seemed very warm where I stood.

There was something uncanny about how he looked at me. I would swear that I'd met him before, but with those distractingly gorgeous eyes, and his absolutely perfectly chiseled features, there was no way I would have forgotten if I had.

"Do I know you?" I asked, and then wished I'd asked something more clever. My question sounded like a pickup line that a man like him probably heard too many times, especially on an island like this.

"I doubt it. Why are you here?" His voice gave me chills. There was a rich smoothness to it. He almost sounded like someone who'd lived in so many countries that he maintained a mixture of many accents. It added to the air of mystery about him.

If I closed my eyes and he kept talking, I would swear he sounded like Nicolas. This man wasn't black though. At least I didn't think he was. His skin was definitely darker than mine, which wasn't saying much. But his features were Caucasian, and his hair, although very dark, looked thick and smooth, and hung straight, with soft looking waves that passed his ears.

"I was taking a walk." I half turned to point toward the sidewalk that brought me here. But then turned completely when Rose approached me, driving a golf cart.

I swore her expression appeared outraged, but when I gave her my full attention, she smiled broadly and waved. "You have a very unique gift," she said, her soft-spoken manner the same as it was when I first met with her, although her eyes glowed brightly in the darkness. They were a rather unique tan color that I didn't notice when we spoke before. "I don't think I've ever seen two grown men so upset."

She stopped the cart next to me and then patted the passenger seat. "Hop in," she continued, her pitch rising just a bit, making me think she fought to sound cheerful. "I'll give you a ride back. You sure took quite a long walk."

"What is this place?" I turned around to say something to the man I'd just spoken to, but he was gone. An odd feeling of regret swept over me that I didn't understand, and numbly, I climbed into the cart and tucked my robe around my legs as I continued studying the buildings. "And who was that man I just spoke to?"

"What man?" Rose sounded surprised.

I shifted my attention to her in time to see her scanning the grounds around us, almost appearing nervous.

I pointed to where he'd been standing. "He was right there."

Rose turned the cart around quickly and almost sped out of there. She flipped a switch and headlights came on, lighting the wide sidewalk that I'd managed to walk along in the dark before.

"These facilities aren't open to our guests. I'm sure you can see they don't possess the magnificent grandeur that helps create an air of paradise."

"I didn't ignore any sign or rule," I said, instantly feeling myself being pushed into the defense chair. I added confidently, because damn it, I knew I was right, "And nowhere in the handbook does it say anything about guests being forbidden to walk alone on the grounds."

"Of course not. I hope you enjoyed your outing." Rose

smiled, all businesslike and professional. The woman could run for a political office and win with her reserved beauty and calm aura, and her ability to avoid every comment and question I put out on the table, without making it obvious she was doing so. "Allow me to call Nicolas and Tomas. They are out searching for you as well. How does a hot, scented bath sound to you?" She smiled as she pulled out a cell phone from her dress pocket. "Rose petals? I love rose petals in a garden tub. I'll have your men prepare it for you immediately."

I don't think I'd ever driven so fast in a golf cart before. The night air slapped against my cheeks and sent chills rushing over my flesh. I wrapped the robe around me tighter, suddenly wishing I were warm again.

As long as it took me to walk to those buildings, Rose made record time in returning us to the mansion. She spoke quietly and calmly to Tomas on the phone and finally slowed and hung up the phone at the same time as we neared the edge of the gardens.

One of the servants from the house stood waiting as she brought the cart to a stop. "Jonah will escort you to your room, my dear. Please feel free to call me personally if there is anything I can do for you."

She stopped the cart but I didn't get out. Instead, I turned and placed my hand on her arm. Rose stared at me, her expression blank, but relaxed. She wasn't going to offer any information, and for some reason, that made me want to push harder.

"What were those facilities?" I asked directly, then paused, holding her gaze and waiting out the moment of silence for her answer.

"Simply storage and maintenance buildings." She smiled and moved her arm, then patted my arm. "Allow Jonah to take you to your room, dear. It's late."

"Yes, it is. And thank you for the ride back," I said graciously, wondering if I was making something out of nothing. What I saw bothered me though, and it bugged me further that Rose didn't seem to notice. "Why do you have medical supplies in maintenance buildings?"

"What medical supplies?"

"I recognized the company name on the boxes the men were unloading," I explained. "They don't sell generic first aid items that one would think you'd store here, but supplies for large hospitals. I didn't understand that, anymore than I understood why the men ignored me when I tried speaking to them."

Rose's laughter was melodic. "They don't speak English, Natalie. I apologize if you feel anyone here has been rude to you. Not all of my employees are trained to entertain our guests. But as I'm sure you realize, you did enter an area that is not designed to be open to the public. If your time here so far hasn't stimulated or satisfied you, I will do everything in my power to make sure the rest of your stay with us is completely to your liking."

She wasn't exactly reprimanding, but damned close.

"Everything and everyone here is perfect." I wanted to add that she should know that already, but I didn't see a need to create more friction between us. It was late. I was suddenly very tired. And more than likely I was trying to make something out of nothing. It made sense that the workers would ignore me if they didn't understand me—I guessed. "Thank you again for coming to get me. Good night."

"Good night, my dear." Rose nodded her head politely as I climbed out of the cart. She turned around and drove off quickly, back in the direction from where we came.

Jonah stood quietly, waiting for me when I turned around and fell silently into stride alongside him as we walked backed to the mansion.

I declined the hot bath when I returned to my room, but couldn't pass up on the wonderful massage that Tomas offered me when I climbed into bed. In fact, it was the last thing I remembered before drifting off into blissful sleep.

* * *

I don't remember the last time I slept until almost noon. In fact, I'm not sure I ever have. Tomas and Nicolas were both awake, and freshly showered, sitting facing each other at the table alongside the bed when I moved, and felt all the stiff muscles in my body attack at once. I stared at them for a moment while they simply stared at each other, neither one of them saying a word. When I cleared my throat, it was like they both snapped to life.

Odd.

"How does that hot bath sound to you now?" Nicolas stood easily and moved with the grace of a deadly cat. He walked over to the cappuccino machine and poured a cup for me.

"Sounds perfect." I probably looked worse than shit when I sat up in the bed and then noticed I was naked. I didn't remember removing my robe, but then even the massage was foggy in my memory. What did stand out were the odd dreams I had about a man who seemed to be a mixture of Tomas and Nicolas. Deadly and gorgeous, breathtaking and exhilarating. "I'm sorry if I upset or worried anyone last night," I added sheepishly.

"You are fine." Tomas took my hand and helped me out of the bed, and then pulled me against his virile body as he kissed the top of my head. "Allow us to spoil you with a hot, perfumed bath. Once you are awake and refreshed, we can plan out our day."

"Do you have any suggestions?" I sipped at the hot cappuccino and then closed my eyes as I took another drink. It was the best cup I'd ever tasted.

"I can think of many things I'd love to do with you." Nicolas's deep voice brought the image of the man I'd seen the night before to mind.

For some reason, I couldn't get him off of my mind. Worse yet, I found myself plotting for ways to get to see him again. Somehow I doubted it would be as easy as it was last night to get back to those buildings. I'd done something the people here on Paradise Island didn't want me doing. Again, that rebel inside me raised its defiant head, the same one that brought me here to this island, and had me adventuring out at night by myself. I wanted to return to those buildings and explore some more. I wondered what had changed inside me. I didn't used to be this daring. Whatever it was, I kind of liked it.

"We'll start with the bath. Then I'm sure the two of you will be more than able to entertain me afterward."

The bathroom was equipped with a garden tub, and showers large enough for several people on the opposite side. The glass walls were still damp from my two men showering, and the tub was filled with water heated to the perfect temperature. With Tomas holding my hand so I wouldn't slip, I stepped into the water, and then sunk into the warmth with a contented purr.

Nicolas climbed in as well, sliding off his loincloth and tossing it on the floor outside the tub, and then moved behind me so that I relaxed against corded muscle and smooth skin. Talk about heaven.

If only I hadn't taken that walk last night. Now my mind was full of questions and the compelling urge to learn more. It wasn't fair. Two of the most gorgeous men I'd ever laid eyes on were at my beck and call, and my thoughts drifted to another man, a mystery, an absolutely gorgeous-to-the-point-of-distraction mystery.

"What were those buildings that I walked to last night?" I asked after almost falling asleep in the hot water while Nicolas washed and conditioned my hair and massaged my scalp until I tingled from head to toe.

"What buildings?" he asked.

"They were past the trees. The cobblestone turned into a paved walk."

"Huh." He didn't say anything else.

Tomas offered me a small smile but didn't comment. Maybe

they wouldn't know about buildings on the island that didn't have anything to do with guests. But after last night, I suddenly ached to know all I could know about my men and Paradise Island.

"It was nice of Rose to give me a ride back," I said dismissively.

"She's a wonderful woman." Tomas pulled his loincloth off and slipped into the deep, perfectly warm water and kneeled in front of me. "Almost as wonderful as you are."

I wasn't ready for such sincere sounding praise and made a very unladylike snorting sound. Tomas didn't bat an eye at my reaction but instead reached for a large glass that sat on the edge of the tub.

"You underestimate yourself, Natalie," he said, his voice gruff. Thick strands of blond hair clung to his neck. He dipped the glass into the water and when he looked at me, I again noticed the brown flecks scattered amidst the green in his eyes. "Your honest, open personality adds to your natural beauty." He lifted the glass over my head. "Close your eyes."

I was barely given time to react before very warm water flowed over my head and face.

"Lean your head back," Nicolas said, his firm, strong hands gripped my shoulders and then his fingers glided up to my neck. "Relax and we'll clean you."

"I'm not sure where you two are the most talented." I leaned back against rippling muscle that felt better than the warm water while Tomas expertly massaged my head. "What did you do before you came to the island, Tomas?" I asked lazily.

"I had no life before coming here."

I blinked but couldn't focus on him until he finished his massage. He stared at me intently, his brooding expression serious, if not concerned.

"What kind of work did you do?"

"Anything I could find."

I tilted my head and my body slid over roped muscle and

smooth skin. "What about you?" I asked, looking up at Nicolas's firm jawline.

He looked ahead as he answered me. "I didn't work much. Paradise Island is the perfect place to be."

They weren't going to talk about themselves. For some reason, after having sex with both of them, and then having them close themselves off to me today, put me in a sour mood. It wasn't that I expected or even wanted a relationship with either of these men. But I guess I expected at least mutual respect and at the moment I felt pushed out of their tight little clique. They knew everything about me and I didn't know shit about them.

Although both of them eagerly suggested I wear a scanty minidress, I opted for pleated shorts and a tank top. By the time I started my second cup of cappuccino though, my mood lifted somewhat. I was ready to explore the island and still wanted to learn more about what was going on here. But I'd play by their rules and explore legally. Or at least, hopefully so.

"You two can do more than just have sex, right?" I asked, somewhat sardonically. It struck me as odd when both of them looked at me placidly, apparently not taking offense at the question. "I mean, how about we do some hiking today. The island is so beautiful. Are you game?"

"That sounds wonderful," Nicolas said.

"Perfect idea," Tomas agreed simultaneously.

More than likely they would agree to do anything I suggested. "Good. Have either of you hiked up that mountain?"

"There are many things we've done on that mountain." Nicolas winked at me and then walked over to the phone. "Would you like for the kitchen to prepare a picnic lunch for our outing?"

An hour later I wasn't sure what I'd been thinking. The walk I took last night was more walking than I'd probably done all year, and now this today. "Just a small break, boys." I slid my rear onto a smooth rock and stared off toward the ocean. "My God. It's beautiful."

A breeze wrapped around me, lifting the loose strands off of my neck. I'd pinned my hair up before we left, looking incredibly unappealing, I'm sure, and really not caring. Maybe yesterday's sex left me so sated that I just wasn't horny today. Although I wasn't positive about that speculation. Nothing I'd done so far managed to wipe the image of that man I'd seen last night out of my head. Tomas and Nicolas were gorgeous but neither of them held a flame in comparison to the stranger who'd been there one moment and gone the other. Thinking about him now created a pressure between my legs that made me ache to go search him out.

Which was insane. I wasn't the kind of lady who stalked a man simply because he physically appealed to me. Paradise Island obviously encouraged sexual behavior, but even at that, I was levelheaded enough not to assume I could jump the bones of any man here that I wished. Maybe it was that Tomas and Nicolas were willing partners and there was a thrill in seeking out someone that wasn't a sure thing. At the same time, though, my heart couldn't get trampled on by a sure thing. As I shifted my attention from the magnificent sea sprawled out before me I noticed the roof of a building.

The building I was at the other night.

Tomas reached for me when I slipped off my rock. "Ready to head out again?"

Neither man had sat when I took my break but simply stood on the path without speaking. I swore sometimes it seemed they just shut themselves off when I didn't require anything from them and then snapped to when I moved. They reminded me of the guards at Buckingham Palace the way they stood silently until ordered to move.

"Yeah. I think so." I didn't mention the buildings this time since the two of them already told me they didn't know anything about them.

Leading the way, Tomas followed me with our picnic lunch

strapped to his back in a backpack and Nicolas bringing up the rear, also carrying a small load of a change of clothes and a blanket. I stopped again when we reached a clearing where trees partially enclosed us from the world. They were bursting with gorgeous flowers. A rich, intoxicating scent almost demanded that anyone approaching them stop and admire their beauty.

"This is the perfect place for our picnic," I decided on the spot.

"It's almost as beautiful out here as you are," Tomas whispered into my ear and wrapped his hands around my waist.

"I'm all sweaty." I laughed but eased out of his grip and then turned around, making sure I smiled at both of them. For some reason, remaining happy, or at least acting like I was, made it easier to hang out with them, although their touching me, watching me, their attention in general didn't stir me like it did yesterday. I wondered if that made me shallow, wishing to seek out a mysterious stranger instead of enjoying time with two men who appeared to enjoy my company. "What did you have packed for us in our lunch?"

The two of them almost tripped over each other trying to create the perfect setting for our picnic. I made a show of laughing at their antics and suggesting how the plates should be laid out, but then left them to their task that they seemed to enjoy as much as sex. Turning, I walked through the trees and found myself staring down at the courtyard between the buildings where I'd seen the compelling stranger last night. A third building faced the other two—the building the man had come out of and then disappeared into when Rose showed up.

Who was he? And who were the other men who didn't speak English and whose faces appeared to be not quite done?

10

Malachi

"How in the hell can you possibly blame me for this?" I stared out the large window from my personal quarters, but didn't focus on the courtyard below.

Rose sighed heavily into the phone, then spoke as if she were reprimanding a child. "Your companions were obviously not keeping her occupied. Then to boot, more of your companions didn't notice her approaching until it was too late."

"Don't even accuse the Adams," I hissed.

"Why in the hell do you keep those mutated atrocities around anyway?" Rose's tone hit that pitch of annoyance that made me want to grab the nearest object and hurl it. "Your companions need work. They aren't good enough. I told you yesterday I didn't like that woman. You know I'm always right. Now look at what she's doing, taking walks and snooping around. She can't be trusted."

"She's out of line for taking a walk?"

She hung up on me. I pulled the phone away from my ear slowly and simply stared at it. I wasn't sure if I was more pissed at how she spoke to me, or the fact that she possibly berated the companions in front of Sharay, who more than likely was in earshot throughout the entire conversation.

"Fucking bitch," I growled. I tossed my cordless phone on my bed, knowing that if I left it there too long, one of the companions would hurry into the room and return it to its cradle. My companions were perfect.

Humans were flawed. It wasn't my fault that Miss Natalie Green would rather wander alone on the island than have sex with her two companions. Something nagged at my pride that I didn't like, though. Tomas and Nicolas were both modeled after me. Although far from clones, I'd given them my characteristics. Tomas had my nose. Nicolas had my eyes. Both men had really close versions of my body—all of my body. If Natalie wasn't impressed by those two, she sure as hell wouldn't like the original.

Like I had time to dwell on how much I didn't impress women when Queen Bitch was breathing down my neck and reminding me daily that my work wasn't good enough. Something moved in my peripheral vision and I squinted, staring up the mountain behind the warehouse.

There it was again. "What the hell?" I combed my hair with my fingers, probably messing it up more than anything, and turned, tilting my head and trying to figure out what I just saw. If I didn't know better, I'd say someone was waving a large blanket in a clearing up the mountain.

I didn't become a scientist without an intense sense of curiosity. Heading over to the shelves by my dresser, I grabbed binoculars and returned to the window. After training them on the spot where I saw something flash, I started scanning the side of the mountain until I found what I was looking for.

"Goddamn," I whispered, pressing the binoculars against my face as I stared at Natalie Green who appeared to be staring right back at me.

She was small but held herself in a way that made me think

she didn't realize it. A strand of brown hair blew across her face and she raised her hand, brushing it out of the way and then reached for her clasp that confined the rest of her hair. I watched, entranced, as she let her hair down and then struggled, with the ocean breeze making her task difficult, to put her hair back in the clasp at the nape of her neck.

When she turned, I adjusted the binoculars, pressing the hard plastic against my cheekbones and feeling them pinch into my skin while trying to bring her into better focus. Scanning her backside, I got one hell of a view of her round, perfectly shaped ass for my efforts. She wore shorts that weren't too short, or too long. Although I could tell she wasn't out in the sun very often, and prayed Tomas and Nicolas would remember their instructions to make sure guests were properly applied with sunscreen when necessary, I loved the shape of her slender, creamy white legs.

There was movement behind her and I twisted the outer rim of the lens to pull back a bit from the area where Natalie stood. Nicolas came up behind her and wrapped his arms around her waist then nibbled at her neck. Was I wrong, or did she appear annoyed by the act?

There wasn't any question that she pushed away from him. She turned away from the clearing and although I struggled to see through the trees, too many branches blocked my view of what appeared to be an intimate picnic.

"Well hell," I grumbled, walking away from the window and dropping the binoculars back on the shelf. No way in hell would Queen Bitch prevent me from spending time with another living, breathing person if I felt like doing so.

I refused to question my actions when I headed outside, sunscreen in hand, and headed past the warehouse toward the mountain behind it. Honestly, I didn't know when the last time was that I hiked up the mountain, but I was definitely out of breath when I finally heard them talking. Nicolas and Tomas weren't expecting me, but one advantage of being their creator, I knew I wouldn't offend them when I sent them away so I could spend time alone with our curious lawyer guest.

Quite an elaborate feast was spread out on the blanket. Natalie must have had her fill, either that or she wasn't enjoying Nicolas and Tomas's company, because as I appeared in the clearing, once again she stood facing the ocean where I'd seen her standing when I watched her through binoculars. My two companions were on either side of the blanket, watching Natalie while she stood with her back to them, ignoring both of them.

I tapped Nicolas on the shoulder and then held my finger to my lips so he wouldn't say anything. Nicolas's expression sobered and he straightened, then nodded when I gestured that he should leave. Rose might not be satisfied with my companions but I had their loyalty and no matter what I asked from them, they obliged without question. It sucked at times that humans weren't like that. But then I wasn't delusional enough to believe that anyone could be manipulated or controlled. I just wanted to be alone with Natalie.

Tomas squatted over the blanket, having started to put food away. When he saw me, he stopped his task and stood slowly. I gestured with a nod of my head for Tomas to follow Nicolas and he did as he was told, leaving his task unfinished. Both of them disappeared around the curve in the path when Natalie turned around.

"Oh, God," she gasped, startled, and covered her mouth with her hand as her green eyes widened and she stared at me. "What are you doing here? Where are Tomas and Nicolas?"

"What were you looking at?" I stepped around the blanket, moving in closer. She didn't look like she really cared where either of her companions had gone, and although I obviously surprised her, as she narrowed her gaze on me, she didn't appear frightened. "Does the ocean appeal to you more than your companions?" I asked quietly.

"I wasn't looking at the ocean," she said, her voice suddenly softer as if she just admitted a secret to me.

"Oh?" I was close enough now to touch her and I rubbed my fingers together at my sides, fighting the urge to brush a strand that once again was loose from the clasp behind her head. "You've got an incredible view up here. What were you looking at?"

"Who are you?"

"Malachi Cohen."

Her green eyes were bright, but changed as I watched. I didn't have a clue what emotions were surging through her at that moment, but damned if I didn't want to find out.

"What do you do here on the island?" she asked, her voice so soft it had a sultry appeal to it.

If I didn't know better, I'd swear the slight flush on her cheeks and the way her gaze dropped as she gave me a quick once-over were signs of interest.

"I make sure everything runs smoothly," I told her honestly. "Now you tell me what you were looking at. Something held your attention."

"I was looking for you."

Her honesty and admission surprised me. But when she blushed so beautifully, a rosy hue spreading over her face and to her neck, something inside me stirred that I'd almost forgotten about. I needed to explore this a bit more thoroughly. It had been years since a woman moved me like this, creating a pressure that tightened in my groin and ignited something that burned hotter the longer I stood in front of her.

"Why were you looking for me?"

Natalie turned around and covered her cheeks with her hands. She wore a silver hair clasp that covered her neck and gathered her thick brown hair together. It pooled past the clasp, flipping around itself in soft curls that made my hands itch to touch it.

"I guess it doesn't matter now, does it?"

"It matters to me." My hands moved to her shoulders and

although she flinched under my touch, she didn't move away or try and shrug me off of her. "I'm curious to know why, when you were with Nicolas and Tomas, you would search for me."

"Why did you come up here? Did you know I was here?" She appeared relaxed yet I would wager if I tried turning her around she would be pinned where she stood.

"Yes." I didn't want to lie to her. There was enough deception and frustration in my life already. "I have a feeling I'm here for the same reason you were looking toward my buildings."

"Oh?"

"I want to know more about you, and I think you feel the same."

"But you disappeared without saying a word to me last night," she complained quickly.

And just as quickly, she spun around to face me. My hands slid from her shoulders, but as she looked up at me I again grabbed her arms. She still didn't shrug away from me and the imploring look in her eyes impressed me more than I was ready for it to. Something about her drew a sensation out of me that I wasn't sure I'd experienced before. It had been years since I'd been in any kind of relationship with a woman. But I knew I'd never been this eager to get to know a lady.

Although that should terrify me, have me running from her and not looking back, it didn't. I understood the physical part of it, but I also knew enough about myself to know a woman turned me on with her mind as well as her body. Natalie Green sought me out, and now searched for me. Possibly that fed the ego, but I wanted to know why she did it.

"There wasn't anything I could say last night."

"So there is something going on down there. I knew there was." She searched my face and her eyes widened, once again bright while she searched my face. "Is it Rose? Would you get in trouble if she knew you were talking to me?"

I could see her imagination forming conclusions although

she didn't have a clue what was really going on. There was no way to question her to learn what those conclusions might be, but I was dying to know. Hell, I wanted to know everything about her.

At the same time, remembering Rose accuse Natalie of being up to something, came to mind. I would love proving the bitch wrong. "I don't answer to Rose."

"Who do you answer to?"

"No one." It was right there to add that I owned half of the island, but for some reason I stopped myself. As compelling as she was, I didn't know anything about her. Although I was ready to change that. "I make sure the companions do their job right," I offered instead.

"Oh?" She frowned and her long lashes hooded her pretty eyes when she dropped her attention to my chest. "Nicolas and Tomas didn't know anything about those buildings down there."

I shouldn't have been surprised that she questioned them about what she saw outside the warehouse. And Nicolas and Tomas wouldn't say anything to jeopardize the companions. It was in their programming.

Suddenly Natalie stiffened and then she jumped around me, almost tripping over the plates still scattered on the blanket. She regained her composure quickly and when she turned to face me, the cautious curiosity that had her flushing a moment ago was gone.

"Someone is lying to me and I don't like it." She was pissed. Natalie pointed past me toward the buildings below. "I tried talking to Rose about it and she changed the subject on me. Your companions that you oversee claim to not know those buildings even exist. And although it doesn't state anywhere that I can't walk where I want, I felt like I was being punished because I followed a path to a place that apparently I wasn't supposed to see."

As hot as Natalie was, she was a lawyer and a guest. I might hate Rose's guts, but I didn't want everything I worked so hard on for the last ten years destroyed because a hot, sexy, enticing lawyer got a bit too curious. I might not agree with Rose's tactics on many things that happened on the island, but that didn't mean I would jeopardize the success of my work because Natalie had a heightened sense of curiosity.

"Rose simply worried that you weren't enjoying your companions."

She studied me a moment and a small frown tugged at the corner of her mouth. I relaxed my expression and moved around the blanket, once again closing the distance between us.

"Are you enjoying them?" I asked quietly.

"Would you reprimand them if I told you no?" Her gaze locked with mine and once again her eyes were bright, although the slightest droop of her lashes gave them an enticing edge. "Or would you encourage them to fuck me more?"

"No," I said without hesitating.

The flush that spread over her cheeks was sexy. But when she slowly licked her lips and inhaled deeply, the sensation that came to life inside me earlier now spawned something that made it damned hard to keep my dick from swelling painfully in my jeans.

"Oh." Her lips formed a perfect circle when she whispered the one simple word. "I'm sure they're doing their job perfectly. They both are continuously eager to keep me happy and content."

I noticed she didn't mention that they were fulfilling her sexually. That wasn't something I'd ask her about. Not that she would ever know it, but watching her take both men at once was so fucking hot. It was something I wouldn't forget watching soon and I doubted Natalie could complain she wasn't completely satisfied that day.

Natalie obviously believed something other than the ordinary was going on here. Any intelligent person who stumbled on to my part of the island would wonder the same thing. For the sake of my work, for the companions, for Paradise Island, I had no problem distracting her so she'd never learn the truth.

Her expression didn't change, nor did she stop me when I

cupped her chin and tilted her head slightly. Her lashes draped heavily over her eyes, hooding her gaze. So when I lowered my mouth to hers and tasted her, I couldn't tell where she focused her attention. What I did realize instantly was that she didn't stop me.

And brushing my lips over hers wasn't enough. I wanted to taste her, experience the heat that made her eyes glow. Pressing my hand against the curve of her hip, I encouraged her to move closer while brushing my fingertips over her jaw and then her cheek.

I wouldn't call myself the skilled seducer, but my knowledge wasn't that rusty. After all, I created sexual beings all of the time. There wasn't anything wrong with using some of the techniques that I taught them. I parted her lips with my tongue and then dove into her mouth, feeling greedy and anxious to take as much as she offered.

Natalie sighed, the sound soft and sensual yet ripping through me like a tidal wave. I breathed her in, catching a whiff of sunscreen and feeling a tang of regret that I wouldn't be able to rub the lotion on her. Nonetheless, I ran my hand down her arm, feeling how smooth and warm her skin was. Blood rushed through my veins, creating a ringing in my ears while every ounce drained to my groin. I got so hard for a moment I thought that just kissing her might make me come.

No way would I humiliate myself like that. I wasn't some teenage virgin who didn't know how to control his body. Nor would I scare her when she'd just opened up to me. At the same time, Natalie wasn't a virgin either. I'd watched her fuck my creations, an image that was damned hard to get out of my head, and which made it even harder to maintain control.

I let go of her face and dragged my fingers into her hair. I ached to release the clasp so that I could feel her silky hair tumble over my hand. Instead I cupped the side of her head and started a slow sultry dance with her tongue while feeding off the taste and feel of her.

Although tall women usually appealed to me, Natalie's average height was perfect. When she arched into me, and her fingers brushed over my arm, thoughts of lifting her, placing her on the blanket at our feet and sending the remaining food scattering so that I could ravish every inch of her seemed like one hell of a good idea.

I moved my hand from her hip to her ass and cupped her soft flesh. My fingers wrapped around her curves like she was created just for me. There wasn't a thing about her that wasn't perfect.

I couldn't stop the growl that rumbled from deep in my throat as I moved my fingers lower and felt the edge of her shorts and then her inner thigh.

"Malachi," she whispered, moving her lips against mine as she abruptly ended our kiss.

I loved the sound of my name when she spoke it, especially when her tone was heavy with lust.

She shook her head, stiffening and edging away as she looked down. "I'm sorry. I mean—I'm not sure what came over me."

"I initiated it," I reminded her, reaching to pull her back into my arms. "And I know what came over me."

"But this is wrong." She stepped farther backward, wrapping her arms around her waist as she shook her head. "We're strangers."

She knew Nicolas and Tomas less than a day and fucked them. "Isn't that what Paradise Island is all about?" I immediately regretted the crass question, knowing the sexual freedom encouraged here had nothing to do with why I sought her out.

She looked up at me quickly, her defenses rising quickly when she pressed her lips into a thin line and looked at me defiantly. "That was different."

"You're right. I was out of line. I didn't seek you out thinking you would treat me like one of your companions."

"You don't understand," she snapped, but then looked away

from me and turned toward the path. "I've got to go," she told me without looking back.

Like hell was I going to let her head down the mountain by herself. I would send Nicolas and Tomas up here to gather the picnic remains. Hurrying after her, I took her arm just as she started to slip on loose rocks.

"I can make it back on my own," she informed me.

"And what if you slip? I don't think so. You're my responsibility until I return you to the mansion."

"Because I'm a paying guest?" she snapped, and slapped the strand of hair that I'd itched to play with earlier away from her face.

"Because I'm a caring man."

"I see. So you make it a habit of caring for all of your guests? I'm sorry. I don't recall seeing you at the mansion. Or do you care for them in their rooms?"

The bottom of the mountain was within sight and she picked up her pace, obviously trying to get away from me. But when she slipped again, I grabbed her arm and flipped her around, not minding one bit when she slapped her palm against my chest to steady herself.

I started to say that I didn't mean to embarrass her, but her green eyes were darker than a stormy sky right before a hurricane.

"Are you like the companions?" she snarled, her tone so venomous she could put Rose to shame. "What do I owe you for the kiss?"

"Goddamn it. Stop it." I yanked her into my arms, not being that gentle, grabbed her hair and tugged until she tilted her head back and glared at me. Then I covered her mouth with mine.

For a moment I thought she'd struggle, and I'm definitely no rapist. If she fought me, I'd let her go. Although she stilled, and didn't respond for a moment, when her body relaxed and her hand moved from my chest to my shoulder, I softened the kiss.

"I'm in charge of the companions, but I'm not one of them," I whispered while my lips still brushed over hers. Lifting my head slightly, I rubbed her cheekbone with my thumb and watched her lashes flutter. "You're going to have to want to kiss me on your own accord. I'm not for sale."

Natalie licked her lips, which were swollen and glossy from my attention, and then swallowed. "I don't remember being asked if I wanted to be kissed." The huskiness in her tone belied her blunt words.

"So next time I'll wait until you ask to be." I didn't want to wait for her to voice her interest, especially when she fought so hard to sound like the tough guy. Her soft curves and sultry gazes, along with the way her voice became a rough whisper when she was turned-on was all the asking I needed.

"Sounds like a plan." She backed out of my arms and then turned around carefully. "I can make it from here," she said, again not turning around when she spoke.

I doubted she believed I would let her walk alone back to the mansion. Although the island was about the safest place one could be, I walked behind her quietly, enjoying the hell out of the view as she sashayed her ass in a way I would swear was an invitation. When I managed to get my brain to work again, and not think with my dick, I simply enjoyed watching her until we reached the gardens surrounding the mansion.

She didn't turn around, and I didn't say good-bye. She knew where to find me. Instead, I veered off when the paths split and hurried back to my buildings. It wasn't that I cared what Rose thought if she saw me with her. But my mood was higher than it had been in months, and Queen Bitch wasn't going to ruin my day for me.

11

Natalie

Three days had passed since I arrived on the island, and already I didn't feel eleven more days was enough time before I would have to leave. I needed to explore, to understand what this place was about. And damn it, I wanted to understand Malachi better—a lot better. Nicolas and Tomas didn't comment on my sudden lack of interest in having sex with them. Possibly many guests who came here didn't have sex every day. But they were by my side like they were glued there. I never asked them why they disappeared during our picnic, and they didn't bring it up. I simply added that to my list of the odd things going on here on the island.

I didn't want to go back to the buildings where Malachi was because of his challenge. Like I would ever ask him to kiss me. I wanted him though. Damn it if I didn't try and convince myself otherwise. But the more time I spent with Tomas and Nicolas, the more I thought of Malachi. They didn't challenge me the way he did. I saw now how much that turned me on. I'd always heard that men were the hunters, but I knew now there was quite a bit of the hunter in me, too.

I wanted to return to the buildings for answers. I don't know why I thought the answers were there. Maybe it was because I was free to roam around the mansion, go in any room—other than the other guests' rooms—and be welcomed. And I'd more or less been forbidden to return to Malachi's buildings. Although, as I pointed out to myself while sliding my scoop of ice cream around my bowl after lunch, Malachi never forbade me to return to the buildings.

"I'm going to lie out by the pool," I told Tomas and Nicolas as we sat around the table after lunch in the dining hall.

"I look forward to rubbing oil on you," Nicolas told me. His gaze traveled down my front and when he returned his attention to my face, I swore he looked just like Malachi. At least around the eyes. "Or if you prefer, we can show you a little alcove where you can lie out nude."

"That is, if being naked around the other guests bothers you," Tomas added. He also looked like Malachi, although it wasn't his eyes, but something about his face.

I was obviously loosing my mind over a foolish obsession. Attracted to the man I couldn't have while two gorgeous hunks were right here at my beck and call. And I had no intentions of hunting Malachi. As I sat brooding over my last encounter with him, he'd hunted me. And captured me.

"I think I'm going to lie out alone, if you two don't mind," I said, testing the waters. As close as they'd clung to me since I returned from the picnic, disappointed and a bit pissed that Malachi simply disappeared on me even though I ignored him all the way down the mountain, I wasn't sure how they'd react to me announcing I would do something alone. "You two can hang out in the room. Enjoy some downtime. Sound good?"

I scooted my chair back and started toward the door. Although they were still by my side, anxious to make sure I had everything I needed to enjoy time by the pool, they didn't follow me outside when I left. I was free. It was odd that I suddenly had the urge to laugh out loud and start skipping.

Although I headed toward the pool, when I neared it, I veered off on a path that I now knew would bring me to the buildings if I walked long enough. Having intentionally eaten a light lunch, I managed the walk in good time, enjoying the warm sun that peered through the trees and warmed my bare skin.

The short dress I'd opted to wear today brushed against my thighs, and my sandals slapped my feet as I walked. I didn't care though. I was on an adventure, and this time I wouldn't return without answers.

When I reached the clearing where the buildings were, the sun shone brightly. I felt it immediately on my shoulders and back, knowing if I didn't get inside quickly, I'd be burned. Not to mention, sweaty and smelly. Perspiration beaded down my spine and on my forehead as I walked closer to the warehouse where I'd seen the men who wouldn't talk to me the other day.

I focused on the other two buildings today, doubting I'd find answers in a storage area, which was all the warehouse appeared to be, although there was an elaborate computer system set up along the wall that caught my eye. It appeared the handful of monitors might be some kind of security device. As I stared at them from outside the large doors my skin began to crawl. They didn't appear to be on, but what if there was another system somewhere else on the island? Would Malachi or Rose already know that I was here?

I walked past the large open garage doors and again saw the men moving boxes inside. The brightness of the day made it a bit difficult to focus too far into the interior of the building, but I managed to get a good view of the men. Of their faces.

My stomach constricted and a lump rose to my throat so quickly I couldn't breathe. They weren't ugly. That wasn't the best way to describe them. But three men stood just inside the warehouse, moving boxes from one side of the room to the other. Muscles bulged and flexed and the simple loincloths they wore left little to the imagination. They had perfect bodies, mouthwatering in fact. It was their faces—like something out of *The Twilight Zone*.

Instead of noses like everyone else had, they had lumps, as if their noses had melted and never reformed to their proper shape. Their eyes seemed larger than they should be and as I watched I never once saw them blink. If one of them were disfigured like this, I might accept a catastrophic accident made him this way. But all of them appeared the same. Maybe it was some tribal ritual where all men were disfigured once they were married so no other woman would look at them.

Lord. And maybe the sun was making me hallucinate as well as warping my imagination.

Sweat tickled my belly and I rubbed my dress against the moisture. Then, realizing I'd been staring, and damn near melting in the hot sun, I hurried forward like I knew where I was going. And I didn't stop until I reached the doors of the far building where Malachi disappeared the first day I saw him.

I silently gave thanks when I closed the door behind me and felt the heavily air-conditioned entrance instantly dry the perspiration against my skin.

My heart quickly swelled to my throat again when I heard voices.

"Carry the patch cord for his laptop," a man said.

I stared wide-eyed at the hallway in front of me. Like a deer caught in headlights, for a moment I couldn't move or breathe. Some detective I made.

"He won't shut us down after he makes new companions, will he?" The woman sounded worried.

"Don't be silly. There are only four of them. He's just doing it to get Rose off his back."

I didn't have a clue what they were talking about, but interrupting their conversation and asking questions wasn't an option. I darted up a flight of stairs to the right just as a man and woman appeared and pushed against the doors to go outside.

"I don't want to be shut off," the woman said, sounding miserable. "It's not my fault no one chooses me. Half the time Rose doesn't even put me in the line up."

"Tell Malachi that."

The doors closed behind them and I couldn't hear any more of their conversation. I thought it weird they would refer to losing their jobs as being "shut off" though.

I peeled myself off the wall where I'd plastered my body and stood quietly for a moment, listening for any sign that there was anyone else around me. Then, glancing down the hallway on the second floor, I stared at the heavy looking wooden doors that were closed. The hallway was wide and airy and reminded me of an old-time office building. I wouldn't think the building itself would be that old. From what I read in the handbook, Paradise Island had only been around for ten years. For some reason the architecture of the building matched my image of Malachi. Strong and solid, and unchanging in spite of his environment around him. And although the conversation I just overheard confused the hell out of me, it also appeared that Malachi was somewhat understanding.

One thing I knew, he was a hell of a kisser. I thought Nicolas and Tomas were incredible but they didn't do anything without my consent. Which of course made sense. But Malachi, he took, demanded, and made me so weak in the knees that just thinking about him raised my blood pressure. I was going to break out in a heavy sweat all over again in spite of how air-conditioned the building was.

Halfway down the hallway, I realized I would need to try one of the doors if I was going to explore this place at all. The hallway ended ahead of me and apparently there was only the one flight of stairs. I turned, glancing at the two closed doors

I'd already passed, and then continued turning as I stared at the door next to me and the one at the end of the hall.

"Eenie, meenie, miney, moh," I said quietly and pointed at the doors before shrugging and approaching the one next to me. I was actually surprised at how easily and quietly it opened. "Apparently theft isn't a problem here. Just another part of paradise," I mumbled and entered the room.

I knew where I was the moment I stepped foot into the room. The large bed, which was made military style and looked like a quarter could be bounced off of it, was pushed up against the far wall, and the solid, wood dressers facing it looked like they were made out of the same heavily stained wood as the doors and floorboards. But it wasn't the furniture that gave away my location. I could feel Malachi in here, smell him, sense that this was where he came at the end of his day. The large, airy bedroom with its huge windows that overlooked the courtyard reminded me of a lord's lair, a place where the master of all that surrounded him would come to lie his head at the end of each day.

I approached one window, finding some solace in the empty courtyard below, and then glanced out the other window, which offered a magnificent view of the mountain I'd picnicked on yesterday. Turning and taking in the contents of the room, I spotted a pair of binoculars on a desk next to the cluttered shelves. Returning to the window that faced the mountain I glanced again at the binoculars.

"No way," I decided, shaking my head. There wasn't any way he would have seen me on that mountain, and then spied on me with binoculars. Or was there? And if he had, would watching me compel him to come seek me out?

That warmth that threatened to overheat me in the hallway now shifted between my legs creating an overwhelming pressure that made it hard to move. I stared at the contents on his desk, unable to focus for a moment while my mind danced around the two times he'd kissed me and imagined what else he could do with that incredible body of his.

I was pulled out of my thoughts, thankfully before I soaked my underwear, and focused on the legal pad in front of me on the desk. Leaning over, I touched the paper, running my finger over the handwritten notes as I read.

I wasn't a scientist, and I didn't know a lot about robotics, but after reading through the first page of notes, and then lifting the page and reading the notes on the second page, my stomach twisted and I started shaking.

I'm not sure what I expected to find while exploring and snooping around the buildings. I knew something strange was going on here. But never in a million years would I have guessed the island was full of robots.

"Oh, my God," I whispered, terror hitting me so hard I dropped the page I'd lifted on the notebook and backed away from the desk.

Hard muscle pressed against my back. I shrieked, spinning around as Malachi tried grabbing me.

"Don't touch me," I growled, my heart pounding so hard that I couldn't catch my breath. I tripped over the edge of his desk, and felt the corner of it stab my thigh. Pain shot through me but I tumbled over the edge, slapping at him when he grabbed me again. "Stop it. No! Keep your hands off of me."

"Natalie." He didn't sound upset that I was in his room, or that I'd just discovered his terrible secret. "Natalie, damn it. Cut it out."

I held my hand out, using it as a shield to ward him off once I put his desk between us. Then trying to keep from hyperventilating, I let my gaze travel up his body until I focused on his face.

"Are you real?" I whispered.

He didn't smile and I stared into his green eyes, noticing specks of brown floating around his irises.

"Very," he answered and then glanced down at the legal pad that I'd been looking at when he entered. His black hair was almost straight and drifted around his face until he slowly raised his gaze back to mine. "Did you just read this?"

I couldn't read his expression and nodded like an idiot. I should deny it, get a grip on myself and continue playing ignorant until I understood what the hell was going on for sure.

"And so what? Now you think I'm a robot, or something? Do I look like a robot to you?"

I didn't answer. Maybe he was an incredible liar. Or maybe his programming wouldn't allow him to admit he was a machine. Or possibly he didn't know he wasn't human. I blew out a breath, still feeling my heart pounding against my rib cage. Or I had an overactive imagination and I needed to watch and observe and learn the facts without jumping to conclusions.

"You shouldn't be yelling at me," he continued when I didn't answer. "I should be yelling at you. Last I heard the laws in the states weren't any different from those here and I do believe you could be charged with breaking and entering."

My jaw dropped and my attention snapped to his face. He was joking, right? I mean, yeah, I was in his bedroom. But he'd kissed me—twice.

"You can't have me arrested," I pointed out. "There are no DO NOT ENTER signs and the building was unlocked. It's not like this appears to be a private home. It looks very much like a professional building."

"I tell you what," he said, moving slowly around the desk toward me. "I won't tell anyone that you managed to break into my facilities, past all of my employees, and you don't let anyone know that I have a fascination with robotics."

"A fascination?" I asked, the harsh adrenaline that zapped my senses into a state of panic now shifting as he moved even closer. "What do you mean by fascination?"

"Well," he began, and reached for a strand of my hair that always managed to fall out of my ponytail. He rubbed it between his finger and thumb and watched the action while he continued speaking. "More than a hobby, but not quite an obsession. Maybe you could compare it to something that has you so intrigued that you go out of your way to learn more about it. Can you relate to anything like that?"

When he looked into my eyes, all the energy that pulsed furiously through me turned into a throbbing pressure between my legs that swelled painfully the longer I drowned in his gaze.

"Maybe," I whispered, and my voice cracked.

"Good. Then you understand." He whispered as well and then pulled on my hair, wrapping the strand around his finger until I felt it pinch at the scalp.

When he kissed me, the pressure inside me exploded, need rushing through me at a dangerous rate. There were other things that I should be focusing on. But his mouth did dangerous things to my body when he pressed his lips against mine, and it was damn near impossible to dwell on anything other than holding on.

He ended the kiss before I was ready and I fought the blush I felt creeping over my flesh when I opened my eyes to catch him watching me. I knew he saw my complete surrender and I didn't want to offer that to him. It wasn't fair that he possessed skills that Tomas and Nicolas would beg to have. Just the way he demanded, didn't ask but made me crave more of what he offered, created a throbbing between my legs that didn't subside while I stared up at him.

"Natalie." He spoke my name with reverence while letting my hair slip through his fingers and then caressing the side of my head. "Why did you come here?"

It was my chance. The fog of lust filling my brain didn't completely dissipate but I saw my opportunity to play coy. I still could learn more so that I could understand the mystery that I knew was wrapped around this island.

"To see you." I swallowed, not daring to pull my gaze from his and waiting while he simply studied my face for a moment. If I said another word, I'd blow it. He would know there were ulterior motives. And it wasn't like it was completely a lie. I would be fooling myself if I believed I came here solely to learn about the island. I knew I wanted to see him, too.

Malachi stepped back, taking his hands off of me, and then turned for his door. I didn't understand his actions until he closed it and then turned the lock. Then he walked over to his desk and pulled out the top drawer where he pushed several buttons on something that looked like a security pad. It struck me as seriously odd that when I'd come here, I'd been able to enter the room without any problems, yet Malachi had a security system that would put some financial institutions to shame. Why would he invest in something like that and then not lock his door?

My mouth went dry when he walked back around his desk and stepped out of his shoes. Before he reached me, he'd pulled his shirt from his body and dropped it on the floor next to him.

"I'm really glad you did," he said, his voice gruffer than it was a moment before. "You've become quite a fascination to me, too."

He turned me around without asking and I felt his knuckles press against my back as he pulled my zipper down to my ass. I thought of raising my arms, something to slow this sudden process that I wasn't sure I was ready for, but he took the straps from my shoulders and pinned my arms to my side as he lowered them to my elbows.

I was actually surprised when he turned me around again, not forcing the dress off of me but leaving it up to me to lower my arms and let the material fall to the ground.

"My God, Natalie," he whispered, his gaze dropping to my breasts. "You're perfect."

"Are you sure someone isn't paying you?" I needed to lighten the moment and made a face at him when he lifted those dark, brooding eyes to mine. Before I started blushing, I lowered my head and stared at my 34Bs. When I gulped in a breath of air, flesh pressed against my satin bra, which was strapless. There actually was a small amount of cleavage, very small.

"No one is paying me to adore you," he said. His finger brushed under my chin. "Let go of the dress, darling."

He wasn't going to force me. Somehow, I believed that took some effort on his part. In just a few days, and only seeing him at odd interludes, I felt I knew a small bit about this man. One thing rang true. Malachi was aggressive, determined. God only knew what he was doing on this island. That thought buzzed me back to reality and to the fact that he was probably a large part of this mystery.

There might be something erotic to playing detective and having sex with a man to gather information. A sex game. The thought was rather hot, and a fantasy I could hold on to while enjoying a man who'd successfully crawled under my skin from the moment I'd laid eyes on him.

I licked my lips, trying for the part of seductress, and straightened my arms. My dress fell to my hips, and then stopped.

Damn it. I couldn't even pull off seductress. One glance at his dark, lust-filled gaze and I could tell that the dress not falling to the floor didn't disappoint him at all. In fact, he appeared to wait, with bated breath, as if there were more to the show, and my dress stopping at my hips was simply part of the act.

I decided to give it one more shot. "Do you often fuck guests on this island?" Conversation helped keep me grounded while I took my time turning around and then walking a few paces away from him.

Malachi obviously didn't want physical distance between us. "You would be my first," he told me, and placed his hands on my hips. "Crawl onto the bed, sweetheart."

I didn't want to let go of my fantasy of seducing him, and

following orders didn't fit into the role-playing I'd devised in my mind. If I kept this a game, focused on my actions and not how he made me feel, then possibly I could gather more information.

The only thing that sucked was that I didn't have a clue as to what direction my questioning should take. Talk about going into this blindly.

"Hands off, dear," I said, hoping I sounded sexy, and glanced over my shoulder at him for good measure while pressing my palms on his bed. Not that I could hold eye contact for long. His penetrating gaze would make him one hell of a hard shell to crack on any witness stand. He seemed to bore deep into my mind as he watched me, as if he could read my every thought and know my next action before I did. "I'm not through undressing," I added, and felt a small wave of satisfaction when he dropped his hands from my waist.

Now I've watched probably as many porn movies in my adult life as most people have. And believe me, those actors and actresses have skills, and not just the obvious ones. Crawling onto a bed while slipping a dress down your hips—and not removing the matching underwear and strapless bra—is quite a feat. I paid good money for my designer underwear though, and I'd be damned if I wasn't going to show it off, even if just for a minute.

The dress tangled around my ankles. Before I could free myself of it, Malachi once again took control. This time when he pulled the dress from me and discarded it, it didn't bother me. I went to all fours. My ass isn't one of my worse features, and I actually grinned when I felt his hands grip it before I'd reached the middle of the bed.

"Woman, you're a feast I can't wait to devour," he growled.

I rolled over, keeping my legs slightly spread and leaned back on my elbows. But one look at that hungry glaze that made his eyes almost as dark as his hair, and I worried for a moment that

I was dangerously out of my league. Honestly, I wondered how I'd made it through having sex with Nicolas and Tomas when being alone with Malachi had me tripping all over myself.

"You're definitely not waiting," I murmured, and smiled when he cocked his eyebrow. Although I managed not to blush, being so brazen twisted my stomach into knots of anticipation. And I was so damned wet between my legs I wondered if I wouldn't have been smarter to remove my panties before he did.

"Maybe I decided I'd rather fuck you than allow Nicolas and Tomas to continue enjoying you." When he spoke I saw another side of him instantly. He looked so serious.

"If we were back in Chicago, I'd take that comment rather seriously." I doubted he wanted a relationship. And I made a note that Malachi possessed every characteristic to break a woman's heart with his strong sex appeal and way of saying everything a lady craved hearing.

I turned my attention to him when he unsnapped his jeans and pulled down the zipper.

Without ceremony, he peeled his faded jeans down his legs and stepped out of them. Along with them went the boxers and Malachi stood at the edge of the bed naked, facing me. My mouth went so dry I couldn't have spoken a word if my mind was able to tell it what to say.

Perfection didn't begin to describe him. Dark tight curls sprayed over his incredibly muscular chest. There was a tan line at his waist, proof he spent a fair bit of time outside without a shirt on. If I believed this place was called Paradise Island for any other reason, I now knew the truth. Malachi was by far the most gorgeous man I'd ever laid eyes on.

"You put your companions to shame," I uttered, barely able to get the words out as he crawled onto the bed and then over me. I collapsed onto my back, spreading my legs around his and then rubbing them against his hard thighs. The roughness of his body hair tortured my flesh. "My God, Malachi."

"You know, it's funny that the companions have condoms but I don't." He paused, not lowering himself any closer but simply staring down at me while his black hair fell around his face, giving a darker edge to his expression as he searched my face. "And I think it's only fair that you should know, I haven't had sex in a long time. My performance level might not meet your standards."

I couldn't believe that all of a sudden he sounded so vulnerable. It didn't fit my image of him, and although his concern for protecting our sex made my heart swell, his showing me yet another side of him was more than I expected at this point.

"I've been on the pill for years and your companions did wear condoms. Malachi, I'm definitely not sexually active back home." I was doing a piss-poor job of pulling off the seductress. It was just too easy to be myself around him.

"Good," he whispered and lowered his mouth to mine.

His kisses were more addictive than fine wine, and just as powerful. As he nipped at my lip and then growled into my mouth when I allowed him in, I wondered if he was pleased that I was on the pill, or that I wasn't having sex regularly with any other man. Just as fast as that thought entered my mind, it occurred to me that I liked the idea of him wanting me to be with him instead of my companions. Other than through the lives of characters in my romance novels, I hadn't ever experienced a man coveting me the way Malachi did.

He scraped my lip with his teeth again, bringing me back to what he was doing to me. His face was too close to mine to focus on him clearly, and his eyes were closed. He had long, thick, black lashes and small lines at the edge of his eyes as well as underneath. There was just a hint of stubble on his cheeks and jaw, adding that rough edge to him and creating a dark shadow over his tanned face. If this man were a robot, an undiscovered genius lived on this planet that the world would fight to have control over.

Was that why Rose didn't want me walking to these buildings? Was Malachi her personal companion?

"I want to taste all of you, every inch," he growled and dragged his tongue to my jawbone and then farther down my neck. As he adjusted himself over me, he opened his eyes and caught me watching him. "Touch me, Natalie."

My hands were already on his shoulders so I immediately understood his request. "If you keep moving down me, I won't be able to reach," I told him, smiling at his serious face.

"Come here." He didn't elaborate but lifted me as he instructed, apparently deciding to put me where he wanted me instead of letting me oblige.

Malachi pulled me to a sitting position and at the same time reached behind me and unclasped my bra. It fell to my waist unceremoniously and I tossed it to the side while he grabbed my waist and lifted me against him.

I kneeled against him, which put my breasts conveniently in front of his face. When he latched on to a nipple, sparks exploded inside me and electrical currents sent a charge that zapped between my legs. I dug into his shoulders, feeling my fingernails scrape his flesh.

"Crap," I groaned, almost biting my lip. "You sure don't act like a man who's out of practice."

I continued dragging my nails down his arms and felt his muscles tremble under my touch. Malachi growled instead of commenting and moved to the other breast, torturing and teasing it until I worried I would come while kneeling in front of him. He pushed me so close to the edge with his attention, making me greedy for more of him.

When I dragged my hands over his body to his waist, feeling his coarse tight curls, I traced the line they created from his belly button to the thicker hair just above his cock. He hissed in a breath and every inch of him hardened, which gave me a boost of confidence. Once again I was the seductress, capable of controlling this dominating and aggressive man. I moved my hand lower and then slowly wrapped my fingers around his shaft, pressing my other hand against his chest. His heart pounded so hard that I swore the reverberation of it pulsed through me even though our bodies weren't pressed together.

I shouldn't be thinking about any other man while being so intimate with Malachi. I remembered with Nicolas and Tomas I didn't notice their hearts beating. How weird that I would even search for a man's pulse while experiencing such hot, erotic sex. And then now, distracted once again by how hard his pulse beat against my fingertips. And Malachi's skin was rough, damp, not smooth like Tomas and Nicolas's was. Maybe those two did receive special baby oil massage treatments to make their bodies more enticing for their partners. Honestly, I preferred rough, coarse haired flesh gliding over mine.

Malachi bit my nipple, making me jump and squeeze his dick in my hand. He looked up at me quickly, appearing very pleased with my reaction. If I didn't know better I'd swear he knew my thoughts had strayed to another and he was silently informing me that wasn't acceptable.

I brought my finger up to the swollen tip of his dick and then flicked it with my fingernail. Malachi hissed and his eyes glazed over while his expression hardened.

"Two can play that game," I said, surprised at how husky my voice sounded.

"Who says this is a game?" He pushed me backward and then grabbed my legs, lifting them and forcing me to straighten on my back as he brought my feet to his shoulders. He ran his fingers down my legs toward my panties. "Your skin is so soft," he praised, watching his hands as they traveled over me.

Goose bumps appeared over my flesh and I shivered when he reached the small amount of fabric that was all the clothing I still wore. I knew my panties would disappear in the next moment and didn't fight when he grabbed them and pulled them down my legs.

I raised my feet off his shoulders, bringing them together and allowing him to drag my underwear over my feet. He didn't give them a bit of attention but dropped them next to him and then took hold of my ankles, opening me and spreading me while he stared in admiration.

"So smooth," he muttered, and then slowly raised his attention to my face. "I don't want you holding back," he said while running his hands down the outside of my legs. "I'm going to bring you to the edge and when you get there let go. Give me everything, sweetheart."

I couldn't think of anything coy to say and admitting that I wasn't experienced enough in lovemaking to control when or how I came sounded stupid. So I stared at him, not answering.

I held my breath when he moved one hand over my shaved mound and then parted my moist lips with his fingers.

"Perfect. So wet." He adjusted himself while cupping my ass and lifting me slightly off the bed.

When his mouth covered me, the heat from his breath and the perfect stroke of his tongue made me leap. I felt like a fish out of water, as well as foolish. Even as I cried out, I closed my eyes, loving how wonderful he made me feel. I let myself drift dangerously close to the edge while my insides swelled and throbbed.

"God, you're good at that," I told him, running my fingers through his hair and then pressing against his head, never wanting him to stop. "So damned good." I swear I purred.

And when he rumbled, the sound coming deep from inside him and rising until I felt the heat sear my insides, I was sure I would explode right then. I tightened my leg muscles, determined to hold out and enjoy how wonderful he made me feel.

Anything—think about anything so that I wouldn't come

and end this glorious experience. I forced myself to think about Nicolas and Tomas and found myself comparing their skills. All three men were well built, muscular, and in perfect condition. Tomas and Nicolas had skills that made them worth every penny I'd paid to enjoy them. But Malachi possessed something they didn't. I couldn't put my finger on it, but the way he moved with such certainty, and came on to me aggressively yet could display more compassion than most men, pushed him into a category of his own.

"You're holding back on me." Malachi moved his lips over my soaked, shaved flesh as he spoke. The sensation damned near made a liar out of him when I almost exploded.

"Just don't stop." I wasn't going to argue with him. I couldn't. I had to concentrate on not coming yet. More than anything I wanted to enjoy every minute that he adored me with his mouth.

He clasped his lips around the most sensitive part of me and sucked the overly sensitive nub into his mouth. I cried out and then pulled his hair, holding on more than trying to control his actions. But it wasn't any good. The dam broke and the pressure that had swelled painfully inside me exploded. My orgasm ripped through me with so much intensity I could have pulled his hair out of his scalp from the roots and wouldn't have realized it.

If I hurt him, he didn't give any indication but growled proudly while lapping my juices. It seemed I floated and for a minute wasn't sure I would come back down. When he rose over me and I saw the wet sheen surrounding his mouth, I would have smiled if it weren't for the intense look on his face.

He lowered his face to mine and then ravished my mouth while he found my entrance and sunk deep inside me. I held on, knowing as he fucked me that returning to Tomas and Nicolas for the rest of my two-week stay here would be damned near impossible for me to do.

12

Malachi

I would have labeled it a perfect day if Rose hadn't walked into the laboratory. I glanced at the clock, noting that it was almost eleven. I didn't want to think about Natalie sleeping with Tomas and Nicolas. No matter that they weren't really alive, she didn't know that. Or at least I was almost positive she hadn't figured it out.

"I heard the good news," she said smiling.

For a moment I thought she met that Natalie and I spent time together today but then realized before the thought fully developed that any pleasure I found in life wouldn't be good news in Rose's eyes.

"What I don't understand is why you didn't tell me yourself." She stopped at my side and stared at the companion lying naked on the examination table. "How many are you making? And will they be better?" She grinned like a child on Christmas morning.

I glanced past her at Sharay who stood silently, her serious expression in check until she met my gaze.

"I don't know that I can pull off better than what we already have." I offered Sharay a small smile and she returned it, but then quickly grew serious when Rose turned and scowled at her.

She then blessed me with the same disgruntled look that I wouldn't doubt would be her permanent expression before she turned fifty.

"You know what I mean. I swear Malachi, you cut yourself short getting so close to the companions. They're machines." She placed her cold fingers on my arm and then squeezed. If the smile she offered was an attempt to show compassion, it was proof she didn't have a clue about such emotions. "You're a genius, Malachi. The best that there is. But imagine a companion who didn't need instructions, who could enter any situation, evaluate it, and act accordingly."

"I'm not God," I reminded her, although I doubted seriously she meant half of what she said. Rose didn't think anyone was better than she was. I let it go at that, knowing if I pointed out the obvious reasons why a companion like that would be disastrous would start an argument that I wasn't in the mood for.

"Are you saying I was misinformed when I was told you were making these companions different from the ones we have right now?"

I didn't answer and her triumphant smile would sour my mood if I allowed her to continue staring at me like that.

"I have no idea what you heard. All I plan on doing is implementing a personality chip that I've been working on for a while now," I said quietly and walked around the examination table to check the monitors attached to the not yet "born" companion lying on the table. "If I'm successful, these new models will be able to process material faster. They will be able to adjust to any personality and adapt, which will hopefully help our guests always enjoy their first choice of companion when they arrive here."

"When will you wake it up?" She rubbed her hands together and focused on the nude male lying on the table.

"I doubt I'll finish him tonight." I'd planned on working until I was done, but if I told Rose that, she wouldn't leave.

"I want to be informed the moment you have them ready," she told me, turning toward the door. Rose stopped before leaving though and looked over her shoulder, giving me a quizzical look. "I meant to ask you. Miss Green, our lawyer, went missing again today for a few hours. You didn't by chance see her here, did you?"

"Nope."

"And did you know several of the camera systems were down over here today as well?"

I wasn't surprised that she would discover that I turned off all the cameras in the main building while Natalie was with me. "Yes. I noticed that. They should all be in working order now."

"I see." She nodded once and turned to leave.

I got the strong impression that she didn't quite believe me, and honestly, I didn't care. I looked up, astonished and immediately leery when Rose glanced at Sharay and then pushed her out the door. She closed it in her companion's face and then crossed her arms, her back to the door while watching me for a moment. A sudden impending doom settled around me and I stared back, wondering what bomb she planned on dropping this time.

"What?" I finally said, wishing she would leave and considering giving her the same treatment she just gave Sharay.

"You were with Miss Green earlier today," she announced.

Rose was guessing. She had no proof because there wasn't any proof. I saw to that. "Your story," I mumbled and returned my attention to my monitors.

"Malachi," she said softly, her voice dripping with sweetness that turned my stomach. "The world we live in is changing. There will be more women like Miss Green, women who are rich, successful, and know exactly what they want. You mark my words though. She's here to bring us trouble. You knew it was

just a matter of time before your past crept up to haunt you.
And now I'll have to do damage control."

"That should make you happy," I said, sardonically.

"You're missing my point." She dragged her fingernails up
my bare arm. I remembered Natalie doing that exact same thing,
yet when Natalie did it, my dick turned harder than stone.
Rose's touch repulsed me. She didn't notice. "Intelligent, beautiful women want more than a boy toy. They want a gorgeous
man who can stimulate them physically, and stimulate their
mind, too. Like you, darling," she purred, gripping my shoulder
and trying to make me turn to face her. "Malachi," she pleaded.

There wasn't any getting rid of her. Her condescending tone,
talking down to me like I was a fucking idiot, pissed me off. I
stared at her heavily made-up face. Once she did a fair job of
concealing her age, and the face-lift I gave her a year ago did
wonders. Today though, I saw how her cold-hearted nature
made her too ugly for any miracle to repair.

"I'm not God and honestly don't want the job." I knew
what it meant when she pressed her lips together. She hated it
when I stood up to her and challenged a decision she'd already
made.

Once she'd been easy to get along with, but after a few years
of working with her, and experiencing the success of the island,
she'd turned hard, ruthless, to the point where I doubted if the
side of her that was easy to like even existed anymore.

"Regardless of how well I perfect the circuits that make my
companions come to life, they will always have faults. But
Rose, there really is something else you should focus on. What
are you going to do if one of your clients learns that the companions aren't human?"

"That isn't going to happen," she snapped without hesitating. "Because you're making them so real that even you forget
they're machines." She laughed, a shrill sound that grated my
nerves. "Once you bring it to life, send it to me. If these new

companions are good enough to stimulate my mind and body I might keep one of them for myself." She laughed again and headed toward the door.

I returned to my work, willing myself to calm down so I could think. Rose opened the door but then turned once again and pointed her finger at me. "And remember, Malachi, no mingling with the guests. A lot of your companions are modeled after you. Don't come around and allow any of our too-smart-for-their-own-good clients to get any ideas." Her glare turned even more evil as I watched. "And stay the fuck away from Natalie Green," she hissed.

She slammed the door and I wanted to slug her.

My lack of sleep the night before hit me when I walked out into the morning sun. The golf cart shielded me from the rays while driving to the main mansion, but as I headed toward the back entrance, a wave of exhaustion attacked me. I should have stayed home, possibly gotten in a nap before returning to the lab, but the smallest excuse worked for coming up here in hopes of seeing Natalie.

Rose had a lot of nerve telling me that I couldn't mingle with the guests. I knew damned good and well that many of the male companions had certain features of mine. But none of them were my twin. My brain throbbed at the thought that she might be jealous. The last thing I needed was Queen Bitch making my life hell when for a week or so I might be able to enjoy myself. It wasn't like Nicolas or Tomas would mind.

Not to mention, I knew without a doubt that Rose fucked my companions on a very regular basis. She loved making them her slaves. And as much as she toyed with them, enjoyed lewd and raunchy sex with all of them, my companions still remained one hundred percent loyal to me. More than once we enjoyed a good laugh as the companions shared their sexual adventures that they had with Rose with me.

She might be able to get off anytime she wanted, but that didn't mean I could. There was no way I could have sex with any of my companions. Not ever. Rose would just have to get over me seeing Natalie—and get over her fucked-up notion that Natalie was coming to me for some conspiratorial reason. I knew how to read people. Natalie wasn't some covert spy. She was a bored lawyer, more than likely with too much money and not enough love in her life. I took my time researching her the night before online and found nothing even remotely suspicious about her.

Unfortunately, my reason for coming here meant seeking out Rose. Maybe it was my exhausted state. Possibly incredible sex for the first time in years cleared the cobwebs out of my brain and I saw things as they should be. Whatever the reason, Rose and I were going to have a talk. Then I might seek out Natalie again.

"We need to talk," I informed Rose after tapping on her closed office door once, and then pushing it open without invitation.

Rose glanced up over her reading glasses and then narrowed her gaze. "I'm busy."

"So am I. But I'm not doing any more work until we talk."

Rose sighed and then leaned back in her expensive leather chair, crossing her arms over her narrow waist. Many bracelets slid over her wrists as she placed her hands on her arms and focused on me.

"Fine. What do you want?" Rose obviously felt her outburst last night was adequate. When she didn't want something from me, her cold nature could chill a room.

"Sharay, hon," I said calmly, smiling when she glanced up from her small desk alongside the wall. She was my pride and joy. Sharay could work around mathematical equations that would put some leading scientists in this world to shame. "Give us a few minutes alone, please?"

She nodded and stood, but then possibly remembering her

training at Rose's hand, she glanced over at her, as if making sure Rose approved. I stood patiently, allowing Rose to authorize Sharay leaving the room.

"I know this isn't something you give any thought to," Rose began coolly once Sharay closed the door. "But our island is a business, and there are books to keep and accounting matters to deal with. Say what's on your mind and then get back to making my new companions."

"I think we need to announce publicly that the companions are robots." I was in the perfect mood to watch her jaw drop as she gaped at me.

As quickly as she paled, Rose regained her composure and then laughed easily. "You're funny, Malachi. Now if that's it, I have work to do, and so do you."

"You won't have any work to do if your secret is revealed."

Rose leaned forward, putting her elbows on her desk and then wagged her finger at me. "Don't you ever threaten me, Malachi."

"It's not a threat."

"Listen here. This island supports your research—your mistakes as well as your successes. No other organization anywhere would give you the freedom to develop the companions the way you have here. Jeopardize that, and you might as well go work somewhere in the states installing computer software in cars or something. Is that what you'd like to do?"

"What I'd like to do is sleep with a clean conscience. I'm making these companions more and more human, but no one knows but you and me."

"And Jonah," Rose added, and smiled like she just won the argument.

"And Jonah. What would you do if one of the guests learned they were having sex with a machine?"

"That's not going to happen."

"You can't guarantee that," I told her.

"Oh yes, I can. It won't happen because you won't let it happen," she said venomously, glaring at me. "You'll protect your creations to the death. I have no doubts. Now head back to your lab and quit wasting time. I want those new companions. And they better show more intelligence and be absolutely gorgeous."

"I'll finish making the new companions when I'm damn good and ready," I growled at her.

"You'll finish them today and you'll remember why it is that you're able to do your life's work. If it weren't for me, you'd never have your precious companions. Now get the hell out of here."

I almost lost it. It was damned close. Rose's eyes widened and I saw the fear cross her face when I lunged toward her. "Don't ever threaten me or my companions. And if you don't start showing a bit of respect, you won't get the quality of companions that you're dying to have. So watch yourself," I snapped, and then stormed out of her office.

I yanked open the office door and stepped out into the hallway. Before turning toward the back delivery entrance, I glanced at the main entrance at the other end of the hallway. Every inch of me tightened. Running down the hallway, hurrying around other guests and looking like she raced from a fire, Natalie raced away from me.

Goddamn it! If she'd overheard my conversation with Rose, after reading my notes yesterday—shit. Instead of lunging after her, which was exactly what I wanted to do, I turned toward the back door, stalking out of the mansion and to my golf cart.

Jonah hollered a greeting as I climbed behind the steering wheel and I probably would have eliminated any suspicion that something was up if I'd taken just one moment to answer him. Instead I tore out of there, not even concerned with a couple guests who strolled lazily along one of the paths as I sped past them. But when I reached my buildings and realized Natalie wasn't there, I got worried. I only stood in the middle of my courtyard for a few minutes, pondering the possibilities as to where she might have gone, before jumping back in to the golf cart and heading out again.

Rage still burned inside me, but I was thinking a bit more clearly when I drove around the outer edge of the gardens and then over by the swimming pool. When I didn't see Natalie anywhere, worry replaced my anger. Finally, stopping at the path that led up the mountain where she'd picnicked the other day with her companions, I pulled out my cell phone and scrolled down my names until I reached Nicolas.

"Yes, Malachi," Nicolas answered after two rings.

"Is Natalie with you?" I asked.

"No. She told us to stay in her room and wait for her." There wasn't concern or frustration in Nicolas's tone, just acceptance. And Nicolas would wait, along with Tomas, more than likely either sitting or standing, not talking or moving, until Natalie returned and suggested they did something different.

"That's fine. You're doing a great job."

"Thanks, Malachi."

"Bye, Nicolas."

"Good-bye."

My companions weren't perfect. I understood that. They weren't human, and in spite of Rose's insistence that they be made to act more human, that just didn't rub right to me. Truth be told, I liked my companions just the way they were. There was something about messing with a good thing that often led to trouble.

I'd run on gut instinct a good portion of my life and hadn't been steered wrong yet. Although there were days when I wondered why I continued letting Rose run the show here. She preached about all this money we earned, but what the hell was I doing with my share of the take?

"Not a goddamned thing," I muttered. Slamming the transmission into park and then cutting the engine, the reality I'd been living in for years suddenly came crashing in around me. "All these years," I groaned. Ten years I'd been on this island convincing myself I was doing my life's work when all along I was simply playing it safe, living a fantasy right along with everyone who came here. It was time to take charge and demand what I wanted.

It was one hell of a warm day and my shirt stuck to my back as I hiked up the path. I don't know why I was so sure I'd find her, and when I did, it was as if I was supposed to meet her up here. Natalie turned around slowly, the breeze coming off the ocean blowing her dress around her thighs and slapping strands of hair against her cheeks.

"You lied to me," she said, sounding incredibly hurt.

"No." I shook my head, aching from the very depth of my soul to share everything with her and knowing without any doubt that I couldn't. "I've never lied to you, Natalie. What are you doing up here alone?"

"I wanted to be alone." She turned her back on me. The breeze grabbed her short dress and offered a glimpse of her ass and the thong she wore.

I didn't want to leave her alone and wouldn't believe that she really wanted me to go. She was hurt because of how she translated my explanation to her yesterday. If I was able to hurt her, I'd be able to make her feel better. Clearing the distance between us, I wrapped my arms around her waist.

She didn't fight me, or try moving out of my embrace. My suspicions were right. Natalie would give me the chance to make it right with her. The way she fucked me yesterday showed me an attraction existed. Possibly physical, but with physical came loyalty, and compassion. Show her that I respected her and Natalie would forgive me, and I'd be willing to bet, she stood in my arms, not moving, waiting anxiously for me to say the right words so she could forgive me. And she felt so natural relaxing against me, while we stared at the ocean sprawled out before us. Its magnificence put into perspective how small my accomplishments were so far in life. I'd barely scratched the surface on what I wanted. But feeling Natalie's soft body pressed against mine showed me what was out there to have. All I needed to do was maintain control.

"Are Nicolas and Tomas not satisfying you?" I knew both of them had nothing to do with why she was here and so wasn't sure why I opened the conversation with that question.

"It's not that," she said. "They're both very nice men," she added quietly. Then moving out of my arms, she walked alongside the cliff and stopped at the nearest tree. "What did you do before you came here?"

Her question surprised me, but after accusing me of lying to her, I wanted her to believe I was being honest. "I worked in London for a research team underwritten by Devlin Products."

"Devlin Products?" She sounded surprised, but then nodded as if she were familiar with the organization. "What did your team do?"

"I spent about three years fine-tuning antiquated programming." My vague answers weren't satisfying her. And by the look on her face, I knew she was sincerely interested in knowing more about me. Blowing out a breath and forcing myself to relax, I fought for a way to share as much of myself as I could with her. "It was very tedious work and very long hours. The article we published on the future of robotics might be a bit dry to your liking, but I'll show it to you sometime if you're interested."

"I'd like to see it." She sounded sincere. "Why did you leave all of that to come here?"

I glanced at the ocean and then the trees shrouding us in the intimate clearing. "Who wouldn't want to come to paradise?" That didn't answer her question and I immediately saw disappointment in her eyes. "Here I have the freedom to explore my life's work without being restricted by the terms in a grant."

"And your life dream is robotics." It wasn't a question.

It dawned on me how long it had been since I'd truly been stimulated by conversation. Rose and I had so little in common that speaking with her never fulfilled me. My companions simply agreed with everything I said. But with Natalie, I never knew what she would ask next, or in what direction her mind headed. When it hit me that I would have to work to maintain control of this conversation, it also occurred to me how little effort I'd exerted over the years to be in control. Letting Rose run the show kept her off my back and allowed me to work on my dream. It was time to realize that dream and take control.

And since she didn't make her statement a question, I saw no reason to comment on it. "What is your life dream?" I asked, switching the focus of the conversation over to her.

I swore her smile was sad and a bit wary. "All I've ever wanted to do was practice law."

"What kind of law?"

"Right now I do corporate, contracts, that sort of thing." She shifted, suddenly uncomfortable, although I didn't miss the flare in her eyes at the mention of law.

"But that isn't what you want to do," I suggested.

"Ever since I was a little girl I wanted to be in the courtroom, fighting for justice. I wanted to make sure laws were fair, and to bring the bad guy down." She smiled and I believed I saw Natalie actually opening up to me at that moment. "My parents want me to be like my mom, supporting her husband's career with extravagant parties. They want me to marry into money and have babies and stay at home like all the other girls that I went to college with are doing."

"You don't want the country club life?" I saw that she wanted to make her own path, but at the same time doubted she'd have a clue what to do with herself without a padded bank account at her disposal.

"I'm not going to lead a life someone else chooses for me," she said stubbornly, sticking her chin out as she stared at me defiantly. Then swiping a wisp of hair away from her face, she tilted her head and studied me for a moment.

Sensing she was going to try and return the line of questioning in my direction, I moved closer until I could tuck the loose, stubborn strand behind her ear. "You must love your parents very much."

She blinked, then frowned. "I'm sure I do as much as anyone does," she offered.

I couldn't remember the last time I'd allowed my past to rear its ugly head. All these years on the island and what happened mainland seemed like another lifetime. "Not everyone gets along with their parents, Natalie."

"You didn't?"

"I'm sure we'd get along fine." Although I doubted I would ever take the time to find out. Many years had passed since my father disowned me, and just as many years since I'd been labeled a traitor to my own country. Youth had its advantages and faults, but when I allowed the past to appear in my mind all I saw were the faults. And that one, very large mistake I made when signing the papers for the grant from my government. France had a right to know the results of my experiments and I'd refused to produce them, turning instead and running in the night, fleeing from my homeland on principle.

"And I believe you'd make an incredible lawyer, if that's what you want."

"How can you say that? You don't know me that well." Her tone was challenging, but not accusatory.

"I know that you wouldn't condemn someone without learning all of the facts first. In just these few days you've shown your craving to unravel anything that appears a mystery to you."

"Then there is a mystery here to unravel," she said, her eyes widening. "Tell me, Malachi. You can trust me."

"This doesn't have anything to do with trust."

"Everything involves trust," she snapped, and then stepped around me. "You come after me, and then when you find me alone suddenly your hands are all over me. Just because I'm on this island doesn't make me a slut."

"If you want me to make some proclamation that I'm not interested in fucking you again, it won't happen. I'm going to fuck you again, but it's not because I think you're easy."

"Oh, really," she breathed, her face flushing. "What makes you think you're going to have sex with me again? How are you so sure?"

"Because I can see the craving in your eyes, Natalie. I know that you're as interested in me as I am in you. And it's more than physical."

"I don't even know that you're real!" she yelled.

She might as well have slapped me in the face. But her brutal confession made sense. From what she'd learned so far, I could see how she had her doubts. But as much as I wanted her trust, I needed her to know that every inch of me was as real as she was. Turning quickly, I slapped the nearest palm tree trunk, feeling its sharp bark slice into my palm. I ignored the pain, too determined to gain Natalie's trust.

"Malachi," she screamed, her eyes widening as she hurried to me and reached for my hand.

I did a pretty good number on myself, I realized when I glanced down and saw blood dripping down my palm.

"What the hell did you do that for?" she snapped.

She was angry. I just sliced my hand open for her, was enduring the pain, and she glared at me like I was an idiot.

"Because you have some hare brained notion in your head that I'm not real, that's why."

"Hare brained!" She sucked in a breath and offered a nice

view of cleavage over the V-neck cut in her dress. "There's not a goddamned thing hare brained about it, and you know it!"

Natalie turned and stormed away from me, hurrying down the path and out of view. I didn't let her go down the mountain alone last time she stormed off on me. She knew I wouldn't let her go down it again by herself. I kept my distance, though, knowing if I caught up with her right now I would shake sense into her and then probably fuck her right here on the side of the mountain. Once again, when I reached the point where I could cut off and head toward my buildings, I did, leaving her to storm her way back to the mansion.

13

Natalie

I didn't want to return to my room and Nicolas and Tomas. Let the two of them sleep alone in that large bed together. I wasn't in the mood for company.

What I wanted to do was turn around and march after Malachi, and then knock some sense into his thick skull. I couldn't believe he scraped his hand against the bark of that tree and cut it so badly. I cringed, seeing his outraged expression quickly hidden behind a mask of indifference as he glared at me with his bleeding hand.

I didn't mean that I really believed he wasn't real. I meant to get his dander up. And I guess I did a pretty good job. It was always good to know if a man had a temper.

I could hear my father now. "Best to find out now that he has no self-control than later when he destroys your marriage."

My father really believed there was a perfect man out there who couldn't wait to marry me. Well, I didn't want perfect. I wanted . . .

"Whoa." I reached for the smooth banister alongside the wide stairs that led to the entrance of the mansion and stabilized myself, realizing where my thoughts were heading. "Malachi," I whispered.

I'd never met a man like him. And his words, declaring that he knew I wanted him as much as he wanted me, and not just physically, took me by surprise.

"What the hell did that mean?" I grumbled, although their obvious meaning twisted my gut into knots of anxiety that seemed to make the stairs tilt sideways.

It was stupid to even contemplate a relationship with a man whom I'd never see again after another week and a half.

Turning around, I hurried back down the stairs and around the side of the mansion. There were beautiful gardens and fountains around the back that I hadn't explored yet. I didn't realize how terribly I must be scowling until a couple approaching me gave me an odd look. It took a moment to relax my expression but I nodded and managed a small smile before hurrying past them.

As it did all over the island, or at least in the areas where guests were obviously allowed to roam, the wide cobblestone path split and I opted for the direction away from the mansion. I'd barely walked far enough to cool my temper when I approached a large stone fountain with a stone figure of a boy carved in the middle of it. He held a pitcher and water flowed freely from it. As tranquil a sight as it was, I still fumed over Malachi calling me hare brained.

I didn't notice the old man until he straightened and then brushed off his pants. "It's a gorgeous day, isn't it?" When Jonah smiled, his face looked like leather and even with a few teeth missing, there was something compelling about him. "I don't suppose the weeds will mind if I take a break for a few minutes. Join me and tell me your problems."

"What makes you think I have problems?" I asked, and then wondered why I should be so cras when he was simply being polite. "I'm sorry. I wouldn't say exactly that I have a problem."

Jonah sat on the edge of the fountain and patted the smooth surface next to him. "Come. Sit. You remember me, don't you?"

"Hi Jonah. Of course I remember you."

"Miss Natalie Green. I know all about you."

"You do?" I froze, wondering what he might know.

His laugh was raspy and faded away even as he continued grinning at me. "I promise I'm a harmless gardener. Will you sit with me?"

"Sure," I sighed, shrugging at the same time and then plopped down next to him in a rather unladylike fashion. For some reason I felt like the pouting child who'd run home after fighting with her friends. Jonah appeared the wise grandfatherly type who in the next few minutes would say just the right thing to make everything better.

What an odd analogy.

"Malachi didn't mean whatever he said that upset you."

Those weren't the words I expected to come out of his mouth.

"How did you . . ." I caught myself but couldn't help staring at his peaceful, old expression. "I mean, what are you talking about?"

He patted my bare leg but then held his hands in his lap. They were arthritic and smooth as leather. "I've been working this ground for ten years now, as long as Rose and Malachi have been running this place. There isn't a lot that I miss."

I nodded, deciding there on the spot that the next words out of my mouth better be carefully chosen. At the same time it occurred to me that if this old man lived on this island and knew everything that went on here, then possibly he could help clear up the mystery about this place. Obviously it would take some clever tactics to draw information out of him, but I was good at interrogation.

"I bet you see a lot then." I glanced sideways, offering a small smile.

"You're in paradise." Jonah returned the smile but then stared ahead, his gaze turning thoughtful. "What you've got to remember is that everyone has a different idea of what paradise is. I've learned what is one man's paradise isn't necessarily another man's idea of the same."

I studied his profile, how his tanned, weathered skin and his thick silver hair that once was probably black made him look older than he possibly was. "So whose paradise is this?"

His dark eyes were bright and focused when he snapped his attention to mine. "You're very insightful. Good question," he added, nodding once but not answering my question.

"Don't get me wrong, I'm not complaining."

"Never said you were."

"It's beautiful here. The gardens are definitely my idea of paradise."

"I'll remember that," he said seriously, although I wasn't sure why it would matter to him if he did or not.

"My companions are very . . . nice," I said, hesitating only for a moment before choosing the right adjective to describe Nicolas and Tomas.

"I'm sure they are," he agreed, once again looking straight ahead as he nodded.

"Maybe my idea of paradise would include a mystery, or an adventure," I mused, looking ahead as well at the incredible flower arrangement that stretched as far as I could see ahead of me. The sound of the water pouring behind me into the cement pool was relaxing, but my mind worked around all the information I'd stumbled on over the past day or so. "It just doesn't add up. And I hate feeling like my intelligence is being insulted."

"I would too," Jonah said.

He didn't say anything else for a moment until I focused on his profile again. Then he looked down at his folded hands in his lap and examined his cracked and dirty fingernails. "Possibly if you're searching for adventure and a mystery, you're complicating things that are more than likely quite simple."

"But they aren't simple," I complained. "And I was insulted."

Jonah looked at me, and his dark eyes seemed to fill with compassion and understanding. Or maybe I wanted that from him and so saw what I needed to see. At the moment nothing seemed simple. Everything was beyond complicated.

"Possibly talking it out, voicing your problems to a neutral party, will help clear things up for you."

"How do I know that you're a neutral party?"

He didn't smile, but instead looked even more serious as he spoke. "I'm not a neutral party," he conceded, surprising me. "I'm as sick of Rose's greed as Malachi is. But I see and understand his frustration more than you do, my dear. I assure you that you can talk to me and it will bring you no harm. I won't even say a word to Malachi if you don't want me to. There isn't much that I miss around here. I've told you that already. More than likely I won't have to say a word. Malachi is a smart man and he'll figure out what is the right thing to do soon enough on his own without me having to coach him." He winked and smiled. "Unless you want me to give him a nudge for you."

"Maybe a smack upside the head," I mumbled and received hearty laughter for my voiced frustration. "And you're not helping at all so far. You're speaking in more riddles than anyone else I've met since I've been here."

"What have you learned?" he asked, indifferent to my accusation that he wasn't consoling me as he promised.

"That's the problem. I'm not sure. I can't figure out how to piece everything together yet." I licked my lips and then drew in a deep breath, filling my lungs with the heavily fragranced air from so many varieties of flowers surrounding us. Maybe sharing what I'd learned so far would help. I really did want someone to talk to about everything. "When I was over in Malachi's buildings, I saw some notes. He says he's got a fascination with robotics, and then admits that he worked in that field prior to coming here, but those notes didn't look like just a fascination. They looked real."

"How do notes look real?" he asked, frowning at me.

"There were comments in the margins, formulas crossed out and adjusted, and so many notes scribbled all over the pages I could tell he'd obviously struggled with something."

"And do you know what it is that he's struggling with?"

I shook my head, honestly not having a clue. "But earlier when I was inside, he was talking to Rose, or more like arguing."

"The snake in the garden," Jonah muttered under his breath. And then louder, added, "That doesn't surprise me."

"It wasn't so much what they were arguing about but something was said that bugged me. I heard the same thing from some of his employees over at his buildings."

"What was that?"

"Both times they said, 'when he makes more companions,'" I said, and studied his face for a reaction to my words.

Jonah either kept his emotions well under lock and key, or the statement was very clear to him and he assumed I'd guessed its meaning, too. He nodded for me to continue.

"Why would he *make* companions?" I asked, still searching his face for anything that might enlighten me.

"Because more are needed?" Jonah suggested, meeting my gaze and looking like his response should make sense to me.

"Why wouldn't they say they were going to hire more? Don't you see? They said 'make', not 'hire'."

"Rose wouldn't let anyone on this island other than the guests, and that is only because all of you pay such an exorbitant price to be here. Honestly, I'm surprised she lets me stay on. I keep waiting for the day when she replaces me with one of the companions."

"I'm sure no one else could take care of these gardens like you do. Just look at this place."

"You flatter an old man." Jonah stood slowly, patting my leg with his leathered hand as he took his time straightening, again making me wonder at his age. "And it sounds to me like you have all of the answers."

"How can you say that?" I immediately complained.

Jonah stared toward the mansion but didn't respond. Then pressing his hand against his lower back, he glanced over his shoulder at me and smiled. "Anytime you get tired of your companions and want to talk to a real old man, you know where to find me."

I nodded and watched him walk toward the house then dropped my head into my hands and sighed heavily. "If you're a real old man, what does that make everyone else around here?"

It made them all robots. Lord. I straightened, staring at the mansion. "Have I had sex with robots?"

I stood quickly, and then reached out to balance myself when my legs felt wobbly. Malachi was creating robots and Rose made butt loads of money off guests like me by providing them with perfect companions.

"I need proof." And to think I left my laptop at home expecting I wouldn't need it in paradise.

I ran my hands down my dress and then pressed my hair back into shape before heading back to the mansion. If I acted like something was wrong, Tomas and Nicolas would be all over me trying to make me feel better. At the moment, I wasn't sure I could stomach either of them touching me.

"I wonder if they would bleed if they rubbed their hands down the bark of a palm tree." For some reason, that image made me smile and by the time I reached the mansion's back entrance, a compulsive fit of giggles threatened to take over. "Get a grip," I whispered.

"Where have you been?" Rose asked in a low whisper, stepping outside but turning and not noticing me.

I jumped to the side, frantically looking for a good place to hide, or at least a position to look natural in if I were discovered.

"Just took some cold medicine to one of our guests. He apparently has a terrible cold from being out in the rain last night." Jonah didn't speak as quietly, although if I weren't just outside the back service entrance, I wouldn't have heard him.

There was a single chair next to the door and I plopped down in it, then bent over to grab my sandal, making a show of messing with it in case anyone were to see me. I wouldn't be accused of eavesdropping but something compelled me to listen.

"Why would anyone want to be out in the rain during the night?" Rose used a tone that I hadn't heard before, although somehow her condescending tone fit her.

"Apparently his companion was giving him a blow job and the rain didn't bother her. She didn't want to stop and he didn't have what it took to stop her, I guess." Jonah chuckled as if this were the kind of conversation he had with his boss on a daily basis.

Oddly enough, it probably was. This was an island for sex.

"I guess you can't blame Malachi for this one." Jonah continued chuckling. "You wanted the companions to be more waterproof. She came through the experience just fine."

"Don't you dare take that tone with me," Rose snapped, her voice dripping with venom. "When's the last time you had a dime in your pocket? You don't want for anything on this island, but try making it a day anywhere else."

"How true," Jonah said, not missing a beat, nor sounding that remorseful. "There's no place I'd rather live than here. And no worries about your guest. I gave him some cough medicine that Malachi shipped over for me. He'll be good as new in no time flat."

"This just goes to prove my point. I'll get Malachi to do what I want. You watch and see. That companion was too much of an idiot to come out of the rain. It could have harmed a guest. What if he'd caught pneumonia? Malachi needs to make the companions smarter."

I jumped and covered my mouth to hold back a shriek when Jonah walked out of the service door a moment later. He smiled at my shocked expression.

"Just another puzzle piece," he told me calmly. "Might make it easier for you to piece together the entire picture."

I was too shocked to answer him and simply gawked as he walked past me toward a small cottage to the side of the back door and then disappeared inside. I snapped my jaw shut, feeling a sharp pain at my joints and continued staring, slowly digesting what I'd just heard.

A couple hours later, after resigning to return to my room to shower and spend time with Nicolas and Tomas after my hike up the mountain and walk in the garden, I again left the two men in my room and headed to the dining hall. If I insisted Nicolas and Tomas do something, they didn't argue or question me. I tried imagining Malachi obediently following my instructions and almost tripped myself as I walked down the stairs. The thought was simply too preposterous.

"Where are your companions, my dear?" Rose asked me at the bottom of the stairs.

"They're resting in my room." I gave her a knowing smile and thought I saw something cold in her gaze that I hadn't noticed before. Otherwise she returned my relaxed grin and wrapped her arm around mine as I turned toward the dining hall. "A nap wouldn't hurt me either but I've got a serious case of the munchies. I thought I'd see if your kitchen offers some good old-fashioned chocolate cake."

"You really should have read your contract more thoroughly.

I'm rather surprised since you're a lawyer. But it clearly states your companion, or in your case, companions, are to see to your every need." Rose's hands were cold as she squeezed my arm and guided me into the dining room. "It would be smart next time to have one of them bring your munchies to you. We wouldn't want anything happening to you while you aren't escorted, now would we?"

"I wouldn't even make the servants at home get my late night munchies for me," I said, and then my overactive imagination read double meaning into her words and I glanced sideways, catching her pursed expression and wondered if I spoke too soon. "I'm very capable of taking care of myself."

"Now are those the servants in your parents' home, or in the summer cottage where you stay?" This time Rose's cruel tone wasn't missed.

But I'd be damned if she'd get a rise out of me. "Either," I said, shrugging, and deciding I wouldn't flatter her by asking how she knew the address I put on my paperwork was the summer cottage and not my parents' home. We reached the dining hall and I tried pulling my arm free of her cold grasp. "I'm going to see if they have any cake."

"I'll personally make sure you're brought a nice slice. Would you like coffee as well?"

"That sounds perfect." I headed toward a small table in the corner of the room and Rose held on tightly until I reached for the chair and pulled it out from under the table. "Oh," I added, when she let go and turned to the approaching waiter. Rose turned and her gaze traveled down me before she arched her pencil-thin eyebrows. Not one wrinkle appeared around her eyes. I relaxed into my chair and moved my folded napkin from the center of my place setting. "Would it be possible to bring me a laptop? I really need to get online for a bit."

"I'm sorry, we don't have Internet access here."

I knew she was lying and told her as much with a look. In-

PLEASURE ISLAND / 165

stead of accusing her of such though, I simply continued with an explanation. "Obviously my firm doesn't know where I am. I might not be a senior partner, but I know when they take vacations they check in online. It would do me well to do the same," I lied, positive my lie was more convincing than hers. "I tell you what," I added, keeping my voice low so the waiter who stood patiently a few feet behind Rose wouldn't overhear. "Bring me the laptop and add the charge to my account. I'm sure you still have my credit card on file."

Rose's expression hardened just a bit, but she recovered with the blink of an eye and once again smiled easily as if she didn't have a care in the world. "I'll see what I can do. It seems to me if you wanted to get online while here you would have brought your own laptop though," she added, her friendly smile not fading.

She turned again without bidding me good day and whispered something to the waiter who simply nodded and then retreated to the kitchen. He reappeared with an elaborate place setting, including a coffee pot and coffee cup along with beautiful china bowls filled with sugar and cream. I'd barely prepared my coffee when he once again was at my table with a very delicious looking slice of layered chocolate cake. I was in heaven.

Rose didn't reappear with a laptop. I'd finished my cake and second cup of coffee and stared out the windows across from me at the incredible gardens that offered a panoramic view. There were a few others in the dining room and I tried not staring at a couple, who were getting very intimate a few tables away. But it became impossible not to watch when the young woman, who sat next to the older man, slipped under the table.

I blinked, surprised in spite of what Tomas, Nicolas and I had done, but then remembered that this was Paradise Island and what was considered unacceptable anywhere else on the planet, was encouraged here. It still seemed odd witnessing such a scene in public but after a couple of minutes, I couldn't stop myself from watching.

The woman disappeared under the tablecloth but when the man adjusted himself in his chair, making room for her head between his legs, I could see her face appear and watched when she looked up and smiled at him.

He unzipped his pants and appeared to be pretty good sized when he pulled his dick out and gripped it with his hand. I swear I heard him hiss when she placed her hand where his had been. He gripped the edges of the table, closing his eyes, and although his arm now blocked a good portion of my view, I knew she'd taken him into her mouth.

It was wrong to get excited watching strangers have sex. Everything I'd been taught to believe, to accept about proper society and public behavior, demanded that I look away, or better yet get up and leave the table. I found myself watching though, and in fact, felt a need rise and swell inside me that was stronger than anything I'd felt since I arrived here.

I didn't want to return to my room. As the throbbing increased between my legs, and I watched the man tilt his head and bite his lower lip as pleasure racked his body, I wanted to offer that same treat to Malachi. More than anything, I wanted to leave the mansion, go find him, and do whatever it took to make up after arguing with him so I could experience him inside me again. It wasn't just sex I was after. I wanted to make love to Malachi.

There was more of a mystery on this island than I'd first thought. Possibly everyone here were robots, or androids, or whatever they would be called. Maybe Malachi, and possibly the old gardener, Jonah, were the only humans here, other than the guests. I'd flown in on the plane with some of them so I knew they were for real. Rose might be for real, but I'd love to know she was nothing more than a robot and could be turned off at will. There was something grossly unnerving about her.

But now I believed there was something in the air as well. Possibly having sex, and encouraging sexual acts everywhere, created a charge that affected part of my mind. Because I swear no man ever made me want him to the point where I would swallow my pride and seek him out, but that was exactly what I wanted to do.

The man sucked in his breath and his head fell backward. I watched as he fought to maintain his composure and saw his knuckles turn white as he gripped the table. When he growled under his breath, I realized I'd been holding my breath and released it quickly, then reached for my coffee cup. It was empty and my hands were shaky. I folded and unfolded my napkin before glancing back up in time to see the lady crawl out from underneath the table. The man helped her, taking her hand and continuing to hold it when they both stood. Then kissing her gently, he stroked her hair and slid his arm around hers as they turned to leave.

The man glanced over his shoulder and winked at me before focusing ahead and guiding his date out of the room. I blushed and there wasn't any stopping the blotches that spread down my cheeks to my neck. I sat alone in the dining room, my cup empty and mere crumbs on my plate while a need swelled inside me with such a vengeance that I doubted I'd be able to move as gracefully as the woman did when she climbed out from under the table.

When I did leave the dining room, no one paid any attention to me so I headed down the hallway I'd discovered that went past the stairs and led to the back service entrance. I hoped to find Jonah. He was the gardener, but I'd grown up with servants and knew they weren't to be underestimated and could often manage things that others couldn't pull off.

"I hoped to find you back here," I said in greeting after walking out the backdoor and finding the old man sitting outside his cottage in a wicker chair and carving a piece of wood with a pocket knife.

The scene was so out of character with the rest of the island that for a moment I felt transported to another time, a simpler place, without controversy, lies, or vindictive behavior.

Jonah glanced up at me but then returned to his carving. "What can I do for you, Miss Natalie?" he asked slowly, his raspy voice calm and sounding like he didn't have a care in the world.

"I asked Rose if I could get online for a while and she told me that wasn't possible on the island. But I know there's Internet service here."

Jonah looked up at me again and nodded once but didn't confirm or deny my statement.

I continued, getting to the point. "Do you think you could find a computer that I could use for just a bit?"

Jonah stared at me for a long moment and then returned to his task, slowly rubbing the small knife over the wood and peeling off long strands that fell to the ground. A pile of shavings were on his shoes and the ground around him.

He didn't look up when he spoke. "Go to your room and spend time with your companions. I'll come to you in a bit." He turned his piece of wood and took his time peeling a long paper-thin slice of wood off of his carving.

"Thank you," I said, and when it appeared he wouldn't say anything else I left him to his craft and returned inside.

Tomas and Nicolas looked toward the door at the same time when I entered the room. Both sat at the table, which didn't have anything on it. The TV wasn't on. Maybe they'd been engrossed in a conversation I interrupted when entering. Or maybe they simply sat in the quiet room, not talking and staring at each other the entire time I'd been gone. That thought gave me chills.

"There you are!" Tomas said, grinning broadly and pushing his chair away from the table.

"We missed you," Nicolas added, smiling a toothy smile and standing at the same time Tomas did.

"You two sure know how to make a girl feel good," I said, consenting to hugging each one of them.

When I plopped down on the bed and kicked off my shoes both were immediately on either side of me, caressing my arms and back.

"Did you enjoy your snack in the dining room?" Nicolas asked, his deep voice like a dangerous purr from a deadly cat.

"I did. And I'm absolutely stuffed," I admitted. "I think I'd like to lie here and watch some TV. How does that sound?"

"Perfect." Tomas scooted off the bed and reached for the remote, then turned on the set.

When I reached for the remote, he handed it to me without comment. Proof enough in my mind that he couldn't possibly be a real man. Any guy I know would have fought for rights to control all channel surfing.

I'd barely flipped through a handful of channels, noting that they were all movie channels and not finding any major networks that might offer the news, when someone knocked on the door.

Nicolas slid off the bed without saying anything and walked to the door. I followed him with my eyes, not bothering to move from where I lay on my stomach facing the TV, and noticed how perfect his body was. Although a black man, I thought I saw a bit of Malachi in him. Something about the confident stroll, the way he moved silently, reminded me of Malachi. I watched him open the door and at the same time wondered what Malachi was doing.

Jonah said something to Nicolas that I didn't hear and then stepped into the room, carrying a large serving tray.

"Compliments of the kitchen," he announced, walking past the bed and placing the large, heavy looking silver tray on the table.

"Is something wrong with Jackie?" Tomas asked, moving to a sitting position next to me.

I slid off the bed and reached for my purse that was on the floor alongside the wall. Remembering Rose's comment about Jonah never having a dime in his pocket, I opened my wallet and pulled out a twenty dollar bill.

"Jackie is just fine. But she's running her ass off tonight with room service orders. Miss Natalie here deserves the finest of treatment." He winked at me and lifted the daily newspaper that appeared to be from Hawaii, revealing a closed laptop underneath it. The silver coffee set looked similar to the one brought to me in the dining room. Jonah replaced the newspaper and then lifted the cover from a large bowl. "I was in the kitchen helping myself to some of the rolls. They are exceptionally good tonight and I thought you might enjoy some as well."

"You're so thoughtful," I said, reaching and taking his leathered hand in both of mine and sliding the twenty into his. "Thank you very much."

"Anything I can do," he said and glanced at his hand when I let go. "This isn't necessary," he said.

"I want to," I insisted, taking him by the arm and walking him to the door. Thankfully, Nicolas and Tomas didn't follow. "You've been very nice to me since I've arrived and I consider you a friend."

Jonah wasn't quite my height but when he turned to face me we were pretty much eye to eye. I saw honesty in his gaze, but there was something else.

"Do you always buy your friends?" he asked.

"No, of course not." I frowned and his meaning created an uncomfortable settling feeling in my gut. "I try very hard to take care of those who are kind to me though," I added and placed my arm on his shoulder. "This means a lot to me, Jonah. Thank you again."

Jonah stuffed the twenty into his pocket and turned, reaching for the door handle. "Be careful. Computers never made much sense to me but I notice when people use them they often get mad when they find out Rose seems to know what they were doing on them."

With that he left, and I wondered how much he might actually know about them. Although Jonah was also a mystery, I believed that he wasn't a threat. And I needed to trust someone. Don't ask me why, but possibly with everything around here getting stranger every day, knowing I had an ally helped. And he was definitely an ally if he would go to the effort to let me know she had some way of monitoring her computer systems.

"Here is your coffee," Tomas said, handing a cup to me. "Just how you like it."

"Thank you, Tomas." I accepted the cup and moved around him to the table where the tray still sat. "You two find a good movie to watch. I'm going to do some work here for a while before calling it a night."

"You're going to work?" Nicolas sounded disappointed.

"Just for a bit." I smiled, admiring his dark handsome features until he smiled back and then watched as he stacked several of the pillows against the headboard and got comfortable, stretching out his long legs. "I won't take too long and will join you soon," I added.

"Good." Tomas sat at the edge of the bed, and started changing channels, his expression blank as he stared at the set.

I watched both of them for a moment longer, still not believing they could possibly be machines. They looked human, acted human, felt and interacted like they were human. I didn't know a lot about robotics, or how far along we'd come with making robots appear human, but I was going to find out.

Neither Tomas nor Nicolas said anything when I moved the newspaper and then opened the laptop. It booted up quickly and a handful of icons appeared on the desktop, the usual generic search engines and e-mail programs installed on most systems.

I wondered where Jonah got this computer but wasn't going to question his ability to present me with Internet capabilities.

Clicking on Internet Explorer, I waited for the page to appear and remembered Jonah's parting comment. As soon as the search bar appeared, I typed in the Web site for my law firm and then entered my screen name and password. From there, I used that search engine so no one could track my history on the computer. Not that I didn't plan dumping cookies and clearing all record of my activity before returning the laptop.

Sitting there, browsing one site after another, I felt energy build inside me, course through my veins. Playing the investigator, doing research, and trying to find the final pieces to put together a puzzle turned me on almost as much as being with Malachi. Again, while waiting for the Web site page to download, I wondered where he was and what he was doing right now.

The Web site opened and I read the article posted by Devlin Products twelve years ago. A team had been formed that would work to improve some of their latest inventions. Three names were mentioned but none of them were Malachi. A sinking feeling hit me that I fought to make go away. If he lied to me about Devlin Products, what else did he lie about? I read over the rest of the article, learning how the team was praised for helping to improve many products already invented by Devlin Products.

One of the three on the team, Mac Kowan, received a majority of the praise for the work done by the team. A link in the article led to several pictures, and after clicking on it, I stared at an image of a younger Malachi. His hair was shorter and his body not quite as muscular as it was now but his dynamic presence stood out even in the old photograph.

Why did he change his name? Instead of getting answers, I realized my puzzle was larger than I originally thought.

After staring at the picture for a moment I decided I liked

the way he looked now better. The article explained modern devices that would be available to the public soon, such as interactive maps in cars, homes offering a new level of security, as well as tracking devices for military use were being tested and refined by this highly trained team.

Malachi was responsible for technologies that were common household items today. I shook my head, surprised at how incredibly intelligent he was. At the bottom of the page were several links to related articles. I clicked on each one of them but nothing told me anything more about Malachi.

Going back to the main search bar, I tried another tactic and typed in robotics. The search engine came up with thousands of possible Web sites to go through. I wondered how long Jonah would let me use the laptop. Trying a different angle, I typed in Mac Kowan and then robotics.

"Bingo," I whispered under my breath as I glanced down the page at the few Web sites that appeared.

Malachi apparently didn't cover his tracks well enough. The search matched him to his fictitious name. I clicked on a link titled, *"Cohen Labeled Traitor, Father Refuses Comment."*

"Holy crap," I said too loudly.

"Is everything okay?" Tomas asked.

I'd honestly forgotten I wasn't alone in the room and looked up at the two men who stared curiously at me. "Everything's fine," I said tightly. "I'll be done soon."

I stared in disbelief at the article that filled the screen.

Inventor Malachi Cohen, native of Bischheim, just outside of Strasbourg in France, is charged with withholding information requested by his government. Cohen accepted grant money and signed papers which clearly stated he would turn over all results found while working under the grant. The French government accused Cohen of violating the terms of his grant by refusing to disclose the results of his experiments. Cohen released some of his notes on an invention that would revolutionize robotics as we know it today. Although Cohen insisted during a recent interview that the notes he turned over at the request of local authorities were inclusive, after extensive review by a panel devised to interpret them, it was determined that all factors needed to assemble the chip that would give robots personalities were not included. Also missing from information turned over to the government were schematics for the robots. While being interviewed separately, other members of Cohen's team reported there were schematics, which showed how robots could be designed to appear human. Tests conducted while the team presented their work to Devlin Products were inclusive. It was impossible to determine which was the robot, and which the human. Devlin Products' representative, Jean Luc Beuerlein, announced to the press they were not in possession of Cohen's complete report covering all details of his robotic discoveries. The files containing all test results appear to have disappeared.

Cohen refused further comment. When authorities returned to his last known address to question him further, his landlord reported he'd moved with no forwarding address. Cohen's family, long established in the predominantly Jewish community, refused comment other than stating they didn't know Cohen's whereabouts.

I blinked and looked over the laptop screen at Nicolas and Tomas, who stared at the TV. Was I looking at the results of this personality chip that Malachi supposedly invented, but then refused the French government, almost fifteen years ago?

14

Malachi

"Am I in time?" Rose hurried in to my laboratory and then froze. The look on her face was priceless.

I managed not to smile, or gloat, but I knew admiration and envy when I saw it. If Rose could manage to create the companions and get rid of me, she'd do it in a New York minute. But she couldn't. Nor could she threaten to replace me with anyone else. I wasn't conceited over the fact, or thrilled with the knowledge that no one else could figure out what I knew. There were days when I wished someone else would create mechanical human beings. Even a little competition would probably be good for me.

For two days I'd been buried in the laboratory, fine-tuning their programming and making sure every wrinkle was ironed out. Although I was sure I looked like shit, and desperately needed a shower, adrenaline still pumped through me. I was sane enough, though, to know that pride came before the fall.

Usually I kept that mantra in my forethoughts. Today, however, wasn't one of those times. Watching Rose's smug expression fade as she stared at the six companions sitting on each of the exam tables, gave me a sense of pride and satisfaction that she would never understand. It was like she stared at my newborn child for the first time and raved over how beautiful he or she was.

"Looks like I'm right on time." Her expression changed and she smiled tightly. Rose fought hard not to sing my praises.

I reminded myself that I didn't need an ego boost. Not from her or from anyone. My companions were enough to let me know I was good.

"They still need to be run through an extensive round of tests." I walked around each table, smiling at the three males and three females as I moved past each one and checked their vitals.

"What tests do we have to take?" The male next to me, Samuel, named after my grandfather, frowned as he asked.

"Standard tests that all companions take before starting work," I explained.

"I want them working by tomorrow," Rose announced.

"They'll start working when I say they're ready." I didn't want her to know yet that I'd implemented a new chip, and until I was sure I had all of the quirks out of it, I would be a lot happier if Rose would just leave me alone. "I'll give you a call when I know they're ready."

"Put their outfits on them and they'll be ready," Rose snapped, but then sighed and smiled at me. "Malachi," she said softly, using the tone she employed when she believed she could sweet-talk her way into getting what she wanted. "How could they not be ready? Have you ever created a companion who hasn't worked perfectly? Look at you. Look at them. You're a genius, Malachi. I know I don't tell you this enough, but your intelligence is the backbone of the island and . . ." She paused, took a deep breath, and met my gaze. She was laying it on so damned thick that it was hard for even her to pull it off, especially if it meant humbling herself and singing my praises. "And, well, I couldn't do this without you."

"I know you couldn't," I mumbled, not enjoying her compliment as much as I thought I would. "And it's nice to hear you say that," I added, unwilling to bite her head off in spite of the fact that I knew she had ulterior motives. "Intelligence isn't always a blessing, Rose. Any more than paradise is a place that's perfect."

"Why isn't intelligence a blessing?" Rebecca, who was named after my grandmother, leaned forward to see me since she sat on the last examination table.

They were questioning our conversation, already learning and adjusting their programming to be part of the environment they were in, just as they were programmed to do. I had to have been grinning like an idiot when I walked toward her. Her confused expression told me as much.

"Good question, sweetheart." I reached for the sundress that was folded on the table by her examination bed. Handing it to her, along with brand new underwear I'd ordered just for them, I noticed she didn't do anything to cover her breasts. I stroked her cheek, feeling how warm and smooth it was and also noting that her nudity didn't bother me. She was my child and I loved her. "What I meant was that when we're considered to be very smart by our peers, often they expect answers from us faster than we can provide them," I explained. "Sometimes providing information as quickly as its demanded becomes overwhelming. Especially when I want to make sure everything I do is perfect, like with you, my dear."

She looked at me with soft blue eyes, and then blinked. God, she blinked. That small movement, something I'd finally mastered with my companions, appeared before my eyes like a small miracle. It was all I could do not to pull her into my arms and hug her for showing me my victory.

Rebecca looked down at the dress I'd handed her and brushed her fingers over the material. "I'll do my best to make sure you don't feel overwhelmed by your work anymore," she said softly, and then looked up at me quickly, her blue eyes flashing with brilliance.

Chills rushed over my flesh, although I wasn't sure why. Nodding, I stepped away from her and walked alongside the row of exam tables.

"All of you have clothes on the table next to you. Go ahead and get dressed." This was their first test. They were adults and therefore should know how to do things that human adults knew how to do. If my programming was correct, there were certain "memories" already installed in them.

"What?" Rose snapped. "Why are you putting them in clothes? They will wear loincloths or the two pieces that all companions wear on the island."

"You're wearing clothes. Why can't I?" Samuel challenged as he pushed one leg into his shorts, and then the other.

"Don't you ever question anything I say," Rose said coldly, marching up to Samuel and pointing at his face. "You're a machine, a companion, and your only purpose is to serve me. You will obey without question or I'll unplug you. Is that clear?"

Samuel smiled down at her, his expression clearly looking like he fought to tolerate her insults and condescending tone. "You just go ahead and try unplugging me, Rose," he said quietly. "It might prove to be a rather incredible feat, if you can pull it off, since I've never been plugged in."

Rose stepped backward, her face turning ghostly white. Samuel reached for her but she slapped him away.

"Fix them so they aren't like that," she told me, looking terrified.

"You're a hypocrite, Rose," I said, walking over and taking her arm and then pulling her toward the door. I left the companions to dress and escorted her to the hallway. "You've got what you asked for," I hissed at her, letting her go and then scratching my head. God, I needed a shower. "The new companions can process what happens around them, adjust accordingly, and will respond to any stimuli you throw at them. If that happens to be rudeness, you'll get it in like."

"No! I don't want them to be rude. I want them to obey me."

"They will obey you if you treat them with respect." I looked at her smugly, crossing my arms over my chest. "Sounds like you're going to have to get accustomed to treating them like human beings, if you're capable of treating anyone with decency. That personality chip you've been whining for, you've got it. Now live with it."

I reached for the door to return to my new companions.

"Malachi," she said.

I turned and looked at her. She still looked rather shaken. "There's something else I need to talk to you about."

"What's that?"

"Natalie Green."

It had been two days since I last saw Natalie and we'd parted ways pissed off at each other. "What's wrong?" I asked, thinking for the hundredth time that I should have taken a break from my work and sought her out.

"I told you she was up to no good." Her color returned to her face along with her venomous stare. "Her companions informed me she was on a computer last night, plotting and communicating with her connections in the states. She told me in the dining room she didn't have a computer. Yet she managed to steal one out of the office and get it to her room. Then, while ordering her companions to sit and not move or speak, she sent information to whoever she's working with about the island. She's here to destroy you. I just don't want trouble for you."

"Nicolas and Tomas told you all of this?" I found that really hard to believe.

"No, they didn't tell me all of that," she snarled, tossing her thick long hair over her shoulder and looking very sure of herself. "I cover my bases, Malachi. You'd be smart to do the same, but since you don't, I have to take care of you, too. I went over the laptop after I got it back and learned what she did while she was on it."

"You're full of shit, Rose," I said, shaking my head in disgust. What at first I believed might be jealousy toward Natalie now appeared to be delusional behavior. Rose sounded like she believed what she said. "You don't have any programs on your computers that allow you to trace what anyone's doing on them. I've checked. And if Natalie were snooping around online about either one of us, more than likely it would be you. She probably would be curious how a single woman managed to acquire so many employees who calmly do as they're told when their boss is such an insane bitch."

"How dare you," she growled, drawing out each word slowly while her eyes widened and she shook with rage. "You're the fool here, not me. I tried to be nice about this, but you leave me no choice. Stay away from Natalie Green. That's an order!"

"Go to hell, Rose. I'll do what I want." Turning, I entered the lab, closing the door on her and shutting out her rude response.

My six creations looked at me as I entered, and I was positive I saw concern on their faces.

"Would you look at all of you," I said, intentionally relaxing my voice and letting them see how pleased I was that all of them were dressed. "I have to say, I have good taste in picking out clothes."

"She's a bitch, Malachi," Samuel said, obviously taking the position of spokesperson. The others nodded their agreement. "What are you going to do about her?"

"There are people in this world that you'll like, and others that you won't. Unfortunately, we can't get rid of the ones we don't like."

"Why not?" Bruce asked. He was shorter than Samuel, and had fair features where Samuel was dark like me.

"There are laws." I looked at each one of them, watching them watch me and knowing they were like sponges, eager and excited to learn everything they could. "It's against the law to murder someone. So we have to put up with people we don't like or who aren't nice to us."

Or we could run to the other side of the world and start life over. My companions wouldn't understand that. Not to mention, something told me they wouldn't approve of the action. I didn't create cowards. My companions would fight for what was right. I turned from them, heading to the far wall where a group of computers were installed.

"I don't think we should have to put up with her." Samuel put his hand on my shoulder. "She upsets you and that's wrong. And who is Natalie Green?"

"She's a lady here on the island. You'll treat her with nothing but respect."

"Of course," Samuel agreed.

"And you'll put up with Rose as well. If she gives you trouble, just let me know and I'll handle it."

"Like you did out there?" Samuel challenged. "Malachi, you aren't handling her. You're hiding from her."

I turned, ready to argue with him. "It's complicated. In order to do my work, I need to be here alone, or I wouldn't have succeeded in bringing you to life."

Samuel searched my face, and I swore I could see him digesting what I'd told him and translating it in his circuits so that it made sense to him.

"There's a difference in being alone, and hiding," he said slowly.

"Yes."

"So now that we're created, will you honor her request and stay away from Natalie Green? If she's one of the guests, and you own this island, are you being alone, or hiding if you honor Rose's request and leave this female alone?"

"Call her a lady, not a female," I instructed. "And no, I don't plan on listening to Rose. In fact, I'm looking forward to seeing Natalie soon."

Samuel nodded, and the others around him smiled. "Good. You deserve to be happy, Malachi. Happiness is a measure of success."

"You're amazing, Samuel," I said, patting his arm, and then looked at the others surrounding us. "All of you are. And now, for the tests I told you about. Each of you take one of these laptops. I'll explain the tests that I'm going to run you through."

The six of them each grabbed a laptop while I headed to the storage pantry for the cords to plug them in so we wouldn't have to worry about battery life. My fingers slid off the door handle when I pulled on it and I frowned. I couldn't remember ever having locked this door. Turning it again, this time using some force, the door was obviously locked.

"Do you need some help?" Abram, the last of the six to grab his laptop, moved to stand next to me and stared at the door. "I can open it for you."

Although I didn't create my companions to think on terms that they were stronger than humans, the fact still remained that he could pull or push longer than I could because he wouldn't feel the pain or friction against his skin.

"Sure Abram. Try not to break the door handle if you can help it." As I spoke, I thought I heard something move on the other side of the door. Frowning, I looked at Abram and could tell he heard the same thing. I stepped to the side and pointed toward the door. "Force it open," I instructed.

Abram didn't hesitate. He was a bit stockier than the other new male companions, and his muscles bulged and flexed under his muscle shirt as he grabbed the doorknob and twisted it until I heard the lock snap. He pulled the door open.

I saw movement inside and lunged forward, hurrying into my storage closet and grabbing one hot looking ass before Natalie could crawl out of the window she'd obviously jarred open to sneak inside.

"You're not going anywhere," I said quietly and pulled her into my arms.

Natalie twisted around quickly, a wild look in her eyes when she looked past me at Abram. "Is this your personality chip that you refused to turn over to your government fifteen years ago?"

I froze. Letting her slide down me, I kept her in my arms while studying her face. There was no triumphant expression, or scrutinizing gaze, as if she'd just busted me and would bask in her triumphs. Her question sounded sincere and not confrontational. I wasn't sure if I was impressed that she'd discovered my past or pissed that I didn't do a better job of burying the blemishes on my record. One thing I knew, Rose lied. If she'd known Natalie read on the Internet somewhere about me refusing to turn my results of my work from their grant over to the French government, she would have spit it out at my face while grinning from ear to ear.

"Are you okay?" I asked instead of answering her question.

"Yes." She didn't fight when I ran my hands down her arms and inspected her with my eyes. She looked more than okay to me.

"What are you doing here?"

"I didn't know I'd be stuck in this closet." She also didn't answer my question. "I mean, I didn't know that all of you would be in the other room . . ." She stopped herself, again looking at Abram. "I don't believe it," she whispered. "You really are amazing."

"Thank you," Abram said easily.

I knew the compliment was directed toward me and put my arm around her, deciding I'd be mad at her later. Right now, I needed to know exactly what she'd overheard, how long she'd been in the closet, and what brought her here in the first place. Grabbing the cords that I needed out of the closet, I escorted her into the lab.

"Everyone, this is Natalie," I announced. "Abram, get your

laptop. Do the rest of you have yours turned on?" I walked Natalie over to the chair behind my desk and pressed on her shoulder. "Sit," I ordered, meeting her gaze for only a moment but knowing I got my message across that she better stay and be quiet. "Take these cords and plug them into your laptops then into the outlets next to each of your examination tables. Turn on your laptops and then click on the icon on the desktop that says IQ TEST."

"Why was she in the closet?" Samuel asked, studying Natalie.

"I'm going to find that out," I told him. "I'm also going to instruct each of you not to mention that you saw her here. Do all of you understand? This is very important."

"We understand," Rebecca offered. "Rose will do anything to protect her island and if she knows Natalie is here, it could jeopardize Natalie's safety. You've already told us that she's never to be put in danger," she added, nodding toward Natalie.

Natalie's jaw dropped while her complexion went pale. Rebecca spoke the truth and although I might have presented it to Natalie differently, the situation remained the same. Rose couldn't find out Natalie was here or, God forbid, that she'd learned the secret behind the island.

After leaving them to take the test, I took Natalie by the arm and escorted her out of the lab, closing the door behind us. After making sure there wasn't anyone around, I moved quickly, practically dragging her until I reached my small office where most of my files were kept. Opening the door, I ushered her inside, flipped on the light, and leaned against the door to push it closed.

"Talk. Talk now." I crossed my arms, knowing I needed to keep them off of her. I would ravish her or shake some sense into her. Either way, I could tell by the fear in her eyes that she knew she stumbled on to more than she anticipated. What I needed to know was if there was any truth in Rose's accusations. And I wouldn't learn that by fucking Natalie instead of forcing her to explain her actions.

That look of trepidation disappeared quickly though. Confidence and determination spread over her pretty face. In spite of the soft pale pink strapless dress she wore that hugged her body and showed off her enticing figure, I forced my gaze to remain on her face. One thing was crystal clear: nothing would jeopardize my companions. Nothing and no one!

"I needed to understand," she said, her voice soft and compelling. Then, sucking in a breath that forced her breasts to press against the top of her dress showing off a nice display of cleavage, she looked at me and bit her lower lip. "The other day I spent some time talking to Jonah in the garden."

"Oh?" Jonah wouldn't betray me. But I knew he didn't like Rose. "And?" I encouraged.

"He didn't make any sense." She crossed her arms against her waist and turned, glancing at the contents of my small office and at the filing cabinets, then turned from me and stared out the small window covered with blinds that were open just enough to offer a broken view of the foliage covering the base of the mountain behind the building. "He left the gardens before I did and when I headed toward the back door to enter the mansion without being noticed, I overheard him talking to Rose. I asked Rose if she'd bring me a laptop, and although she said she would try, she didn't. So I asked Jonah and he brought one to my room."

"Oh, did he?" If Jonah brought the laptop to her room, Nicolas and Tomas would have known that. "Your companions were with you?"

I asked, confirming what I already began believing.

"Yes," she said, her brow wrinkling as she stared at me, confused. "Nicolas let him into the room."

I stared at the ornate clip that captured her hair at her nape. Thick brown waves of hair fell out of it and curled just past her shoulders. It would take nothing to release her hair and watch it fan over her bare shoulders. As much as standing so close to her, breathing in the soft fragrance that she wore, made me itch to bury my face in her neck, we weren't going to end this conversation until I knew everything that had happened. And confirm that every word out of Rose's mouth earlier was a lie.

"Why did you ask him to bring you the laptop?"

"I wanted to find answers," she said, exhaling and letting her shoulders droop some as she lowered her gaze so that her long, thick lashes hooded her green eyes. "Don't be upset with Jonah. He's been trying to help me, in his own way, I think."

"What has he been trying to help you do?"

"He cares about you." She stuck out her chin, hardening her soft features, but not making them cold like Rose. Natalie's face glowed with discovery and excitement. She'd figured me out, and to her that meant solving a complex riddle and nothing more. "And I think he wants you to be happy," she added softly, her voice cracking.

Natalie's cheeks flushed a luscious rose shade. I could see where her bathing suit straps had been tied around her neck from tan lines that showed she'd found time to be outside and hadn't spent every minute of the last two days closed in her room online conducting some illusive investigation. But her words hit me, and I returned my attention to her face.

"Jonah is a good man," I said simply. It was time to cut to the chase. I knew from years of experience that Rose lied more often than she told the truth. But I believed I'd see a lie in Natalie, too. "Why did you come to the island, Natalie?"

She blinked, and I prayed her innocent look of confusion was sincere.

"I found a brochure for this place in a taxi a month or so back and I guess I wanted an adventure." She didn't add to her story and waited out the silence while I stared at her. Then, nibbling her lower lip again, she breathed deeply and searched my face. "Did you come here to hide so that no one could force you to use your discovery in ways you didn't want to?" she whispered.

"I didn't come here to hide." I didn't want to think about my past, but the only way I could learn Natalie's motives was to do just that. Worse yet, I didn't like the insinuation that I was hiding, which I'd now heard twice in one day. I wasn't some damned coward. "Coming here was an opportunity, a chance to advance my work."

"Without worrying that it would be taken away from you," she finished for me, nodding. "I understand, Malachi. No one wants to be controlled and told what they can and can't do, especially when it comes to unfolding their dream."

"You don't understand though. Paradise Island has been running smoothly for ten years. Rose inherited this island and with my help turned it into a lucrative business that she isn't going to allow to be compromised. For that matter, neither will I."

"And you think that I would do something to harm you?" she snapped, raising her voice. "Is that what you think, Malachi?"

"I don't know what to think, Natalie, which is why you're going to continue explaining yourself until I'm sure of your motives."

Her jaw dropped. "I don't have sex with men I don't care about."

"You had sex with Tomas and Nicolas."

She opened her mouth to say something and closed it again. "They don't count," she said, waving her hand dismissively. But then looking down and suddenly fidgeting with her fingers, she turned away from me again and walked over to the window, adjusting the wand so she could see outside better. "I don't know how to make you understand. When I found that brochure, it called out to me. Life was frustrating, unfulfilling, and I was dying for a way out. You don't know my life, Malachi. You don't know my family. There wasn't a way out—isn't a way out. But for a couple weeks I could escape."

She paused and looked down, not saying anything else. I forced myself to remain leaning against the door. The last thing I could allow was for our conversation to be interrupted. Although I didn't want to leave my new companions alone for too long, learning what Natalie was about mattered. I needed to know beyond any doubt that she wouldn't jeopardize my work, but more so, if I believed she had, I was prepared for the consequences I would have to take.

"The fact that you and I have slept together doesn't change the situation, Natalie," I said, keeping my emotions at bay. Goddamnit, I wanted to fuck her again. Every inch of my body craved taking the steps toward her and pulling her up against me, feeling her body next to mine. I wanted to ravish her until I had my fill. But taking that step could compromise myself more than she might possibly already have done on her own. I stayed put.

"You need to understand," she said, practically whispering, and continuing to look down at her hands with her back to me. "When I got here I did what was expected of me. I've always done what was expected of me. Always." She flung around, her eyes almost wild as too many emotions to decipher made them moist. "Do you understand what that kind of life is like? No one has ever asked what I wanted. I reached a point where I blindly followed the path I was pointed toward and hated every minute of it. But then I met you." She faltered, then lowered her head and cleared her throat, dabbing her eyes with her fingers and then looking up at me, the determination in her expression returned. "I don't know if you care, but I haven't had sex with either one of them since I met you."

"Good," I said before thinking about it.

She exhaled as if my admission to what she told me meant a lot to her. "Malachi, they're machines. Why do you hide from the world that the companions we pay so dearly for when we come here are machines?"

"That isn't my doing."

She stared at me. "You're still hiding. You've created something the world would fall at your feet to acknowledge and appreciate and you refuse to let anyone know. I spent hours online searching for information on you. And I guess I have my answers. But they don't make sense, Malachi. Are there charges against you? Would admitting you're here and the work you've done somehow bring you harm?"

I shook my head, knowing I couldn't make her understand. "It's not me I'm worried about," I admitted.

"You can patent your inventions. I'll help you." She suddenly sounded excited and took a step toward me. "No one will take your inventions away from you. I can write up the paperwork and make sure of it. Is that what you're scared of? Is that why you're hiding?"

"I'm not hiding!" I bellowed.

She reached for me and I crossed my arms, not wanting her touching me out of pity. I couldn't bear her thinking I wasn't the man that I was, and I didn't need her help. She was excited to learn the truth, and in fact, my hat was off to her for discovering what no other guest in ten years had figured out.

"You don't get it," she cried out, dropping her hand and glaring at me while her eyes welled with moisture again. "You've got the wrong opinion of me and what I want. I'm not a slut. I don't have sex with just anyone. I came here prepared for an adventure that I would remember for the rest of my mundane life. That's why I had sex with Nicolas and Tomas. But you were different. I researched you because I wanted to know more about you, not because of this island." She waved her hand around her but then turned and slapped my chest. "Move and let me out. If you think I'm out to destroy you, then I don't want to talk to you anymore."

"I can't let you leave, Natalie."

15

Natalie

"What do you mean, I can't leave?" As excited as I was to learn the truth, it terrified me too. But those emotions paled compared to the pain I felt over Malachi not trusting me. "What do you think I'm going to do?"

"I know that you aren't going to do anything," he said firmly.

"I'm glad to know you at least trust me on that one." I couldn't hide the hurt that seeped through my words. Closing my eyes for a moment, I fought to control my emotions. "I accept that you feel your life work has just been compromised," I said, fighting to keep calm and sound convincing. "And I know we've barely known each other a week," I added. I wouldn't cry. No matter the pain over realizing how badly I wanted to know this man better and realizing that learning the truth also meant he would push me away, he wouldn't see me make a fool of myself. "But I didn't fight to learn this about you to bring you any harm. I just wanted to know what was going on around here."

"Natalie, this knowledge puts your life in danger." He spoke so calmly that I couldn't look away when he stared down at me.

It was like looking into the eye of a storm, the calm before the explosion. "If anyone besides me learns that you know the companions aren't human . . ."

"Your companions in there know." I don't know why I added that and closed my mouth quickly. His words hit me at that moment and I tried to keep my heart from racing as fear gripped me. "What are you going to do, Malachi?"

"I'm not worried about my companions," he said. "None of them would ever do anything to harm me. And they've been ordered to protect you under all circumstances. I need to get back to them. They were just brought to life."

I almost corrected him and told him that they weren't alive, but I understood. In fact, knowing the truth and talking to him now helped me see how things were. These companions were like his children, and Malachi the mother of all of them. He would fight to the death to protect and defend them, and if that meant keeping his existence here on the island a secret and creating them without the world knowing about it, he would do it.

At the same time, I didn't miss how the glow in his eyes disappeared. I still didn't know what he meant when he said I couldn't leave but already I saw how stubborn and determined he was. What extreme would he go to in order to allow his companions to exist without being threatened?

I wasn't sure, but I knew I needed him to see I wasn't a threat.

"I'm sorry I said you were hiding," I said, wiping my damp palms down my dress and willing my heart to quit pounding so painfully hard in my chest. "I think I understand even more now. If I could grab hold of the life I wanted, I wouldn't let it go for anything. I envy you for living your dream."

"You're right. I won't let anything or anyone harm the companions, even if they didn't think they were causing harm." He almost looked sad when he gazed down at me. "They should be through with their tests by now."

"I'll come with you."

Malachi shook his head. "You want my trust. I'll give you more than I probably should." For the first time since we started talking, he touched me. I felt his large, warm hand cup my cheek and couldn't stop myself from tilting my head, leaning into his touch. He rubbed his thumb over my cheek. "Go back to the mansion. Don't let anyone see you leave here. You don't know how important this is. Go back there and don't come back here again."

"I want to see you," I said, surprising myself that I would open up to him when he obviously planned on shutting me out.

Which was why I probably didn't notice any sign of his next action before he did it. Malachi grabbed me, pulling me against him with enough force that all air swept out of my lungs. He leaned into me and forced me to bend backward as he held me securely in his arms and devoured my mouth. All thoughts drained from my brain and were replaced by one demanding urge to fuck him. With that one kiss, he turned me into a throbbing, overly sensitive nerve ending that craved his touch, required his attention, and ached to keep him by my side. I frantically thought of something to say that would convince him I should stay here.

My brain was mush when he let me up for air. All I did was stare into his smoldering gaze and sighed noticeably to see that it had returned. I reached for his face and caressed it, feeling at least a day's growth of facial hair rub roughly under my fingertips.

"Leave now, Natalie." His voice was gruff.

"Figure out a way to see me," I said, hoping I sounded firm and not like I was begging.

He didn't answer, and that hurt. In fact, as he stepped away from the door and then opened it, the amount of pain racking through my insides made it hard to move. I didn't want to leave without knowing that my actions hadn't ruined the first chance

I'd had in my life to spend time with a man who appealed to me, and not a man who appealed to my father.

Malachi slid his hand underneath my hair and gripped the back of my neck, then guided me down the hallway in the opposite direction of his lab where the companions were.

A rush of warm, saltwater air hit my face when we stepped outside. The doors barely closed behind us when Malachi pulled me close and then almost tripped me when he practically lifted me and put me on the other side of him. We stayed close to the building as he walked me to the back of the building. That's when I noticed several companions standing in the middle of the courtyard. If they saw Malachi, or both of us, they didn't give any indication.

"Would they not notice us?" I asked, wondering at the level of their programming.

He didn't answer until we were behind the building where the window was that I'd slid into earlier. "They would notice me. Hopefully they didn't see you. My companions aren't security guards. They won't harm anyone, or do anything unless instructed."

"I've noticed." I must have grumbled enough to cause him to pause and look down at me. He frowned as if I'd just insulted him, and I knew I needed to elaborate but worked to choose my words carefully. With every moment that we openly discussed his companions, I realized that Malachi held each one of them very close to his heart. Oddly enough it occurred to me that he'd make one hell of an awesome father. "What I meant," I began, still searching for how to explain to him about Nicolas and Tomas. "Nicolas and Tomas, although confident in their actions, immediately adjusted to what I wished if I didn't go along with how they started doing things."

"As they should," he said, but watched me so closely that I worried I would blush under his scrutiny. Not only were we discussing the quality of his companions' actions, but we were also talking about when I had sex with them.

I wanted to point out again that I hadn't fucked either of them after meeting Malachi, and that anything either of us did prior to meeting each other shouldn't be held against us. But then I reminded myself that he was sending me away, which meant there wasn't reason to defend a relationship that wasn't going to develop. Malachi was seeing to that.

"I don't think you're following me," I said, deciding I would be blunt and honest. Maybe it wouldn't be to my advantage, but Malachi had a right to receive honest feedback on his work, as well as constructive advice. "A lady, even an intelligent one who knows her mind and what she wants out of life, doesn't want a man who is submissive. At least I wouldn't," I added, feeling the impending red blotches that I feared would appear all over my face and neck any moment now. I exhaled and forced myself to continue. "My two guys were fine, until I met you. Even when we argue, I feel your passion and see desire in your eyes. And I know you sense the same in me. When you want something from me, you take it. Not because you are brutal, or inconsiderate of my feelings, but because you know my feelings. You are aggressive and can command a situation. Your companions can't do that. And please don't take this the wrong way, but that was a turnoff for me once I was with you."

We'd reached the almost hidden, rough path that I'd taken down the mountain. I'd discovered it after walking down half of the mountain through the underbrush and almost falling on my ass more than once. But when I found the path, coming here without being noticed had been surprisingly easy. Instead of sending me on my way though, Malachi started up the path alongside me, taking my hand and holding it tightly as we began up the incline together.

I wasn't going to question why he remained with me, but enjoyed the fact that he did. "I'm not a coward, Natalie," he said after we'd walked a short way in silence. I'd worried that I'd offended him with my honesty and was surprised when he spoke and changed the subject.

"I never thought you were," I told him.

He tightened my grip and pulled me up the first steep incline. "Coming here took more courage than I expect you to understand," he continued, turning when he reached the top and pulling me into his arms. He finally let go but still held my hand as we walked single file on the narrow path. "I had a good job in London and it appeared that the French government wouldn't pursue finding me and demand I return home."

"Changing your name probably helped," I added.

He didn't comment but continued with his story. "Devlin Products offered large grants for me to produce results that were easy to do. There wasn't stimulation. Possibly like you, I was bored with my work. But the pay was good and I lived well."

"What about your family?"

He ignored my question. "Rose Bontiki sent me a certified letter asking if I was interested in going in on a joint venture and asking for a personal meeting. I ignored the letter and three months later she arrived in London, this time seeking me out personally. I'll never forget that rainy night when she approached me in the parking lot where I worked. I was heading home for the day and thought she was insane to be seeking out a stranger at night in an unprotected parking lot."

"But you met with her."

"Yes," he said, acknowledging that I'd spoken for the first time since we'd started climbing the mountain. "I went to dinner with her and listened to her pitch. I was amazed at how much she knew about me and was intrigued by her proposition."

We reached another steep incline and Malachi took the wall of rocks with a few quick steps then turned around and reached for me. He grabbed me under my arms, lifting me and then placing me on the ground next to him. I held on to his shoulders and he didn't let go when I gripped his muscular body and stared at his brooding expression.

"Did you sleep with her?" I asked, practically whispering.

Something softened in his eyes. Maybe I was getting through that thick skull of his that in spite of the short amount of time we'd known each other, I wasn't a threat and didn't want to be returned, only for him to disappear from my life. I wouldn't think about what would happen in another week when I left the island, but I didn't want to go through the next week without spending time with him.

"No. My relationship with Rose has always been only about business," he said, and then lowered his head and kissed me.

It was brief, too brief, but when he spoke his lips brushed over mine, sending chills rushing over my flesh that left me far from cold.

"During that dinner meeting, she offered me half of the island, and profits of this place if I would come live here and help her establish the business."

"How did she know you could create companions if you hadn't done it yet?"

"I didn't move here believing I would create companions. The men you saw working in the warehouse, the Adams, were my first attempt. During that time, Rose hired companions and started inviting guests to stay at the mansion. The Adams were supposed to do the physical labor. And they did an incredible job. Rose saved hundreds of thousands of dollars thanks to the Adams. They finished building the mansion, Jonah's home, and my buildings. Plus they laid the paths that we use to drive around the island."

"When did you decide to start using them for companions?"

"After I was here a few years, I created the next group of companions. Nicolas and Tomas came out of that group."

That explained why they wouldn't share what their lives

were like before coming to the island. They didn't exist any-where else but here.

"Rose convinced me to let them work in the mansion, at first in the kitchen and doing housecleaning. They were all so convincing as humans that Rose didn't tell the guests they were androids. She put several of them into rotation as companions for guests without telling me. I found out after a month or so, but by then she'd already booked every room in the mansion and used the money to purchase new equipment for me to cre-ate more companions."

"Would it be so terrible to let your guests know that their companions are androids, or whatever you call them?"

Malachi stopped walking and glanced around us. Something dark passed over his expression and I couldn't label it. Frustra-tion, maybe contemplation, or possibly a mixture of both. I fol-lowed his gaze, taking in the thick rows of trees around us and then glanced up as a bird made a unique sound above us. All I saw was a flash of bright-colored feathers as it flew from a nearby tree away from us. I focused my attention on Malachi and caught him staring toward the ocean.

"I should have fought her on that," he said, sounding regret-ful. "For the first time in my life I was able to create the way I wanted to create, without the threat of my creation being taken from me the moment I got all the wrinkles out."

Malachi led the way off the path far enough that we soon stood in a narrow clearing. The ground ahead of us dropped down and when I stepped forward to see how far it went down, Malachi grabbed my shoulders and pulled me back. His hard, warm solid body pressed against my backside, and he ran his hands over my bare shoulders, caressing me and igniting a fire inside me that swelled and spread quickly.

"It's so beautiful here," I whispered, feeling like if I spoke too loudly I would ruin the magic that seemed at play here. I ached to know everything about Malachi, and for him to gain confidence in me so that he would open up to me. Something told me that he'd never done that with anyone before. "I can see how easy it would be to get lost in work you love while living here. You can almost believe the rest of the world doesn't exist."

He lowered his head so that his face was close to mine and when he spoke, his breath scalded my flesh. "Beauty isn't always what it appears to be," he whispered, while fingers moved down my front, making my nipples harden. I damn near trembled with the sexual craving that swept over me. His deep baritone did a number on my system. "Be very careful about what you think you might want. What you see as intelligence and beauty could be cloaking something much darker."

"I think I'm seeing the picture clearly," I told him, ignoring the chill of trepidation that rushed over me. I turned my head but was unable to adjust my body when he pressed his hands against me, his fingers grazing the swell of my breasts.

"What appears to be paradise, or a beautiful island, might simply be a volcano waiting to explode." His hands moved and he quit touching me.

Following him away from the cliff, I scowled, keeping up with him when he started down the path. "If you're trying to scare me away, then why are you staying with me instead of simply telling me to go back to the mansion and leaving it at that?"

"I'm not going with you to the mansion." Malachi slowed and then turned and reached for me, once again taking my hand. "I decided to walk with you for a while to make sure you understand the danger you've put yourself in. I'm not talking about legal ramifications, or the kind of danger that you know in your world." His grip on my hand tightened when he stopped and turned to face me. "This is the kind of danger that could cost you your life. People will kill for the knowledge that is now in your head. And now that you know, you will never be safe again."

I walked to the mansion alone, my knees wobbling enough that twice I parked my rear on stone benches and stared, not seeing the beauty around me for the first time. Malachi had hugged and kissed me when we reached the gardens, then turned and headed back, leaving me to go to the mansion alone as he promised. I didn't feel alone though. I felt haunted, nervous, almost scared. Malachi appeared content sharing more information with me about the companions, but at the same time stressed how my knowing changed everything. What exactly would change?

Would I not be allowed to leave the island? God! That thought alone almost made me sick. No one knew I was here and it would take a while to find someone to fly me off the island. I didn't know the name of the charter plane service that flew me here. And it could take a while to get someone to come get me. They could keep me here and who knew how long it would take for anyone to trace my whereabouts.

I left my room later that evening with Tomas and Nicolas on either side of me. The moment we stepped into the hallway, I could hear the music outside. A party was scheduled for a group of guests who would be leaving the island in the morning. I barely remembered showering and preparing to head down to the festivities, my mind still buzzing from my conversation with Malachi earlier.

The knowledge I now possessed would harm me only if others knew what I'd learned. That wasn't going to happen. I couldn't forget. I didn't want to forget. But I wanted to live. Maybe I didn't have the best life on the planet, but I could change that. Malachi had. I doubted I'd go to the extremes he did, that didn't seem to be my nature, but I could always try practicing law somewhere else. My family would disown me. Hopefully, though, they would eventually see that I was happy and therefore be happy for me. Hopefully.

In the meantime, I was a Green. If there was one thing I

could do it was appear to be having a blast at a party when in actuality I was miserable.

"There's no better party than one thrown on Paradise Island," Tomas whispered in my ear as he wrapped his arm around mine.

I looked up at his smiling face, knowing he'd never been to a party other than one on the island. But I smiled and allowed him to escort me outside while Nicolas held the door for us. "I can't wait. Look at everyone. We're missing all the fun."

Torches were burning throughout the gardens and tables lined both sides of the orchids that stayed in full bloom even though it was dark.

"Where would you like to sit?" Nicolas asked.

"Do you want to eat first?" Tomas asked.

Everything smelled wonderful but I seriously doubted I could eat a bite. "Let's go over by the pool," I suggested and then glanced at each of them, ready to ask if either was hungry. It hit me they probably didn't get hungry so I didn't say anything. They would just agree to whatever I suggested anyway.

"The pool sounds great," Nicolas said, rubbing my back.

"I didn't bring a suit, though." We entered the gate that surrounded the lit pool where a handful of people were already splashing in the water. "Let's sit here."

Tomas pulled the chair from the table I pointed to and held it while I sat. Immediately a waitress appeared, dressed in a short skirt similar to the loincloths my companions wore and a piece of material that barely covered her ample breasts.

"What can I get you to drink?" she asked, smiling at all of us.

I ordered for all of us and then leaned back, watching everyone play in the pool. It was time to play guess who's human and who wasn't. After an hour of small talk with Tomas and Nicolas, and the drinks loosening me up a bit, the pool started to look appealing.

"I think I'm going to get my bathing suit," I informed the two of them. "Stay here and save our table."

Both nodded amiably and stretched out in their chairs, sipping at bottles of beer and watching those already in the water. As I walked through the gardens toward the mansion, I spotted Rose with a Blue Tooth in her ear, the blue glow radiating against her thick black hair. When she spotted me I looked away, but couldn't help wondering who she was talking to. Was it Malachi?

He wouldn't tell her that I knew their secret, would he? Then I immediately wondered if anyone else might share with Rose that I'd been there. Malachi trusted his companions but they were machines. Could Rose get them to tell her what she wanted?

I held my stomach and hurried to the mansion, worry and panic threatening to make me sick.

I decided on the elevator and hurried down the second-floor hallway to my room, then slid my card to let myself in. My heart pounded in my chest when I dropped my bag on the bed and began searching for my suit. Malachi wouldn't tell Rose that he found me in the storage closet. I knew he wouldn't. But at the same time, he made it clear that nothing would come between him and his companions.

Maybe I was being a fool to believe that knowing a man barely a week and sleeping with him once would create any type of relationship. Malachi didn't have any reason to trust me. What was my word to him?

"Crap," I groaned, pulling my suit free from several pieces of underwear and then stripping out of my dress as I headed to the bathroom to grab a towel.

What if Malachi didn't say anything but his new companions did? Rose was very anxious to have them start working. Granted she didn't think much of them and possibly wouldn't seek them out for conversation or information, but what if they wanted to impress her? Tomas and Nicolas were always tripping over each other for my attention.

By the time I'd put my suit on, my palms were sweaty and I was shaking like a leaf. And all because I wanted to know answers to questions that people wouldn't give me.

"Someday you'll learn," I muttered, and turned to grab my bag. I put my key card in my purse and left my room.

Heading down the hallway, I glanced over the balcony as I walked to the elevator. Rose stood in the middle of the entryway looking up at me. The moment we made eye contact, she turned and stomped toward the back end of the mansion. I fought to keep from hyperventilating as I waited for the elevator.

The mixture of salt water and exotic flowers filled the air with a rich aroma that helped relax me. It was a warm night and there weren't any stars in the endless black sky. I stared up at it, deciding that heavy clouds meant there was probably a storm coming in.

I needed to relax. This was my vacation, damn it. An experience of a lifetime. Memories that would keep me going for the rest of my life. I hadn't planned on the memories being nightmares that would keep me up at night. Rose had stormed off when she saw me. That wasn't how someone behaved when she was out to get someone, it was how someone behaved when she didn't like someone.

So Rose didn't like me. I could live with that. Letting out a calming breath, I walked through the serene gardens. I was imagining a fiasco that hadn't even happened. Malachi said I possessed knowledge that could get me killed, but only if the wrong people knew I possessed that knowledge. I would be cool, remain relaxed and have fun with the evening. No one would be the wiser. I could take Malachi's secret to the grave.

It was my job to create my own memories. I was getting damned tired of someone else running my life. I reached the pool and opened the gate, letting myself in and managing a smile when Tomas and Nicolas noticed me and stood. I was in charge of my life, I was the one calling the shots, but up until now, I'd allowed others to manipulate my actions. First my parents, and now Malachi with his implications that discovering the truth about him put my life in danger. It was time I did what I wanted to do.

"What do you say we walk down to the beach?" I suggested.

"We can do that," Tomas said, reaching my side first.

"We got you a fresh drink," Nicolas offered, bringing me a fruity drink complete with an umbrella. "This way is the fastest," he said, slipping his arm around my waist and guiding me along the path.

I hadn't been to the beach yet and immediately wondered why not once we were walking on the warm sand and watching the dark water ripple against the shore. There were reclining chairs lined in a row with more torches that gave off a soft light.

"Do either of you swim?" I wasn't sure how wet androids could get but put my drink down on a stand next to a chair and then hurried toward the water. Kicking off my sandals, I splashed in the water.

Maybe it was the alcohol or maybe fear peaked inside me and finally released me from the stress I'd felt since being with Malachi. But running into the waves laughing and splashing was more therapeutic than anything else I could have thought to do. Although, I couldn't help but glance in the direction of any newcomer to the beach, wondering if each one might be Malachi.

Nicolas and Tomas never answered me about swimming, but at the same time didn't join me, instead holding our drinks and towels. I headed back to my chair, accepting the large towel Tomas wrapped around my shoulders, when a man approached me from the side. I jumped, startled when he stopped next to me and touched my arm.

"I didn't mean to startle you," he said. He had dark hair that was curly and wet and a finely chiseled face. His skin was tan, obviously from a tanning bed, and he was in incredible shape. "My name is James Martin. I couldn't help watching you enjoy the waves."

"Hi, it's nice to meet you." I'd reached my chair and sat down, taking my drink from Tomas and sucking up a good-sized swallow as I watched the man recline in the chair next to me. "Are you one of the guests, or do you work here?"

"I'm a guest, and I assume you are too. I'm from St. Louis, and you?"

"Chicago."

"We're practically neighbors." Even in the dark I could tell when a man looked interested. "Are you heading back to the mainland in the morning?"

"No. I'm staying here for another week."

"Oh?" He frowned, looking confused for a moment but then nodded. "Too bad. We might have been on the same flight. But we have tonight, right? I'm here over the weekend so maybe we can spend some time together."

"Sure." I wasn't sure why I allowed him to continue flirting with me. When a very pretty woman approached him from behind, and he waved her on and told her he'd return to the room later, I honestly wondered what he thought of me. This man didn't know the woman he just sent off wasn't human. Did he really think I would spend the evening with him knowing another woman waited for him back in his room? "I think I'll call it a night as well."

"Allow me to walk you to your room." He helped me to my feet and then pulled me into his arms. "Send your hired help away. I want to be alone with you," he whispered into my ear.

"You don't like your companion?" I asked, walking with him, but not sending Nicolas and Tomas away. As I suspected, they didn't look put out that another man escorted me along the path but dutifully walked behind the two of us.

"She's a gem. But there's something about enjoying the mystery of what might or might not happen in the evening. How do I say this?" He looked down at me and flashed a brilliant smile. "She's a sure thing and I don't know if you are."

"I'm not." I paused and stared up at his handsome features while he eyed Nicolas and Tomas standing now on either side of me. "James, I'm sure you're a very nice man, but I'm not the kind of woman . . ."

"Gentlemen," James said, interrupting me and focusing on the men on either side of me. "If you would excuse us for a moment, please."

The two of them nodded and walked away. It crossed my mind to call them back, but I was sure I could handle James alone.

"There isn't anything to say that they couldn't hear," I began.

"I don't think you're easy," he began, taking my arm and trying to lead me away from the mansion and the remaining guests lingering in the gardens. "But I would like to spend the evening with you. We can send our companions out of our rooms if we want."

"I don't want to send them away. And I don't see the point . . ."

"The point is I've been watching you since you arrived," James said, his grip on my arm tightening when I tried pulling free. "I happen to know you're with a very successful law firm."

"How do you know that?" I yanked free of his grip and then rubbed my arm where it stung from his hold on me. "And why have you been watching me?"

All the panic I'd managed to let go of earlier this evening came back with a vengeance and I took a step backward. James's expression relaxed noticeably and he held his hands out in a feeble attempt at looking harmless. He looked more like a slimeball to me.

"Forgive me for alarming you," he said, his tone suddenly sweeter than honey. He held his arm out, as if I would take it willingly, and turned to walk toward the mansion. "When a woman interests me, I research her. Maybe I'd do better to not tell her that. Obviously you see why I'm here. My pick-up lines are dismal at the most."

"I'd agree with you on that one."

"Is there a problem here?" Malachi interrupted as he appeared from behind James. "Natalie, I've been looking for you."

James got a strange look on his face as he stepped aside and made room for Malachi to take my arm.

"Have a good evening, James." I put my hand over Malachi's, letting James see that Malachi was someone I knew better than just casually.

"Very interesting. I see how it is," he said, and turned from us, heading toward the mansion.

Malachi kept a firm grip on me as he led us down the path, back toward the beach, and into the darkness where no one else was.

"How long were you listening?" I asked.

"Long enough." He didn't elaborate, nor did he sound pleased.

16

Malachi

I was so wound up after leaving the laboratory. My new companions tested off the scales. After sitting and talking to them, it was like being in a room with colleagues, people who understood what I said, and challenged me with their responses. It was exhilarating and I wanted to tell someone about it. I was in my golf cart and halfway to the mansion before it hit me I was seeking out Natalie. There wasn't anyone else I could share my excitement with.

"Malachi, where are we going?" Natalie hurried alongside me, her hand warm in mine.

I slowed, noticing when she spoke I was dragging her toward the beach. "I'll show you when we get there."

There wasn't anyone left on the beach, thank God, but still I kept us along the tree line, walking in the shadows. When we reached the cliffs I slowed even further and then pulled the flashlight out of my pocket.

"Malachi?" she questioned, gripping my hand harder but not trying to pull free.

"It's okay. It's your turn to trust me." I didn't look to see her expression but her silence was enough. She understood now the leap of faith she was asking of me earlier when she insisted I could trust her.

I helped her around the first rock and then turned on the light and flashed it ahead of me. Water splashed at our feet and I knew we were close.

"Be careful," I said unnecessarily. "The rocks are slippery and sharp. I don't have to tell you where one wrong step will take you."

"No, you don't." Her voice was tight behind me and she held on firmly, her smaller hand in mine. "Why are we climbing the cliff? If we fall . . . Malachi, those waves down there look really dangerous."

"They are but I've got you."

There was one place I could go and not be found. And right now, I wanted just a bit of alone time. It sucked I couldn't be seen with the woman I wanted to be with on my own damned island.

"We're here."

"Where are we?" Natalie grabbed my shirt when her foot slipped.

I turned and grabbed her and then lifted her around so that she faced me and then moved in on her, forcing her to step backward and into my cave.

"We're in my sanctuary." I flashed the light around us to show her.

"Oh, wow," she said, her hand on my chest as she glanced around us at the black rocks that provided a perfect hideaway. With the waves slapping the rocks outside the cave it would be hard for anyone to hear us. "Why did you bring me here?" she asked, returning her attention to me.

"So we wouldn't be bothered." I gripped her jaw and kissed her, showing her instead of telling her why I needed to be alone with her.

Hunger soared to dangerous levels inside me as I devoured her mouth. My need for her was so intense I almost staggered. Ever since this afternoon, sending her away, and knowing I scared her, I needed her back with me. As overwhelming as my day was with my new companions surpassing even my prognosis on how close to human they would act, Natalie never left my thoughts.

She tasted sweet, whatever alcoholic beverage she'd been drinking still fresh on her breath. It was strong, potent, and I felt the fumes from it and from the heat of her body tear through me, intoxicating me.

Lifting her as I continued kissing her, I situated myself on the smooth hard floor of my cave and adjusted her on my lap. I took her hand and moved it over my cock, showing her how much I needed her. She whimpered into my mouth. That was all I needed to know. I wouldn't try making love to her if she didn't want me to. Although there was little doubt that she needed this as much as I did.

"It might not be as comfortable as a bed," I whispered against her mouth.

"I'm good," she said, and ran her fingers along the length of my shaft.

"Yes, you are."

Her eyes opened and she smiled, the glow from the flashlight highlighting her cheekbones. "Let me show you how good I am," she said, licking her lips and moving her hands to my shirt.

She tugged until I let go of her, raised my arms, and allowed her to undress me. Natalie made good work of it, and I wouldn't question how much the alcohol in her system had an effect on her actions. I wanted this, and drunk or not, she was here, in my arms, touching me, kissing and nipping while caressing and exploring. Later I would think about the practicalities of spending more time with her. For now, I believed she wanted this as badly as I did and would give her what we both needed to have.

"Take your bathing suit off," I instructed when she'd managed to peel me out of my clothes. "I need to feel all of you when I make love to you."

Even in the darkness of the cave, her eyes appeared to glow from the flashlight when she met my gaze, holding it only for a second before obliging. She slid off my lap and stood in the small cave, reaching behind her and unhooking her bathing suit top. She dropped it next to her and then slid her thumbs under her bottoms, easing them down her legs. When she straightened I was eye to eye with the part of her that I needed on top of me, craved sinking deep inside of.

"Come here," I said, my voice gruff as I grabbed her hips and pulled her back into my lap. "Natalie," I said, but she found my mouth and kissed me.

She was right. There weren't words that needed to be said, not right now. Maybe there wouldn't ever need to be words. I wasn't sure what it was about her. A part of me was flattered that she'd dug deep enough to learn the truth about me. Granted, she would be better off if the facts had remained buried. But she knew, and she was here with me. For now, I would let it go at that.

Knowing we'd need the flashlight to return to the beach when we left the cave, I positioned it next to me and then turned it off. The two of us sunk into an inky world of blackness, so dark that it didn't matter if our eyes were open or closed.

"Malachi," she whispered, her tone urgent as her hands groped my arms and then my chest.

"I'm right here," I whispered. "Feel your way, sweetheart."

Natalie hummed, her lips brushing over mine before the kiss ended. She'd let her head fall back, although I only knew from brushing my fingertips over her jawbone and then down the narrow length of her neck. Her heart pulsed strong and solid as

I stroked her, and her soft breaths were like gentle caresses against my frazzled brain. Being with her now made me wonder how I endured years of having no one prior to meeting her.

I ran my hands over her breasts, feeling how hard her nipples were as they brushed against my palms. Then, running my hands down her waist, gripping her hips, I helped her straddle me. Immediately I felt how wet she was. I didn't have to help her further. Natalie adjusted herself over my cock and then slid down, taking me deep inside her.

"God, yes," she cried, slowly sinking down on me while her hands ran up my arms and then grabbed my shoulders.

I held her hips, keeping my eyes open although I couldn't see her at all in spite of how close we were to each other.

"This is so hot," she whispered, giving me a clue as to how far her face was from mine. "It's like without my eyes I can feel you so much better."

I would have loved to tell her I planned it this way, but she voiced her thoughts the same moment they came to me. "Eliminating one sense heightens the others. And darling, I love how you feel."

Again she hummed. Letting her run the show, move over me slowly at first and then building momentum, I kept a firm grip on her, drowning inside her.

"Why did you interrupt me when I was with that man?" she asked, panting as she spoke.

Her fingers pinched my shoulders and I felt her inner thighs quiver when she lifted herself off of me and then sheathed me again with her hot, soaked pussy.

"Were you enjoying his company?"

"Uh-uh," she said, her breathing coming hard. "That's not what I meant."

"I didn't want him touching you," I told her honestly. Not to mention he was a fucking slimeball treating her like that, but adding how much I instantly hated his guts for coming on to

Natalie would ruin the mood. And I was going to enjoy every minute of this.

"Thank you for saving me," she whispered and then brought her face to mine until our noses bumped in the darkness.

She found my mouth and impaled me with her tongue. I moved into her mouth, taking control of the kiss while grabbing her hair and angling her head so I could explore deeper. She made the most incredible sounds, humming and moaning at the same time as she slowed her pace and tortured me to the point where it took more effort to kiss her than I could bear. I wasn't ready to come yet.

"I wasn't saving you," I told her, moving my lips over hers as I spoke and loving the hell out of how soft they were. "Let's just say I was marking my territory."

She stilled over my cock while so many tiny muscles constricted around my shaft. I could feel her breath on my face while her fingers moved to my neck, and then my jaw. She touched my face, gently caressing me as if she could learn my facial expression and understand the meaning behind what I said without having to ask.

It would be mighty damned clever of her if she could, and would save me the effort of explaining what didn't make sense to me either. In a week she would be back in her own world— too far away for me to protect her. And I didn't want her to question that fact right now.

Adjusting my grip on her hips, I rammed her. She howled, scraping my face, but I didn't care. Doing it again, I took over fucking her. I thrust deep, hard, grunting as I gave her all I had and felt her open for me, and then immediately constrict around me like she would suck the life right out of me without asking.

"That's it, sweetheart. All of it. Now," I grunted, thrusting my hips upward and feeling her soft thighs slap against mine as I buried my cock deep inside her drenched heat. "You feel so goddamned good," I growled, as my balls tightened with the pressure that quickly moved beyond my controlling it. "So damned good," I muttered, giving way and feeling more than a physical release when I came.

"You're amazing," I whispered, wrapping my arms around her when she finished with me and collapsed in my arms. "Now to get you back without being seen."

She didn't lift her head, but kept it cradled on my shoulder. "Not yet. This feels good."

It felt more than good, holding her naked in my arms. Her heart pounded against my chest, her breasts were smooth and round, and her skin moist with a sheen of sweat as she cuddled closer and relaxed.

"I wish you could have seen the six of them today," I said, burying my nose in her brown hair. Running my finger up her spine I then reached for the fancy hair clasp and released it, setting her locks free. "They aced every test I gave them and even challenged me on a few of the answers. I swear we spent several hours discussing so many different topics."

She lifted her head and I could feel her trying to see me in the darkness. "Why are you telling me this?" she whispered. Her hand moved down my body until I felt her reach for the flashlight. In the next second the beam flashed off the wall behind her as she held it backward.

The immediate light where before it was darker than night made us both squint.

I met her gaze, still feeling her muscles quiver around my dick as it remained semihard inside her. "Even after they finished all the standard tests that I always put new companions through, I knew in my heart I really hadn't pushed them. The new chip I installed in them allows them to feel. I wasn't sure if it would happen like this, but I thought maybe when we feel, we crave processing information and running with it. Natalie, that's what they're doing. Any knowledge I gave them, they processed, accepted, or questioned. Hell, they've already found numerous faults and contradictions while studying world history and the political evolution of several countries."

"I'm not surprised," she said dryly, still searching my face. "You're cool with me knowing about the companions now?"

"No," I told her honestly. "It terrifies the hell out of me when I realize what could happen to you with this knowledge in your head."

She shook her head slowly, looking sad all of a sudden. "Nothing will happen to me with this knowledge in my head, because I won't tell anyone. That isn't how I am, Malachi. You intrigued me. All my life I've dealt with an overbearing father who steered me away from any man I found interesting and pushed me toward men who were lacking a single drop of testosterone."

She made a face that was impossible not to smile at. "I seriously doubt I would fall under the criteria of what your father is looking for."

She shrugged. "You've got money."

I brushed her hair from her face with my fingers. "It's more than just money, though. Your father wants a name. He wants someone respectable who is good enough for his daughter. I'm willing to bet that any connection he would manage to associate with my name would give him a heart attack."

When she laughed it echoed in the small cave and made her muscles constrict around me until I was hard as steel once again. I tightened my grip on her waist, holding her in place while my expression caused her to sober.

"This is my life, not his," she whispered, and leaned forward to kiss me.

"I understand," I told her, made love to her again, unable to do anything else.

The longer both of us were gone the more danger I put Natalie in. I hated making quick work of it. More than anything I wanted to make love to her all night long, this time with light to watch how fucking sexy she was when she came. I wanted to take her home with me and wake up with her in the morning. I wanted to show off the new companions and my accomplishments with her by my side.

"Your father might have a problem," I said, and this time held her in place, thrusting deep inside her. "He's going to have a hell of a time finding a man good enough for you."

Natalie blushed, biting her lower lip, which I guessed was to hold back whatever response came to mind. I imagined a little girl, so willful and intelligent, but incapable of hiding her emotions when color would rise so beautifully to her face with her feelings. That's when I caught Natalie watching me intently, seeming to stare deep enough into my gaze to see my thoughts. And goddamn, what the fuck was I thinking anyway—having children with Natalie.

"Maybe I should save him the trouble," she whispered, but then closed her eyes, as if she could prevent hearing my response if she lost herself in our lovemaking.

And maybe I would save her old man the trouble, not that I didn't doubt for a minute that claiming his daughter would probably bring me more trouble than I needed.

When she stiffened, pushed over the edge once again, I continued driving deeper and deeper drowning in her cream, and finally losing myself to her once again.

The cold night air, thick with salt water, clung to my body but did little to soothe the heat still tearing me apart inside. I ran my hand down her back, soothing her while she fought to catch her breath. Damp curls clung to her cheek when she looked at me and blew out a breath.

"Sitting on your lap can be dangerous," she said, her voice husky.

"A lot of things about me are dangerous." I lifted her, hating to leave the warmth from being inside her but knowing I couldn't risk more time alone with her, especially with no one knowing where I was.

She didn't say anything and we dressed in silence, but she frowned as she stared ahead of her and I could only guess where her mind headed.

"You said you understood," she said, finally looking at me. "Your father pressed you to do things you didn't want to do?" The way she looked at me made me fear I'd already revealed more of the answer than I cared for her to see. She searched my face and then sighed. "He wanted something for you that you didn't want."

"Something like that." I didn't want to talk about my father.

"You've never mended bridges with him?"

"No." I'd sought her out to discuss the success of my day, not the failures of my past. "I'll walk you back to the gardens."

I should have slept like a baby, but I was stiff when I woke up, and dreams throughout the night unnerved me. Fragments from my past, my father's determined and disapproving scowl, along with my own stubborn willfulness to take my experiments in the direction I wanted them to go, mixed with current events. Everything from the island to the new companions and of course Natalie preoccupied my brain and left me feeling distracted as I started my day.

Traipsing barefoot to my desk, I made coffee and then walked over to the large windows overlooking the courtyard below. The Adams were dutifully working in the warehouse and a few of the other companions walked out of the dormitory across from the warehouse. I watched two of the new companions leave my building and head over to parked golf carts. After speaking with the older companions briefly, they all piled in the golf carts and headed toward the wide sidewalk that led to the cobblestone paths and the mansion. I hadn't authorized the new companions leaving yet.

That thought barely had time to register when I realized that my new companions were driving. I didn't teach them to do that. Yet they took off in the golf carts as if they drove them every day. The oddest sensation that I was a king looking down at my subjects created a very uncomfortable knot in my gut.

"Coffee," I growled, turning from the window and staring at the coffeemaker while the black brew slowly appeared in the glass pot.

By the time I headed outside, the morning sun was taking the dampness out of the air. "Did Rebecca and Bruce say where they were going?" I asked Pierre, one of my oldest companions who was in charge of overseeing the Adams.

"No," Pierre said, turning to face me and stared with his nonblinking blue eyes. Although it hadn't been my intention at the time, Pierre always reminded me of a life-size Ken doll, with his not quite real looking brown hair that was parted on the side and waved over one eyebrow. "Maybe you could ask Samuel though."

I sipped my coffee and then almost choked on it when Pierre made the suggestion. The two companions I made after the Adams were a simple program, capable of answering questions with a yes or a no, but not of offering advice, or suggesting a way to gain my answer if they didn't know it.

"Pierre," I said, coughing to clear my throat and then staring at him. "Has someone tampered with your programming?"

"I don't understand," he said, frowning.

Backing away from him, I damn near stumbled as I headed across the courtyard to the laboratory. Pierre should have said yes or no, not, "I don't understand." Chills rushed over my skin and I wondered if possibly I were still sleeping and this was yet another unnerving dream.

By the time I reached my small office where I'd taken Natalie yesterday, I needed more coffee.

"Good morning, Malachi," Samuel said, looking up from my computer in my office and smiling at me. "Coffee is brewing in the laboratory. Honestly, though, I don't see why you like it so much." He made a face at me and returned to whatever it was he was doing at my computer.

He shouldn't be doing anything on my computer. I didn't tell him to do anything. Instead of explaining the importance of coffee, I turned and headed to the lab then poured myself a cup from the full pot. Whoever brewed it did a pretty good job and I sipped greedily while heading back to my office.

"What are you doing?" I asked, moving in behind him and immediately recognizing the file he'd opened. "And how did you get the password for that program?"

Samuel smiled again, looking like I'd just sang his praises. "It wasn't hard to figure out. Yesterday when we were discussing family trees, you told me your first dog's name was Pluto. Jonah's dog is named after him. You really should create different passwords for each program, Malachi. Someone who shouldn't be in your files could access them."

"Apparently," I said, leaning against the table next to the computer stand and watching Samuel enter the notes that I'd taken yesterday and planned on entering this morning. "Where are Bruce and Rebecca headed?"

"Rose insisted the new companions start working today," Samuel said, although he didn't stop typing while he spoke. "I thought those two might appease her until you woke up." He finally did stop and look up at me. "I can send more if you think they're ready."

"Those two are fine for now."

Samuel nodded and returned his attention to his task.

"What did you do to Pierre?"

"Pretty impressive, huh?" Samuel said, typing so fast that I could barely see his fingers as they flew over the keyboard. "This latest chip that you installed in us can be modified. Obviously his circuits wouldn't be able to handle the technology I'm using, but I'll pull up my notes for you here in a minute. Let you take a look. By the way, where were you last night? I couldn't locate you or I would have shown you the results immediately after I installed the new program in him. His work efficiency is up over 50 percent."

I stared at Samuel. "The programming installed in you doesn't allow alteration of programs that you aren't currently using."

Samuel didn't stop typing until he reached the end of my notes and then lifted the paper on my legal pad, confirming there weren't any more notes and then dropped it. He moved the chair, turning so he faced me and leaned back, stretching out his long legs and crossing one foot over the other. Clasping his hands behind his head, he grinned up at me while his blue eyes flashed so brightly they were the only thing about him that suggested something more than human.

"Would you like to see the adjustments I made to your programming?" he asked. "You did an incredible job, Malachi. Amazing actually, since your process levels don't match mine."

I fought the urge to remain quiet, hear him out. The pride I'd felt yesterday and this morning seemed to teeter as I listened. I should be angry, but that wasn't what I felt. Instead, it was almost like my defenses were up. No one messed with my companions—not even my companions.

"You don't have my permission to alter my programs, Samuel," I said, remaining calm. "Get up. Let me see what you've done."

Instead of moving out of the chair, he turned around again, grabbing the mouse and clicking out of the program he'd been using and then reached for my laptop. He sighed when the computer didn't move as quickly as he wished. Before I could follow what he was doing with my eyes, the printer hummed to life and began printing. Samuel clicked out of the program and returned to the desktop.

"Rose asked to speak with you as soon as you were awake. Why don't you take this and read it over? I'll have one of the Adams bring around a golf cart for you."

"Slow down, Samuel," I said, making myself smile and relax while gripping his shoulder. "You're dealing with a mere mortal here, and one who hasn't had his caffeine kick in yet. I'm not going anywhere, and neither are you. Sit. Tell me what all you've done while I slept."

"You don't trust me?" he asked, and looked hurt.

There wasn't a wash of pride this time when I stared at such human emotions easily read on his face. Instead, the oddest sensation that I was being played, offered the emotion I would most easily respond to, hit me like a punch to the gut, and I didn't like it.

"From now on you won't implement any changes without my consent." I watched him nod once but still felt that peculiar twist in my gut that Samuel might not listen to me. I needed to hear him out though, and then decide what I would do with him before my newest companion started revamping my entire system. "Show me everything you've done and spare no detail."

I listened while Samuel explained what he'd done to my programming, not only to Pierre, but also in his own programming. Intrigued, I sat there with him for the next hour, not even bothering to get up for more coffee, and discussed programming with my own creation.

"You're amazing," I said, realizing how dried out I was suddenly and standing to refill my cup. "However, the Adams aren't compatible for this programming. There's no way with their existing database that we can upgrade them as you suggest."

"By upgrading a few of your older models, they can handle the warehouse work and do the job faster than the Adams."

Samuel followed me to the lab and stood next to me while I re-filled my cup. "There's no reason to keep them in service."

I stared at my cup after filling it. The Adams were my first attempt at imitating life. Shutting them down just seemed wrong.

"Why does that bother you?" Samuel looked confused.

"They were my first," I said, and thought of how to explain the emotion of loss to him. He watched me and I could tell he was like a sponge, anxious to learn and process all information around him. "It's okay, though. You're right. Pierre can handle their workload and I can put John with him. I'll put the Adams in storage until I have time to mess with their programming and see if they can be upgraded."

"They can't."

I shook my head at Samuel. "Never say can't, my friend. Be-sides, I'd like to come to that conclusion myself."

Samuel looked contemplative but didn't say anything. I headed out of the laboratory and back to the office with him at my heels. Then sitting, finally, at my own computer, I cleared the screen and clicked on the icon that held my notes and pro-grams for the companions. A box popped up indicating that I enter a password.

"The password is Elijah."

"Elijah?" I asked, frowning when I turned to look at him. "Why did you password protect my files? And why Elijah?"

"If you gave me a middle name, it would be Elijah, right?" Samuel beamed like he'd just discovered the secret to life. "You did name me after your grandfather. Elijah was his middle name, so I figured it would be mine also. As for the password itself, in a way, they aren't just your files. They're our files. And no of-fense, I really don't want anyone knowing how I tick."

"Unbelievable," I muttered, turning back to the screen.

"You never did say where you were last night."

"Top secret, classified information." I typed in the password and then clicked on the file that held my notes.

"You were with Natalie."

I didn't bother looking up but focused on the notes Samuel typed in for me. Then glancing at my legal pad still sitting next to the computer, I read over my handwritten notes. Samuel had made some changes.

"Why is she a secret? Is it wrong for someone to mean something to you?"

"No, of course not. In fact, usually it's very right."

"Then why the secrecy?"

I sat back, wondering for a moment if he persisted with this conversation to distract me from the alteration of my notes. On more than one page, I noticed he'd edited my notes. Fortunately, they were all backed up to disc. Sometime I'd explain to him the harm in altering how history is recorded. But then pulling my attention from the monitor and focusing on him for a moment, I'd noticed he'd reclined on the table in the exact positioning that I had when we were in here a few minutes ago. The overwhelming sensation that my son sat facing me, imitating his father, and trying to learn to be just like his old man damn near distracted me from the conversation. Once I ached to be just like my father. Now I pitied his narrow-minded attitude.

"It's not secrecy, Samuel. It's more that I want my privacy and don't want everyone knowing what I'm doing when I decide to take some much needed downtime."

He nodded, appearing to accept what I said without questioning it. I turned back to my notes.

"Did you fuck her?"

"Samuel," I yelled, glaring at him. "That is none of your goddamned business."

"Okay," he said, not appearing riled at all by my outburst. "What is it like to fuck?"

Dear Lord. I did have a son. But unlike any other father on this planet, my answer would differ.

"You'll find out very soon. As far as I'm concerned, you're ready to go to the mansion."

"I'm not sure." Samuel rubbed his chin and stared at me with those bright, intense eyes. "I don't know that I want to be so distracted by a woman like you are by Natalie."

"What makes you think I'm distracted?"

"You're comparing your notes from yesterday to those you wrote down last night and growing frustrated because they don't match." He pointed at the computer.

I jerked my head to the screen, and then down at the notes. "Crap," I muttered. Samuel was right. Closing the file I had opened, I then went in and opened the correct file. Samuel was more to me than just programming and circuits, though. He was making that more than clear to me the longer we sat here. I owed him an explanation, but damned if I knew the right thing to say. "When you are a companion to a guest, it isn't like what you're seeing between me and Natalie."

"Because you aren't her companion?"

"It's more than that. I didn't want to get to know Natalie. In fact, I did everything I could to scare her away."

"Do you want me to get rid of her?"

"No," I bellowed, turning on him fiercely. "You will never harm her. Do you understand?"

"Clearly." Samuel nodded slowly. "About the not harming part. The rest of it I don't think I've processed yet."

"Neither have I," I admitted. "And don't say processed. Say that you don't understand it yet. That makes you sound more human."

He nodded but didn't say anything, watching me intently until I continued. "Samuel, I feel something for her that I tried not to feel, but I couldn't prevent. She makes me happy," I said finally when I couldn't manage to explain what it was about Natalie that made me seek her out when I knew damned well that doing so quite possibly could cause both of us more trouble.

"Do you love her?" He asked calmly, his expression the same as it had been throughout our conversation. There wasn't any way he could understand the seriousness of his question.

"That isn't normally a question one man asks another man, Samuel," I said, remaining patient with him although the conversation was irritating me. I didn't want to think about how I felt about Natalie. "Honestly, it doesn't matter how I feel about her. In another week she will leave the island and you and I will continue to live here."

"That makes you sad." Samuel was quiet for a minute.

I took advantage of his silence and read what he'd typed into my file, which did indeed match my notes. Then minimizing the file, I stared at my desktop, realizing the work I'd come over here to do was already done. I needed something to occupy my thoughts so I wouldn't dwell on the accuracy of Samuel's observation concerning Natalie. In eight days, she would be gone. That was the last thing I wanted to think about.

"There are quite a few scenarios I can reference from classic literature, as well as movie clips I've seen so far online," Samuel began.

"What?" I frowned and looked over at him.

Samuel tapped his finger against his lips and looked at the wall behind me. When I questioned him, his attention snapped to me and he smiled.

"I know, a romantic evening will make you happy." His grin broadened. "We will prepare a candlelight dinner for you and Natalie. How does tomorrow night sound?"

17

Natalie

Malachi's expression seemed exceptionally dark as I stared across the small table. Tall candles flickered between us, and I honestly wasn't sure I'd ever enjoyed better food. Several companions that Malachi introduced proudly served us, and halfway through the meal he informed me it had been one of his new companions who suggested our romantic meal by the beach.

"This was wonderful," I told the young lady who cleared our table.

A young man, whose freckles and impish green eyes added to his youthful, roguish appearance, appeared after the dishes were cleared and poured wine.

"I don't see any of you in them," I mused after the young man left us.

"The six are completely unique," he told me, but didn't elaborate, instead he lifted his wineglass. "Here's to ..." He hesitated, staring deep into my eyes while our glasses clinked quietly against each other.

I saw a bit of Tomas and Nicolas in him. Something around

the eyes and the way Malachi held his head reminded me of both of them.

"Here's to trust and learning about each other," I offered.

"To trust, and knowing each other," he said, and then brought his glass to his lips and sipped, without taking his gaze from mine.

I could drown in him, in the good wine, the candles, all of it was so damned perfect. "This seems more a fantasy than the times I spent with Tomas and Nicolas," I murmured.

"Why do you say that?" Something tensed in his face, and the way he pressed his lips into a flat line made him look very determined, if not displeased.

I guessed I'd upset him by mentioning the men I'd been sleeping with. "Possibly because I wish this were real," I admitted quietly. There wasn't anything to wish for with my companions. Although lately I wished I could have my room to myself.

"This is real, Natalie," he said, and then pushed his chair back and set his glass on the table. Reaching for me, he took my glass from my hand and set it with his. "Let's walk along the beach."

I fell into stride alongside him, and Malachi put his arm around me, pulling me close. The warmth from his body made the cool breeze coming in off the ocean tolerable. And after walking in silence until we reached the steps that led down to the sand, every inch of me tingled with anticipation.

"Malachi, where are you going?" The urgent question came from one of the companions.

I turned along with Malachi and saw the young man who'd poured our wine and another man hurry toward us. Their expressions were stricken with concern and something that looked like panic.

"Where are you going?" The blond man I hadn't seen before

stopped when he was close enough to take Malachi's arm. "You shouldn't wander in the dark. It isn't safe."

The other man took my arm and started dragging me back up the steps.

"Malachi," I complained.

"Let go of her, now!" Malachi's firm tone made me jump but they let go of both of us. Malachi ran his hand through his hair, leaving it tousled when he scowled at his companions. "We're fine. We're going for a walk."

"I'll come with you," the blond suggested.

"Alone, Samuel," Malachi stressed. "Natalie and I are taking a walk alone."

Samuel looked stricken and then frowned, looking at me as if I might be the cause of taking Malachi away in the dark. His intense blue eyes were unnerving and I looked away first, turning my attention to Malachi. For some reason, Samuel gave me the creeps.

"How long will you be gone?" Samuel asked, his handsome features and perfectly shaped body making him the best looking companion that I'd seen so far. Although, the way he slowly put his hands on his hips as if he were the parent demanding to know when our date would end almost made me wonder if he were really a companion. He didn't behave at all like Nicolas and Tomas. They were eager to please and never once questioned that any decision I made might not be right. "It would also be wise if you informed me of the direction you will be walking," he added.

"Go clean up and then head to your rooms. We don't need a babysitter." Malachi sounded stern.

Samuel turned his attention to Malachi and for a moment looked like he might argue. Then without saying anything, he turned, and when he did, the other companion followed suit.

"Samuel," Malachi called to him.

Samuel turned. Maybe it was the dark shadows that made me misread his facial expression, but he looked pissed as hell.

"Remember what I told you," Malachi said in a low, commanding baritone, making it sound like a warning.

It was a tone I hadn't heard from Malachi before and I stared from one man to the other, swearing I sensed a testosterone battle at play here. Which would be impossible since Samuel didn't have testosterone. There was tension in the air though and it didn't appear to be coming completely from Malachi.

"I remember," he said and then turned and walked back up the path with the other companion at his side.

"What did you tell him?" I asked.

Malachi once again pulled me against him, quickly warding off the chill of the night. "That under no circumstances is he to tell anyone that you and I are together."

I looked up at him but he focused ahead of us, his expression unreadable. "I guess that's for the best."

He continued staring ahead, and kept the pace slow, probably for my benefit since my legs were so much shorter than his.

"It's not how I'd like it to be," he said finally. "You accused me of hiding, and seeing you secretly makes me feel you're right."

"It doesn't matter," I said quickly, rubbing his forearm and searching for something to say to pull him out of his brooding state. It occurred to me to mention how different Samuel was compared to Nicolas and Tomas but something told me that would upset Malachi further. If there were problems with his new companions, he wouldn't want to discuss that with me. "Just spending time with you is great. In a week I'll be heading back to Chicago anyway."

"Is there anyone waiting for you there?"

His question surprised me. "No. I thought you knew that. There isn't anyone."

"You've mentioned several times that your father tries to

find men for you. I wasn't sure," he said, and rubbed his thumb over my shoulder.

"I'm not a cheater," I told him, feeling like I should be offended, at least a bit. "If I had a boyfriend, I wouldn't have come here."

He nodded once, slowing the pace more until he stopped. The moon was full and glowed over the ocean, creating a surreal atmosphere that was breathtaking. I snuggled into Malachi, sighing, and wishing time would just stop for a while.

"Tell me about your work," he suggested.

"What do you want to know?"

"What do you do every day?"

"Nothing as exciting as what you do." I laughed and admitted to a bit of envy that he was living out his dream. "For the most part I handle cases that never go to court. I don't get the good cases, even when I ask. My father doesn't want me buried in my work. He feels it robs me of time to socialize and be seen in the right circles."

"But he must pay you well." His fingers traced my spine, giving me chills. "Or is that too personal?"

"I live in my parent's summer cottage, and so have no mortgage or utilities to worry about. My paycheck is more than I deserve for what I do but nothing compared to what I could earn if I worked somewhere else."

"Then why don't you work somewhere else?"

"The thought's crossed my mind." I relaxed against his powerful body and stared out at the waves that rippled toward us. At that moment, everything seemed so perfect. "I've done some pro bono work at the legal aid office," I offered. His arms tightened around me and we shifted so that my back pressed against him. He rested his head on top of mine and grunted, which I guessed meant for me to continue. "I really enjoyed that, fighting to help people whose rights were being stripped from them.

There wasn't any money in it, but I felt like I was doing what I was supposed to be doing, if that makes sense."

"Yup. It does." He shifted again, and we walked alongside the waves that fought to reach us as they raced up the beach and then receded just before soaking our feet. When we neared the cliffs he released me and then slid his hand around mine. "Don't worry. I'm not taking you to another cave."

"I'm not worried. Tonight is about trust, right?"

"And us," he added.

I loved how that sounded. And as my heart skipped a beat, I fought to keep from getting too excited that there could be an us. "Yes," I said, clamping down on my emotions but not quickly enough to keep the pain from swelling in my chest. "Although us is just for now, here on the island. After next week we probably won't see each other again."

Malachi stopped and grabbed me, his actions turning rough for a moment as he lifted me off the ground and then wrapped his arms around me, capturing my mouth. His kiss was demanding, aggressive, and turned my world upside down.

"Never say never," he growled into my mouth and then lowered me to the ground. His hand slid under my shirt and slipped my bra over my breast. He pinched my nipple hard enough to send a rush of electrical currents straight down my center until they exploded between my legs. "Is this just sex, Natalie?"

"God! God," I cried, turning my head sideways in the sand and not caring that so many granules sunk into my hair. "It doesn't feel like it is," I confessed.

"Good. Because it isn't." Once again he filled my mouth with his tongue, his hands undressing me while he feasted.

I couldn't dwell on his words. It was too painful to let myself go there. Instead I explored his body, moving my fingers under his shirt and then tangling them in the many tiny coarse curls that spread over his chest. I'd never known a man so perfect and so determined to keep me by his side. Malachi made me feel special, wanted, and so sexy.

I arched my back off the ground when he moved his fingers between my legs. "Damn, you're wet," he growled, and then lowered his mouth to my breast.

I dragged my fingers through his thick hair while he sucked on first one and then the other breast and would have held his head in that spot forever if I could. When I opened my eyes and stared at the black sky stretching forever overhead and the countless stars that blinked brightly at me, I couldn't stop my heart from wishing that this could last forever.

For the first time in my life I'd met a man that I really wanted. Malachi was perfect in every way. From his incredible good looks, to his intelligence and mysterious nature, every bit of him appealed to me. I couldn't imagine how we could continue any kind of relationship from damn near opposite sides of the world, and that knowledge caused the pain to constrict around my heart until I could hardly breathe.

Malachi moved lower and his hair slipped through my fingers. When I realized where he was headed, I stared at him, wide-eyed, feeling something close to an out of body experience as he spread my legs. But when he ran his tongue over my shaved flesh, I jumped, scratching at the sand, and cried out.

"Malachi," I wailed, reaching for him.

He growled against my soaked skin, dipping his tongue inside me and then slowly devouring me. There wasn't any holding on. As good as he was at fucking me, his skills in this department took me over the edge faster than I ever imagined I could go. When I cried out again, he held my hips firmly, continuing to feast upon me until I was sure I would pass out.

I heard myself yell his name, but my release came so hard, and with so much fury, that the ringing in my ears drowned out the sound of my voice. Every inch of me throbbed when he hovered over me and eased inside.

I couldn't say how long we made love on the beach, but I knew without a doubt as he pulled me on top of him after we finished that my world had changed. So many emotions ransacked my body that I didn't know whether to laugh or cry.

Never say never, I thought to myself, and listened to the solid rhythm of his heart pound a steady rhythm to my mantra.

"We can't go back like this," Malachi decided as he pulled me to my feet a few minutes later. "What do you say to a shower?"

"A shower?" I watched him gather our clothes and then guide me across the beach, both of us naked. "Where are we going? What if someone sees us?"

"Afraid of an adventure?" he asked, glancing down at me. Mischief danced in his eyes and I decided he had to be the most well-rounded man I'd ever met. I'd never known anyone who could go from brooding and almost sullen, to looking like he was ready to pull a good prank and enjoy every minute of it.

"You're asking *me* that?" I challenged, picking up the pace and forcing myself to smile at him. "You're talking to the lady who put her life in danger out of an incredible sense of curiosity."

"This is true," he said. "Come on."

He didn't hold my hand this time but carried our clothes as he walked ahead of me up a slight incline and around a wall of rocks. I focused on buns of steel and how muscles flexed and stretched in his powerful legs as I followed. The sound of rushing water finally managed to pull my gaze away from my perfect view.

"Oh, my," I breathed and watched Malachi put our clothes down and then step into a pool of clear water. A waterfall tumbled off the rock, creating the perfect outdoor shower. "Wait for me," I said, reaching for him as I gingerly stepped into the water.

Malachi took my hand and held on as I stepped over the slippery rocks and then wrapped his arms around me. Together, we moved under the spray of fresh water that immediately soaked my hair and body. I closed my eyes, turning slowly until I was sure all the sand was washed from my skin. Once we were clean, we moved to a large smooth rock and sat naked next to each other, staring out at the dark sea, while we dried our bodies in the moonlight.

It was the best date I'd been on in my entire life. I hated entering my quiet, dark room later that night, wishing more than anything I could have spent the night with Malachi. He didn't offer to have me stay over, and I knew, although I didn't like it, that it would create more trouble than we were already causing for ourselves if I did.

Climbing into bed between Nicolas and Tomas seemed wrong. I felt like I was cheating on Malachi by sleeping with them. I procrastinated while they stumbled over each other to try and take care of me.

"I think I'm just going to relax in the chair for a while," I told them, sitting quickly and then pulling my legs up against my chest. I'd put on my sweats in the bathroom and stared at my bare toes, knowing both of them stared at me. "You two can go to bed," I said weakly.

"Is everything okay?" Tomas asked, sitting on the edge of the bed and facing me. "If you don't feel well we can get a doctor for you."

I remembered overhearing Jonah tell Rose how he took medicine to a guest with a cold after being out all night and wondered what doctor Tomas referred to.

"I'm not sick." At least not the kind of sick that a doctor could fix. "Honestly, and please don't be offended, I wish I could be alone for a while."

"What's wrong, Natalie?" Nicolas's deep baritone and the sincerity of his voice reminded me of Malachi.

I didn't want to look at either one of them. I shouldn't feel this way. They were Malachi's creations, a part of him. And I was starting to believe they meant as much to him, if not more, than I did.

"Nothing's wrong." I didn't sound convincing even to myself.

Tomas reached out and touched my foot. "Something isn't right. You can talk to us, you know. I don't understand why you want to be alone when you're hardly ever around us," he said.

When I looked at him, and then glanced over at Nicolas who stood at the end of the bed, it was hard to keep back the tears. I could see Malachi in both of them. As much as I should treasure these two since they were his creations, all I wanted was for them to go away.

"That isn't true." I shook my head. "I really enjoyed all of the time we've spent together. Maybe I just have a bit of a stomachache," I lied. "Go to bed, please. I'll be fine."

"We'll wait for you to go to bed." Nicolas moved and leaned against the low dresser and stared at me.

"I can't stand you both just staring at me," I wailed, knowing the dam holding back my emotions was too close to breaking. I jumped up and ran between both of them and into the bathroom and slammed the door. Then, sinking down to the floor with my back to it, I let the tears fall. I didn't want to believe that coming here to this island was a mistake. But it seriously sucked that I'd met the perfect man and would have to walk away from him. I didn't have to say never. My heart already knew how it would be.

As I sat on the bathroom floor, wallowing in self-pity, I stilled when the door to my room opened. Barely daring to breathe, I listened and heard a woman speaking very quietly. Slowly, I brought myself to my feet and then stared at myself in the mirror. My hair was a wreck and I didn't have any makeup left on my face from showering in the waterfall. Damn good thing it was dark outside or possibly I would have scared Malachi off.

As hard as I strained to hear what was being said on the other side of the bathroom door, all I could pick up were the low baritones from Nicolas and Tomas and the quiet whispers from a woman. What the hell was a woman doing in my room?

I quickly applied base and blush to my face and did my best to straighten my hair before putting it back in a ponytail. If Rose were out there, she wouldn't be whispering. That didn't strike me as her style. There was only one way to find out.

"Hello, Natalie," a young lady with very long, very blond hair smiled at me as she crossed her arms over very large breasts. "I'm Ruth, Rose's new assistant. Your companions were very upset that they weren't pleasing you. I've talked to them and I think you'll find them much more understanding of your feelings now."

With that she walked past me and as I turned to say something, she let herself out of my room and closed the door behind her.

I woke up too fast, sitting up and positive I'd overslept. It took a minute, and Nicolas and Tomas sitting up on either side of me, to get my bearings.

"I've got to use the bathroom," I mumbled, crawling out from under the covers and then moving on all fours to the end of the bed. There was a wall of muscle and brawn on either side of me. "When did I come to bed?"

I grabbed my sweats, which were folded neatly on the low dresser and didn't wait to hear their answers as I hurried to the bathroom.

"I'll get coffee going," Tomas announced, sounding too chipper for first thing in the morning.

I locked the bathroom door and stared at my naked body in the mirror. I know I'd never crawled into bed, and I sure as hell didn't take my clothes off. This was wrong. They had no right to undress me after I was sleeping. Not to mention, I couldn't imagine sleeping through being undressed. I felt violated and grew grouchier the longer I stood there.

"Open the door, Natalie," Nicolas said from the other side. "I'll shower with you."

"I don't need any help," I snapped. Then turning around, I started the water and ignored what he said after that. After adjusting the water, I climbed in and stood under the spray for a moment, unable to remember much after Rose left the night before.

"Are you sure you don't want some help in there?" Nicolas asked.

I damn near slipped in the shower. "How did you get in here?" I demanded.

"It's really not safe to lock yourself in a bathroom, Natalie." Nicolas pulled the shower curtain back and his gaze traveled down my body. "Let me scrub your back."

"Out. Now," I demanded and yanked the shower curtain closed.

I stood under the water, no longer enjoying the hot spray massaging my body, and listened for the bathroom door to close. When I didn't hear it, frustration grew inside me, making my stomach hurt, as I resigned to finish my shower and deal with the two of them when I got out. If Nicolas wanted to stand outside the shower curtain, fine. But I was going to enjoy the hot water and decided to shave and take my time.

As I suspected, the moment I turned off the water, Nicolas was right there handing me a towel. I sighed, accepting it, and then dried off in the shower. Although in order to wrap my hair, I would have to get out of the tub naked. I told myself I wasn't being unfaithful to Malachi by doing so. One, Nicolas was a machine. And two, I'd only known Malachi a week. It wasn't like there was a voiced commitment of any kind between us.

Never say never.

I ignored the tightening in my gut and stepped out of the tub.

"There aren't as many guests here now," Nicolas informed me as he held another towel in his hands and reached for my hair. "What do you say to breakfast poolside? Afterward, we can go for a dip. I'll call down to have them send our breakfast out and have it ready for when we arrive."

"Nicolas, did you drug me last night?"

He studied me with his dark brown eyes and then took me by the shoulders and turned me around. I could have fought him but he was commanding with his attention and had me facing the bathroom wall in the next second. I let him towel dry my hair while I focused on the flowery wallpaper, waiting for his answer.

"We would never do anything to harm you."

"Is that a no?"

"No," Nicolas said, but didn't elaborate.

I didn't know if he meant no they didn't drug me or no it wasn't a no. Playing word games with an android wouldn't get me anywhere.

"If you two want to head down to the pool, I'll join you after a bit. I think I'll just sit up here with my coffee and wake up."

"We're not leaving your side at all today. I think it would be good for you if you spent the rest of your time here on the island with just us," he said.

I spun around and gawked at his calm expression. "What are you talking about?"

"It's apparent that you're not enjoying your vacation here as much as you should. We know you're sneaking off to see Malachi. I think if you quit seeing him, you'll have a lot more fun and enjoy yourself more."

I pushed him out of the way and stormed out of the bathroom. "And I think I'm a big girl and can make my own damned decisions," I snapped.

"Of course you can make your own decisions," Tomas said as he reclined in the chair I'd tried sleeping in the night before. "Nicolas is simply making a suggestion. We're both concerned, Natalie. Look how uptight you are this morning. Coffee?" He nodded toward the pot that was full and smelled good enough that I actually calmed down a bit as I headed toward it. "If you don't want breakfast at the pool, we can do something else. How about some morning sex?"

"No," I said firmly and poured myself a cup.

"Then possibly a massage would help relax you." Tomas stood and moved in behind me. When he grabbed my shoulders it was like Malachi stood there instead of him. The moment Tomas continued speaking though, he pulled me away from imagining Malachi behind me. "You're wound tight, darling. The sooner we can distract you and help clear your head of Malachi, the happier you'll be."

"What is this?" I turned around so quickly that I almost spilled my coffee. "Why do you keep mentioning Malachi? I don't know what you're talking about."

I stared Tomas down, daring him silently to call me a liar. But for all anyone on this island knew, he and I weren't spending time together. I remembered Malachi telling Samuel last night not to tell anyone that we were heading toward the beach. Possibly Samuel broke his word to Malachi. He cared about his companions so much though. And Malachi didn't strike me as the kind of person that would be a bad judge of character. He would know if his companions could be trusted or not.

But if they'd drugged me, they couldn't be trusted.

Somehow these two learned where I'd been. The only thing I could think of was that Ruth told them when she stopped by my room last night. I'd never met her before, so someone told her. An uncontrollable urge to find Malachi, or call him, hit me so hard it took a moment for me to realize Nicolas was talking to me. I needed to tell Malachi there was something wrong with his new companions. I seriously doubted he meant for them to go against his direct orders.

"We know you're spending time with him," Nicolas said.

I sipped my coffee and then walked slowly to my clothes, making a show of deciding what to wear today. "I honestly don't know what you're talking about. You two are the only ones on this island I'm spending time with." Then to make it look good, I put down my cup, pulled out a sundress, and then looked from one of them to the other. "Oh, yeah. I almost forgot. And Jonah. I've spent time with him. He's such a nice old man. But other than that, I don't know where you're coming up with these ideas about Malachi. He's the man at those buildings you claimed not to know about, right?"

I had them there and hid my smile as I looked down and stepped into my dress. It had an elastic waist and spaghetti straps and I pulled it up my body and then twisted in it until it hung on me properly. Finally, looking from one of them to the other, I stared at their unreadable expressions.

"I think you both have some explaining to do." They wouldn't push me in to a corner with lies. Two could play their game and I was going to win. "How come all of a sudden you know about a man whom the other day you claimed to know nothing about? And I also want to know how you undressed me without waking me up last night."

18

Malachi

I stared at my cell phone before slowly closing it. It was the third time this morning I'd tried to reach Rose. Each time it went straight to voice mail. I hung up this time before having to listen to her voice purr in my ear. The sound of it raised my blood pressure.

Maybe calling Natalie instead would put the morning to a better start. I'd much rather talk to her anyway. I always checked in with Rose after sending new companions to her. Although Rose usually contacted me first. She was always quick to tell me anytime one of my new companions did something stupid or didn't behave according to her definition of how a perfect companion should behave.

It wasn't my fault the companions couldn't get her off. The Queen Bitch probably dried up years ago. More than likely she couldn't have an orgasm if she tried.

"John," I called out as I headed down the hallway toward the doors.

My older companion turned, smiling as he saw me. "Good

morning, Malachi," he said, stopping and waiting for me to reach him.

"Do me a favor." I patted his shoulder and walked with him toward the doors to the courtyard. "Run up to the mansion and tell Rose I need to talk to her. For some reason, she's not answering my calls."

"Sure thing," John said, shaking his head. "I don't know why she wouldn't answer you though."

"Beats me." I wasn't sure why I worked so hard to talk to her. After last night, all I wanted was to talk to Natalie.

I followed John but entered the dormitory building when he headed toward the path to the mansion. Each companion was issued his or her own room where they stayed unless they were with guests. I walked down the hallway, surprised to see the doors to their rooms were shut. They were always kept open. I stopped at the end of the hall, turning slowly and frowning. The hallway looked so different with all of the doors closed.

The new companions were more independent than any others I'd made so far. Maybe that instigated a need for privacy. I glanced down at the nearest doorknob and tried remembering where the keys to the dorms were. Obviously the companions found them. I continued focusing on the closed door, getting the strangest sensation I was being closed out of their lives. From Samuel changing my passwords yesterday, which I had half a mind to change again to something he wouldn't figure out, to his outburst last night when I walked with Natalie on the beach, and now this.

Before I gave them life I needed to take control and put a tap on Rose's manipulative nature. Now the urgency to regain the helm on the island was paramount. If I weren't careful, my new companions would take over. That wasn't going to happen. I didn't answer to anyone.

It crossed my mind after learning that Natalie discovered not only my past but also the truth of the companions that I should heighten security. If someone else learned the truth about me, and who I was, it could be damning. Other than the cameras I used to monitor the companions so I could intervene if their circuits malfunctioned before anyone noticed, I didn't concern myself with anything being stolen. In all truth, I was the only living person on this side of the island, and I wouldn't rob myself. I headed outside again and crossed the courtyard. I was pretty sure there was a master key for all the locks in the storage room in the warehouse.

I stopped at the entrance of the double garage doors and watched Pierre and John load boxes off of golf carts onto the shelves.

"John, I thought you'd headed up to the mansion." I bit at the twang of regret that hit at not seeing my Adams unloading the boxes. "I need you to check on Rose for me."

"Samuel told me to stay here and work instead," John said, and then grunted when Pierre loaded another box into his arms.

"Oh did he?" I grumbled and turned, staring at the courtyard before heading back to my office and laboratory. This wasn't the way I wrote their programming. I pushed open the door in the hallway, letting it slam against the wall and echo as I stormed down the hallway. It pissed me off even more when I entered my office to find Samuel diligently working on my computer and not bothering to look up when I stood over him. "Don't ever override an order I give to anyone," I growled.

When he kept typing, ignoring me, I grabbed his shoulder and spun him around in his chair. "Do you understand me, Samuel? You do anything again without consulting me first and I'll shut you off faster than you can get your next word out."

Samuel stood slowly and stared at me, his expression looking annoyingly amused as he tilted his head and studied me. "It would be a lot easier for me to turn you off, Malachi, then for you to turn me off."

"Out, now," I barked, pointing to the door. My companions had never scared me, and Samuel wouldn't frighten me now. In spite of how powerful he appeared within a day of being turned on, I was too damned pissed. "You're behavior isn't acceptable. Get the fuck out before I use you for spare parts," I yelled loudly enough my heartbeat throbbed in my temples.

It was all I could do to restrain myself from pounding that smug expression off his face when he walked out the door. Standing in the hallway, fighting for control before I acted, I watched Samuel walk away from me.

Goddamn it. I was so fucking impressed with his test results, and the results of the other new companions that I obviously missed something incredibly crucial. I was so damned angry I shook as I closed the office door and sat at my computer. Fisting my hands, I glared at the screen a minute fighting to calm down. I needed to think clearly in order to handle matters and fix them. Clearing the screen by moving the mouse, I growled when the box popped up in front of me requesting my password.

"To access my own fucking computer," I mumbled. I punched in the password and was promptly informed it was incorrect. "Crap," I yelled, clearing the box and then taking my time typing in the name Elijah. Again it said incorrect password. "What the fuck?"

Two more tries proved I wasn't typing the password incorrectly. "The son of a bitch changed the password. I'm going to have to bypass through the back door just to gain access to my own goddamn computer." I was going from angry to royally pissed.

An hour later when I couldn't access either of my computers in the laboratory, nor in my private quarters, I went in search of

Samuel. No one could tell me where he was. The bastard was hiding, and probably for the best at the moment. I was livid. I didn't bother explaining where I was going when I hopped into a golf cart and took off toward the mansion. If Rose's computers wouldn't give me access, so help me, I would take down the entire computer system. Teach some machine to mess with me.

I couldn't remember the last time I parked in the front of the mansion. And it had been forever since I entered through those doors. Storming over the marble floors, listening to my shoes echo in the large open foyer, I didn't remember the place looking so abandoned. There wasn't anyone around anywhere. A group of guests had left the other morning, but there were still a handful on the island. One of them being Natalie.

I glanced up at the balcony overhanging the entryway just as a man walked to the elevator. It was James Martin. He looked my way but then turned his back on me and pressed the elevator button. I glared at the asshole's back, noting his solid build and leathered skin from tanning made him look even more like a pompous creep.

But wait a minute; Martin was supposed to leave this morning. He'd told Natalie as much when I'd eavesdropped on their conversation the other night. What the hell was he still doing here? Like I fucking cared. As long as he kept his paws off Natalie, and treated my companions with respect, I didn't give a rat's ass about the jerk. Heading down the main hallway, I stopped at Rose's office. The door was closed.

Years ago, when I learned that Rose enjoyed my companions for more than just padding her pocketbook, I'd learned to announce myself before entering her office. The last thing I wanted to see was one of my creations getting the Queen Bitch off.

I rapped on the door with the back of my hand, taking a deep soothing breath. I'd accomplish a lot more with Rose if I didn't barge in and start yelling. No one answered.

I stared at the door a moment. If the thing was locked I was going to rip it off its hinges, guests or no guests. Scowling, I grabbed the door knob and turned it. For the first time today something went right. The door opened easily.

"Ruth," I said, staring at my new companion sitting behind Rose's desk. It seemed different not seeing Sharay in here. "Why didn't you answer when I knocked?"

"Oh, Malachi, hi," Ruth said, and glanced at the computer screen on Rose's desk before giving me her attention. "I'm so sorry. I guess I was trying to get this done."

"What are you doing?" Ruth was sent to the mansion before I'd really finished testing her, although Rose hadn't complained. And she sure as hell would have if Ruth didn't do something to her liking. "Where's Rose?"

"I'm just doing some work for her while she is getting a massage and pedicure." Ruth brushed her long blonde hair over her shoulder and licked her lips as she studied me.

I had to admit, she was probably the hottest looking companion I'd pulled off so far. Her thick long lashes fluttered over her blue eyes several times in the moment that she stared at me. No one would know how much those small, natural facial movements that every human being on the planet did thousands of times a day without giving it any thought made me prouder than any parent who'd biologically given birth to their own child could ever be.

"You look stressed, Malachi. I can arrange for you to have a massage, too. When is the last time you took some time for yourself?" she asked, her tone dropping to a sultry purr.

I didn't doubt for a moment that any other man would agree to anything Ruth suggested. Damn, she was perfection in all caps.

"Don't worry about me, sweetheart," I said, approaching the desk and moving to walk around to her side. "I need to get on Rose's computer for a moment. Hop up."

"I can't do that." Her expression didn't change, nor did she move.

She looked up at me, her calm appearance making it easier to keep my frustration from rising as quickly. "Don't worry about Rose, hon. This is important."

Ruth shook her head slowly and again brushed long blonde strands away from her face. She wore a low-cut sleeveless sweater that hugged her shapely figure. The amount of cleavage I had a view of would have rendered any other male speechless. If her shirt were cut any lower, she'd be showing off nipples. She turned in the incredibly expensive high-back swivel office chair that Rose insisted on ordering a few years back and exposed her long, thin bare legs from underneath the desk. Her skirt was short enough that if she parted her legs, there wouldn't be a damned thing left to the imagination. I knew I didn't authorize the clothing she had on and wondered sometimes at Rose's thinking when she approved having an office assistant who was dressed like a prostitute. It wasn't exactly what I'd had in mind when I decided not to put this new round of companions in loincloths and small scraps of material that barely covered anything. There was something to say about having an island that sold sex and appearing as classy and not slutty. I'd take that up with Rose later.

"I'm sorry, Malachi," she said, her tone still soft and sultry. "Rose specifically ordered me not to show these files to anyone. They are her personal files and do not pertain to the island. You look really upset. Are you sure you're okay?"

At least I knew that Samuel didn't run and confide in his fellow companions. Another time I might have been curious to know what personal files Rose might have that didn't pertain to the island. If they were financial, island money was as much mine as it was hers. Right now, that wasn't a concern. I wanted my fucking computer network back. I needed to do some serious damage control immediately before my companions grew unruly.

"Ruth, close the damned file and get up. I don't care about anything pertaining to Rose's personal matters. I need the computer and I need it now."

"I can't let you have access, Malachi. Rose won't allow it. If she were here it might be different, but in her absence, I can't allow anyone to supersede her orders."

"Close the file or I'll move you and close it out myself," I told her, getting fed up with my own companions repeatedly telling me no.

"Tell me what you want, and I'll do it for you," she suggested, turning back to the computer.

I came the rest of the way around the desk and spun her chair around. Ruth looked up, surprised, and her legs spread as she braced herself in the chair. I was right about little being left to the imagination. Ruth's naked body didn't impress me. I created her. And at the moment I was wondering at my sanity level to listen to Rose about wanting companions who were more human than they'd been before.

"I want you to move so that I can sit at the computer," I said, gritting my teeth and fighting to keep from yelling. The beginning of a serious headache threatened at my temples. "Ruth. Move."

She finally stood, and I sighed, relieved that I didn't have to yell at her, and stepped back to allow her around the desk.

"Malachi, tell me what's wrong," she said, dropping her tone to a seductive whisper. She placed her slender hand over my heart and searched my face, batting her thick eyelashes like a seductress with years of experience on how to manipulate a man into doing or saying whatever she wanted. "My, my, sweetheart," she drawled. "You're wound so tight you're about to explode. I tell you what. I'll order you a good strong drink from the bar and send for someone immediately to give you a full-body massage. Would you rather have a man or a woman massage you, sweetheart?"

I didn't like how she spoke to me. I wasn't her fucking sweetheart. That term of endearment was meant for someone she might flirt with, or meant to manipulate. Ruth was going to get a serious circuit adjustment if she thought she could manipulate me.

"Ruth, I appreciate your concern," I said, taking her hand off of my chest and holding her by her wrist as I backed up and pulled her with me. "And you're probably right. I don't think of what I do as stressful because I love every minute of it, especially when I create perfection like you."

She smiled and licked her lips, moistening them as she stared me in the eye. "Would you like me to show you how perfect I am?" she whispered, allowing me to guide her around the desk. But then, instead of stepping to the side so that I could move around her, she walked into my arms and draped her slender arm over my shoulder. "Maybe that is what you need to relax. I can't imagine any human female could offer you the pleasure that I could give you."

"I'm sure you're right." I took her hands off of me again and this time held on to her wrists and tried guiding her to the other side of the desk. She didn't budge. Damn Rose to hell and back for informing her companions that her orders outweighed mine. "That isn't why I'm here though, Ruth."

"Why are you here, Malachi?" Her expression changed, the seductress disappearing and a small frown appearing. "You know this is Rose's office. If you want information from her, you'll have to wait for her to return."

"I don't want anything from her. I want to use the computer. I don't want to see any of her files, just clear everything out to the desktop and move if that makes you feel better."

"It would make me feel better if you would calm down, Malachi. It would be awful if you upset yourself so much that something happened to you," she said, her face looking more serious by the moment. "You may come back when Rose is here."

"Ruth, I don't need Rose. I need the computer." And I'd be damned if I stooped low enough to remind her that she answered to me before answering to Rose. I had enough faith in my programming to know she already understood that. "You can close that file if you want. But do it now or I'm going to see whatever precious information Rose feels is so important that it's being protected this well."

I crossed my arms, waiting for Ruth to listen to me.

"Malachi, you can't use the computer."

I sighed heavily, about done with the insubordination that swarmed through my new companions like a fucking virus. "Ruth, sit down. We'll discuss this in a moment." I pointed to one of the chairs at a table along the wall in Rose's spacious office.

Then turning from her, I walked around Rose's large wooden desk. Ruth grabbed my arm with enough strength to pinch my flesh. I turned on her quickly.

"I just gave you instructions. Do as you're told," I hissed at her, ignoring the pain in my arm from where she gripped it.

"No, Malachi." This time she didn't bother moving the long straight blond hair that tumbled over her shoulder and one breast.

"What is wrong with you?" I snapped, grabbing her by the wrist and yanking her hand off of me. It took some effort and her nails scratched my flesh before I succeeded in releasing myself from her grasp.

The question was rhetorical, but obviously Ruth didn't take it that way. I watched her pretty face scrunch up into a vindictive scowl. If I didn't know better I'd say she mastered the look from watching Rose. Another improvement I needed to make in her programming, having the good sense to know who to mimic and who not.

"There is nothing wrong with me," Ruth said, her tone turning cold as she puffed out her breasts to the point where they looked like they would explode out of that tight-knit sweater any moment. "I've been more than generous in offering to help you relax and also offering to do whatever computer work you wished done."

"And I appreciate it. Now go sit down." I turned toward the computer and caught a glimpse of the screen.

Ruth was working on a program, and it wasn't an accounting program, not from the code that I caught a glimpse of before she grabbed me again. I howled from shock probably more so than from the pain when she dug her nails into my arm and pulled me over the desk.

Scrambling out of her grip and damn near falling off the side of the desk I fought to regain my balance. At the same time I worked to keep my thinking straight. Once, years ago, a companion malfunctioned and I had to physically restrain him. But he hadn't been strong enough to lift a grown man off his feet by one arm, and practically dislocate that arm in the process.

I rubbed my arm, which did little to stop the excruciating pain that shot up through my shoulder. Something was seriously wrong with her programming and I could only guess where to begin looking for the problem. I wouldn't be able to fix her until I shut her down though, which contrary to what Samuel informed Rose the other day, was possible. Maybe they couldn't be unplugged, and every computer had a crash protector, but they definitely could be turned off if problems persisted.

"Stay away from the computer, Malachi," Ruth said and walked around the desk to me.

"What is your processing telling you, Ruth?" I asked, hoping I could help her correct herself with the right questions. "Run a diagnostic, sweetheart. You're not functioning properly."

"I'm functioning exactly how I want to be functioning, Malachi. There isn't any reason for you to enter the system. I'm controlling everything from the mansion now. Rose is relaxing. Now you can leave on your own, or I can have you removed."

Dear God. I stared at the blonde beauty as she moved closer, her expression hardened and serious. First Samuel, and now her. If the pain wasn't ransacking my body at the moment, I'd be crushed that my new chip I'd been so proud of was obviously beyond disastrous. Worse yet, if my companions were trying to take over, there were still guests on the island. I wouldn't say I was fearful for their lives, but if I was forced to shut down the island until I could fix this nightmare, the less people around, the better.

"Run your diagnostics, now!" I ordered.

She ignored me and instead tried to grab me.

"Ruth!" I yelled, although yelling the name of a computer when it's malfunctioning is ridiculous.

I ducked, then jumped out of her way and tried darting around the other side of the desk. All the wiring for Rose's computer was in the way but I pushed her small filing cabinet toward Ruth in an effort to block her, and then jumped over the small end table, knocking over a potted plant.

Ruth leapt onto Rose's desk and jumped on top of me when I tried reaching for Rose's office chair. Almost every man knows not to strike a woman. It's engraved into our brains at such an early age that even in extreme, critical, if not life-threatening situations, we hesitate, even when that one moment of not reacting could risk our lives. Ruth grabbed my shoulders and shoved me against the wall. The large window behind me was covered with Venetian blinds but still rattled when my body crashed into it.

"Damn it," I yelled. "What the fuck has gotten into you?"

"You're not listening, Malachi." In spite of her aggressive actions, Ruth's tone remained calmer than one would expect a woman to sound when she was preparing to beat the crap out of you. "I told you to leave and you didn't. Now I have to shut you down."

I wasn't going to ask what the hell she meant by that. But my worst fears surfaced quickly. And I sure as hell wasn't going to die at the hands of one of my own companions.

Panicking right now would give her the upper hand. It was hard as hell to think straight when a woman with ten times my strength was getting ready to attack again. I needed to think quickly, and my next move had to do the job, or she would "shut me down."

Ramming the office chair into her, I jumped back the way I came, falling over the small filing cabinet that I'd moved and coming down hard on my knees. My arm already burned with pain and I'm not as young as I once was; my knee popped loudly while the air flew out of my lungs with the impact.

Worse yet, I bit my tongue when I clenched my teeth together to keep from howling in pain. As many he-man movies that I'd seen all my life, pain fucking sucked. Nothing immobilized me faster. Bolts of severe, throbbing jolts shot up from my knee into my thigh. It hurt so fucking bad my balls tightened quickly, adding to the misery. My eyes watered and now, biting my tongue added to the distractions that made it impossible to focus immediately and prepare for Ruth's next attack.

Ruth jumped over the desk and landed on top of me. I barely registered the fist she aimed at the side of my head before managing to flip her over my shoulders.

"Damn it to hell," I yelled, and reminded myself that she was nothing more than circuits and programming. To hell with hitting a woman. Ruth was a machine.

I slammed my fist into the middle of her back, hoping to

crush her main navigation equipment housed where her lungs would be. She was stronger and faster than I anticipated, though, and flipped over, grabbing my fist with one hand, and sending a blow straight to my face. The last thing I saw was long blonde hair flying in front of my eyes before it seemed my world exploded and an overwhelming rush of excruciating pain made everything go black.

Fear hit me so hard I couldn't breathe. I crashed to the ground, a ringing in my head drowning out any sounds in the room. My new companions were malfunctioning worse than I ever imagined. Fight as I did to overcome the pain and make the ringing go away, I couldn't. My stomach jerked, nausea reaching my throat and choking me. It hurt too much to puke. I couldn't get up. I couldn't see a thing. I could lose the island but the pain overtook me. There wasn't anything I could do, and worse yet, Natalie was in the mansion somewhere and the companions knew I cared about her. Somehow, I needed to protect Natalie.

19

Natalie

When I followed Tomas out of my room, I swore I heard someone yell. It had to be my imagination. Neither Nicolas nor Tomas reacted to the sound. But damn if it didn't sound like Malachi. I wondered if he was in Rose's office, and if they were fighting. It was definitely a man howling, sounding outraged. If it was Malachi in Rose's office, they were downstairs. There was no way others wouldn't hear.

"You two didn't hear that?" I asked, staring at their backsides and then searching their relaxed expressions when they turned and looked at me questioningly. "Someone just yelled."

Nicolas smiled and Tomas's mouth curved at the corner when he reached for me. "Darling, it's very normal to hear someone cry out from pleasure on the island."

"That didn't sound like pleasure," I said, listening but not hearing anything now.

"Some people have different ideas of pleasure," Nicolas offered.

He was right, but I still didn't like it. Growing unease filled me when they turned toward the elevator.

"Let's go down the back way. I want to find Jonah." I turned before either of them could say anything and hurried to the smaller staircase that led to the back end of the first floor near the service entrance.

"Why do you want to find Jonah?" Nicolas asked, reaching my side as I started down the stairs.

The stairwell was too narrow for both of us to go down at the same time and we were forced to descend single file. Which was fine with me. I led the way. I had wanted alone time but if I were going to hang out with these two, we were going to do things my way.

"I thought I'd ask if I could cut some flowers for my room." I said the first thing I could think of and was relieved to see the back service entrance door closed. "I guess he's busy. Maybe we'll find him outside."

"I'm sure he'd love to arrange a bouquet for your room." Tomas smiled down at me and took my hand in his, then led me toward the front hall and past Rose's office.

The door was closed but as we walked past I swore someone yelled "Ruth." It really did sound like Malachi. Panic forced bile to my mouth and I prayed I wouldn't start shaking with apprehension as I continued walking between both men. Something crashed in Rose's office and then it seemed the entire mansion was too quiet.

"Don't worry. At least none of us will be in trouble for whatever just broke," Nicolas teased, taking my other hand and giving it a squeeze.

"Oh, shoot. Did we remember my suntan oil?" I asked, making a show of stopping when we reached the large foyer.

Letting go of their hands, I opened the bag that hung over my shoulder and looked at the contents. At the same time, I glanced up and spotted Ruth coming out of Rose's office. She was carrying a very large bundle of blankets, or possibly carpets, over her shoulder. Ruth turned toward the service entrance without looking in our direction.

"Your oil is in there," Nicolas said, taking the bag from me. "We have everything we need. Shall we go?"

Something was wrong, grossly and incredibly wrong. The sinking pit in my gut swelled and made it hard to breathe.

What if something had happened to Malachi?

"Natalie."

"What?" I snapped realizing Tomas had said my name more than once and I didn't hear what he asked. "I'm sorry. What did you say?"

"Do you want to play volleyball before we go swimming?" he asked, smiling down at me although I worried there was concern in his expression when he searched my face.

"Fine. That's fine."

"Natalie, there you are. I've been looking for you." James Martin stood from one of the chairs inside the main doors and stopped in front of the three of us. "I would love to buy you a drink. Where are you headed?"

"Volleyball, I think." I was too distracted to deal with James right now. "Maybe later, James," I added, my voice cracking so that my words were barely audible. I needed to figure out a way to get around to the back of the mansion and find Ruth. There wasn't any way I would be able to think until I knew she'd carried out garbage and not Malachi's body.

"We'll join you at the volleyball court then."

I didn't care enough to ask James who he meant by "we." Nicolas and Tomas led me outside and over to the net where a handful of people were already into their game.

Damn good thing, too. I was so shaky there wasn't any way I could play right now. Worse yet, Tomas and Nicolas clung to me, moving whenever I moved until I worried I might scream. And it wouldn't be from pleasure. I needed to get away from them and they were determined not to leave my side.

"Hi there, gorgeous." James walked over to me with a young blonde on his arm. "Care to join us? We were thinking about taking a walk over to the hot springs since the game has already started."

"The hot springs sound good." I needed to get my wits about me. "How about if you escort me alone?"

James's face lit up like I'd just told him he'd won the lottery. "Don't tell me you're jealous of Darcy here. She loves to share, don't you, sweetheart?" he asked and gave her a quick hug, which made her giggle. James slapped her ass. "Why don't you hang out with Natalie's companions, Darcy? Is that all right with you?" he asked, glancing at Nicolas and Tomas, and then back at me.

I didn't answer him, although somewhere in the back of my head I was yelling at myself for agreeing to be alone with this pushy chauvinist. It might possibly be my only way to get away from my companions, though. Once I shook free of them, getting away from James would be easy. I hoped.

"I'll meet you back here in a bit," I said. And that's when I saw the small group playing volleyball in a sandy area blocked off by cement.

I should have noticed sooner but I didn't and that proved how upset I was about what I heard and saw inside. There were six people playing volleyball, three on each side, and not once did that ball touch the ground. More so, the men and women playing continually tapped the ball over the net, causing it to arch into the air and come down so that their opponent could tap it back to them. The players barely moved and the ball appeared to create the same arch—the same height and curve—every time it went up in the air.

"They're good, huh?" James put his arm around me and I damn near jumped out of my skin.

Making a show of laughing off my jitteriness before he could make a big deal out of it, I shook my head in disbelief. "Amazing," I muttered.

I would swear the only people on that sand were companions. For some strange reason, knowing James was here, walking beside me, brought solace that I wasn't alone and surrounded by androids. Androids that were changing over the week that I'd been here. Or maybe it was just the new group that Malachi turned on, or started up, or whatever he did to make them "come to life." Tomas and Nicolas were less amiable since Ruth stopped by my room the other night.

They were just as eager to see to my every need, but also watching me. The moment I moved, they moved. They questioned my every action, and before we left, we almost got into an argument.

When I woke up and simply wanted to watch TV and brood over Malachi in peace, they wouldn't leave me alone. It wasn't until I agreed to coming out and doing something that they quit pawing me. If I hadn't conceded to leaving the room, we might have actually fought. Now all I had to deal with was James fondling me as we walked along the wide stone path.

"I'm thrilled that you've decided to give me a second chance," he said, pulling me closer to him as he gripped my waist. "How about we go soak in the hot tub?"

I reached for his hand and took it off my waist. "Tell me, James," I said, paying no attention to anything he just said to me. Somehow I needed to figure out what Ruth hauled out of Rose's office. The longer we walked the more I tried convincing myself that just because I heard Malachi yell and then saw Ruth with a large bundle that was about the size of a grown man meant absolutely nothing. Knowledge of all of these androids running around was causing my imagination to run rabid with morbid ideas. "Are you enjoying your companion? I mean, has she been good for you since you got here? She hasn't changed or anything, has she?"

James laughed and I looked over at him quickly, again shifting how I walked to dodge his hands when he tried grabbing me.

"Why, darling," he said, his rich tone sounding thick, like he might have an accent that he worked hard to hide. "You make it sound like you're not happy with your companions. How could you not be happy with perfection?" he asked, eyeing me shrewdly.

He tried stopping me, wrapping his arms around me and then bringing his face to mine for a kiss.

"James, please. I'd rather just talk," I told him, seriously doubting that would stop his advances. But he did back off and I smiled my appreciation. I headed down the path quickly, reaching the gates where several hot tubs released steam into the air. "It just seems to me that my companions are growing bossier the longer I've been here," I offered quietly.

James opened the gate for me and I looked around, surprised that no one else was in the hot tubs. It appeared most of the guests left the morning after the party. I wondered how many were actually still here.

"They will do as they're told if you just maintain the upper hand with them." The gate closed with a clang and I turned around quickly, my heart exploding in my chest from the sound. James looked at me, his expression tight. "Do you know why I want to be with you so badly?"

James definitely had an accent. It was slight, not overly obvious, but definitely not native St. Louis.

"I can guess," I said dryly, and then walked around the steamy water toward a rack of towels on the other side.

James arms snaked around me. I grabbed his wrists but he tightened his hold on me, pressing against my already upset tummy.

"Can you guess?" he whispered hoarsely into my ear. "Do you think I would wonder why you are so willing to be with me now when you left me for Malachi Cohen the other night?"

I froze. James shouldn't know Malachi's name, and he especially shouldn't know his last name.

"I think you are starting to understand," he said, loosening his grip.

I tried stepping out of his arms but he grabbed my waist and turned me around. The steam from the water suddenly made me feel nauseous. I stared into James's dark eyes. His black curly hair bordered his face, which added to his brooding expression while he stared at me for a moment. If I was supposed to respond, I didn't, which didn't appear to upset him. Instead, a slow smile appeared and his gaze dropped to my mouth.

"I need your help and I think you will cooperate with me, no?"

"French," I whispered, suddenly figuring it out. "Your accent is French."

James raised one eyebrow. "We already know you like French men, don't we?" he suggested, his smile disappearing as quickly as it appeared. He looked sinister while his fingers pressed into my waist. "You are from a very successful law firm, Miss Green. And you have a great deal of money, too."

"James, you're making me very nervous," I said, wondering if agreeing to come here, where we were very much alone, might not have been a good idea after all. "What are you talking about?"

"I also know you are a very intelligent woman. I think you will decide to work with the winning side. Already you see what I see, and that is how incredibly successful this island is. And you know why it is so successful, don't you, Natalie?"

"Why?" My mouth was almost too dry to speak. I pushed against his wrists. "Please let go of me."

Surprisingly, James complied. He didn't move and with the gate closed, and him standing between it and me, my only means of escape would be jumping over the stone wall surrounding us.

"Malachi Cohen has something that belongs to me—that belongs to my government." James's words seemed to hang in the air between us, not registering at first. He kept speaking, his cool, soft tone slicing through me as his words slowly sunk in.

"When I came to the island I believed I would have to sneak." His accent thickened as he continued. "You are a wonderful bonus because I see how he cares for you very much. But you two are strangers and you will see what the right thing is to do, for your country, and for ours. You will help me, Natalie. We will return to France what belongs to her, and you will be a hero for your actions."

"Help you?" I stammered, shaking my head. I crossed my arms over my chest, the steam from the water no longer feeling hot. A chill ransacked my body while my brain stumbled over possible ideas on how to get away from him, and warn Malachi—if Malachi was okay. "I don't understand. What are you talking about?"

"You will go to Malachi and get his files. Seduce him, whatever it takes. You will bring those files to me." James took my arm and walked me to the gate. After opening it, he pulled me to him, although seduction appeared the last thing on his mind. "If you betray me, Malachi will die and I will still take the files. Do you understand now? With your help, no one will be harmed. And that is how we want this to work out, don't we?"

I nodded dumbly, hearing only that he wanted me to go to Malachi. "I'll do it," I said, pulling away from him and praying my legs wouldn't give out underneath me as I shook from head to toe.

"Good. I will be waiting for you. You can't leave the island. Don't think you can change the inevitable. Remember, I will take Malachi's files, and him if possible. If you are good, no one will get hurt. If you try and deceive me, many will die."

I glanced back at him once before hurrying out the gate and down the cobblestone path. It wouldn't be more than a five minute walk to Malachi's buildings. I prayed he was there, safe and sound. My stomach twisted into a mean knot as fear gripped me. My knees were wobbly and I tripped more than once as I almost ran to Malachi—at least I prayed I was running to him. And I didn't have a clue what I would do if I couldn't find him.

20

Malachi

I wasn't sure which was worse—the terrible throbbing in my head or the stench I breathed in with every breath. Turning my head almost made me nauseous and I blinked a few times, willing my surroundings to come into focus. It took another moment to realize I couldn't straighten my legs.

"What the fuck?" I muttered, and then cleared my throat when my voice didn't want to work.

After running my hands down my body, and determining there weren't any broken bones, I then touched my head and felt something sticky matted to my hair.

"Blood," I grumbled after bringing my fingers to my face and smelling them. My blood.

Then I remembered. Ruth knocked me out. But where the hell was I? And what the fuck was that smell?

Still unable to straighten my legs, I reached out, fighting to see in the dark. My right hand touched a cool flat surface and I stretched as far as my arm would reach and felt a metal wall next to me. It was close in front of me as well, which was why I couldn't straighten my legs. Twisting around, and then making an effort to try and stand, I hit my head hard on the very low ceiling and damn near passed out again.

All I could do was sit there. My brain didn't want to work and I imagined I had a concussion, but that didn't explain the smell. And God, it was fucking putrid. With every breath my stomach turned, but I couldn't place what it was.

The longer I sat there, the more I remembered. Samuel blocked me out of my computer system. Obviously Ruth did the same thing, although she never confirmed she was working with Samuel. My own companions, my creations, my children, had turned against me and now apparently had me locked inside some small container.

At least I was alive. Although I questioned why they didn't kill me. Their programming was so fucked up, I couldn't speculate on what thought processes were at play here. But for some reason, my companions decided I was better off alive than dead. This wasn't exactly my idea of being alive though—locked in some kind of metal box.

What if they were punishing me? Crap. I would fucking kill to straighten my legs. The longer I sat here trying to determine why I was here, the more my muscles ached, and pain racked my body.

Maybe they needed me alive. Samuel might have access to all of my files, but that didn't mean he could interpret them. Over the years I'd devised my own form of shorthand, of writing in code intentionally, so that if anything ever were to happen to my notes, no one else could decipher them.

No possible reason I thought of appealed to me at all. My stomach churned and nasty acid rose from my gut. I swallowed, cursing under my breath, which caused a fit of coughing. I wasn't going to puke all over myself while locked in a metal box.

I needed to think, try to move. My head throbbed and figuring out a way to lie down and sleep off the pain wasn't an option. I wasn't a doctor but I knew and understood medicine. A head injury, any trauma, needed attention, and until I could treat myself properly, I needed to stay awake and at least try and think clearly. I started by trying to learn every inch of my prison.

Once again reaching in front of me I found the hinges to a door and determined it was very narrow, and possibly five feet tall at the most. That explained why I couldn't stand without hitting my head on the roof. I was next to a wall but couldn't tell by looking how wide my prison was.

The darkness surrounding me reminded me of the cave where Natalie and I made love. Odd how the sensations I experienced while engulfed in complete darkness were so different then than they were now. Natalie better be all right. My companions beat me this round, but the war wasn't over, and I was their creator.

"I brought you into this world, and I can take you out," I grumbled, my throat burning when I tried speaking out loud. If they harmed Natalie in any way, I would see to it that they understood the meaning of pain before turning them off permanently.

Devising idle threats in my mind helped clear my head, but didn't accomplish shit other than that. I needed to get the fuck out of my prison.

I moved my legs and tried stretching sideways to determine the width. My shoe pushed against something that gave with my weight and I reached out in the darkness. My stomach damn near shot up to my throat and I yanked my hand back when I touched something soft, like skin.

"Crap," I yelled, willing my heart to quit pounding so loudly it was drowning out my thoughts. Taking deep breaths turned my stomach as well. The smell in my pitch-black prison was making me sick.

Slowly running my hand along the cool floor, I found the soft lump again and willed myself to explore until I felt hair.

"Oh, my God," I whispered, choking and forcing myself not

to get sick. "Please, no. Crap." I choked on my own words, hating to believe the truth but fearing the worse. "Natalie. God, no!"

I stared wide-eyed into the darkness, unable to see. Finally, I blinked, then rubbed my eyes trying to take the burn away. The companions had killed—committed murder. As to whether or not they could be charged was another question. But I sure as hell didn't kill her.

The lump in my throat made it hard to breathe. Gulping in air turned my stomach. My eyes burned while images of Natalie from when I first laid eyes on her on my monitors, to fucking her in my bedroom, seeing her triumphant gleam when she learned about the companions, and feeling her warm body against mine when we made love in the cave, pranced through my mind. I pictured her on the beach, more beautiful than any other woman I'd ever known. She was perfect for me, in so many ways.

"Natalie," I whispered, my voice cracking while my eyes watered.

I reached my hand out, moving through the darkness until my fingertips rubbed against clammy skin. Enduring my stomach revolting, I touched her, stroked her arm, while a tear streamed down my cheek. When had I last cried? Not for my country, not for my family, not for any of my companions' triumphs or failures. But for a woman I'd known a week and a half out of my life and who'd given me more than anyone else I'd ever known.

I reached her elbow and felt hair, long, thick, coarse hair.

"Fuck," I groaned, feeling nauseous all over again but experiencing a wave of relief at the same time that made me dizzier than shit. "Rose," I hissed, identifying the body next to me correctly as my fingers moved over her body. "Fucking crap, Rose."

I imagined her and Ruth getting into it. For whatever reasons, Ruth killed Rose, but not me. Maybe she didn't understand what death meant. Possibly when I stopped moving that was good enough for Ruth and she stuffed me in this compartment with Rose.

"Rose, I'm so sorry," I whispered, finding her cheek and caressing it a moment while a tear reached my jaw. Then wiping it off, I disregarded how relieved I was that the person next to me wasn't Natalie. All that meant was that she was still out there with my companions, who were capable of killing.

Returning my attention to the door, I ran my fingers along the seam until I found the lock. Exploring in the darkness it was clear there wasn't a handle or doorknob of any kind on the inside. From the best I could tell, it appeared I was locked inside one of my own storage lockers. Which meant I was in the warehouse.

I wondered if I was strong enough to kick open the door. If I was, the noise would be loud enough to alert anyone outside that I was escaping. If they'd killed Rose, they wouldn't hesitate in killing me, too. Possibly they might believe they already had. I needed to get out without drawing any attention to myself and then somehow I had to break into my own network and stop my companions before anyone else got hurt.

"Natalie," I moaned, my gut once again rising to my throat as fear gripped me hard enough I swore I would choke to death on it. She was in danger, serious danger. They would go after her in a second if they wanted to stop me, or control me. She was my only weakness. Goddamn it. Why hadn't I left her alone?

As I tried to figure out what to do I swore I smelled her perfume. She was consuming my thoughts and making me believe that I could breathe her into my system. It was part of the concussion. My mind wasn't working right.

Then something moved outside the locker. I heard someone. Shit. I needed a plan. I appeared to be okay, other than a deadly headache and a flesh wound, as well as possible trauma. Yeah right, I was just fucking peachy.

Whoever was in the warehouse outside the lockers was

moving quietly. It wasn't Pierre or John working; the footsteps were too soft.

The smell of her perfume was almost strong enough to drown out the god-awful stench inside the locker. I sat there staring wide-eyed and not blinking in the direction of the door. Please tell me that Natalie hadn't snuck into my buildings again. If she was looking for me and one of the companions found her here . . .

Shit. Fucking shit.

Reaching out until I felt the cool metal press against my finger-tips, I tapped the metal. Then I tapped it again. The footsteps outside the locker stopped.

"Malachi?" I heard her whisper.

"God. Natalie." A rush of panic and relief hit me so hard I damn near passed out again. "Natalie, don't talk. Don't say a fucking word."

"How do I get you out? It's locked," she whispered, ignor-ing what I'd just said.

I sucked in a breath and almost threw up. "At the end of the lockers there is a shelf. The key should be there," I whispered, fighting the urge to break out in a coughing fit. "Be careful. God. Don't make a sound."

There wasn't an answer and I didn't breathe, fighting to hear when there wasn't a sound. My world was eternal blackness and devoid of noise. It seemed minutes passed and I didn't hear anything. The silence was replaced with the painful throbbing of my heart pounding in my head, I wondered if I imagined her being there in the first place. I could be hurt worse than I thought.

Suddenly the door opened and I was hit by brightness that split my head in two. My eyes weren't ready for the light and pain racked my senses.

"What is that smell? Oh, my God!" Natalie whispered.

I focused on her just in time to watch her face turn green as she covered her mouth and looked like she would puke all over both of us if I didn't move quickly.

Pushing myself forward, I stood and then almost fell over on top of her. Natalie proved to be stronger at the moment as she wrapped her arms around me and held me up.

"Is that Rose?" she hissed, her voice cracking.

I turned and closed the locker, knowing I would have to deal with her later but for now there was an emergency to tend to.

"Thank you for trespassing again, sweetheart," I said, kissing her forehead.

Natalie backed up, her hands all over me while she looked at me, worry etching lines in her pretty face. "God, you're hurt, Malachi. Your head . . ."

"I'll be fine," I promised her. "But we need to get you out of here. I want you to return to the mansion. Lock yourself in your room and stay there no matter what happens. I'll come for you once it's safe."

"Safe?" She searched my face. "I saw Ruth carry you out of Rose's office, didn't I?" She was pale as a ghost as she looked up at me. "I'm not leaving you. There's something you need to know," she whispered, glancing toward the entrance of the warehouse.

"It's not safe for us to be together right now." I looked around the empty warehouse, wondering where the companions were. It was too early for them to return to their dorms. "I don't know what went wrong, but until I fix it, our lives are obviously in serious danger. I'm not going to lose you because I fucked up."

"James Martin," she whispered.

I frowned and my head pounded. "Not right now." I didn't care about the creep.

"He's not who he claimed to be. He's not from St. Louis at all, but from France."

It hurt to look at her, my head pounded so furiously. "What are you talking about?" No one came to the island from France.

I wouldn't allow it. It was one of the ground rules I'd laid down years ago that Rose never disputed. We couldn't risk anyone from my country coming here, no matter how much time passed. There wasn't any way I could explain that to Natalie right now.

"I thought if I agreed to walk with him, it would get me away from Nicolas and Tomas and then I could figure out if you were okay or not. So I went to the hot springs with James."

"Why are you telling me this?" Hearing that she willingly went off with another man ripped me in two. The pain was almost more than I could bear. But I couldn't acknowledge it right now, not with my life's work ready to destroy me and everything I'd accomplished so far.

"He's here to steal your notes and return them to France. He told me to come here and find the information on your companions and bring them to him. If I do what he says, he won't kill you." She sucked in a deep breath and then cupped my face with her cool, smooth hands. "We've got serious problems to figure out. But I need to know you're okay, first."

"I'm fine." Everything she just told me sunk like a heavy rock, falling quickly to my gut. It was a matter of time before someone caught up with me. My escape plan had been in effect for years. The numb resolve settling over me helped eliminate the pain, although the sickening trepidation that settled inside me didn't feel a hell of a lot better. "Do as I say and return to the mansion. Don't let anyone from this island into your room. Do as I say, Natalie."

"I didn't just run here through the trees, scratching my legs and arms, to be sent away, Malachi. I want to be with you. I can help. What should we do?"

I stared at her, the pain over the mutiny of my own companions subsiding momentarily as I lost myself in her gaze. If there were time, I would kiss her and let her know how much her wanting to be with me meant to me. She was staring at a failure, at the man responsible for one death and possibly more unless I acted quickly. Yet, as I saw her lips flatten into a thin line and determination replace her panic, I believed she really did want to be by my side.

"I've been locked out of the computer network. I went to the mansion to get on Rose's computer when Samuel informed me that he wouldn't release control of the laboratory to me. Ruth refused to give me access to the system there, attacked and obviously won round one."

"She won't win round two," Natalie told me, looking determined. "We're human, they're not. Tell me how I can help."

I ran my fingers through her hair and wished I had her faith. But there was only one way to stop my companions. As for this James Martin creep, until I knew what he was about, he was the least of my concerns. If I couldn't get to my files, he sure as hell couldn't.

"If we can get to my room, we have a slim chance at victory," I decided. There wasn't time for an explanation. And fortunately she didn't demand one. Taking her hand, I headed toward the open garage doors. "If we run into anyone, stay quiet. Let me talk."

"No problem. No offense, Malachi, but I've had enough of your companions for a while."

If the matter weren't so serious, I would have laughed. The fact that the urge hit me proved that I needed to tend to my head injury as soon as possible.

I paused when we reached the warehouse doors and looked around the courtyard while we remained in the shadows. There wasn't anyone anywhere, which was odd. At the least, John and Pierre should be out here working. Unless Samuel pulled all of them in for serious upgrades.

Although it pissed me off that he would take my notes and my formulas and try implementing them into the older models, it bought me some time.

"Let's go," I said, holding her hand firmly and hurrying across the courtyard to my building.

Running wasn't an option, and although I was sure I didn't stagger, when we entered the building where my room was, I realized Natalie had her arm around my waist and I was leaning against her.

"The stairs," I said, pointing to them.

"Are you sure?" she asked, looking up at me.

"I'm fine," I told her, but looked ahead, not wanting her to see the pain I was in.

"Malachi," she said.

I thought she meant to argue with me but then realized Maggie and Maria came through the doors off the first floor and headed toward the exit. I didn't answer Natalie but held her close to me as we ascended the stairs. Neither companion acknowledged us but kept going out the door.

Natalie sighed loudly, voicing her relief, when we reached the second floor without being stopped. Although I prayed our chances of getting to my room just increased drastically, Natalie would never know the new pain that hit me when Maggie and Maria ignored us. Just yesterday, both of them would have stopped and smiled, greeting me by name. They would have asked how I was doing and offered to help with anything I might need help with. And they most definitely would have been all over me once they saw I was hurt. Now they didn't even notice me. I no longer held any rank in their eyes. And that knowledge ripped through me, causing more pain than my head injury.

"In the bathroom cabinet is a first aid kit," I told her when we entered my room.

Natalie left my side, hurrying into the adjoining bathroom while I closed my bedroom door. Any other time I would have been in high heaven to have her here in my bedroom, but right now wasn't the time to enjoy her being with me. I hoped I would have the opportunity to know Natalie better once this nightmare ended. But knowing what I had to do, and praying I could pull it off, I forced myself to face the facts that today would probably be my last day with her.

My fingers shook as I reset the code that locked my bedroom door. Walking over to my desk, I sat down, fighting off the dizziness when it hit, and then pulled out my top drawer and reset the code that controlled the camera system in the courtyard and this building.

Round two had begun. Already I'd regained control of my building. But once Samuel learned that I was here and fighting back, he would attack. I prayed I had time to disable him before he could.

"Sit still," Natalie ordered, moving in next to me and opening the first aid kit. "Malachi, you're really hurt," she said, kneeling next to me and brushing her fingers over my forehead. "You really should shower, or at least let me wash your hair before we bandage that wound. It could get infected."

"Sweetheart, there isn't time." I looked in the kit and pushed through the surgical tape and wrapped bandages until I found what I wanted. Pulling out the small bottle of pain meds that I kept in there, I flipped the lid and poured a couple pills into my palm.

"I'm going to at least clean it up with the antiseptic pads you've got here," she insisted.

I wouldn't tell her I doubted it mattered if I were cleaned up or not because it gave her something to do. Her fingers trembled as she fumbled with the packages until she had prepared all the supplies she needed. She continued pulling supplies from the first aid kit and working to clean the wound on my forehead while I turned my attention to my computer. That's when I remembered that I couldn't access my own system.

"Damn it," I swore, hitting the desk next to the keyboard with my fist.

Natalie yelped and made me feel like shit. She was fighting so hard to be strong for me, yet she was so out of her element and was suffering more than I was. She didn't know what to expect. At least I knew how it would all end.

"What's wrong?" she asked. "Did I hurt you?"

"No." I looked away from the computer long enough to stare into her worried expression and brushed my fingers over her smooth cheek. "Thank you for being stubborn enough to stick with me. I just remembered that I don't have the password to my computer anymore. Samuel changed it."

"That's right," she said, shifting her gaze to the monitor. "Well, you created them. So they can't possibly have any thoughts or memories that you don't know about. I'm sure you can figure out what the password would be."

I remembered Samuel telling me how he chose Elijah for the password and stared at the box in the middle of the screen and the small icon blinking and waiting for me to enter the right order of letters or numbers so it could allow me entrance. After trying a handful of times and failing, I couldn't believe it when I typed in the date that I brought the six to life and the computer screen blinked and then displayed my desktop.

"You did it," Natalie shrieked and reached down to hug me.

Pain throbbed in my forehead and the pressure from her body was almost more than I could bear. But I felt her excitement right along with her and covered her hands with mine, holding them against my chest for a moment while we triumphed over our small victory.

"What was the password?" she asked.

"Their birthday," I told her, finding it interesting that family and genealogy meant so much to Samuel. My ideal creation craved life so much he ached for family history and put merit into the day he was born. And here I was, ready to destroy him. I swallowed the additional pain that it had to be this way.

I was sick to my stomach as I slowly started deleting file

after file. Cross-referencing the path to each main program file, I managed to log into the other computers on the island and wipe out the copies of the files that I found hidden under different paths. Samuel knew the importance of my notes, of the files that held the diagrams and codes that showed how to create the chip, which made him unique from the companions before him. He'd done an incredible job of hiding them in remote files under bogus code names, but I found several of them, and after a few hours passed, prayed I'd found them all.

Returning to my desktop, I then started in on the main system. The room was dark and the sky outside the windows an inky black as I continued to delete everything. Natalie lay on my bed, relaxing on her side with her head on my pillow as she watched me in the darkness.

"You look so sad," she mused, breaking the silence that had carried on for quite a while.

I glanced over the monitor at her, and paused for a moment, stretching and realizing the pain meds were doing their job. The throbbing in my head had settled into a numbness.

"I'm erasing years of my life," I told her, knowing there weren't better words to explain it but doubting she would understand.

"It's all still in your head though, right?" she said, sounding sleepy.

"Yes." I returned my attention to my task. If I slowed down or started thinking about my actions, I might have second thoughts.

I forced myself to remember Rose. Goddamn, she'd pissed me off more times than anyone ever had, but she didn't deserve to die. I did this for her, for my father who never forgave me for not taking my discoveries to my government and dutifully handing them over. If I had done that, I possibly wouldn't have had the power to destroy the creations that my country would have made once they turned and started trying to take over the human population. At least here, on the island, the virus was contained.

My heart weighed so heavily in my chest when I finally stood. It was done. My computer system was wiped out, and control was back in my hands. Walking around the desk and moving in the darkness toward the large windows I'd stared out of for so many years, I looked out them one last time. They were all out there somewhere. I didn't doubt for a moment that they were very aware of what I'd done. If I gave them enough time, they would regain control. There wasn't any doubt. I'd made them, and it was my job to destroy them. Not just the files that made them, or could make more, but each and every companion on the island had to be shut down. My work was far from done.

I glanced down at Natalie who was now sleeping soundly on my bed. Walking to her, I bent over and kissed her gently on her forehead.

"Malachi," she whispered, shifting on my bed.

I loved how she said my name in her sleep. What I wouldn't do to be next to her, stretched out alongside and feeling her warm soft curves caressing me while we slept.

"Good night, sweetheart," I said quietly and straightened.

Then backing away from the bed I turned, leaving the room and closing the door quietly. I could barely swallow. My heart was now swollen and lodged in my throat. The night wasn't over yet and wouldn't be until I'd finished what I'd started.

"I didn't teach you well enough, Samuel," I said as I walked down the dark, quiet hallway to the stairs. "You don't realize what happens when you try to play God. It's time I showed you. Pay attention because there will only be one lesson."

21

Natalie

Something exploded so close to my head that I screamed and almost fell out of the bed.

"Malachi," I yelled, grabbing the blankets and staring at the darkness surrounding me. It took a minute to remember that I'd fallen asleep in his room. "Malachi?" I repeated, searching the quiet room and realizing I was alone.

That's when I noticed the glow from outside the window. I'd managed to pull the covers over me while I'd slept and now fought to untangle my legs and finally threw the blankets to the other side of the bed.

"Oh, God! No! Malachi!" I screamed and stared in disbelief at the buildings outside that burned, flames dancing out of the windows. Then another explosion forced bright orange and yellow flames to dance furiously out of a far window at the far side of the building to the right of me.

Hurrying to the door, I grabbed the doorknob and found little solace when the handle wasn't warm. I yanked the door open and ran down the hallway then almost fell down the stairs, continually calling for Malachi. But as I hurried outside and ran toward the mountain and away from the intense heat from the fire, I didn't see him anywhere.

When I reached the gardens another explosion had me slamming myself to the ground. My knees and palms stung badly enough to bring tears to my eyes. I wasn't positive but it looked like the building I'd been asleep in had just exploded in flames. I got out just in time.

"Malachi, where are you?" I cried, unable to stop the tears as I crawled several feet before pushing to my feet again and running toward the mansion.

There were others outside the large house that was quickly engulfed in fire. I didn't see any companions anywhere and turned my back to the mansion to see flames dance in the dark night. Malachi's world was burning to the ground and with it all of his dreams and successes.

I don't know how long I stood there but was so stiff I couldn't move when a man touched my arm. I barely acknowledged his uniform and the helicopters that whipped their blades through the morning air. Everything smelled of smoke and the air was black in spite of the bright morning sun that failed to warm the depressing chill that settled deep inside me.

"Ma'am, are you hurt?" he asked.

"I need to find Malachi," I said, turning to look at the uniformed man. "I don't know where he is."

"Everyone is getting on the choppers. Are you hurt?" he asked again.

I didn't answer him and he kept his hand on my shoulder as he guided me to the helicopter where the others were already waiting. Turning, I stared at the island, at the gardens and the flowers that stubbornly opened yet were no longer part of paradise. Ashes floated through the air and the smell of fire and burned wood drowned out any beauty they offered.

"I've got to find Malachi," I said and tried turning from the helicopter. "We can't leave without him."

"Ma'am, we've searched the island and there are still men out there looking for survivors. But I'm pretty sure that everyone who is alive is already on board." He tried guiding me toward the open door where several people stared weary eyed at nothing in particular.

Malachi wasn't one of them. I didn't see Jonah or James Martin. I tried shrugging out of the man's grip and turned toward the gardens. Something caught my eye by the trees and I started walking in that direction.

"Malachi," I called out and saw the figure stop.

I stared at him when he paused between the trees and looked at me. His face was dark from ashes and his hair tousled, but he was alive.

"Malachi!" I started toward him.

He turned from me and disappeared into the trees.

"Malachi," I whispered, my voice cracking as I lost him among the foliage.

"Ma'am?" the man behind me said, slowly approaching and taking my arm. "The helicopter is leaving. There isn't anyone out there."

"But . . ." I complained, searching the trees and seeing no one.

"Let's go," he instructed, staying by my side until I was in the helicopter with several other people I didn't recognize.

All I had were my possessions in my purse. I'm not even sure who shoved it in my arms. I didn't have any luggage, and wasn't sure how I managed to get on the right planes as I flew back to my world. Even enduring the chaos at O'Hare Airport didn't pull me out of the daze that settled heavily in my brain. I climbed into the shuttle and sat there, staring out the window at the city where I'd grown up, but didn't pay attention to the familiar buildings or the driver when he announced each section of the parking lot that we arrived at. For all I knew I drove through the many parts of the reserved parking over and over again before I heard the driver announce the section where my car was parked.

I drove home in a daze. When I pulled my car into my driveway at the summer cottage and turned off the engine, the older man who approached me, smiling and calling my name, reminded me for a moment of Jonah. But it wasn't.

"Miss Natalie, welcome home." Stefan opened my car door and stood to the side.

I smiled at my butler who'd lived with me most of my life and cared for the cottage while I'd been gone.

"Where are your bags?" he asked.

"Airport lost them," I said and walked past him up the path toward my home.

I didn't even shower or change clothes but walked to my bedroom, shut the door behind me, and headed to bed. There wasn't any comfort in the familiar things of home. I knew I'd seen Malachi, knew he was alive, but he'd turned from me, leaving me, and returned to his destroyed world. He didn't want me.

The pain over losing the man I'd known just over a week but knew in my heart was my soul mate didn't lessen over the next few days. After I'd showered and walked into the kitchen that following Monday morning, Stefan looked up from where he had just set the table for one and frowned at me.

"Your father called and expects you at the office today," he told me, taking in the clothes I wore. "We really should get you changed."

"Okay," I said, shrugging.

I declined breakfast and sipped coffee while Stefan drove me to my father's firm an hour later. There wasn't anything for me here. There never had been. Everything I lived for, the whole purpose for my existence was back on that island, and I wasn't sure how I could continue without him.

I ignored my father's concern when I refused to attend the party scheduled for that Friday night. Instead, staying late at the office, I browsed the Internet, searching for news of Malachi. There was nothing. No news of the island burning, nothing about androids, and no mention of Malachi at all. In fact, as I continued searching, no matter what search engine I used, his name didn't appear at all. There was no mention from the French government on robotics, or any reference to breakthrough technology of any sort. It was close to midnight when I finally leaned back in my chair, certain I'd exhausted every avenue there was trying to find him.

The Web sites I'd found while on the island seemed to have vanished. It was as if Malachi Cohen never existed. Even the article from Devlin Products was no longer there. Oddly enough, that brought me a bit of solace. Malachi was alive. And he'd not only wiped out the past ten years of his life, but also successfully erased all mention of his name and his past. He was a ghost. But he was still very alive in my heart.

Another week passed and I finally accepted that I couldn't remain in Chicago. This wasn't my life. Honestly, it never had been. For almost thirty years I'd managed to do what my parents wanted, but I couldn't anymore.

I loved my mother and father, and didn't want to part ways with them the way Malachi had with his father. I owed them my life, and in spite of the pain that was permanently wrapped around me now, I would show them respect and gratitude for giving me what I had.

I sat in my living room, watching the clock and knowing they would be punctual. I'd invited them to dinner at seven, telling them I had an announcement, and knew they would show up. And then berate and condemn me for making such a foolish decision. But it was time to do what my heart wanted.

"Miss Natalie," Stefan announced, appearing in the doorway.

I stood, glancing past him but my parents weren't behind him. "What, Stefan? Where are Mom and Dad?"

"I'm sure they will be here promptly at seven," he said, his reserved tone never changing. "But this just arrived for you." He approached carrying a plain white envelope.

I frowned at it before accepting it and turning it over. There wasn't a return address, just my address and postal stamps that indicated it had traveled through several post offices before arriving here, priority mail. Returning to my couch, I reached for the letter opener in the oval bowl on the coffee table and then slipped the pointed edge under the glued flap.

A folded piece of paper slipped out and then an airline ticket floated to the floor. Something tingled inside me as I bent over and picked up the single ticket. Turning it over, I stared at the flight itinerary, along with a ticket for a charter plane, while my heart fluttered so furiously in my chest that I couldn't breathe.

Then I jumped up so quickly I banged my shin on the coffee table. "Who brought this?" I asked, for a moment thinking that Malachi might be outside.

"The mailman, Miss Natalie." Stefan watched me, an odd look on his face. "Are you okay?"

"No. Yes. Damn. I don't know." I started laughing, and then realized I hadn't heard that sound come out of me in almost a month. "It's a plane ticket. I'm leaving, Stefan. I need to pack right away."

"When are you leaving?" he asked, his expression not changing.

"Right now," I said and then hurried over and hugged the old man. "Isn't it great? He does want me."

"Who does?"

"Oh, Stefan," I cried, feeling the tears well in my eyes. "My soul mate. The man who still has my heart."

I laughed and cried when I stared at his puzzled expression. The doorbell rang and Stefan turned, hurrying out of the room. I looked at the ticket, reading again the itinerary that had me flying out to a small island in the Pacific. That's when I noticed the piece of paper that had been folded around the ticket had writing on it. I stared at the hand-written message.

Come if you dare. Stay if you like.

Stefan announced my parents and I hurried across the room, positive they were convinced their only daughter had lost her mind as I hugged both of them and cried as I told them I was moving away.

None of their lectures bothered me. Even when my father threatened to cut me off, all I gave him was a stupid grin. I was still grinning the next morning when I made sure all my luggage was packed. Double-checking my room and the rest of the house before heading back to the car, I made sure I had everything I needed.

"Good-bye," I told the summer cottage and then climbed into the backseat. Stefan closed the door and I felt like it was closing on the first half of my life. I was embarking on an adventure, the rest of my life. And I couldn't wait to get there and start living—finally.

This time I was the only one on the small chartered plane that flew low over the ocean and then landed roughly in an undeveloped field alongside a magnificent white beach. Waves splashed against rough looking rocks when I stepped out of the plane. The pilot stared around at the quiet and apparently abandoned island.

"Are you sure you want me to leave you here?" he asked, scratching his head as he took in our surroundings. "I know these are the right coordinates, but shouldn't someone be here to greet you?"

"I'll be fine." My stomach was so twisted in knots that I wasn't sure at all that I would be, but I wasn't turning back now. "You can leave."

He shook his head, mumbling something about the eccentric rich and then walked around to the back of the plane and tossed my luggage to the ground. I watched as he took off and then flew into the pale blue sky, leaving me on the island. It did appear that I was here alone. For the first time since I'd left Chicago a bit of fear seeped into my gut. I squinted at my surroundings, shading my eyes with my hand, searching for signs of anyone.

Someone appeared through the trees, walking toward me and I grinned broadly. "Hello," I called out but then my smile faded. The fear that started in my gut swelled quickly and damn near choked me as I stepped backward and almost tripped over my luggage.

Samuel stopped when he reached me and then reached down and methodically organized my luggage, managing to carry all of it with both hands. He didn't say a word as he turned and started walking in the direction that he'd come.

"What's going on, Samuel? Where's Malachi?"

Samuel didn't answer but instead walked into the dense forest ahead of me. "Hey, wait up!" I ran after him. "Wait! The least you can do is tell me where we're going." Apparently the least he could do was tell me nothing.

After dodging branches and swatting at bugs for a few minutes, we reached a clearing and I saw a simple, unadorned thatched-roof cottage. Samuel walked toward it and the front door opened.

"Jonah!" I cried out, happy to see the old man.

"It's about time," he said, grinning and then moved next to the door, holding it open with his body and clasping his hands behind his back. "Welcome home, Natalie."

I wouldn't become a blubbering idiot. And obviously, by the way Jonah stood, he didn't want to be hugged.

"Where's Malachi?" I asked, unable to stop myself.

Jonah looked at Samuel. "Put her luggage in the bedroom, and don't open it."

Samuel didn't say anything but entered ahead of me and then disappeared into a room off the large living room. Half of the walls were bamboo, and the other half netting, I assumed to keep bugs out. I glanced at the furniture, guessing a lot of it was homemade. The place was very simple, but a fan overhead moved silently, assuring me that at least there was electricity.

"This way, Ma'am," Jonah said, walking through the living room and into another room.

I followed him into a spacious kitchen and noticed several pots steaming on a wood burning stove. Whatever was cooking smelled really good and my stomach growled in appreciation. Jonah tapped on a wooden door off the kitchen with his arthritic knuckles.

"Malachi, we have company," he announced.

"What?" a gruff voice snapped and the door flew open.

I stared at him. Malachi stared back and from the look of shock on his face I could tell that he didn't have a clue I was coming here. His hair was longer and a thick growth covering his jaw showed he didn't shave often. He wasn't wearing a shirt and his skin was leathery, almost like Jonah's, his dark tan adding to his foreboding, incredibly appealing good looks.

"Malachi?" I whispered, suddenly worried he wasn't happy to see me. Memories of his turning in the woods, ashes floating in the air between us, attacked as I felt weak in the knees and sick to my stomach.

"Natalie." As he spoke my name his face softened and then with one large step he cleared the distance between us and swooped me into his arms.

I wrapped my arms around his neck, no longer able to hold back the tears. He hugged me like he'd never let go, and my fears dissipated, along with the depression I'd felt over the past month. The dark cloud that had submerged in my brain vanished and I was light as air. Laughing and crying at the same time, I wrapped my arms and legs around him and couldn't get close enough to him while he continued holding me fiercely in his arms.

"What are you doing here?" he breathed into my neck and

then slowly let go of me enough that I could slide down his body. He stared down at me, his dark eyes filled with more emotion than I'd ever seen in him before. "I can't believe you're here. How did you find me?"

"Someone had to bring her home." Jonah rocked up on to his toes, looking very pleased with himself.

"I left within hours of getting the plane ticket," I whispered and dared to reach up and brush my knuckles over his whiskered jaw.

Malachi pulled his gaze from mine and looked past me at Jonah. "How dare you spend my money without discussing it with me first," he growled, although there was no bite in his tone and he continued holding me close against him.

"Supper will be ready in an hour. I told Samuel to put clean towels and soap in the bathroom. I'll go make sure he did as he was told."

I watched Jonah leave the kitchen and then returned my attention to Malachi.

"You're really here," he whispered, and then lowered his mouth to mine.

I drowned in that kiss, knowing I wouldn't come up for air the same person. All of my fears and concerns dissipated, and I leaned into him on tiptoe, returning the kiss with as much energy and burning passion that he showed me. When he did let me up for air, he stared at me, not saying a word while holding my face in his calloused hands.

"That shower sounds good," I whispered, having to say something but unable to think clearly with his dark gaze devouring me.

"Yes, it does," he growled, pulling me close again.

Something clattered in the other room and I jumped, but Malachi didn't let me go. I turned when someone walked up behind me and then pressed closer to Malachi as I stared at Samuel.

"Bring more firewood in and make sure the table is set for four," Malachi instructed.

Samuel didn't answer but walked past us and out a back door.

"He can't speak," Malachi told me, and then guided me back into the living room. "I made him a promise on the other island not to turn him off. But his thought processes are a lot simpler. He doesn't remember anything about Paradise Island."

"It hardly seems a fitting name anymore," I mused and looked around the spacious bedroom we'd entered.

The furniture in here also looked homemade. There was a large bureau on one wall and a very large bed pushed up against the opposite wall. A fan circulated above the bed and the walls were identical to the living rooms, half bamboo and half netting.

Jonah walked out of another adjoining room and around us. "I've started the bath," he announced, then left the room and closed the door behind him.

"Well this place definitely isn't paradise." Malachi looked at all of my luggage stacked neatly against the wall next to the bureau. "Are you here to stay?"

"I guess that's up to you," I said, suddenly feeling nervous.

"Good," he answered, not elaborating.

My stomach fluttered though, as more of my nervousness disappeared and anticipation and excitement replaced it. He took my hand, leading me into the bathroom that was already steamy. A sweet perfumed fragrance floated in the moist warm air and I stared at Malachi's muscular, tanned back as he bent over and tested the water.

When he turned and looked at me, the anticipation inside me swelled into something that ached. Malachi didn't speak but reached for me. I didn't stop him from undressing me and then melted in the intensity of his gaze when I stood before him, naked.

"It won't be an easy life, Natalie," he said gruffly, taking my hand and guiding me to the large tub. "There's electricity and we won't starve, but none of the amenities you're accustomed to are here."

"You're here," I said quickly and felt heat rush to my face and neck. The blotches covered my skin before I could stop them.

"Tell me you're here to stay. It won't be easy and it sure as hell won't be perfect. But this is it for me. I can't ever return to the civilized world, and as far as any government is concerned, I don't exist."

"I don't want easy and I don't want perfect. I lived with both for thirty years but there was no pleasure, no joy or happiness until I met you."

"I'll give you that."

"What?"

"Pleasure, happiness," he began, and then looked down. "And love," he mumbled.

"Oh, Malachi," I cried out, jumping into his arms and breathing in his all male scent as my breasts swelled and ached and my insides throbbed with a fierce desire to make love to him. "There isn't anywhere else in the world I'd rather be."

I let go of him and he stripped out of his drawstring shorts. His cock was hard and swollen as he stepped into the water and then held my hand as I climbed in to the water with him. This was truly paradise. I sat between his legs, feeling the hard length of him throb against my ass. His muscular arms wrapped around me and I slipped deeper into the heavily fragranced warmth, knowing Jonah was right. I had come home.

We made love in the water, splashing most of it out of the tub and soaking the wooden floor, but not caring. I was at last fulfilled, complete for the first time in my life. As I straddled him, gliding down and feeling him take me completely, I wanted to cry tears of joy. I'd spent a week with this man and known him for a month, but there wasn't any doubt in my mind.

"I love you," I whispered, kissing him gently and realizing how natural it felt to say those three simple words.

"I love you, too, darling," he growled into my mouth and then impaled it as he did my pussy.

My world shattered at that moment. All the frustration of not living how I wanted, of searching for something more disappeared. I didn't know what lay ahead of me, and that was fine. I would walk alongside Malachi and that meant life would be perfect. Maybe not paradise, but definitely perfect.

We soaked in that tub until the water turned cold and chills covered my sated body, when we finally climbed out and wrapped ourselves in towels.

"I need my overnight bag," I said as I stared into the long narrow mirror that hung over the large bathroom counter.

"Yes. Let's get it unpacked." Malachi walked out of the bathroom with the towel wrapped around him hanging low on his hips. He'd lost some weight since I'd last seen him but he glowed from our bath and his black hair was shiny and wet as it clung to his neck and curled against his shoulders. "Remind me to thank Jonah. You don't know how many times I thought about contacting you."

"Why didn't you?" I asked after pointing out the bag with my bathroom supplies and then following him back into the steamy room. I watched as he unpacked my personal items and arranged them on a shelf next to his sparse toiletries.

"After leaving Paradise Island, I used money I'd saved over the years and bought this island."

"And you worked hard to delete the rest of your history," I added.

He gave me a pointed stare but then returned to his task. "I knew you would notice and figured it was a small way of letting you know I was alive."

"I knew," I whispered. But didn't add that I saw him turn from me the morning I left the other island.

"And there is so much work to do," he continued, standing back and watching while I applied some makeup and then brushed my hair. "It will take at least a year. I've got a skeleton crew and we all work together, but eventually, I'll open this island up as a resort."

"You'll need to make sure it's legal," I suggested, and let him take my towel when he reached for it.

"Definitely," he agreed, walking naked ahead of me into the bedroom where we dressed together for dinner. "I'll need you. I've known all along I couldn't make this place work without you."

"I'm not going anywhere." I brushed a damp curl from his face and then leaned into him, kissing him and knowing also I couldn't get enough of him. Already I ached to have him inside me again.

"I don't have a theme yet. I figured I'd create a few companions," he said and paused when he felt me stiffen. "Simply as servants," he added quickly. "I've created perfection and know now that not so perfect is how I need to live."

"Sounds like paradise to me," I whispered, wrapping my arms around his neck. "It will be my pleasure to work alongside you."

"It is paradise now. Now that you're here," he added, and devoured my mouth.

Malachi lifted me into his arms and carried me to his bed and I stretched out next to him, climbing over his virile body and feeling him enter me once again. With my dress raised to my hips, I straightened over him, and rode him until I couldn't take it any longer. My orgasm hit me hard and the room tilted as I came harder than I ever had in my life.

Malachi grabbed me, wrapping his arms around me tightly, and growled fiercely as he shook, filling me with everything he had.

"There's no preacher here, or anyone who could marry us."

His words shocked me and I raised my head, surprised by the seriousness of his expression. "But if you'll take me, Natalie, I promise to give you the best of everything for the rest of our lives."

"Yes, Malachi. Oh, God, yes!" I laughed and felt him quiver inside me.

"I want you to name our island," he said, his black damp hair falling around his face, as he looked more relaxed than I'd ever seen him look.

"It's not Paradise Island. No way."

"Agreed."

"But we will have the pleasure of making it home, so therefore it will be perfect."

"Perfect Island?" he asked, his expression comical.

"I like Pleasure Island." I nibbled his lip and combed his hair with my fingers, wondering if I could make love to him again. "Although now that I'm with you, it will be paradise."

Jonah yelled from the other room that supper was ready and Malachi's arms tightened around me. "It is now," he whispered, and I had a feeling we'd be late to supper.

Join Lorie O'Clare
on a new journey to
SEDUCTION ISLAND!

Coming in November 2009 from Aphrodisia!

Jordan Anton squatted on the edge of the volcanic rock and stared at the white foam as it raced up the sandy beach. It receded into crystal clear, bright blue water. Coral reefs added to the magnificence of the view. Too bad the small island was nothing more than a dried up old volcano.

Jordan picked up a loose rock and hurled it at the ocean. Prisons came in many shapes and sizes. At least this one offered a view.

He jumped the three feet to the sandy ground and walked the length of the rocky wall. Beyond the thick grove of some erotic-looking flower-type plant, a worn path led away from the beach. He started up the path, taking in the thick trunks of possibly what might be a hybrid of a palm tree. If he were in Wyoming he would know the names of the trees around him.

Jordan wondered how many Antons had been sent to the island when they didn't meet the approval of Pierre Anton, his grandfather. He would only be here a month, and the terms weren't completely unbearable. But he was begrudgingly here against his will.

He paused, tucking a thick black strand of hair that had come loose from the ponytail at his nape behind his ear. The "long" hair bothered his grandfather, but then everything about Jordan bothered Grandfather Pierre. Which, of course, was why he was here.

"Why bother with a Harvard degree if you aren't going to use it, boy?" Grandfather asked him more than once during their last visit.

Jordan wanted to ask exactly how he was *not* using his degree. There was knowledge in his head that hadn't been there before going to Harvard. Life experiences and memories that he wouldn't have had if he hadn't attended the Ivy League school. Jordan didn't have any regrets. He wasn't sure why it bothered Grandfather so much that he went to help Aunt Penelope with her ranch in Wyoming. His grandfather, of all people, should see and understand that Jordan was yet again learning and gaining life experiences and memories by helping out on the ranch that his aunt would otherwise lose after divorcing her husband.

Of course, since she divorced an Anton, more than likely Grandfather Pierre didn't want her ranch to make it.

Jordan could spend weeks trying to understand the mind of someone like his grandfather. Or he could put those thoughts out of his head and figure out what the incredibly gorgeous woman, standing no more than ten feet in front of him, was doing on this island. His grandfather spelled out the terms of their agreement very clearly before Jordan flew to the island. He would meet the Princess Tory, a Sicilian princess who possibly came from more money than the Antons. His grandfather wanted to merge the families, a business deal in his eyes, loosely called a marriage.

Jordan had no intention of marrying anyone but knew if he didn't agree to come here and spend a month with the princess on the pretense of possibly announcing an engagement, Grandfather would make it hell for Aunt Penelope and her ranch.

Princess Tory would arrive tomorrow, which meant the sexy little thing wandering from the castle was one of the hired help, probably taking advantage of her boss not being here by exploring. He wasn't supposed to arrive until tomorrow either.

He finished tucking the stand behind his ear and watched her studying the bark of the tree she stood in front of. "What are you doing?"

She jumped, yanking her hand back from the tree she was about to touch as if it might bite her, and turned and stared at him, wide eyed. In the next moment she regained composure, straightening, and narrowing her gaze on him.

"I'm not sure that's any of your business. Who are you?" she demanded, obviously clueless as to whom her employer would be while on this island.

There were advantages to people not knowing his identity. It gave him the upper hand, and the opportunity to learn their true nature before revealing his name and watching the fake appreciation and respect gloss over their face like it did every time he mentioned his last name.

"I asked you first." He hid his smile when she appeared frustrated, obviously realizing she didn't have the upper hand with him.

Jordan moved closer, admiring her straight brown hair that was pulled back in a ponytail. His guess was it fell close to her ass. And he'd bet she had a nice ass too. The curves he saw from the front view were beyond mouthwatering.

"I seriously doubt you have permission to be away from the castle. And I don't approve of taking advantage of breaking rules to gain information." She had an American accent, probably northeast, New York or one of the nearby states. The way her hackles went up, turning her dark blue eyes almost violet, proved she knew how to defend herself.

Definitely not old money. Not to mention, if she were from his class, or the class his family so proudly held on to, she wouldn't be out here without an escort. Jordan wouldn't put her much past twenty-five at the most. No rings on her finger, not even a school ring. Maybe he'd run into his social organizer, although Grandfather boasted the reputable social organizer ran only in the best of circles. Jordan seriously doubted his grandfather would hire a social organizer who shopped at Wal-Mart and not Neiman Marcus.

"Sometimes there are advantages to breaking the rules." He decided not to ask further who she was, doubting she'd confirm anyway. The anonymity on both sides allowed him to see her in her natural form. It would go away soon enough and she'd start kissing his ass. At least for a few he could enjoy the fiery temper he doubted she'd let him see otherwise.

"Not that I can see." She turned, walking away from him, along the path she'd probably come, which more than likely led back to the castle. "And if you believe there are, I doubt you'll hold on to your job long."

Jordan liked playing the rogue. In truth, he didn't feel he was playing too much. But his damned last name, and supposed "position in society" got in the way too often to allow him to interact with another person like this. Especially a gorgeous woman. Hell, when was the last time a lady walked away from him?

"What's life, if you don't take risks?" He caught up with her easily enough. Although it didn't bother him a bit that the path wasn't really wide enough to walk alongside her. The view of her backside was as extraordinary as he imagined.

"A safe place," she said tightly, her ass swaying beautifully in her snug, new looking blue jeans.

"You must know how to take risks if you're here," he pointed out.

"You'd be surprised what I know."

"We might both surprise each other with our knowledge."

"Huh," she snorted, picking up her pace. "I know your type."
The path curved around thick foliage and inclined and de-

clined as it brought them closer to the large castle, visible now ahead of them. It was an anomaly, the only structure on this small island, and probably built during a time long forgotten. Jordan wouldn't be surprised if it were the selling point when his grandfather decided to pick up this little rock surrounded by the Pacific, and not too far off the coast of New Zealand.

"Do you now? And what is my type?"

"The type I'm not interested in," she said, her arms swaying on either side of her as she kept a steady pace ahead of him. He liked how her long thick ponytail flowed from side to side, matching the soft curves of her hip and ass as it moved to a tantalizing rhythm.

"You don't know anything about me, how do you know if you would like my type, or not?" he asked.

She stopped, the edge of the path just ahead of her, where it broke off into the well maintained gardens surrounding the castle. It amazed him when he arrived, just a few hours ago, and learned a skeleton crew maintained the land and castle. There were only a few household servants, and there had to be a gardener, with as magnificent of a view the yard around the old structure provided, although he hadn't spotted any outdoor staff yet.

Jordan snapped his attention from her ass to her face when she spun around and shoved her long ponytail over her shoulder. He decided he liked how her spaghetti strap to her haltertop almost crept over the side to her arm, aiding in showing off her small bone structure and slender shoulders.

She shoved a nicely manicured finger into his chest. "I know enough about you," she hissed, stepping close enough he could see cobalt flecks bordering her irises. They helped her blue eyes darken when her emotions were running strong, as they obviously were now. "You are the one who thinks acting like a bad ass will impress a girl, make her take a risk, invite an adventure. You think you can play me, take what you want, and then gallivant on to the next pretty girl who strikes your fancy."

"Ouch." Jordan noticed she said "girl," and not "lady." That would definitely make her not Harvard. Probably not Yale or Stanford either, although he wouldn't swear to the latter. He also concluded she wasn't from New Zealand, although her American accent already gave hint to that. Kiwis were usually pretty friendly folk, and this woman came equipped with a double-edged dagger. He hated admitting his intrigue. What he did know was he couldn't let her see it, or she might very well hand his head to him on a platter. "You've pegged me wrong, my lady," he drawled, using his best Montana accent. "And as well, you've offered me a challenge. One I'm up to, I might add. For now though, I'll bid you good day." If only he wore a hat. Tipping it in parting would play the part out so perfectly. Instead, Jordan stepped around her, forcing her to jump to the side to avoid brushing against him. "I'm sure we'll see each other again very soon." He picked up a pace, heading to the castle, and on an afterthought, opted to head to the backside of the building, instead of the front. Making it look like he would enter through the servant entrance, or possibly even head to the stables, would keep her guessing.

Soon enough she would know who he really was.